RAID 42

By the same author

GRAHAM HURLEY

RAID 42

HEAD
of ZEUS

First published in the UK in 2019 by Head of Zeus Ltd

9 7 5 3 1 2 4 6 8

A catalogue record for this book is available from the British Library.

ISBN (HB) 9781788547505
ISBN (ANZTPB) 9781788547512
ISBN (E) 9781788547499

MIX
Paper from
responsible sources
FSC
www.fsc.org   FSC® C020471

Printed and bound by CPI Group (UK) Ltd, Croydon, CR0 4YY

Head of Zeus Ltd
First Floor East
5–8 Hardwick Street
London EC1R 4RG

WWW.HEADOFZEUS.COM

To Ute, Fiona,

And the memory of Sgt Ollie Kemp

'This place is full of corpses, dancing and playing at war'

Erich Maria Remarque, *The Night in Lisbon* (1962)

PRELUDE

London. A full moon rose on the night of 10 May 1941. It happened to be a Saturday. *Luftwaffe* bomber crews ate an early supper on their bases across the Channel and hours later the first wave of Heinkels and Dorniers lined up for take-off as the last glimmers of daylight died on the western horizon. Past ten o'clock, radar stations on the south coast were warning about the imminence of a major raid and within minutes ground observers in Kent and Essex reported enemy aircraft in sight. German aircrew peered down at the Thames estuary, silver in the moonlight, as RAF controllers scrambled night fighters and air raid sirens in the capital emptied the pubs.

One of the first bombs to hit the Palace of Westminster was an incendiary. The Victoria Tower was already under repair and a police sergeant climbed a tangle of scaffolding to extinguish the burning magnesium with a sandbag. Minutes later, high explosive bombs killed two auxiliary policemen, shattered windows and brought down a wall.

By midnight, with the bombs still falling, firemen were battling to save the House of Commons and Westminster Hall. Fifty fire pumps struggled to contain the blaze, hosing water directly from the Thames, but by daybreak both the Commons chamber and the Members' Lobby had been destroyed. The Speaker's chair was a pile of ashes and the padded green leather seats in the chamber, famous worldwide, were charred beyond recognition. Onlookers that Sunday morning stared at the drifts of smoking rubble, uncomprehending. The mother of parliaments had survived months of savage bombing throughout the blitz. Now this.

That same night, 340 miles to the north, a lone Me-110 appeared on another set of radar screens. It roared over the tiny coastal town of Bamburgh and disappeared into the darkness towards the west. Three Spitfires and a Defiant night fighter were ordered to intercept but failed to find the enemy aircraft. Thirty-four minutes later, his fuel tanks close to empty, the lone pilot baled out.

Word of the fast-developing raid on London had already reached Scotland but no one suspected that the two events might be linked. By now, radar controllers in the north had assigned the mystery intruder a codename.

Raid 42.

BOOK ONE

1

Six months earlier, on 14 November 1940, *Major* Georg Messner was trying to find a dentist. Messner was assigned to the *Reichsregierung*, Hitler's personal transport squadron out at Tempelhof airfield and spent his working days at the controls of a Ju-52, ferrying his Führer and an assortment of other Nazi chieftains to the far corners of the Reich. On this particular day he'd just returned to Berlin with Goering and a couple of aides from the *Reichsmarschall*'s private office. A rogue tooth and ulcerated gum had been bothering Messner for weeks. Vague promises of dental help from the squadron's medical officer had come to nothing. Now, the pain was close to unbearable.

He telephoned his wife from the main squadron office. She and their two-year-old daughter lived in a summer house on the shores of the Wannsee. So far Beata and young Lottie hadn't been troubled by the increasingly frequent RAF raids on the capital, though Messner, like many of his colleagues, wasn't sure how long this blessing would last. First thing this morning, moments before Messner had set off for the airfield, Beata had promised to lay hands on a dentist. Now all her husband wanted was a name and an address.

'Kohnsson.' She spelled out the name.

'Jewish?'

'I'm told not.' She gave him an address in Charlottenburg.

'You've talked to the man?'

'Only his wife. She sounded nice. They're leaving for Leipzig tomorrow but he can see you tonight as long as you're there between nine and half past. They live above the surgery. And if you've got the money he might be able to find a little gold for the filling.'

Messner pulled a face. These days, if you could even lay hands on a dentist, they plugged teeth with tin alloy. Gold would be a godsend but it would cost a fortune.

'You couldn't find anyone else?'

'No.'

'You tried?'

'Of course I tried. And I'm your wife, by the way, not your secretary.'

Messner mumbled an apology. Getting by on nothing but soup, he said, did strange things to a man.

Beata wanted to know whether he'd need something to eat when he finally got home. Messner was checking his watch. Nearly seven.

'I imagine that depends on Herr Kohnsson,' he said.

Under normal circumstances, Charlottenburg was half an hour from Tempelhof and as far as Messner knew there were no expected raids this evening. In any event, the English bombers – few as they were – rarely turned up before ten and so Messner settled down to sort out some of the last week's paperwork.

Within minutes, the door opened and he was looking at the squadron adjutant, an ex-Heinkel pilot who'd lost a leg in a pre-war training accident but whose web of connections seemed to include everyone in the Wilhelmstrasse.

'You're off home tonight? Or sleeping here?'

'Home.'

'Best leave early. *Luftgaukommando* are calling a raid for nine thirty.'

Luftgaukommando was the organisation responsible for the night-time defence of Berlin. They were in constant touch with a chain of Freya radar stations stretching all the way to the North Sea. Flying time from the coast to Berlin was nearly three hours.

'We believe them?' Messner asked.

'We believe anything. Goering's at the Russian Embassy tonight, along with Ribbentrop. Molotov's in town. If I was British I'd know where I'd be dropping my bombs.'

Molotov, Messner knew, was the Russian Foreign Minister. He'd heard his name mentioned on today's flight back from Munich. Both times by Ribbentrop, the Reich's Foreign Minister, and one of the VIP passengers in the Ju-52.

'Nine thirty's early,' Messner said.

'I expect it coincides with the cheese course. The Russians are mad about *Handkäse*, especially these days. The British spend their lives spoiling everyone else's party. It's one of the few pleasures they have left.'

The adjutant shot him a grin and limped out of the office. Messner listened to the tap-tap of his false leg as he disappeared down the corridor. The sensible thing would be to leave now, while driving in the blackout was still legal. The moment the sirens sounded, all traffic had to come to a halt and park. But leaving at half past eight would still give him plenty of time and so he picked up his pen again, running his tongue over his throbbing gum, determined to get the better of the paperwork.

Nearly an hour later, he'd finished. Nearly half past eight. The adjutant was still at his desk down the corridor and looked up when Messner said goodnight.

'You're crazy,' he tapped his watch. 'They're twenty-five minutes away.'

'The British?'

'*Ja.*'

Messner ran across the hardstanding to the allotted parking spaces. His own BMW was under repair and he'd borrowed Beata's Volkswagen for this morning's trip. Now, in the darkness, he had a moment's difficulty getting the door open. Then he stirred the rattly old engine into life and headed for the long curl of concrete that led to the exit gate. A guard on the gate brought him to a halt with a torch. The adjutant had been right. The sirens would sound any minute.

Messner gunned the engine. Travelling at night without headlights was, as he knew only too well, an acquired art. In the gloom of the blackout you had to grope your way from landmark to landmark, constantly alert for the sudden loom of other vehicles. The official speed limit of 20 kph was often the triumph of optimism over blind faith but Georg Messner prided himself on his night vision and tonight of all nights he was determined to get to the dentist's chair before the RAF arrived and made life a little more difficult.

The air raid sirens began to wail seconds later. Messner was following what looked like a lorry, probably full of coal.

The driver stood on the brakes and Messner hauled the tiny Volkswagen to the left, hoping to avoid any oncoming traffic. Nothing. Just darkness and the sudden glimpse of the whiteness of a woman's face as she ran across the road.

Traffic had come to a halt. Cars were pulling into the kerbside. Doors were opening. Drivers were looking for the nearest shelter. Messner watched them for a moment, his pulse racing, his ulcerated gum on fire. He flicked on the interior light and checked his watch. Twenty to nine. The raid would last at least an hour, probably longer. By which time Kohnsson would have gone.

Messner hit the throttle again. Anything was preferable to another sleepless night, another day trying to pretend there was nothing wrong with him, another bowl of tasteless slop masquerading as soup. He clawed his way past the truck, sensing nothing beyond. 10 kph. 20 kph. Up into top gear. For at least a minute, probably longer, Messner rode his luck, straddling the unoccupied middle of the road, tallying the intersections as they came and went, urging the little car faster and faster. Then, as if from nowhere, came a dim red lamp waving in the darkness. A ghostly uniformed figure. A shouted warning.

Messner stabbed at the brakes, feeling the car shudder. He tried to brace himself at the wheel, arms straight and locked. Ahead was a wall of something blacker than everything else, something solid, something that – in less than a heartbeat – stepped into his life and changed it forever. For a split second he caught, very faintly, the tear of rending metal and then came the brief kiss of the night air as his head went through the windscreen, and the pain in his gum vanished and the blackness grew blacker still.

*

That same evening, in a café in Stockholm, Tam Moncrieff was nursing a beer. He'd been in Sweden less than two hours, the time it took for the taxi to bring him in from the airport, and he was basking in the novelty of a city lit at night.

Outside, the street was still thick with passers-by. Already he'd lost count of the blonde girls shrouded in bright ankle-length coats, the kids kicking their way through an inch or two of snow, the older folk with their knitted mufflers and their string bags full of shopping. These people had a freedom and a confidence he could only envy. They were carefree. They looked well fed. Their very presence on the street spoke of a life he could barely remember.

Wilhelm Schultz, he thought. Would he share this feeling? Would he arrive from a Berlin as grey and disenchanted as the London Moncrieff had just left? Would he be tired of a life measured out in ration coupons and stern reminders about digging for victory? Or might his tiny corner of the Reich be treating him rather better? On balance, Moncrieff favoured the latter, partly because Schultz was a born survivor, but mainly because Moncrieff had always assumed that their relationship had ended a couple of years ago, the day the Germans sent him packing from Berlin. Which was why the invitation to meet here in Stockholm had come as such a surprise.

The message had been routed through a Swedish businessman with a ball-bearing factory in the Home Counties. Birger Dahlerus, like a handful of other intermediaries, had never believed in the war. War, he often said, was no friend of international commerce. Neither was it sensible to kill people en masse for no better reason than the mess that politicians made. Hence the neatly typed letter that had landed on Moncrieff's desk. *Your friend Wilhelm Schultz presents his compliments. He proposes a meeting on neutral territory. This I am only too happy to facilitate.*

With the letter came a map of Stockholm with directions to the Café Almhult. The Almhult, Dahlerus assured Moncrieff, was owned by a good friend. He'd provide a room upstairs with the guarantee of privacy and something half decent to eat. There, Moncrieff and Schultz could talk to their hearts' content.

Hearts', content had raised a smile among Moncrieff's bosses. This was vintage Dahlerus, they assured him. In a darkening world, the man remained an idealist. More to the point, he knew many of the people who mattered in Berlin and one of them was Hermann Goering. The trusty Hermann, they told Moncrieff, had performed well at Sylt. Sylt? They wouldn't say. This, only yesterday, had irritated Moncrieff but his reaction had simply raised another smile. Ask Wilhelm about Sylt, they'd said. He knows.

Schultz arrived nearly half an hour later. Moncrieff watched him climb out of the back of an ancient Volvo and bend to the driver's window to haggle over the fare. Three more years with the *Abwehr* at the heart of German military intelligence had done nothing to soften his appearance. The same shaven head. The same overpowering physical presence. The same black leather jacket. The same hint of menace in his battered face as he pocketed his change and turned to gaze at the café. The man walked from his shoulders, anticipating life's next blow, the way ageing boxers did. Old habits, Moncrieff thought, die hard.

Inside the café, Schultz stamped the snow from his feet. The blond young man behind the bar got a smile as well as a nod. Then Schultz muttered something in Swedish that made the bartender laugh.

Moncrieff extended a hand, wanting to know whether he'd been here before. His German was fluent.

'Twice,' Schultz grunted. 'The herrings are good. So is the cured salmon. Avoid the bread. These people are still at peace yet their bread is *Scheisse*. They have no excuse.'

Schultz settled on the bar stool. His eyes, pouched in the wreckage of his face, gave the lie to everything else about him. They spoke, to Moncrieff, of the essence of the man: watchful, alert, giving nothing away.

Schultz ordered a beer and then studied Moncrieff for a long moment. The expression on his face might have been a smile.

'So what did they do to you?' he asked at last.

'When?'

'At the Prinz-Albrecht-Strasse. Basement corridor, was it? Big room at the end? Man in a white coat with a hosepipe? Shit your pants and pray to God to get it over?'

'Something like that.'

Schultz nodded, reaching for the beer. Two gulps and most of it had gone.

'You did well, my friend.' He wiped his mouth with the back of his hand. 'One minute twenty-two seconds. No one's managed that before. Believe it or not, they still talk about you.'

Moncrieff managed a faint smile. The night before leaving Berlin for the last time he'd spent hours in the hands of the Gestapo. One of their party tricks was slowly drowning a man and the terrifying sensation of water in his lungs had never left him. He'd never discussed it with anyone since and he'd no intention of starting now.

'So is life good, Wilhelm? Is the *Abwehr* keeping you busy?'

'The *Abwehr* is up its own arse. One day someone will come along and put it out of its misery. If you were a betting man you'd pile your money on that little bastard Schellenberg. The trick he pulled at Venlo was crude as fuck but it did the trick. Do you want the pair of them back, by the way? I might be able to sort something out.'

The two men looked at each other for a long moment and then Moncrieff began to laugh. Time obviously meant nothing to Schultz. Three years ago they'd worked together in Berlin and Nuremberg while the world held its breath over the Czech crisis, Moncrieff the callow novice, Schultz the one-time SA brawler with a new perch in the *Abwehr* and powerful allies in the German military. Moncrieff, with his Royal Marine background and his language skills, was in Berlin to make contact with the opposition to Hitler and Schultz had the ear of the people who mattered. In the end the operation foundered, neither man's fault, but the respect and the beginnings of a friendship were still there. Moncrieff found himself smiling again. September 1938 might have been yesterday.

Schultz was digging in a pocket of his leather jacket. At length he produced a small cigar. The barman supplied a light.

'Dahlerus tells me you're at St James's Street. True?'

Moncrieff nodded. The former MGM building in St James's Street was part of MI5's London estate. He had a desk in a small office on the third floor.

'Yes,' he said. 'I joined the day after war was declared.'

'Your idea?'

'Theirs. I'd have been very happy back in the Corps but everyone told me I was too old. So it was either Five or something noble in Civil Defence. I could never wear a blue uniform so it had to be the Security Service.'

'And?'

'And what?'

'You like it?'

Moncrieff hesitated, wondering quite where this conversation was heading.

'Is this between friends?' he asked.

'It is.'

'Then the truth is that I love it.'

'Why?'

'Because it stretches me. And because I'm good at it. Back in the old days, up in Scotland, my dad had a couple of dogs. One of them was old. Her days in the field were over. But the other one was much younger, almost a puppy. She'd be out in the hills most days, chasing a neighbour's sheep, and it was my job to get her back. I used to try every trick in the book to get inside that little dog's tiny head. Work out what appeals. Lure her. Trick her. Tempt her. Bend her to your will. In truth nothing's really changed. Except the weather's better down south.'

'And you're dealing with people.'

'I am.'

'Our people.'

'Possibly.'

'Counter-espionage. Emptying a man of everything he knows.'

'Lovely idea.'

'So tell me,' Schultz's face was very close. 'Are any of them as stupid as the puppies Schellenberg took at Venlo?'

Moncrieff ducked his head. Venlo was a Dutch town on the German border. A couple of months into the war, two MI6 agents were kidnapped by Walter Schellenberg, whom they believed to be heading a plot involving senior *Wehrmacht* officers to kill Hitler. In real life, Schellenberg was a rising star in Himmler's intelligence organisation, the plot was a carefully baited trap, and the damage the *Sicherheitsdienst* inflicted on MI6 networks across Europe was substantial.

'You could really get them back?' Moncrieff reached for his drink. 'If we asked nicely?'

'No.' Schultz caught the barman's eye and nodded at a door towards the back. 'But would you really want them?'

They ate in a smallish room upstairs clad entirely in wood. When Moncrieff asked Schultz whether this might once have been a sauna, he said it was more than possible. The building was old. The harbour was a sprint away. Half an hour in the oven and then a plunge into this corner of the icy Baltic? Difficult to refuse.

There was no menu. A buxom woman in her fifties who'd clearly taken to Schultz offered a list of dishes in Swedish. Schultz didn't bother to consult Moncrieff on any kind of choice and sent the woman on her way with their order.

'Let me guess...' Moncrieff was emptying the glass he'd brought up from downstairs. 'Fish?'

Schultz ignored the question. First they had to attend to

business. He'd invited Moncrieff over to point out what seemed, at least to most Germans, the obvious.

'It's over,' he grunted. 'It's finished. It's a numbers game. Austria, Denmark, Norway, Belgium, France, Luxembourg, Poland.' He tallied the countries that had fallen to Hitler's armies on the fingers of both hands and then looked up. 'Only the British have forgotten how to count.'

'You missed out the Czechs, my friend. Easily done.'

'*Ja*, them too. Do I hear a yes? Are we right to consider the war won?'

Moncrieff didn't answer. Instead he wanted to know about Sylt. He'd looked it up on the map. A tiny Friesian island off the German–Danish border.

'You don't know what happened?'

'That's why I'm asking.'

Schultz nodded. Moncrieff's question seemed to surprise him.

'We organised a meeting there,' Schultz said carefully, 'a couple of weeks before the war began. If you really want to know what happens next in life you ask a priest or a businessman. They both have a stake in the future but on this occasion we stuck with the businessman.'

'We?'

'Goering was in charge. He wanted somewhere quiet, somewhere offshore, somewhere no one would notice us. He wanted to talk to the British face to face. He wanted to look them in the eye, explain the facts of life. The whole thing was his idea.'

'And you were there?'

'Yes. The Fat One's thick with Canaris. I was the Admiral's man at the table.' Admiral Canaris was head of the *Abwehr*, an inscrutable old-school warrior who'd never bothered to hide his doubts about Hitler.

'And?'

'Goering was pushing for a treaty to keep Britain out of a war that everyone knew was a couple of weeks away. The British brought a selection of businessmen and a couple of aristocrats who all agreed it made perfect sense. Fighting each other would be crazy. Goering thought another four-power conference might do the trick. Get the French and Italians on board and we could have the whole thing tied up in no time at all.'

'Like Munich?'

'Exactly. Except you'd be shitting on the Poles this time, not the Czechs. It never happened, of course, but that really wasn't the point. The Fat One made a big impression. This was someone you British could do business with when the time was right. Your phrase, not ours. I remember writing it down.'

Moncrieff nodded. *When the time was right.* At Nuremberg, three years ago, he'd shared a bottle of Spanish brandy with Goering at a late-night meeting brokered by Schultz. Moncrieff had brought word from London that the British would march if Hitler moved into the Sudetenland. He'd known from the start that Goering didn't believe him, but they'd drunk deep into the small hours and laughed a great deal in one of those precious moments of implausible bonhomie stolen from a mind-numbing week of interminable military parades in the gigantic bowl of the Zeppelinfeld. Moncrieff hadn't known what to expect but the father of the *Luftwaffe* had fully measured up to his advance billing. A man of gargantuan appetites and ready wit. A raconteur of the first order. *A man you might do business with.* Perfect.

'So is this Goering's idea, too?' Moncrieff gestured at the space between them.

'He knows we're here, certainly.'

'But he thinks the war's over? As good as won?'

'Yes. And not just him. We all do.'

There was a knock on the door. The woman was back with a tray of food. Moncrieff watched her serving Schultz first, bending quickly to whisper something in his ear. Schultz, eyeing the platter of soused herring, shot her a look, then nodded. Seconds later, she'd gone.

For several minutes they ate in silence. Schultz was right about the herrings. They were delicious. At length, Schultz reached for a napkin and wiped his mouth.

'Hitler, I'm afraid, doesn't understand the British. He thinks you're all Nazis with better manners. In his view you should be making the most of your empire and getting very rich. Europe's always been nothing but trouble as far as you British are concerned. Now he's taken care of that, we might all make a new start.'

'By bombing us every night?'

'By getting rid of Churchill and having a sensible conversation. That man's something else he doesn't understand. You're alone. Your army's fucked. You don't know what to do about our U-boats. There's nothing left to eat. And you're right, every night we help ourselves to another city. How many bombs do we have to drop before you people come to your senses?'

'This is you talking? Or him?'

'Both, my friend. Hitler is a tidy man. He likes things done a certain way. It starts with his domestic arrangements and it ends with most of Europe. Churchill upsets him. Just ask

Hess. Rudolf is the only one Hitler really trusts. Churchill is a schoolboy, a lout. He loves to fight. He *lives* to fight. We all agree you're better off without him. Hess thinks a conversation with the King might do the trick.'

Rudolf Hess served as Hitler's Deputy. Moncrieff could pick him out in a photograph – bushy black eyebrows, piercing eyes – but knew very little else.

'We owe Churchill a great deal,' Moncrieff murmured. 'I think you'll find he's very popular.'

'Of course,' Schultz stabbed at a flake of herring. 'That goes for Hitler, too. As we both know.'

Moncrieff nodded. The operation he and Schultz had tried to mount three years earlier had come to nothing because Hitler knew how to ride his luck. First Austria and then Czechoslovakia had fallen into Berlin's lap while the rest of the world looked the other way. How many Germans would argue with an ever greater Reich?

Moncrieff pushed his plate away. 'If you're asking me whether the British will get rid of Churchill then the answer's no.'

'Even at the cost of all those cities? All that shipping?'

'Even then.'

'So there's nothing we can offer?'

'I doubt it. Unless you're talking withdrawal. Pack your bags and get out of France, out of Belgium, out of Scandinavia, and even Churchill might have second thoughts...'

Schultz nodded, said nothing. Moncrieff had the impression he might have planted a seed but wasn't sure.

'You want me to report this conversation back?' he asked.

'Of course. That's why you're here.'

'The messenger again? Is that it?'

'Yes. And tell your masters something else. That the bombing will continue until peace negotiations start. Our Leader's pleasure, Tam. Neatness is all.'

The waitress had left a couple of glasses and a bottle of white wine on the table. Schultz poured. Moncrieff proposed the toast.

'I hear the Russians are in town tonight,' he said.

'You mean Molotov?'

'Yes.'

'It's true. He's thrown a dinner for Goering and that fool Ribbentrop. Should we be expecting a visit?'

'Fifty-plus bombers,' Moncrieff checked his watch and then raised his glass. 'About now.'

Two *Wehrmacht* soldiers who happened to be on leave were first to the wreckage of Beata's Volkswagen. The little car had telescoped into the back of one of Berlin's big trolley buses, destroying the bonnet. A body hung over the wreckage, thrown through the windscreen by the impact. There was glass everywhere and blood dripped onto the torn metal from a deep gash on the driver's forehead. Other lacerations had webbed his face with more blood.

Another figure emerged from the darkness, a local man in the uniform of a *Blockwarten*.

'You need to get out of here,' he gestured skywards. 'There's a shelter at the next U-Bahn station.'

The soldiers ignored him. One of them was bent over the body protruding from the car. He was trying to find a pulse.

'He's alive. Just.' He threw a look at his mate. 'We have to get the poor bastard out.'

Between them, the two men smashed the rest of the windscreen and eased the driver out of the wreckage of the car before laying him carefully on the road. One of the soldiers picked the bigger fragments of glass from the driver's jacket. Then the other removed his own greatcoat and draped it carefully over his chest and legs. By now he'd recognised the uniform.

'*Luftwaffe*,' he said. 'A *Major*, a big shot.' He looked up at the *Blockwarten*. 'Find a telephone. The man's dying. He needs a hospital.'

The *Blockwarten* started to protest. Regulations were black and white. Bombing raid. Take cover.

'The man's dying,' the soldier repeated. 'He doesn't need a fucking shelter.'

It had begun to rain now and very faintly from the west came the growl of aero engines. The *Blockwarten* glanced up into the darkness, then looked at the figure under the greatcoat. There was a telephone in a ground-floor apartment nearby. He'd do his best.

For the next twenty minutes the soldiers crouched over the driver, whispering to the man, trying to keep him alive. From time to time there were faint signs of movement in one hand and, when the first bombs fell a kilometre or so away, and the ground shook with the impact, one eye flicked briefly open. By now, thanks to the man's ID card, the soldiers had a name. One of them knelt beside his ear.

'Herr *Major*... help's coming... Herr *Major*... you're going to be OK...'

The soldiers took it in turns, bending low, trying to make contact, trying to keep this dying stranger from slipping into oblivion. The bombs crept ever closer, the biggest explosion barely a block away, but they didn't seem to care.

'Georg...' one of them said, 'it's nearly Christmas. Hang on there.'

The ambulance appeared from nowhere. Overhead, the night sky was laced with searchlight beams hunting for the enemy bombers. A uniformed nurse with a flashlight bent briefly to the body while two orderlies readied a stretcher. The soldiers helped lift the dead weight onto the stretcher and manhandled it into the back of the ambulance. Then came the whine of a bomb, the closest so far, and everyone ducked for cover. Moments later a huge explosion rocked the ambulance and the trolley bus, and the street was suddenly full of flying glass and other debris. The men lay still. Nobody was injured. At length, wiping the dust and the rain from their uniforms, they were back on their feet. On the night wind, the unmistakable smell of gas from a ruptured main.

One of the soldiers still had the driver's ID. He handed it to the nurse.

'*Major* Georg Messner,' he said. 'Next-of-kin details on the back.'

2

The following day, 15 November 1940, *Major* Dieter Merz was piloting a twin-engined Me-110 on a flight from Flensburg, on the Danish border, to Zwolle, within touching distance of Amsterdam. The fighter bomber had a glasshouse canopy with room for a crew of three, though on this occasion Merz was alone.

He'd taken off less than half an hour ago, climbing through the early morning mist after a snatched breakfast of hot cinnamon rolls and a welcome mug of strong – and genuine – coffee. For nearly a week he'd been the guest of honour at the *Kriegsmarine* college overlooking the grey fjord that led to the city's busy heart. He'd delivered a series of lectures on ways in which the *Luftwaffe* planned to tighten operational support of the Reich's Navy, and when word spread that – *ja* – this was the same Dieter Merz who'd starred in one of Goebbels' pre-war propaganda films, the draughty classrooms had been standing-room only.

At the end of each talk, Dieter had always been careful to welcome questions. But instead of earnest enquiries about interservice command protocols, and the likely reach of the latest generation of maritime reconnaissance aircraft, everyone wanted to know about the air shows. Was it true that the famous dog fights between *Major* Merz and his comrade Georg Messner had always been fixed in Merz's favour? And when the Reich's aerial pin-up had swooped low over the huge crowd on the final day of that last Nuremberg rally, were witnesses kidding when they swore they could count the rivets on the underside of the Bf-109's wing?

In truth, Merz had been slightly embarrassed by the warmth of his welcome. The last six months had turned him into a warrior rather than a showman, and only once at the college – late last night, in convivial company – had he opened up about the realities of taking on the British. They flew well, he admitted, and often better than well. The Spitfire was a superb aircraft, more than capable of out-turning the 109. In one dogfight after another his squadron had battled to hold their own against the RAF, but exhausting months of close-quarters combat had left far too many of his precious pilots at the bottom of what the British called the English Channel.

Berlin, he pointed out, regarded the *Luftwaffe* as artillery with wings. They were obsessed by the bombing campaign. That's where the money went, into high explosive, into Heinkels and Dorniers, which left pilots like Dieter Merz flying live bait as bomber escorts. No wonder, he said, that the English constantly jumped them and that their losses had been so high. No wonder that even Goebbels struggled to turn those pitiless summer months into anything resembling the expected victory. After the steamroller campaigns of May and June, with capital after European capital offering nothing but token resistance, Goering had counted on destroying the RAF. And he'd failed.

Last night, the frankness of this admission had raised an eyebrow or two among the younger officers in the mess but the older staff had simply nodded. Wars rarely conformed to the script of any politician. So far, Hitler's run of victories had been little short of miraculous so it came as no surprise that the British had thrown a handful of sand in Goering's eye. Who knows, maybe postponing an invasion might turn out to be a blessing in disguise? Maybe there were other countries more deserving of the *Wehrmacht*'s attentions, lower-hanging fruit on the battered old tree that had once been unoccupied Europe?

On this note, the conversation had taken a lighter turn. Dieter's host had ordered another four bottles of Côtes du Rhône seized from the French Navy's mess at Brest, and the evening had ended with a raucous game of skat which Dieter, much to his surprise, appeared to have won.

'You'll find a crate of Mouton Cadet in your room,' his host had whispered. 'Our best to your comrades.'

Now, at 8,500 metres, the Me-110 seemed to be hanging motionless in the limpid air. For the last ten minutes Dieter had been sucking oxygen from the mask on his face. It tasted of rubber with a hint of exhaust fumes, but it had cleared his head after last night and left him with a feeling of immense privilege which – through the summer months – had become a bit of a memory. From his seat up here in the gods, unthreatened by the English, he could see forever. Move his head a little to the right, and the long curl of the Friesian Islands stretched all the way to Denmark. Glance left, and the Ruhr Valley was unmistakable, a long dark smudge, smoke from a thousand factory chimneys, proof that the Reich's engine room was in the rudest of health. More bombs, he thought. More Heinkels, more Dorniers, more reasons for the British to throw in their hands, leave the table, and opt for an easier life.

Would they ever do it, he wondered. Would they ever sue for peace? Somehow he doubted it. Back in the late spring, once the *Sitzkrieg* was over and the Panzers were off the leash, the English had spotted the invasion barges massing in Calais and Boulogne and knew that they were next on the list. Their precious Spitfires were held in reserve for the big battle to come, *der Kanalkampf*, and so for now they sent a two-engined bomber called the Blenheim to try and wreck the German plans.

The Blenheim was a maiden aunt when it came to combat. It had just three guns to defend itself, all of them useless. It could carry less than five hundred kilos of high explosive. In level flight, on a good day, it could manage barely 300 kph, half the speed of a Bf-109. Yet day after day these tubby little impostors would appear from the north, in a perfect V formation, easy prey for the likes of Merz and his eager young sharks.

Dieter smiled at the memory. The Spitfire was a princess among fighter aircraft, a proposition any *Luftwaffe* pilot would take very seriously indeed, but when it came to dropping bombs and making mischief the British were in the hands of designers who were still fighting the last war. The Blenheim was a hopeless aircraft. And so was the Whitley. And the Hampden. Too slow. Too vulnerable. Too *small*. One day all that might change, and you'd be foolish to assume otherwise, but by that time the war would be over.

Dieter checked his watch. He'd been airborne now for nearly an hour and ahead he could see the bright gleam of winter sunshine on the Ijsselmeer. His left hand reached for the throttle levers and the cackle of the twin engines changed note as the aircraft began to descend. On the ground at Zwolle he was expecting to meet an *Oberstleutnant* with whom he'd served in the Condor Legion. Hans Siebert was running the show at Zwolle and had already been in touch by phone. More lectures had been scheduled for the days ahead, a chance for operational pilots to reflect on the lessons of the summer campaign, but for today Hans was promising a long lunch at a fish restaurant in Amsterdam, followed by an afternoon in a couple of bars beside his favourite canal. The fighting over northern Spain had bonded Condor pilots for life. With this new war going so well, the least they owed themselves was the chance to celebrate a memory or two from the old days.

Minutes later, Dieter had the airfield in sight. He side-slipped the last hundred metres, kicked in a dab of right rudder, fed in a little more power to clear a hedge and then hauled back on the joystick until he could see nothing but sky. Then came a trio of tiny jolts as the aircraft settled on the racing turf and began to slow.

Hans was waiting on the broad circle of hardstanding in front of the control tower. Expecting a grin and the usual pumping handshake, Dieter sensed at once that something was wrong.

'Georg Messner?' Hans was never less than direct. Georg had been Dieter's wingman in Spain, and his best friend ever since.

'What's happened?'

'Beata phoned this morning. Here's her number. She's in Berlin. She needs to talk to you. Urgently.'

'But what's happened?'

Hans shot Dieter a look, then gestured loosely up at the sky. 'The English paid Berlin a visit,' he said. 'Last night.'

*

Tam Moncrieff returned from Sweden that same afternoon. An Airspeed Consul took him to Dyce aerodrome outside Aberdeen. He caught a slow train south to Laurencekirk and, after a brief conversation on the telephone with his masters at MI5, took a taxi home.

The Glebe House lay half an hour west, in the shadow of the Cairngorm Mountains. The property had been in the family for generations but recently it had suffered during Moncrieff's long absences in London. After the death of his father in 1938, Tam had done his best to keep the modest family shoot available for parties of visiting businessmen, but the Munich crisis had reduced bookings to a trickle and even these had dried up after the outbreak of war. With killings of another order in prospect, no one wanted to shoot game in the hills.

The taxi dropped Moncrieff at the head of the short drive. It had been raining earlier and water was still dripping from the line of beeches that had been his father's pride and joy. The house revealed itself slowly, glimpsed through the trees as the drive curved towards the mountains: solid granite walls veined with lichen, a curl of woodsmoke from the chimney, doors and windows badly in need of a lick of paint.

Moncrieff paused. A car he didn't recognise was parked among the puddles in front of the house.

Moncrieff let himself in. He could hear voices in the kitchen, then a roar of laughter. He listened a moment longer, making sure, then he dumped his bag on the flagstones, glad he hadn't gone straight back to London. Archie, he thought. After all this time.

He was sitting at the kitchen table, finishing a bowl of what looked like barley soup. The moment Moncrieff stepped in, he was on his feet, hand outstretched. Moncrieff hadn't seen him since he'd left the Marines, back in the mid-thirties, but the intervening years had barely touched him. The same brutal haircut. The same rosy, outdoor complexion. The same hint of mischief in the blueness of his eyes. Lieutenant Archie Gasgoigne had been the youngest of the officers in Moncrieff's company. And by far the most talented.

He pumped Moncrieff's hand, complimented him on his choice of cook.

'She fed you well?' Moncrieff was looking at the empty soup bowl.

'She made me welcome. And then she made me laugh. Bugger the food. Where on earth did you find a treasure like her?'

'In a pub. Where else? Isn't that right, Cathy?'

Cathy Phelps had been looking after the Glebe House for nearly a year. She was small, mid-twenties, with a melting smile and an earthy sense of humour. She had limitless patience and a passion for befriending life's misfits. Moncrieff had yet to meet a man who didn't fall instantly in love with her.

There was more soup in the pot. Cathy ladled a bowl for Moncrieff and let Archie help himself to seconds. There was soda bread, too, still warm from the oven.

Archie asked about the trip. Tam said it had been fine.

'Where did you go? Am I allowed to ask?'

'No.'

Archie held Tam's gaze a moment, then shrugged.

'OK, Boss. Sorry.'

'Boss?' The word made Cathy laugh. 'Is that what you used to call him?'

'It was. Boss and Big Man. Boss because that's what he was. And Big Man because he always put us in the shade. Isn't that right, Boss?'

Tam shook his head, and attended to the soup. Once again, he wouldn't be drawn. He'd loved his years in uniform, the company, the craich, the ceaseless physical challenges, and eager young whelps like Gasgoigne had been a big part of that.

'You're still in the Corps?' Moncrieff asked.

'Sort of.'

'What does that mean?'

'Later,' Archie winked at Cathy. 'I don't want to bore your young lady.'

Gasgoigne stayed the night. Cathy enquired about his tastes in food and when Archie assured her he'd eat anything that had once had a pulse, she busied herself at the kitchen range to cook a proper meal while the two men retired next door to the dining room.

Gasgoigne had brought a bottle of malt. Glenmorangie.

'Still partial, Boss?'

'Try me.'

Moncrieff found a couple of glasses. He wanted to know what Gasgoigne was up to.

'Funny, that. I was going to ask you exactly the same question.'

'Don't want to tell me?'

'Not at all. We're running supplies into Norway. It might sound simple, but it isn't.'

'We?'

'Me and a bunch of other blokes. Most of them are Norwegian fishermen. They shipped out when the Germans arrived. There's an Army guy in charge and a Navy bloke who they've let off the leash. I'm the only bootneck north of Cape Wrath. We run a freight service back to Norway. Tons of stuff you and me know only too well. Ammunition. Small arms. High explosives. Proper Norwegians can't get enough of it.'

'This is from Scotland?'

'The Shetlands. A tiny backwater called Lunna that no one's ever heard of. If you think this place is wild you should try a spell up there. Terrifying weather. And that's *before* you put to sea. Even the sheep plead for mercy but you'd love it.'

'You've come to offer me a job?'

'You're serious? The bloody Shetlands?' Gasgoigne nodded towards the stove. 'With a woman like her in your life?'

'You think we're together?'

'I think you'd be crazy if you're not. She's mad about you. She told me.'

'Nonsense.'

'I mean it. Women open up to me. You know that. It was true then and it's true now. You're telling me she's free? Because I need to know. One weekend might not be enough.'

Moncrieff ducked his head, trying to mask a smile.

'I'm old enough to be her father,' he said.

'So what? We're at war, Boss. Anything can happen and probably will. Peace is a conspiracy to make us behave. That excuse has gone. Take a risk or two. Give her a kiss. Are you serious? You haven't even *tried*?'

The thought made him laugh. Moncrieff asked about his own love life.

'I was married, Boss. Very briefly. Lesson one? Never tell yourself you've fallen in love. Let's talk about something else. Why Sweden?'

'I had to meet a German there.'

'For King and Country? Line of duty?'

'Of course.'

'MI5?'

'Yes. How did you know?'

'I didn't. I guessed. You're not posh enough for MI6 so it had to be Five. Tell me it's interesting. Tell me it's full of like-minded deviants with no table manners and far too much imagination. Am I getting warm here?'

'Absolutely not. Most of my colleagues spend their time locking up vast numbers of detainees. This country's become a giant prison camp. If that sounds interesting, it isn't.'

'And you, Boss? What do you do?'

'I do something different.'

'Because you speak German?'

'Yes. Well remembered. Because I speak German and because my face fits. I did MI5 a couple of favours around the time of Munich. To be frank, that was more than enough for me but then the war happened and they were suddenly back in my life. I work with some clever people. That makes me very lucky.'

Gasgoigne nodded. He sensed his questions had taken him as far as Moncrieff was prepared to go. He grinned and raised his glass.

'To the war,' he said. 'Long may she prosper.'

A little later, Cathy arrived with plates of haddock and settled at the table. Gasgoigne pounced on her at once. She'd told him about meeting Moncrieff in a pub. Now he wanted to know more.

'How come you can cook something as delicious as this? And how come you can meet the Big Man's standards? He's a tyrant when it comes to ironing. Or was.'

The question made Cathy giggle. She said she'd been in royal service for a while. First BP. Then Balmoral.

'BP?'

'Buckingham Palace. My mum had a brother who'd been with the Royal Household. It's the old game, who you know not where you come from. I was lucky. Not many girls from the East End get a chance like that.'

'You're serious? You were working for the *King*?'

'The Queen, mainly. She liked me, God knows why. Maybe we had the same sense of humour. They're a strange lot but that goes for most families. One of the chores they hate is being painted. I could help her out there. We've got the same build, the same height. The painter would arrive and I'd sit for him in whatever clothes the Queen had chosen and he'd paint me for hours on end until the time came to do the face and hands. Then I was back in the kitchen again. Knowing my place.'

'You're serious?' Gasgoigne was spellbound. 'I'm looking at a portrait of the Queen and it's really you in there?'

'Yes.'

'Remarkable.' He reached for his glass and summoned Moncrieff to his feet. 'God save the Queen, Boss. We're in the presence of royalty.'

Moncrieff, who'd never heard this story, motioned Gasgoigne back to his seat. Cathy Phelps had come to him on the recommendation of good friends in Aberdeen. Now he had a question of his own.

'Is that why you ended up at Balmoral? Because of the Queen?'

'Yes. She owns the place. It's hers. She spends as much time as she can there and she liked having me around.'

'So why did you leave?'

'There was a bit of an upset.'

Moncrieff held her gaze, but it was Gasgoigne who insisted on an answer.

'Upset?'

At first Cathy shook her head, reached for the bottle, recharged the empty glasses, but then Gasgoigne asked again and she looked him in the eye, spared Moncrieff a glance, and then shrugged.

'There was a young footman. I really liked him. One thing led to another. He was good at what he did but he never kept his views to himself. He was a Communist and when he'd had a drink or two he'd get on his soapbox and bang on about the Spanish War and Karl Marx and all the rest of it. We all looked after each other below stairs and not a whisper of this stuff went any further, but then he got really drunk one night and by next morning he'd gone.'

'Why?'

'He poured sand into the filling cap of one of the Rolls-Royces. It happened to belong to the King.'

'That's sabotage,' Gasgoigne sounded delighted. 'Give me his details. There's a job waiting for him in Lunna. Does this beau of yours speak Norwegian, by any chance?'

'Beau?'

'Lover. Consort. Prince over the water.'

'I've no idea. I don't see him any more.'

'But you'd like to?'

'I didn't say that.' She got to her feet and stifled a yawn. 'The rest of the fish is on the side in the kitchen. Help yourselves.'

Moncrieff and Gasgoigne stayed up late that night, working their way through the bottle and swapping stories about the old days, and it was nearly three in the morning by the time the two of them climbed the stairs.

Moncrieff now occupied his parents' big bedroom at the front of the house and he lay awake, musing on where the war had taken them both. Gasgoigne, in one sense, had been right about MI5. The Secret Intelligence Service, or MI6 as some preferred to call it, was for the toffs, a collection of public school boys who'd passed through the sieve of Oxbridge or the better regiments. They were responsible for intelligence gathering abroad, a calling which naturally required both foreign languages and a certain *je ne sais quoi*. Their contempt for their lesser brethren in the Security Service was emphatic and undisguised. MI5, they murmured, was for tweedy provincials and burned-out imperial policemen. Their noun of choice to describe these lesser folk was 'plod'.

Moncrieff had never agreed. Once you knew where to look, he suspected there were pockets of MI5 that held much brighter prospects and one of these was Section B1A, which addressed itself to Counter Espionage. This fast-growing empire was run by a softly spoken, balding figure who had the comfortable manners of a country solicitor. Guy Liddell rarely raised his voice but he played the cello to some effect and – to Moncrieff's surprise – sometimes kept raffish company in the evenings.

He was also a talent-spotter of genius and had carefully built a team of individuals – gifted, often difficult – prepared to pool their talents. Between them, in the words of Guy Liddell, it was the business of this coterie of eccentrics to defend the nation's fragile little barque against espionage and subversion. An interesting challenge, Moncrieff had quickly concluded. And a pleasure to be on board.

Now, in the darkness, he caught the sound of footsteps in the corridor outside. Then came the sound of a door opening and – after a while – a brief murmur of conversation. Seconds later the footsteps returned and another door opened and closed. Archie Gasgoigne, Moncrieff thought. Trying his luck.

Moncrieff smiled to himself. One of the attractions of having Cathy around on the rare weekends he could spare away from London was the sheer pleasure of her company. She was bright and lively and brought something to his life that he knew had been missing. She had a natural gift for conversation, for listening and responding, and once or twice – a glance, a smile – he'd sensed that something more might be on offer. That he found her attractive was beyond dispute. She had a physical presence no man could ignore. But he cherished, as well, the simplicity of their relationship, the fact that he could trust her with a house he'd always loved. I'm lucky to have found her, he told himself as he drifted off to sleep. Keep things simple.

Gasgoigne departed the following morning, assuring Tam of a warm welcome should he ever find himself in the Shetlands. It had been a real pleasure to revive a memory or two and he'd be back like a shot if young Cathy needed any company on these dark winter nights. She lingered in the open door as he clambered into his car and she grinned as he blew her a kiss.

Later, after lunch, she drove Moncrieff to the station. Mist had covered the mountains all day and a thin rain had begun to fall. Moncrieff had been round the house after Gasgoigne's departure and now he handed Cathy a list of jobs she might have the time to attend to. She'd parked outside the station. She barely glanced at the list.

Moncrieff had the passenger door open but had yet to get out.

'You'll be careful, Boss?' she said.

'Always.'

'There was a big raid last night. It was on the wireless. Central London. Hundreds killed. Lots of damage. Watch out for yourself, Big Man.' That smile again. 'You promise?'

Cathy was right about the bombing. Next morning, after the overnight sleeper finally crawled into London, Moncrieff took a bus from King's Cross station, a journey lengthened by endless diversions. Southampton Row had been cratered in three places, and a fountain of water was still pumping from a fractured main. A demolition crew had started work on a tottering façade on Bedford Place, while a thin stream of traffic slowed in fascinated anticipation of the building's collapse.

It was mid-morning by now and Moncrieff got off at Oxford Circus to walk the last half-mile to MI5 headquarters in St James's Street. The area around the bus stop had survived Saturday night's raid virtually intact but several Mayfair properties off Conduit Street had taken direct hits and platoons of tailors' dummies occupied the pavement along Savile Row while shop staff cleared up the damage inside.

Moncrieff paused to watch them for a moment. Scenes like this had become routine, a strange mix of the familiar and the bizarre, but what struck him most was the sheer stoicism of Londoners. Maybe they'd been anticipating this for years, he thought. Maybe the real lesson of the thirties is that God and Hitler have no surprises left.

Half an hour later, he was standing in the middle of St James's Street, enjoying the thin winter sun on his face. A huge bomb had demolished a building at the upper end of the street and passers-by were still stepping around drifts of rubble and broken glass. Few windows at number 53 had survived the blast and Moncrieff lingered to watch a small army of carpenters nailing boards to the empty frames. Stepping inside the building, he paused beside the reception desk. Mid-morning, it was unusual to find the burly civil servant in charge working by the light of a candle.

'Electricity off?'

'Until lunchtime, Mr Moncrieff. That's the rumour.'

'And water?'

'Later this afternoon. If it's tea you're after, Miss Barton had the good sense to leave the kettles filled on Friday night.'

Good sense, my arse. Ursula Barton had an uncanny knack of anticipating every single enemy raid. Quite how she managed this Moncrieff had never fathomed, but she was rarely, if ever, wrong. On the one occasion he'd dared to ask, his question had drawn a rare smile and a muttered reference to a secret source. This, to Moncrieff, simply confirmed that she was, in all probability, a witch.

He found her in the first-floor office she occupied next to the Director of 'B' Section. She was thin-faced, blonde, slightly forbidding. She had a stylish dress sense with an overwhelming emphasis on black. Her operational budget stretched to two candles but when Moncrieff enquired about the possibility of a cuppa, she shook her head. Carpenters were working on the windows of the floor above and the noise was deafening.

'I'm nearly out of tea leaves,' she shouted. 'You might be luckier this afternoon.'

Moncrieff nodded at the door that led to Guy Liddell's office. She understood the unvoiced question at once.

'He's been in since eight,' she said. 'Just like the rest of us. I think he might appreciate a word.'

Moncrieff knocked on the door, waited a second or two, and then stepped inside. Liddell's single window had, for some reason, been spared by the blast. A couple of cracks in the glass but nothing missing. Moncrieff stood in front of the big, glass-topped desk, blinking. Already, in a matter of minutes, daylight had become a novelty. Just like peace, he thought. You never know you'll miss it until it's gone.

Liddell was bent over a pile of paperwork. Moncrieff studied the polished oval dome of his head.

'Sir?'

The Director looked up. Moncrieff wondered whether the surprise on his face was real.

'Ah...' Liddell smiled, '... the wanderer returns.'

'We talked on Saturday, sir. On the phone.'

'We did indeed. Very briefly. And now we must talk a little more. But not here, I fear. I don't mind the bloody Germans making the nights so difficult, but this is ridiculous. Maybe we should all invest in a hammer and a ladder and a bag of nails. Make ourselves rich before we all go mad.'

The hammering stopped for a moment and in the brief silence Moncrieff became aware of a scuffling noise and a soft mewing. Beneath the desk, in an empty drawer, the office cat had nested in balls of newsprint. Her name was Brünnhilde and just now she was busy attending to a litter of tiny kittens.

Liddell sat back, his arms neatly folded.

'Gave birth during the raid. Prematurely, we think. Wonderful mother, though, and still loves powdered milk, thank God.' He got to his feet and glanced at his watch as the hammering resumed. 'Anthony Eden has made himself available at noon. Perfect timing, Tam, as ever.'

Liddell and Moncrieff walked the half-mile to the Foreign Office where Eden, as Secretary of State for War, had been attending a meeting. On the other side of St James's Park, Liddell paused at the sandbagged entrance to King Charles Street to show his pass to one of the sentries before escorting Moncrieff towards the steps that led to the main entrance. On the train rumbling slowly south, Tam had expected – at the very most – some kind of internal gathering where he could present what he'd learned in Stockholm and debate its significance. The last thing he'd anticipated was this.

Anthony Eden was occupying a small, bare office at the back of the building on the first floor. The ageing diplomat who'd met them downstairs warned Liddell that the War Secretary was due at a lunch in Downing Street at a quarter to one and that time was therefore precious. He appeared puzzled by the lack of advance briefing papers.

'You people fly by the seat of your pants,' he paused outside the office Eden had borrowed. 'Sometimes that can be a cause of envy.'

Liddell chuckled but said nothing. The aide knocked softly on the door and then stood aside to let his guests in.

Moncrieff had met Eden twice before, on both occasions at diplomatic receptions, a brief handshake and an even briefer exchange of pleasantries, but this was the first time he'd had the chance to take a proper look. In Whitehall, Eden had a reputation for impatience and a certain loftiness. He had little time for small talk and none at all for politicians or journalists prepared to credit the Nazi regime with anything but the most malign of intentions. Before the war he'd spent three years in this very building as Foreign Secretary before resigning over the issue of appeasement. Now, according to Liddell, he was rumoured to be only weeks away from returning. Hence his interest in Moncrieff's brief visit to Sweden.

Now he rose from behind the desk and buttoned his jacket before extending a hand to Liddell. For a politician, he was improbably handsome. His face alone would have won him a career in Hollywood.

'Guy...' he murmured. 'I'm afraid this has to be quick.' He waved the two men into the waiting chairs and resumed his seat. No handshake for Moncrieff.

Liddell offered a brief résumé of the chain of events that had taken one of his key agents to Stockholm. Wilhelm Schultz, he said, had an ear to some important doors in Berlin. His network of trusted confidants extended deep into the upper reaches of the military. As an *Alter Kämpfer*, a brawler from the twenties, he was no stranger to the rougher edges of the Nazi regime. And the message he was sending was impossible to misinterpret.

'You're telling me this is official?'

'We believe so, yes.'

'Proof?'

'There is none.'

'So what's this man telling us?'

Liddell glanced sideways at Moncrieff. Moncrieff described the conversations he'd shared with Schultz in the harbourside restaurant and during another, briefer meeting at the airport the following morning. In essence, the Germans believed the war was as good as won. The British were now isolated with no possibility of recruiting allies in occupied Europe. The Russians were bound hand and foot by the Non-Aggression Pact and the Americans had turned their backs on the quarrelsome tribes across the Atlantic. The British still had an empire, and therefore a future. Berlin would be only too happy to call off the bombers and the U-boats in exchange for a formal peace treaty. In short, Germany's rightful claim to her European destiny should be no concern of London's.

'They've said all this before.' Eden was looking at Moncrieff.

'So I understand, sir. But that was before the fall of France. The point Schultz makes is that time marches on. Much like the *Wehrmacht.*'

'Facts on the ground? We have what we hold?'

'Indeed.'

'So what would this... peace treaty... comprise? What could possibly be in it for us?'

Moncrieff had been anticipating this question since he and Liddell had set out from St James's Street. He outlined the bones of an agreement whereby Hitler would withdraw from France and the Low Countries in return for a permanent peace with Britain.

'He *said* this? Schultz?'

'On the first night, no. It was my idea, my suggestion.'

'You're telling me you're a diplomat, as well as a spy?'

'No, sir. I was sent to listen. To listen, and probe, and maybe sow a seed or two.'

'Go on.'

'As I said, we met again at the airport the following day. Schultz had obviously been in contact with Berlin overnight.'

'And?'

'And he appeared to think some kind of deal might be possible. He called it an arrangement. Between like-minded friends.'

'Including formal withdrawal?'

'That's the impression I got.'

'From Paris? Brussels? Amsterdam? Copenhagen? The full *status quo ante*?'

'Not as far as Norway's concerned. He talked of protecting the ore supplies.'

'Remarkable. And you believed all this?'

'I'm not a diplomat, sir, as you just pointed out. I'm simply reporting back.'

There was a silence. Eden was staring at Moncrieff. He looked, if anything, irritated. Then Liddell fingered the crease in his trousers and cleared his throat. He wanted the War Secretary to be absolutely clear where Wilhelm Schultz stood in the ongoing battle between the key German intelligence agencies. He was an *Abwehr* man, a devotee of Admiral Canaris. He viewed Himmler and the dead-eyed careerists in the *Sicherheitsdienst* with little short of contempt. If we were to put our money on any horse in this race, ventured Liddell, then the odds might favour Wilhelm Schultz. He'd been around for years. He was an *Alter Kampfer*. And, as one of the old campaigners, he had form.

Eden nodded and said nothing. Listening to Liddell, Moncrieff had suddenly realised exactly why this brief meeting was taking place. It wasn't about war and peace at all. It wasn't about some fanciful Nazi ruse to buy the British off and shut them out of Europe. It was about a turf battle much closer to home. MI5, Liddell was implying, had much better sources in continental Europe than MI6. Listen to us for a change, and begin to understand what's really going on in the enemy's black heart.

Eden checked his watch, then he got to his feet. He said he was grateful for Liddell's time and would ponder the implications of what he'd had to say. It was just possible that Mr Moncrieff might be obliged to repeat his story in the presence of others and he trusted that wouldn't be a burden. Moncrieff shook his head. Eden was still looking at him. His irritation appeared to have evaporated.

'The Glebe House?' he said at last. 'Am I right?'

Moncrieff blinked, remained silent

'Cathy Phelps? Been with you a while?'

'Yes, sir.'

'Wonderful girl. She made weekends at Balmoral almost bearable. You're a lucky man, Mr Moncrieff.' He winked. 'I wish you well.'

Walking back across St James's Park, Liddell wanted to know more. Moncrieff, who'd always guarded the privacy of his life at the Glebe House, was reluctant to go into details. A woman called Cathy Phelps was currently keeping house for him. She'd previously been with the Royal Household at Balmoral. With domestic help so hard to find, he counted himself more than lucky.

'That sounds a bit wooden to me.'

'Far from it. Honest? Conscientious? Tireless? Good company? Since when did words like that go together? No wonder Eden was so smitten.'

'Eden's a gourmet when it comes to women. He normally treats himself to other people's wives. That might not have been the case at Balmoral.'

'She was in service, sir. With respect.'

'All the better, Tam. *Droit de seigneur.* While the royals weren't watching.'

'Really?'

'Ask her. Get the full story,' he was smiling. 'Not that it matters a damn, eh?'

Moncrieff didn't answer. They walked on in silence for a while. Then, leaving the park, Liddell was struck by another thought. He fumbled in his pocket and brought Moncrieff to a halt.

'Here. Andrew gave me this first thing this morning. He said it came in the post from your sister. Andrew's over in Washington for the rest of the week but he thought it might amuse you.'

Moncrieff took the card. Andrew Ballentyne worked for another arm of MI5 and had been quietly appointed liaison officer with the FBI ahead of the moment America might be obliged to take up arms against the Nazis. Two years ago he'd been responsible for Moncrieff's introduction to the secret world and the two men had been friends ever since.

Moncrieff was looking at the card. He'd never heard of Gordon Millord Hesketh.

'He's some kind of historian,' Liddell said. 'He's over from Lisbon and paid a call on that sister of yours. Some story about growing up in her house. Lisbon?' His eyes were gleaming in the pale sunshine. 'You think it might merit a conversation or two?'

Moncrieff smiled. Guy Liddell was a man you underestimated at your peril. As the last hour had so amply proved.

'You think it went well? Back there?' Moncrieff nodded at the grey Italianate façade of the Foreign Office looming over the park.

Liddell gave the question some thought.

'Politicians know so much and understand so little,' he said at last. 'From time to time we need to redress that balance.'

3

It was mid-week before Dieter Merz could get away from Zwolle. His host, Hans Siebert, cancelled one of the lectures, combined three others into a single day-long session and drove Dieter to the railway station to catch a train to Berlin. Dieter had talked to Beata twice on the phone and knew that the doctors at the Charité hospital were still fighting for Georg's life. An operation on his swollen brain had released pressure that had nearly killed him in the hours after the accident but he was still unconscious and his vital signs, in Beata's dry phrase, barely kept him ticking over. Even her constant presence at his bedside had failed to raise a flicker of response.

Darkness had fallen in Berlin by the time the train pulled into the Anhalter station. Beata had offered to meet him on the platform, but Dieter said he'd take a taxi straight to the hospital.

She was sitting on a bench outside the neurological ward when Dieter finally arrived. Heavy blackout curtains hung at every window along the corridor and she looked pale and thin in the dim lighting. This wasn't the Beata he'd last met back in the summer. Then, she'd been in the rudest of health, tanned from days in the sun playing with her daughter Lottie. Now, grey and drawn, she might have been a ghost.

She struggled to her feet and Dieter gave her a hug. She pressed herself against him. There were tears in her eyes.

'Any improvement?' Dieter nodded towards the nearby ward.

'None.'

'I'm so sorry.'

'Don't be. He's not dead yet.'

She slipped her arm through his and walked him into the ward. It was bigger than Dieter had expected and the silence was punctuated by the steady ticking of bedside equipment and the clack-clack of their own shoes on the polished wooden floor.

Beata led the way to a bed at the far end of the ward. Dieter barely recognised the swollen face on the pillow. Georg's head was heavily bandaged and his eyes were closed. His long body was covered by a single sheet and Dieter had to look very hard to catch any sign of movement when he breathed.

Georg Messner had always been the man in charge. Over Spain, he'd flown as Dieter's wingmate, but in every other respect he'd taken responsibility for the life they'd led together. He was utterly dependable. He'd been born grown up. In the air and on the ground, he always made the wisest calls. Never for a second had Dieter doubted his immortality. Now this.

A male nurse stepped into the ward from a door at the end. He was carrying two chairs. He offered Dieter a nod and arranged them side by side at the head of the bed before murmuring something in Beata's ear. Then he was gone.

'What did he say?'

'He told me they're going to operate again. Tomorrow afternoon.'

'To do what?'

'He doesn't know. He's seen the operating schedule. He's a friend. He's doing me a favour.'

'Shouldn't you ask?'

'Ask who? It's half past eight in the evening. The doctors are all at home eating supper with their families.'

She wasn't looking at Dieter. Her eyes were on her husband and there was an edge of envy in her voice.

Dieter didn't know what to say. He had no words of comfort to offer. He came from a world that Beata had never understood, the world of dawn take-offs, of strafing missions against enemy positions, of combat patrols, of the seemingly effortless extension of the Reich by eager young men who'd never tasted defeat. Now, as a simple civilian, she was suddenly living with the knowledge that the enemy, too, could play this game. And that there might be consequences. Every night, because of the RAF, Berlin put the lights out. And the inky darkness could kill people.

They sat in silence for the best part of an hour. From time to time there was movement in the ward as nurses came and went, attending to some of the other patients. A handful were conscious and could manage a murmured conversation. Others babbled in their sleep. One in particular, an older figure in the next bed, balding, troubled, was moaning softly to himself. But Georg never moved, not once, a recumbent figure, an object of passing curiosity, as if already preparing himself for the afterlife.

After a while, Beata reached for Dieter's hand. Her cheeks were wet with tears. Dieter asked her whether she wanted to go. She shook her head.

'Lottie?'

'She's with my father. He's moved in with us. He does the cooking, too. Leave if you want. He'll be glad to see you.'

'You want me to stay? In the house?'

'Of course. You will, won't you? Please say yes.' She was staring at him, and Dieter saw something close to panic in her eyes.

'Of course.' He gave her hand a squeeze.

Minutes passed. Beata's attention, single-minded, had returned to the face on the pillow. Dieter, too, was gazing fiercely at the man who'd meant so much to him, as if some inner force could conjure just a flicker of movement, but after a while his mind began to play tricks with him.

He and Georg were back in the bullring at Sevilla, down in Andalucía, the night the young matador despatched three bulls before the fourth nearly killed him. They were up north, months later, flying wingtip to wingtip over some helpless Gallego township, trailing their own capes in a bid to tempt the Ivans into combat. They were in a bar in Vitoria, a dog asleep under the battered wooden table, rain lashing at the tiny windows, the wind howling under the door. That particular night, after a repeat expedition to Guernica, they'd matched the Spanish at the bar, raising glass after glass to Franco and pledging the ugliest of deaths to the hated Republicans. A game, Dieter thought. A roll of the dice, a wrong call, a moment's inattention, and here you were, beyond reach, barely alive, feeling nothing.

The lightness of the hand on his shoulder made him jump. He looked up. Hans Baur.

Baur was Hitler's personal pilot, the legendary flyer who'd brought Georg back from Spain to help fly the Führer to the far corners of the ever-expanding Reich and had later found a brief perch in the squadron for Dieter Merz. He offered Beata a formal nod of greeting before gesturing Dieter to his feet.

'A word, please.'

They returned to the corridor outside the ward. Baur, it turned out, was a regular visitor. Georg had been in the hospital since the raid at the weekend and Baur had checked up on him every night.

'You've noticed any difference?'

'None.' He tapped his own head. 'He's dead in there. It's gone.'

'How do you know?'

'I don't. But sometimes it pays to assume the worst. That way life can only surprise you. You find that?'

'Never.'

'I'm glad to hear it. That was always *der Kleine*'s charm.'

Hans Baur had a habit of sometimes talking in the third person. *Der Kleine*. The Little One. Merz's squadron nickname.

'The *Kanalkampf*? I'm hearing you did well against the British.'

'They never saw me coming. Never fails.'

'Twenty-one kills?'

'Twenty-three.'

'And Beata? The good lady?' He nodded towards the ward. 'You're going to play the gentleman? Look after her?'

'As best I can.'

Baur held Dieter's gaze for a long moment, then asked him about his current posting.

'You're on some kind of grand tour? *Jagdstaffel* by *Jagdstaffel*? Have I got that right?'

'You have. How do you know?'

'Your name came up this morning. Goering, no less. I flew him down to Augsburg and told him about Messner. He thinks as I do. He thinks we owe Beata a little care and attention.'

'You mean me?'

'I do. Goering has a proposition. Nothing to keep you too busy. Just as long as you keep an eye on Frau Messner.' He smiled. 'And Georg, of course.'

Dieter nodded. He hadn't a clue what Baur was talking about. 'Proposition?'

'He'll tell you tomorrow. I'm flying down to Augsburg to pick him up. Eight o'clock at Tempelhof. Come with me.'

Tam Moncrieff's sister lived in an elegant three-storey Regency house overlooking Eaton Place. One of the reasons their relationship had never been easy was Vanessa's lifelong determination to turn her back on life in the Scottish uplands and find herself somewhere more fitting to call home. A six-bedroom mansion in the heart of Belgravia, with the cream of the capital's diplomatic representation as neighbours, had probably outstripped even her own expectations, but marriage to Alec Nairn had won her a perch at the very top of London society. Which was why Moncrieff had been so surprised to find a furniture van at her door.

'You're on the move?'

'We are. Alec likes a good night's sleep.'

'Anywhere nice?'

'North Yorkshire.' She named an estate Moncrieff had never heard of. 'The owners are moving to Canada. Alec's sister passed the word and the rest, as they say these days, is history.'

'You're selling this place?'

'Closing it up for the winter. Or maybe winters. The bloody Germans write the script these days. Don't you find that?'

Tam followed her into the house. Wooden crates lined the big hall, ready for collection, and through an open door into the dining room Tam caught a glimpse of two elderly women on their knees wrapping glassware in sheets of newspaper. The kitchen was in a similar state of chaos: tottering piles of crockery, boxes of tinned food, three old blankets for the dog and a sweetness in the air from the remains of the overnight fire.

'The last of the cherry tree,' Vanessa was staring at the ashes in the grate. 'Where we're going we're spoiled for wood and Alec saw no point in leaving it all. Scorched earth... isn't that the term?'

'You're denying the enemy?'

'We are. Does that amuse you?'

'Only if you're expecting the Germans. I don't think it's quite that bad. Not yet, anyway.'

'You don't? You really don't? Alec thinks there's a peace to be had. So do most of his chums. Sometimes we think someone should spare us all and put that maniac out of his misery.'

'You mean Hitler?'

'Churchill, Tam. Don't be so bloody obtuse. What's the point of fighting on alone when it simply prolongs the agony? I imagine you must have been in London the other night. Are you deaf or something? Blind? Isn't all this suffering, all this bother, a little...' she frowned, hunting for the right word, '...*indulgent*? At this rate there won't be anything worth saving, not if you really care about the country. One man. One bad apple. That's all it takes. Life could be so much simpler.'

'If we all spoke German?'

'If we all looked the situation in the face. Alec says that even Hitler is bewildered. Apparently he's prepared to offer the PM perfectly good peace terms. Why can't the bloody man *listen* for a change? There's no question of us all speaking German. That's cheap, if I may say so. Unless there's something you know and we don't.'

Moncrieff shrugged, said nothing. He'd always been tight-lipped about the exact role the war had assigned to him, though he suspected that his precious sister had guessed most of it. Hence her recent phone call to Andrew Ballentyne.

'Tell me about Gordon Hesketh,' he said. 'Then I'll leave you in peace.'

'Hateful little man. Came calling last week. Uninvited, unannounced, and – on first acquaintance – deeply implausible.'

Hesketh, it turned out, had knocked on her door with some wild story about having grown up in the property as a child. Vanessa's first instinct had been to send him on his way but then he'd mentioned the big old radiator in the attic with the antique guard and the way the sun slanted into the nursery in the early mornings and after that her curiosity had got the better of her.

'Not so implausible after all?'

'Quite the reverse. Alec had been going through the deeds only the other night, a complete record of previous owners, and what the little man said may well have been true. Back at the turn of the century, the house belonged to a man called Hesketh. It's there in black and white. Ronald Hesketh and his wife Violet. Hesketh, it seems, was in the oil business. Worked most of his life in Persia. Got himself some kind of emissary role with the Shah afterwards. Ended up living here.'

'And the little man at the door?'

'Adopted. That made perfect sense, of course. There was something about him, very hard to pin down. No style. No breeding. Talked too much. *Assumed* too much.'

'Didn't know his place?'

'Exactly. It's no sin to be quite so pushy, quite so charmless, but the social advantages, says little me, are limited. That was Alec's view, too. The wretched man was still here, in the kitchen, when he came home. All day in the Upper House is enough for anyone. An extra hour or so with our new friend was beyond the call of duty. For once I almost felt sorry for my poor lamb.'

Moncrieff ducked his head to hide a smile. After the death of his father, Alec Nairn had inherited the family title. On the day of her marriage, much to her satisfaction, Vanessa had therefore become Lady Nairn.

'You telephoned Andrew Ballentyne,' Moncrieff pointed out. 'May I ask why?'

'Because the little man kept telling me about his life out in Lisbon. How he loved the place. How he was writing this book of his. How many people he knew out there, interesting people, well-placed people, people with a story to tell. He was bragging, of course, and to tell you the truth I couldn't shut him up, even after Alec came home. In fact it was his idea, Alec's.'

'To do what?'

'To pass the little man on to you. Alec thinks Lisbon's the root of all mischief. He tells me it's thick with spies.' For the first time, a smile. 'Might he be right?'

Moncrieff didn't reply. Instead, he asked whether – in his sister's opinion – Hesketh had really grown up in Eaton Place. By now, Vanessa was looking for a note she'd made of a telephone number. She looked up.

'Oh, yes,' she nodded down at the remains of the fire. 'He knew exactly where the cherry tree had been.'

'How do you know?'

'I asked him.' She'd found the number. 'Here. Give him a ring. But for God's sake don't breathe a word about North Yorkshire.'

4

Next morning, Dieter Merz flew south from Berlin to Augsburg. Hans Baur was at the controls of the big Ju-52 and invited Merz to share the cockpit with him. As a display pilot before returning to front-line combat duties after the invasion of Poland, Merz had frequently hitched a lift with the Führer Squadron but he recognised none of the Berlin functionaries in the cabin behind him. No wonder, Baur had grunted. The regime eats these people for breakfast. If you want to survive, stick to being a fighter pilot.

They landed at the Messerschmitt factory at Augsburg in a flurry of snow a few minutes short of noon. Baur waited for the passengers to clamber down the metal ladder before checking the cabin and ordering more fuel from the ground crew. Waiting in the warmth of an office in a building next to one of the big assembly hangars was a familiar face.

'Herr. Messerschmitt.' Dieter offered the Hitler salute. He'd met Willi Messerschmitt on a number of occasions, most of them dedicated to post-combat analysis of ways in which the great designer might improve his fabled Bf-109. For someone whose name was on the lips of millions of Germans, he was remarkably down to earth.

'*Der Kleine*,' he ignored the Hitler salute and pumped Dieter's hand. 'A pleasure, as always.'

Baur accompanied them up two flights of stairs. *Reichsmarschall* Hermann Goering was waiting in a spacious office on the top floor. So far, the war had been kind to the *Luftwaffe*'s founding father. Hitler seemed to have forgiven him for not destroying the RAF in the *Kanalkampf*, it was whispered, because he'd never intended to invade Britain in the first place. Whatever the truth, Goering was fatter and more expansive than ever.

'Merz,' he nodded at the chair in front of the desk. 'Sit.'

Merz did as he was told. Baur and Willi Messerschmitt had disappeared.

'Messner?'

'Not good, *Herr Reichsmarschall*.' Merz described his visit to the Charité hospital and the hours he'd spent sitting up with Beata afterwards at the family home beside the Wannsee. 'I'm afraid she's starting to fear the worst.'

'She thinks he'll die?'

'She thinks he may be like this forever.'

'Unconscious?'

'Different. Even if he recovers, that's what alarms her. She says she can see it in his face. She says he's changing in front of her eyes. Becoming someone else.'

'And is she right?'

'I've no idea. But she's an intelligent woman, and strong, too. She thinks the way Georg thinks. She makes it her business to try and understand what might be going on and draws the logical conclusion. That can't be easy, *Herr Reichsmarschall*. Not in a situation like this.'

It was true. Last night, crouched over the log fire, Dieter had listened to her worst fears. Before the arrival of little Lottie, Beata had been a physicist at the Kaiser Wilhelm Institute, the Reich's leading centre for scientific research, and she was no stranger to the unforgiving logic of cause and effect. Her husband, at the very least, was brain damaged. If he survived at all, then it would be at some cost.

The *Reichsmarschall* was playing with one of the rings on his fingers. He said he was sorry. Messner had been a fine addition to the *Reichsregierung*, and his flying had won even the Führer's approval. Merz nodded. Despite everything Beata had said, he'd yet to write his friend off as a pilot and Goering's choice of tense made him feel deeply uncomfortable.

'You'll pass on my sympathies to Frau Messner?'

'Of course, *Herr Reichsmarschall.*'

'And you'll tell her how much we'll miss him?'

'Yes.'

'Excellent. She'll need support. She has friends? Family?'

'She has a father. Her mother's dead. No brothers, no sisters. Friends, of course, but they're all at the KWI. Some of them used to drive out in the evening after work but this time of year that isn't an option.'

'Because of the English?'

'Because of the blackout.'

'Same thing, isn't it?'

Merz held Goering's gaze. It was a direct challenge. Merz had heard the rumours in squadron messes across the Reich that *der Eiserne,* as some called him, was extremely touchy about the growing threat from RAF bombers. *Der Eiserne* meant 'The Iron Man'. In Goering's view, German airspace was sacrosanct. The English had no business appearing over Berlin night after night.

'We're fighting a war,' Merz pointed out. 'We should expect to bleed from time to time.'

Goering frowned, gave the proposition some thought. Then the flat of his huge hand slammed down on the desk and he roared with laughter.

'Blood,' he said. 'That's exactly what I told the Führer. We spill the enemy's blood. They take a little of ours. You know what kind of aircraft they're using now? Blenheims. Hampdens. We wouldn't deliver the post in machines like that. And in any case, the war's as good as won. Messner is unfortunate. Look after that wife of his. I have your word she won't suffer?'

'Of course, *Herr Reichsmarschall.*'

'Excellent. Now then. Rudolf Hess. How well do you know him?'

Dieter blinked. Sudden conversational swerves were Goering's stock in trade. He loved to wrongfoot people, to take them by surprise exactly the way you might jump the enemy in a dogfight. Maybe that was the key to his success. Over the trenches in the last war he'd amassed a decent tally of kills.

'I've met him a couple of times when I was flying with Messner on the Führer Squadron. Once we had a conversation.'

'And?'

'He was friendly. He told me how much he loved flying and how jealous he was.'

'Of what? Who?'

'Of me. We were coming back from Stuttgart. He'd been at Nuremberg that last year, '38, when I flew on the final Sunday in the 109. All his life he'd wanted to be a fighter pilot. We talked for a while. He had a list of questions, really technical questions. He wanted to know everything.'

'So what did you make of him?'

Dieter hesitated. Rudolf Hess was Hitler's Deputy in the Party hierarchy, a man with his fingers in countless pies. He knew all the top bankers. He was on first-name terms with industrialists like Fritz Thyssen and Gustav Krupp. He ran the *Auslands-Organisation*. He could interfere in court rulings. He had a voice on the War Council. And most important of all, he had a unique relationship with the Führer himself, a kinship that went back to the earliest days, something that was immediately evident when you saw the two men together. Hitler seemed to listen to Hess. He even treated him with something close to respect. That made Hess someone to be reckoned with, a man of immense power and influence, and yet – when it came to his private life – he seemed to be an exception to the Party rule.

'He's a modest man,' Merz said carefully. 'And he struck me as shy, as well.'

'He's an anchorite,' Goering said. 'He should be living in a cave. Deserts were invented for people like Hess. No temptations. Nothing fancy.'

Merz nodded. At major rallies he'd noticed that Hess had no taste for elaborate uniforms or any of the other trappings of power. On the contrary, unlike Goering, he favoured a plain brown shirt, unadorned.

'He never uses the government fuel stations when he's driving.' Goering was rocking with laughter again. 'Can you imagine that? At first I thought he was a simpleton. Now I know it's even worse. He's got principles. *Principles?* In a regime like this? In God's name...'

Merz smiled. The government fuel stations, with their rock-bottom prices, were a present to the Party faithful. Pledge your allegiance, claw your way up the Party ladder, and you could drive for practically nothing. Unless you were Hess.

'You're telling me he pays the regular price for fuel?'

'I'm telling you he gives us a good name. He's the conscience of the Party. And he's educated, too. That's why Hitler loves him. Needs him. He keeps the Führer honest. Don't ask me why but no one else can do that.'

Merz had been wondering what kind of assignment he might expect to give him time to look after Beata. Now it appeared to have something to do with Rudolf Hess.

'You liked him?' Goering was always looking for something to play with. Just now, he'd found a small die-cast model of the Bf-109, weighting down a pile of loose paperwork on the borrowed desk.

'He was interesting, someone a little different,' Dieter said. 'I wouldn't claim to know the man, but shyness isn't a sin.'

'Good to hear it.' Goering picked up the tiny fighter, ran an approving finger over the long powerful nose. 'As you know, our spartan friend has a single weakness. He loves to fly. When we went into Poland he begged the Führer to let him join the *Luftwaffe*. It wasn't the glory he was after. He didn't even want a special rank. Just the promise of flying was enough, ideally in one of these.' He tapped the cockpit of the 109. 'Hitler wouldn't hear of it. Hess matters to him. He wants the man alive. He needs the voice in his ear when it suits him. And so the answer was no. But Hess doesn't give in. Ever. He was at the Chancellery night and day. He badgered. He argued. He even pleaded. And in the end there was a negotiation. One year. Just one year. That, believe me, makes Hess unique. Hitler never negotiates.'

'One year of what?'

'Of not flying. Of staying on the ground and doing his job.'

'And now?'

'The year is up. Hess has been counting the months, probably the minutes. And so now, without even checking with the Chancellery, he's come down here to Uncle Willi and ordered himself a nice fat aeroplane.'

'A 109?'

'A 110.'

'He's qualified for twin-engines?'

'No, and that's the point. He needs instruction. Hitler has found out because Hitler finds out everything sooner or later and he's ordered Uncle Willi to find the best men to get our Rudolf flying solo on the 110. You know the other Willi?' Dieter nodded. Willi Stor was Messerschmitt's Chief Test Pilot. 'He's taking Hess through the basics but he's leaving soon for another appointment and so Helmut Kaden will take over as Chief. He'll be with Hess as well, but speaking personally I'd like a third pair of eyes on our friend at the controls.' He paused, carefully returning the model to the desk. Then he looked up. 'How do you find the 110?'

'I like it. I like the power. It's built like a horse. It can take punishment. Nimble? Not really. Reliable? Yes. Quick? Definitely. And plenty of range, too.' Merz frowned. 'So why the 110? Why not a fighter? Single-engine? No need to convert?'

'Hess says he needs the range and the speed. He's everywhere, that man, all over the Reich, day after day, speech after speech.

A personal carriage on a regular train might be fine for the lesser gods but our Rudolf sees no point in wasting all that time. In here' – he tapped his head – 'he's been a pilot since he was old enough to dream. He flew in the last war, just a couple of months before it all turned to *Scheisse*. He tells me the conversion to the 110 is all for the good of the Reich and I think I believe him.'

Think? Dieter said nothing. A third pair of eyes was the key phrase.

'You want me to fly with him?'

'I do. And I want you to talk to him, make a friend of him. It won't be hard. He's a decent man. And he respects you as a flyer. You think you can handle Hess? Turn him into a human being? Tease a little mischief into that cave of his? Daub something interesting on those walls?'

Dieter nodded. He said it would be a pleasure, something he'd look forward to. He was thinking of Beata again. Was taking care of Hess his only commitment for the time being?

'It is. And what's more, I've taken the liberty of warning Hess what might be in store. You know what he said? When I told him?'

'No.'

'He said he couldn't wait. He said *der Kleine* was the perfect addition to his new toy.'

'A toy? He called it a toy?'

'Of course he didn't.' The *Reichsmarschall* was beaming. 'That's my word, not his. The man's a child at heart. Listen to him, take care of him. And then go back to Berlin and do the same with Frau Messner.'

Minutes later, dismissed with a hearty slap on the shoulder, Merz found himself looking for Hans Baur. The Führer's pilot was in the canteen, eating alone, demolishing a plate of *Schnitzel*. Merz queued at the servery counter and then joined him. Baur, who was never less than direct, wanted to know what *der Eiserne* had been after. Merz took his time answering. Something had troubled him about the conversation upstairs – seemingly so cheerful, so innocent, so unforced – but it took Baur's question to put it into words.

'He wants me to spy on Rudolf Hess,' Merz murmured. 'Is that something I should be doing?'

Tam Moncrieff took nearly a full day to track down Gordon Hesketh. The number he'd been given by his sister turned out to be a hotel in Bayswater. A male voice confirmed that Mr Hesketh had been occupying a room at The Limes since last weekend. None of the rooms possessed a telephone but he'd be more than happy to pass on a message. Moncrieff gave him an MI5 number he was authorised to use and said he'd be grateful for a call. Mr Hesketh was to ask for Mr Rogerson.

Nothing happened. Hours later, Moncrieff tried again, this time from a call box on the Bayswater Road. From here he could see the hotel. So far it had been spared the attentions of the *Luftwaffe* but nothing could hide the seediness of the place: pitted stucco, peeling yellow paintwork around the windows and a hand-lettered sign on the door, when Moncrieff had paused to check, that offered rooms with special rates for servicemen. This, as Moncrieff knew, was code for payment by the hour. Hesketh, despite his Belgravia origins, was living in a brothel.

This time it was a woman's voice on the line. She sounded foreign, perhaps Spanish. Yes, Mr Hesketh was aware that he needed to make a phone call. And, no, he wasn't up in his room just now. Maybe he gets in contact later. Or maybe not.

Back in the gloom at St James's Street, Moncrieff attended to various files while waiting for the call that might not come. The office was manned twenty-four hours a day and it had been dark for hours when the phone on his desk finally rang. A call for Mr Rogerson.

'Might I ask your real name?' An English voice, rich, cultured, sure of itself, with more than a hint of amusement.

Moncrieff ignored the question.

'Mr Hesketh?' he asked.

'Indeed.'

'My sister gave me your number. How can I help you?'

Hesketh apologised for the relative lateness of the hour. Nearly eight o'clock was no time to find a man at his desk. However, he'd taken the liberty of checking with the Ritz Hotel and they'd be serving dinner until 10 p.m. Hesketh himself could be in Piccadilly within half an hour and he suspected that Mr Rogerson was even closer. He'd booked a table in his own name. Just ask the maître d'.

Moncrieff said nothing for a moment or two, long enough to make Hesketh break the silence.

'If you're worrying about the Ritz, *Herr wer auch immer*, let me put your mind at rest. My choice of venue and my pleasure in settling the bill.'

The line went dead. Moncrieff, still holding the receiver, was staring at the phone. *Herr wer auch immer* was German for Mr Whoever-you-are. Several messages in one simple phrase. Clever.

Moncrieff took the long route to the Ritz, ducking into Green Park and using his pass to negotiate a path through the ack-ack emplacements. According to Ursula, the *Luftwaffe* were occupied elsewhere tonight, with raids expected on Birmingham and Southampton, and as Moncrieff stepped deeper into the park he paused to savour the calm that descended on the city at this time of night. From surrounding roads came the low growl of traffic moving with great care and if he listened very hard he thought he could hear the clop-clop of a distant horse. From time to time, the flare of a match pricked the darkness and he caught the briefest glimpse of a face beneath a helmet as one of the gun crews lit a cigarette. Then, from nowhere, came a murmured offer.

'Two bob, mister? Whatever you fancy?'

Moncrieff glanced behind him. The boy was barely into adolescence. His thin face was pale in the darkness and he seemed oblivious of the surrounding gun crews. Moncrieff studied him for a moment. More and more kids were coming north of the river, taking advantage of the blackout to earn themselves whatever they could negotiate. This area – monied, raffish – was said to offer easy pickings, especially after the cocktail hour, and for the briefest moment Moncrieff tried to imagine the kind of life this child might lead in daylight. Did he go to school? Did he have a job of some kind? And was it his family who despatched him every night to the land of milk and honey? Moncrieff was tempted to ask. Instead, he fumbled in his pocket, handed over a fistful of small change and watched the boy disappear into the darkness. Then came a throaty cough from a nearby gun pit.

'His name's Danny,' a voice said. 'But his brother's the real looker.'

The Ritz was packed. Stepping in from the darkness of Piccadilly, Moncrieff elbowed his way through the mill of bodies in the lobby and deposited his greatcoat in the cloakroom. When the uniformed attendant offered to take his briefcase, Moncrieff pocketed the ticket and shook his head.

'Stays with me,' he said.

The big dining room lay beyond a noisy swirl of guests. With its walls of gilt-framed mirrors and heavy chandeliers it offered a glimpse of an England that was fast disappearing. The floor-to-ceiling windows were shrouded in thick falls of blackout material, and the floral displays – on close inspection – turned out to be made of paper, but half close your eyes and you could be back in an Edwardian London that had yet to experience a world war.

In truth, Moncrieff had never had much time for the Ritz. Over the past year or so he'd dined here on a number of occasions, line of duty, accompanying Guy Liddell and occasionally Andrew Ballentyne when they were conducting discreet fishing expeditions with highly placed visitors. The Ritz was undeniably popular, partly because it offered much better protection than the Savoy or Claridge's, and partly because the food was still so good, but Moncrieff had quickly wearied of the hotel's mix of minor European royalty, cinema starlets, Fleet Street gossip correspondents, fellow-travellers from the intelligence world and national politicians on the make.

The Lower Bar downstairs, known as the Pink Sink, was the trysting spot of choice for well-connected homosexuals – as well as a clutch of off-duty MI5 faces – and Moncrieff had lost count of the aristocrats he'd watched, titled figures from the House of Lords, ascending the big staircase with their pale young escorts in tow. Did the kid from Green Park ever make it this far? And, if so, had he gone home with proper money in his pocket?

Moncrieff intercepted the maître d' on his way to a table of partying officers in RAF uniform. Mention of a booking in the name of Hesketh prompted a smile.

'Over there, sir. Beside the palm tree.'

Moncrieff nodded. He was looking at a smallish individual who was sitting alone, a glass of wine at his elbow, enjoying a cigarette. His greying hair was cut *en brosse*. He wore a moustache and a goatee beard. His rumpled black suit didn't quite fit, and there was a tiny curl of cotton wool beneath his jawline where he must have cut himself shaving, but he had the composure, to Moncrieff, of a man at peace with his surroundings. Gordon Millord Hesketh might have pitched his tent in a Bayswater brothel but he was no stranger to indulgence of quite another order.

He offered a nod of welcome as Moncrieff approached and got to his feet to extend a hand. Balliol tie, poorly knotted. Deep-set eyes, the darkest shade of brown.

'Your sister suggested I call you Tam. Might that be a good idea?'

'If you wish.'

'Then Tam it is. A '32 Gewürztraminer. Playful at this time of night. May I?'

Without waiting for an answer, he steadied the bottle over the empty wine glass. Moncrieff put his briefcase beside the table and settled into the chair. The nearest diners were conducting a loud conversation in German. Hesketh noticed Moncrieff's interest.

'Émigré bankers,' he said. 'Jews to a man. One of them's fresh in from New York. Arrived this morning. Took the clipper to Lisbon and then onward to Poole. He says the food was shameful and the company en route worse. These days everyone wears a uniform and has absolutely nothing original to say. His words, not mine. Your health, my friend. Happy days.'

They clinked glasses. Already, within less than a minute, Moncrieff felt the conversation slipping slightly out of control but Hesketh had a knowing smile on his face and he was right about the wine.

'Excellent,' Tam took another sip. 'Your choice or the sommelier's?'

'Mine. There are plenty of risks I'm happy to take but wine isn't one of them. Your sister thinks you work for Box. Might she be right?'

Box 500 was a favoured code for MI5. It was Moncrieff's turn to smile.

'My sister has many talents. Discretion isn't one of them. Neither does she always get the facts right. I'm intrigued by what she had to say about you. Is it true you grew up in that pile of hers?'

'I'm afraid it is. How well do you know the house?'

'Barely at all.'

'A pity, if I may say so, and very much your loss. The place is a jewel. My first memory, the day I emerged from the chrysalis, was a spider that must have been bigger than my chubby little hand. I was up on what I later knew as the top floor. The sun was streaming in through the nursery window and the spider was busy webbing the clouds over all those rooftops. My father took me to the circus years later but nothing ever beat that spider. It spun, and it hung, and then it spun some more, and every time it put those threads to the test my tiny little brain waited for the whole thing to fall apart. But you know what? It never did. Ever see a spider eat a fly? The purest magic. One of God's conjuring tricks. The fly alive one moment. Starting to decompose the next. *Prost dem Feind, ja?'*

Cheers to the enemy. The raised glass again. Moncrieff wanted to know how long Hesketh had stayed in the house in Eaton Place.

'Many, many years. Sometimes it felt like forever. Your sister will have told you most of it. I was adopted. I was below stairs. My real parents were Irish. Lots of vigour, lots of dreams, but nothing they could put in the bank. My adoptive parents changed all that. They gave me a new name and they gave me everything money could buy. My father was away most of the time, prospecting for oil. When he found it, he took it to market and made a fortune for everyone within touching distance. That included us. There was a sweet little school round the corner. Blazers the colour of boiling rhubarb. Tiny straw boaters. Prayers every morning and a grace before lunch. At Christmas we walked to Westminster Abbey for the carol service, every spring they took us to St James's Park for the ducks and the daffodils, and every midsummer's day we went to the zoo. They tried to turn me into a gentleman and I'm glad to say they failed. You've taken a look at The Limes? *Chez moi?* Bayswater Road?'

'Yes.'

'Then I rest my case. At my age you learn a thing or two about quality. Her name is Carol, she's cheap, she's grotesquely overweight, and she'll put every other woman you've ever had to shame. An artist. *Unvergleichlich.*'

Beyond compare.

Hesketh smiled, reaching for his glass again. Well-shaped fingers, heavily stained by a lifetime's smoking.

'You're indulging me, Tam. Change the subject. Save me from myself.'

Moncrieff wanted to know about Lisbon. According to his sister, Hesketh had been there for some time. True?

'Yes.'

'Why?'

'Because I love it. Pay attention, my friend. Lisbon is what happens when a million people turn their collective face to the sun, to the ocean, to the west, and shut the door on the world they left behind. It's not a city at all. It's like this place.' He gestured round the busy dining room. 'It's a confection, an illusion, a glorious fantasy scored for fat helpings of everything that's supposed to be bad for you. An earthquake knocked it over several hundred years ago but it got back up on its sturdy little legs and brushed itself down, as good as new. I lived there first in the late thirties. Not a hint of war, not a proper war, not unless you happened to be Spanish, and I loved it at first sight. The Portuguese can be glum people but not there, not in Lisbon. Then the war came and thanks to the Germans us Lisbon *Volk* have prospered. Mightily. We invent. And we trade. And we barter. And when we've got nothing left to sell we invent a little more. In Lisbon, you live on your wits. And then you turn your face to the sun. Believe me, Tam. It never fails. Ever.'

Moncrieff sat back a moment, fingering his glass. At first he'd assumed that Hesketh was drunk. Now he wasn't so sure.

'But what do you *do* out there?' he said. 'How do you make a living?'

'I have an allowance, of course. My ma and pa saw to that. I'm not sure either of them were terribly pleased the way things worked out but you might be surprised to know that adoptive blood is a great deal thicker than the real thing. Then there were the books, of course. They certainly helped.'

'Books?'

'I'm a writer. Your sister never mentioned it?'

'She did. I remember now. What kind of books?'

'Military history. It's a virus I picked up at Oxford. Show me a battlefield and I'll put it between hard covers. Lines of Torres Vedras? Ring any bells?'

'Wellington's campaign. Peninsular War.'

'Excellent,' Hesketh mimed applause. 'That's what brought me to Lisbon in the first place. I'd made a name for myself with a series of tomes about the Franco-Prussian War. Sedan. Gravelotte. The Siege of Metz. All grist to the authorial mill. But the Lines of Torres Vedras will be my magnum opus. Once the book's done there'll be nothing left to say.'

A waiter approached. Hesketh appeared to know him. The manager had warned him that a party of two dozen were about to dine in a private suite. The kitchen was already busy. Might now be a good time to order?

Moncrieff reached for the menu. To the best of his knowledge the Lines of Torres Vedras were a series of fortifications north of Lisbon. They'd spared the city the attentions of Napoleon, and it was easy to imagine this eager little figure in his shapeless suit pacing the earthworks and plotting lines of attack.

'You're close to finishing the book?' Moncrieff had settled for the Dover sole.

'Never. That's the point. Find something you love and never let it end.' He glanced up at the waiter. 'The usual, please,' he patted the beginnings of a paunch. 'But not too many of those gorgeous spuds.'

The waiter made a note and departed with the order. Hesketh's gaze swept the room before returning to Moncrieff.

'You'll know most of these people. I imagine one way or another they'll be in those files of yours. Over there, for instance. By the door.'

Moncrieff stole a glance. A tall, thin-faced figure bent over his table, locked in conversation with a younger man. Lord Londonderry. Family seat in Northern Ireland. Otherwise known as Charlie.

Hesketh nodded. 'You know what else they call him?'

'The Londonderry *Herr.*'

'*Touché.* Excellent. Put most of the people in this room on a London bus and their first port of call would be Berlin. But you'd know that, of course.'

Moncrieff conceded the point with the faintest smile. Charlie Londonderry had been beating the drum for Hitler since the mid-thirties, in keeping with a number of fellow aristocrats. Add most of the City, a sizeable number of industrialists, dozens of leading Tories, plus a longish list of sympathisers from Court circles and it was a miracle that Britain was at war at all. Why pick a quarrel with the Germans, these people asked, when the real menace marched under the red flag, pledged their lives to the Proletariat and couldn't wait to fall on the Western capitalists and tear them apart?

'You'll have a large circle of friends in Lisbon...' Moncrieff began.

'Is that an assumption or a question?'

'The latter.'

'Then the answer's yes. Conversations, a passing friendship or two, the rest I expect you can imagine. That's what Lisbon's about. That's what makes the place so...' the briefest frown, '... intoxicating. It's a ragout, a stew, *une bouillabaisse*. Fascists. Communists. Anarchists. Monarchists. Jews. Slavs. Poles. Gypsies. You dine *à la carte*. And you never go hungry.'

'Anyone especially interesting? Anyone you might like to bring to our attention?'

For the first time the conversation faltered. This was the heart of the matter, the reason they'd stepped in from the darkness outside, and they both knew it. The old dance. You first. Me first. A courtly bow. A murmured word of apology. And then the music restarts. Perhaps a little brisker.

'I thought abroad was MI6 territory?' Hesketh had lit another cigarette.

'It is. Occasionally we hunt in tandem. Operational protocols needn't concern you. I suspect you have something to share. Just tell me what it might be.'

Hesketh gave the proposition some thought. Then he bent over the table and gestured Moncrieff closer.

'June,' he said. 'Magnificent weather. The Portuguese were celebrating the eight hundredth anniversary of their independence and the flags were out the length of the Avenida da Liberdade to prove it. Fiesta time. Dancing and bottles of icy Alvariño and all kinds of other mischief. Lisbon does this kind of thing extremely well. Small wonder the bloody man turned up.'

'Bloody man?'

'George Windsor. The Duke of Kent. He married a Greek Princess in '34 to keep the royals quiet but his heart was never in it. Morphine. Cocaine. A riotous affair with Noël Coward. *Gloria in excelsis Deo*, Tam. Get on your knees and do your worst.'

Moncrieff ducked his head. MI5 kept a file on the maverick Duke and regarded him as a significant security risk. Hesketh was right. The bloody man was frequently out of control.

'You've met him?'

'I have,' Hesketh nodded. 'Thanks to a good friend of mine.'

'And who might that be?'

'Ricardo Espirito Santo Silva.' He beamed with pleasure, savouring each vowel. 'A banker. A man of immense wealth and immense ambition. A man who plays skat with the German ambassador and rarely loses. A man whose knowledge of Torres Vedras is nearly as extensive as my own. We've visited the fortifications together on a number of occasions. And each time, dare I say it, Ricardo left the field of battle a wiser man.'

'Thanks to you.'

'Indeed. He respects knowledge and he respects authorship. Two reasons why we see a great deal of each other. He's also won me a role in the restoration work at the Castelo in Lisbon, for which I'm more than grateful.'

Santo Silva's royal connections, he explained, extended beyond the Duke of Kent. The abrupt collapse of France drove millions south, away from Hitler's armies. Overnight, even the wealthy became refugees. One of them was the Duke of Windsor, George's elder brother. With his American wife, Wallis Simpson, he made his way to Madrid where he enjoyed the hospitality of Sir Samuel Hoare, the British Ambassador.

Moncrieff reached for his glass, sensing what might be coming. The Duke of Windsor had formerly been Edward VIII, King of England. Wallis Simpson was an American divorcee, an unthinkable choice of Queen, and the affair had triggered a constitutional crisis. In the end, offered a choice between kingship and love, the Duke had been forced to abdicate. Exiled to Paris, he'd become a baleful presence on the wrong side of the Channel, not least because of his admiration for Adolf Hitler. Alone, despite the ravages of a spiteful peace treaty, this was a leader who'd restored the fortunes of a great race. The Germans, he assured anyone who cared to listen, were lucky to have him.

'You've met him, too? The Duke of Windsor?'

'I have. The briefest conversation, alas, but fascinating nonetheless.'

The Duke and Duchess, Hesketh said, had arrived in Lisbon from Madrid. Santo Silva had been their host. He'd installed them in a rather pleasant villa at Cascais, on the coast road north from Lisbon. Pink stucco, lots of bougainvillea, and views that fell sheer to the boiling Atlantic surf.

'The local fishermen call this place *Boca do Inferno*. You know what that means?'

'The Jaws of Hell.'

'Exactly. That's why God invented metaphor. That's exactly where they found themselves. You're familiar with Operation Willi?'

'Tell me.'

'The Windsors, alas, were a liability. Still are. Dear Bertie, the current King, was put in to replace his errant brother. When it comes to public events, he can't hold a candle to Edward VIII and he knows it. After the fall of France, the Windsors were desperate to get back home, back to the Mother Country, but Bertie wouldn't have it. He told Churchill to find his wretched brother another job. Preferably on the moon.'

Churchill, he said, was no friend of the current King. He'd taken Edward's side during the Abdication Crisis and George VI had never forgiven him. Churchill had toyed with various postings and finally settled on the Governorship of the Bahamas.

'Imagine St Helena with a nicer climate. Somewhere safe. Somewhere sleepy. Somewhere on the very edge of the map. The Duke and his good lady were appalled. They fought to have the order rescinded. No matter. Churchill's writ runs to every corner of the Empire. What he wants, he gets. And so there they were, the Duke and the Duchess, sitting on a clifftop in Cascais, growing glummer by the day. Churchill had arranged a boat to take them away. The last thing they wanted was to get aboard. Something of which our German friends were very aware.' Hesketh paused for a moment. His eyes were bright. He was a storyteller by trade and he knew he was good at it. 'I'm sure you're aware of all this, Tam, but just imagine the possibilities. You're sitting in Berlin. The once and maybe future King of England is nursing a whole list of grievances. He's marooned in Lisbon. He's on neutral territory. He's on your side. He's there for the taking. All you have to do is be rude about Churchill and assure him that one day, with a little help from his German friends, he might be back on his throne.'

Operation Willi, he said, was the logical consequence of the Windsors' plight. A team was despatched to Lisbon. They had a good look at the villa overlooking the *Boca do Inferno*. They spread a number of ugly rumours about the British and their real intentions. Under cover of darkness, they reinforced these threats with shots aimed at the windows of the villa. And then, once the real peril of the situation was more than evident, they had the Spanish extend an offer they judged the royal couple would find hard to resist. An unlimited stay at the Palace of the Caliph at Ronda, a chance to catch their breath in the safety of Spain before the pressure of events and a sizeable German army bore them back to London.

'If that sounds like kidnap, Tam, then I'm afraid it is. And you know who they put in charge?'

'Walter Schellenberg.'

'Indeed. A king in his own right. The lord of the dark arts. The mastermind who gave MI6 a black eye at Venlo. The ship was due to sail on 1st August. The whole city knew the date. Schellenberg arrived three days earlier. A letter was delivered to the villa that same afternoon. It warned the Duke that his life was in danger and offered him safe passage to the Spanish border. By now Churchill had sent the Duke's trusted friend to whisper in his ear. You know Monckton? Dear Walter? A lawyer of genius and a very civilised man. That did the trick.

Santo Silva threw a farewell party at the Hotel Aziz the night before the ship was due to depart. I was there. And so was Walter. And so were the Germans. They had trick after trick up their sleeves. Talk of a gunman despatched from London to take the Duke's life. Another dark rumour about a bomb aboard the bloody ship. This was *opéra bouffe*, Tam. Music by Offenbach. Libretto by our friend Walter Schellenberg. And you know what happened the following day? The ship sailed. With the Windsors on board. I watched it leave. Hundreds of well-wishers on the pier and two blasts on the steamer's siren as it slipped away. That day was a legend in the making, and Lisbon loved it. Can you guess the name of the ship? *Excalibur.* It sailed at twenty to seven in the evening and the whole episode, if you know where to go, is still the talk of the city. Believe me, Tam, the word Arthurian doesn't do this tale justice.'

Moncrieff was watching an enormous family eating at a table in the middle of the dining room. They were Albanian royalty and their various members occupied a fat file at MI5. A telephone had been brought to the table. The adult in charge, an imposing figure with an impressive beard, finished a conversation and murmured something to the woman who might have been his wife. At her command, the children pushed aside their plates, neatly folded their napkins and made for the door. At the same time, Moncrieff became aware of a more general stir in the room. Then came the wail of an air raid siren and the sudden appearance of the maître d' in the entrance to the dining room that led to the reception area and the staircases beyond. Guests were advised to make their way to the basement bar. He apologised for any inconvenience.

Diners gazed at each other for a moment. For many of them, this invitation was part of the Ritz routine, a prudent retreat in the face of *Luftwaffe* high explosive and the laws of chance. The cannier souls took their food with them, half-eaten kidneys swimming in a pool of jus, the chef's signature fish pie, a glorious assemblage of cod, pollock and rock salmon, nestling in a whorl of mashed potato spiked with butter and dill. The wait downstairs could last hours, often did. A man could die of hunger before the all-clear sounded.

Moncrieff and Hesketh were among the last to leave the dining room. Hesketh insisted on finishing his tripe and onions in a civilised setting and Moncrieff didn't blame him. He was thinking about Ursula Barton. Her predictions for the evening's entertainment were seldom wrong. She seemed to have a direct line to *Luftwaffe* headquarters in Gatow. So why hadn't she foreseen tonight's raid?

None the wiser, he and Hesketh made their way downstairs. The Lower Bar was standing room only. Diners were shouting orders at the barmen from every corner of the room and drinks were circulating from hand to hand until they found the right home. There was no hint of panic or even apprehension. On the contrary, an incoming raid and the prospect of a bomb or two appeared to be a cause for celebration. For those in the know, five sturdy floors above street level was a virtual guarantee of survival.

Hesketh enquired whether Moncrieff wanted anything to drink. When Moncrieff shook his head, Hesketh excused himself and set off in the direction of the bar, worming his way through the solid mass of bodies. En route, he stopped briefly to talk to a tall figure in an RAF uniform before disappearing completely. Moncrieff looked around. In truth, he wanted to be anywhere but here. The crush of dozens of well-fed diners was oppressive. There was an overwhelming fug of sweat and alcohol and clouds of impossible-to-obtain perfume. Maybe now was the time for Moncrieff and Hesketh to make their excuses and take their chances outside in the fresh air.

The bar's normal clientele lurked on the edges of the room, eyeing the women and the prettier boys. Moncrieff recognised faces from Fleet Street and the Foreign Office, from the House of Lords and theatreland. Many of them were drunk. Some of them were visibly resentful. This was their territory, their evening. By what right had these people, with their wretched children, intruded?

Then came the first explosion, far too close to be comfortable. The whole building seemed to rock and in the silence that followed Moncrieff heard a woman sobbing. A second bomb, even closer, filled the bar with dust and plunged it into darkness. Now came a different smell, far earthier.

Hesketh had suddenly appeared again. Instead of a drink, he'd acquired a child who seemed to have lost her parents. When the girl began to cry, Hesketh assured her that everything was going to be fine.

'Just a little bang or two,' he was bent to the child, his mouth to her ear. 'Let's find your mummy.'

The child turned out to be foreign. She didn't understand. Hesketh tried again, first in Spanish, and then in French. French did the trick. The child took Hesketh's hand, consented to be cuddled, stopped crying. Then, from the darkness, came the sound of a harmonica and a tune that Moncrieff must have heard dozens of times, first on newsreels, then on the streets of Nuremberg and Berlin. It was the 'Horst Wessel Song', the soundtrack to the years of Nazi conquests, the marching song that had taken Hitler's armies into country after country.

Was this ironic? A doff of the bowler hat to the unseen *Luftwaffe* bomber crews overhead? Or was there something more complex going on? As the explosions receded towards the west, the bar erupted, male voices, plausibly guttural accents, word perfect for verse after verse.

Die Fahne hoch, they roared, *die Reihen fest geschlossen...*
Die Strasse frei den braunen Bataillonen...

Moncrieff shook his head. Unlike most of the people in this hideous space, he'd tasted the realities of life in Hitler's precious Reich. He'd served in Berlin. He'd attended one of the Nuremberg Rallies. He'd been at the mercy of the Gestapo. He knew the rules they'd torn up, what they could do, what they were capable of. Then he felt a tug at his sleeve. At first he assumed it was the child but he was wrong. The voice in the darkness belonged to Hesketh.

'The British Establishment at play, Tam.' He'd lit yet another cigarette. 'You and I need to talk a little more.'

5

At Goering's insistence Dieter Merz stayed on in Augsburg. His forthcoming visits to squadrons across the Greater Reich were cancelled until further notice and when the secretariat at Hess's ministry in Berlin confirmed that the Deputy Führer was due to address the Party faithful in Munich the following evening, Willi Messerschmitt put a car and a driver at Merz's disposal.

The driver turned out to be a veteran from the Condor Legion. Like Dieter, he'd spent a couple of challenging years among the mountains in northern Spain, trying to get the best of the marauding Ivans, and more recently he'd looked after Hess on a number of occasions.

'He's unlike the rest of them,' he said. 'In fact he's almost human. Nice wife, too. Proper family man when he gets the chance.'

Hess was speaking at a *Bierkeller* in the oldest part of the city. A flat tyre en route meant that Merz arrived late. He slipped in through the heavily guarded main doors and offered his ID to the brown-shirted *Alter Kampfer* in charge. The man ignored the documentation. One look at Dieter's face was enough to trigger a click of the heels and the Hitler salute. He'd had the privilege to witness a couple of Herr Merz's air displays. His wife had scissored Dieter's photograph from an old copy of *NS-Frauen-Warte* magazine and gazed at it far too often. He was more than welcome here in Munich.

Dieter found a perch at a table at the back of the *Bierkeller*. Hess was already on the makeshift stage in the centre of the room. He was a tall man, very erect. Bushy eyebrows. Square jaw. Sallow complexion. Sloping forehead. The knee-length boots were beautifully made, the finest leather, but the brown shirt carried no trace of rank or decoration. He held himself very still, the stance of someone with a back problem, and despite the fact that half the audience were behind him, he made no attempt to address them directly. Inflexible, Merz thought. A man of unbending principle, just as Goering had described him.

Hess's theme for the evening was the struggle in the early years that had finally taken the Nazis to power. He wasn't a gifted speaker, nothing compared to Hitler or Goebbels, but he took care not to insult the intelligence of his audience by pulling any of the usual tricks. This wasn't a harangue. In fact he barely raised his voice at all. Neither did he rely on crude attacks against traditional enemies like the Bolsheviks or the Jews. Instead, with some patience and not a little humility, he described his own experiences trying to come to terms with a *Heimat* he barely recognised after his service in the last war. In city after city, he said, there was nothing but brawling and chaos. Germany had lost its compass. In the face of yet more bloodshed, there had to be a better way.

The years spooled by. Hess was back here in his home city. Then, one night, he found himself spellbound by a voice he'd never heard before. Someone with a vision. Someone with belief. Someone who knew the real meaning of the word 'destiny'.

Mention of the twice-decorated Austrian corporal from the List Regiment in which Hess himself had served brought the audience to its feet. They knew this story by heart.

'*Heil Hitler!*' they roared.

Afterwards, with Hess still disentangling himself from the press of Party veterans, Dieter found himself in the back of Hess's personal Mercedes. His adjutant, Karl-Heinz Pintsch, was at the wheel. Waiting for Hess, he eyed Merz in the rear-view mirror. They'd never met before but Pintsch, like everyone else around Hess, was a byword for loyalty among the Berlin chieftains.

'The older guys want to drink with him all night,' Pintsch nodded towards the *Bierkeller*. 'They can't understand why he never touches alcohol. They think it's one of Goebbels' little lies. An *Alter Kampfer,* one of the old warriors, without a taste for booze? It makes no sense.'

At length, Hess appeared in the street. His calf-length leather coat was the perfect match, thought Dieter, for those wonderful boots. Pintsch was already out of the car, opening the passenger door. Hess ducked inside. Once again, he didn't look round.

'Merz?'

Dieter acknowledged the greeting, extending a hand over the back of the seat. He felt the lightest of touches, flesh on flesh, then the car began to move.

'We go home. You will stay the night. We must feed you, make you welcome. It's the least we can do.'

The matter appeared to be settled. There was nothing left to say. Already, Hess was talking to Pintsch. Tomorrow he had business in Augsburg. Might his adjutant be ready with the car by seven o'clock?

Hess lived in Harlachen, a suburb of Munich much favoured by Party bigwigs who'd made the journey from the pitched street battles of the early twenties and who still lived in the city. Pintsch pulled the big saloon to a halt outside a secluded villa in a street off the tram route. Munich, like Berlin, was under compulsory blackout and in the darkness, waiting for Hess to emerge from the car, Dieter could make out the shape of the property behind the hedge. With its shuttered windows and boxy silhouette, it was neither grand nor tiny. It called no attention to itself. Much like its owner.

Hess led the way to the door. His wife must have heard the car because she was waiting inside the open front door. The house smelled lightly of bleach and furniture polish. The door closed, she pulled a curtain across and switched on the light.

'Ilse,' Hess murmured. 'My wife.'

The handshake was warm. No *Heil Hitler*. Ilse led the way down the hall. Little Wolf, she told her husband, was still running a temperature. She thought he had a bad cold, nothing worse, but she couldn't be sure.

'He's still awake?'

'*Ja.*'

Hess disappeared upstairs. Merz followed Ilse into the drawing room. It was less formal than he'd been expecting and a log fire was burning in the grate. One wall was covered entirely by bookshelves containing hundreds of volumes, and small occasional tables were home for little nests of framed photographs, a mix of family moments and more formal occasions.

Ilse apologised for the lateness of the hour. She'd prepared a little goulash. This was no time to be eating but she hoped that Merz was hungry. Her husband, she said, had no fondness for either meat or fish. She'd learned to live with his dietary fads, as a good wife should, but she wouldn't inflict Rudolf's tastes on any guest.

Dieter said it didn't matter. The lateness of the hour was no fault of hers. She smiled at him, seemingly lost for words. She was a plump woman with lustrous chestnut hair and there was a hint of the Jewess in her features. Quietly spoken and attentive, every gesture suggested a motherliness that could only have been instinctive. Did this protective urge extend to Hess himself, Dieter wondered. Was the Deputy Führer sheltered from the regime's harsher moments by this wife of his?

Hess returned with his young son. Dieter was no expert when it came to children, but he judged the infant Wolf to be two or three years old. Cradled in his father's arms, he regarded Merz with interest. His face was flushed with fever, but he kicked his chubby little legs and reached out for this stranger in the family home.

'He trusts everyone,' Hess was frowning. 'These days it's a habit we might have to cure.'

Ilse served the meal in a smallish dining room next door. Hess had his son in a high chair beside him and paused between mouthfuls of his own to try and coax a thin, pink liquid down his tiny throat. Dieter was tempted to ask what Hess was eating. His first guess was semolina, but he wasn't at all sure. Hess was explaining their guest's role over the weeks to come. Ilse, with a fetching smile, said she needed no introductions. Like every other housewife, she knew exactly who young Dieter was.

'You're going to teach my husband to fly?'

'No need, Frau Hess. He's been flying far longer than me.'

'That's what I thought.' She turned to Hess. 'So tell me again. You drive to Augsburg. You meet Uncle Willi. And then what?'

'I get in a new aeroplane, a different aeroplane. Two engines. Believe me, it makes a difference.'

He turned to Merz for confirmation. Dieter nodded, said nothing. Then came an abrupt change of subject. Ilse had forgotten a call that had come earlier. Something evidently important.

'Albrecht telephoned,' she said. 'He said he's going to be late tomorrow.'

'At Augsburg, you mean?'

'Yes. And he wanted to know whether you'd talked to his father yet.'

'This morning,' Hess said. 'I told him about Wolf. He suggested throat pastilles if the linctus doesn't work. It seems Albrecht had the same problem. He said the child was always ill.'

Dieter slept in a guest bedroom under the eaves of the house. The goulash had settled nicely and he'd enjoyed a brief fireside chat with the Deputy Führer before retiring for the night. Hess had been more than complimentary about Dieter's reputation in the air. Alas, he'd never seen any of *der Kleine*'s legendary displays but he had it on good authority that Dieter Merz was up there with the angels when it came to the Reich's top flyers.

He asked a series of searching questions about the performance of the 109 against the British, leaving Dieter in no doubt about the depth of his own knowledge, and asked for his thoughts on the 110. Dieter obliged as best he could. The 110, he said, was a tough old bird. Establish the right rapport, and it was an aircraft that would always look after you. The phrase sparked a rare smile from Hess and, as Dieter drifted off to sleep, he wondered yet again what had prompted the need for a busy man to subject himself to all the demands of a conversion course. There were a number of single-engined aircraft that could take the Deputy Führer to any corner of the Reich. Why this added complication?

Next morning, up early, Merz descended to the sharp tang of real coffee. Hess was already at the table, carving himself the thinnest slice of black bread. Wolf, it seemed, had enjoyed a peaceful night and was still asleep. The pink linctus appeared to have done the trick.

Pintsch arrived minutes later and Ilse waved them goodbye from the front gate. Dieter, she made a point of saying, was welcome at their little house whenever he needed a bed and in the meantime he was to keep a sharp eye on her husband.

'My husband takes on far too much,' she said. 'Maybe the flying is good for him.'

The drive to Augsburg, on one of the new *Autobahnen*, took less than two hours. Dieter knew that Hess's passion for flying had led him to enter the famous Zugspitze race around Germany's highest peak, an event that would pose a serious challenge for any pilot. On his first attempt, a year before the Nazis came to power, Hess had been runner-up but when Dieter pressed for details he seemed almost embarrassed. He'd made careful preparations, he said, and once he was in the air he'd simply followed the pilot who he knew would win. It had certainly been cold up at three thousand metres, and there'd been an intermittent problem with high cloud, but completing the Zugspitze was nothing compared to flying over Everest.

'Everest? You mean the Himalayas?'

'*Ja.*'

'You've done that, too?'

'Not me. A friend of a friend of mine. An English flyer. My friend calls him Duglo. Properly, one should call him the Duke of Hamilton. He's a Wing Commander now, in the RAF. And I suppose one day we might fly against each other. Such are the fortunes of war.'

'And he flew over Everest? This Duke?'

'He did. I met him afterwards, very briefly, in Berlin. He was there for the Olympics. The flight itself was a couple of years earlier. 1933. And he did it in a *biplane*. Can you believe that? You have to hand it to the English. Not only did they conquer half the world, but they produced men like Hamilton who can survive at nine thousand metres. Remarkable. Anyone who underestimates the British is a fool.'

Willi Messerschmitt was waiting for them at Augsburg. With him was a square-jawed civilian in his late thirties. He had a thick, black moustache and wore a tweed jacket over an open-necked white shirt. In a world of uniforms, to Dieter, this made him unusual.

'My friend Albrecht Haushofer,' Hess did the introductions. 'Dieter Merz.'

Dieter shook the proffered hand.

Hess took Haushofer aside. Never less than intense, the Deputy Führer did most of the talking. Twice, he consulted his watch. Dieter, in the meantime, was talking to Willi Messerschmitt. Hess, it appeared, had been allotted a brand new Me-110, but in the way of these things the aircraft had developed a hydraulic fault. The Deputy Führer's schedule had called for a two-hour training sortie, and with the company's Chief Test Pilot otherwise engaged, the role of instructor would fall to Merz. Alas, yet another complication had just recalled Hess to Berlin and so Willi Messerschmitt was about to kill two precious birds with one stone by proposing that *der Stellvertreter* take another 110 and head north with Merz in the rear seat.

They took off nearly an hour later. Rain pebbled the glasshouse canopy and a vicious crosswind buffeted the aircraft on take-off. Given the circumstances, Hess coped without hesitation and as they climbed up through a thousand metres of cloud Dieter offered his congratulations. In certain situations, twin-engined aircraft needed a delicate touch at the controls as well as an iron nerve. On both counts, Hess had done extremely well.

'I'm flattered, Merz,' he grunted. 'Don't hesitate to speak your mind.'

There was no need. Above the thick canopy of cloud, the sun shone in a clear blue sky. The wind was still strong but Hess, who'd taken care to do his computations on the ground before take-off, offset for the strong easterly drift, and when the time came to start the descent Merz had no doubts that they'd find themselves over Berlin once they broke into clean air again.

And so it proved. Not just the grey sprawl of the Reich's capital but the sight of Tempelhof airfield bang on the nose. From the rear seat, Dieter applauded. Oddly enough, the sound of clapping broke Hess's concentration but seconds later he'd nudged the aircraft back onto the track that would take them onto the runway's threshold. For the second time in the flight the crosswind posed a problem but Hess reduced the flap setting, eased the throttle forwards and powered the aircraft into a perfect three-point landing.

'*Wunderbar*,' Dieter murmured. And meant it.

*

Tam Moncrieff occupied a claustrophobic flat on the first floor of a property on Woburn Square. The letter arrived shortly after dawn in the hands of a postman new to the Bloomsbury round. Moncrieff descended from the first floor, edging around his bicycle parked in the narrow hall, and retrieved the envelope from the mat. The handwriting was familiar. Cathy Phelps. The chance discovery who'd brought both laughter and order to the enveloping chaos of the Glebe House.

Back upstairs, Moncrieff settled briefly at the kitchen table to read the letter. Cathy wrote the way she talked: voluble, winning, a Cockney voice – a presence – that never failed to raise his spirits. She hoped he'd weathered the journey south. She worried a bit about the bombing raids and the reports on the radio about all the damage. She hoped he was looking after himself and keeping warm. And above all she begged him not to take what followed at anything but face value.

Face value?

Moncrieff frowned, checking his watch. He was due for a meeting in the Director's office at a quarter past eight. It was already twenty-five past seven and he'd yet to wash and shave. If he pedalled fast he could make St James's Street in twenty minutes. He returned to the letter.

Cathy had received a visit from a member of the Royal Household she'd known at Balmoral. His name was Jack Riordan and he'd carried all sorts of responsibilities when it came to finding the right people to staff the many outposts of the Royal Court. She'd liked Jack, she wrote. He'd always been fair in his dealings with the below-stairs staff and when her dalliance with the young Communist footman had raised a few eyebrows, he'd protected the pair of them from the wrath of more powerful figures.

Moncrieff smiled. Jack Riordan was a name he recognised. This was the man who'd penned a glowing reference for Cathy once she'd decided to leave Balmoral. Among the adjectives he remembered were 'diligent', 'tireless' and – twice – 'spirited'. In all three cases, nearly a year later, he'd been proved right.

Moncrieff returned to the letter. Jack, Cathy wrote, was briefly back in Scotland after a recent posting to Buckingham Palace where he held a new job as Master of the Household. A vacancy had come up in Housekeeping and he thought this might be the perfect opportunity for someone with Cathy's talents. She'd served there before and she knew how the place worked. The wage was nearly twice what she'd been earning at Balmoral and her responsibilities would allow her plenty of time to explore the capital's many attractions. While candidates for the job were obliged to undergo a couple of formal interviews, Jack had made it plain that the post was Cathy's for the asking. It seemed, in Jack's phrase, that she'd turned a head or two at Balmoral and left her mark where it mattered.

So what shall I tell him, Cathy asked at the end of the letter. I love it here, you know I do. But I could certainly use the extra money and if it felt right we might see a little more of each other.

If it felt right.

This was a woman, thought Moncrieff, who held a fascination for certain kinds of men. Jack Riordan was plainly one of them. The War Secretary, in God's name, was another. Archie Gasgoigne was a third. And Moncrieff himself knew exactly what kind of impact she made. Her smile alone lingered a

long time in the memory. Only days ago, Moncrieff had felt
a pang of deep regret as he'd boarded the train south. Under
different circumstances – no war, no summons to St James's
Street – he might have stayed at the Glebe House. They might
have talked deep into the night, tossed another log on the fire,
abandoned all caution, woken up next morning in a different
relationship, exactly the way Archie had counselled. Might have.
Might have.

If it felt right.

Moncrieff checked his watch for a third time, wondering
whether he might phone her later. The first of his worries should
have been the house itself. Who else could he find to fill her
shoes? Yet he knew with total certainty that she'd never abandon
the modest Moncrieff estate without finding someone equally
suitable to take her place. That's what made her so unique, so
dependable. And it was that same brimming self-belief that had
led her to put an unspoken intimacy down on paper.

If it felt right.

Bold, he thought, heading for the tiny bathroom. Bold, and
more than welcome.

The Director was already at his desk when Moncrieff rapped
on his door. Unusually, Guy Liddell didn't bother with the
usual exchange of courtesies. Instead he wanted to know about
Hesketh.

'What happened? What did you make of him?'

Moncrieff described the meal they'd shared, their hasty
evacuation to the Lower Bar and the conversation they'd
resumed over glasses of Armagnac once the raid was over.

'And?'

'He seems to know Lisbon well. He's been there a while. He certainly speaks Portuguese because he bumped into a businessman from Mozambique as we were leaving.'

'And his connections? In Lisbon?'

'To be honest, I lost count. We started with another businessman, Santo Silva. Then came the German Ambassador, our old friend Schellenberg, a handful of agents working for the *Abwehr*, two Russians he claims knew the Romanovs, and then a host of smaller fry, mainly rogues on the make. All evening I got the impression he was trailing his coat for our benefit, but I suspect he genuinely likes rough company.'

'I see.' Liddell reached for his fountain pen and scribbled himself a note. 'So where, precisely, do our interests lie?'

'He thinks something big's in the offing.'

'Big how?'

'He thinks the Germans are serious about peace.'

'But we know that already. Your good friend Schultz was kind enough to tell us.'

'I know, sir. But this might be a little more concrete. And a little bolder.'

'Specifically?'

'He wouldn't say. Not in terms. All he wanted me to believe was that he was in touch with the right people, that he could open doors for us, that he could make things happen. He wants us to regard him as someone of significance.'

'Make things happen where? How?'

'In Lisbon, obviously, but it would require our presence there.'

'You mean your presence?'

'Yes.'

'He liked you?'

'I've no idea.'

'But you believe him? You think he knows the right people?'

'I think I do, yes.'

'Evidence?'

Moncrieff held the Director's gaze for a moment and then stooped to his bag. From an envelope he extracted a cardboard token the size of a half-crown.

'What's that?'

'It's a cloakroom ticket from the Ritz, sir. On the back is a figure. That's Hesketh's writing.'

He passed the ticket across the desk. Liddell turned it over.

'Seven?' he looked blank.

'There was a raid last night, sir, as you probably know. Nothing major but totally unexpected. Even Ursula was taken by surprise.'

'And?'

'Hesketh says the target was the Piccadilly area and it turns out he wasn't far wrong. He also says just seven aircraft were involved. We need to check that figure.'

'Why?'

'Because he claims to have had a hand in organising the raid.'

'Through his German contacts? In Lisbon?'

'Exactly.' Moncrieff smiled. 'In his own words, it would serve as an act of authentication. He needs to prove the value of his contacts. If he's right, we'd be foolish to ignore him.'

'So what does he want?'

'Money.'

'How much?'

'Last night he mentioned a retainer of ten thousand plus a thousand a month operational expenses. All of it payable to a bank in Lisbon. He seems to think that's cheap. He says the Germans have offered him double that.'

'To do what?'

'To come to London and talk to us. Obviously we have no means of checking.'

Liddell nodded, said nothing. Then he got to his feet and walked through to the adjoining office. Moncrieff caught the briefest conversation with Ursula Barton before he was back again. He was carrying a newspaper.

'Here,' he gave it to Moncrieff. 'Page two. Someone you might recognise.'

The paper was the *Völkischer Beobachter*, the public face of the Nazi Party, on sale daily across the Reich. Moncrieff glanced at the date: 16 November 1940. Nearly a week ago. The main story on page two offered an account of Molotov's visit to Berlin for trade negotiations with Foreign Minister Ribbentrop.

Moncrieff skimmed the text. Despite the many tributes to the Reich's steadfast Soviet allies, he detected a darker tone. In Stockholm, Schultz had told him that Hitler wanted to squeeze the Russians far harder when it came to raw materials. More coal. More oil. More everything.

'The picture, Tam. The photo.' For once Liddell didn't bother to hide his impatience.

Moncrieff's eye drifted down the page. The photo had obviously been taken at the Hauptbahnhof, at the moment of Molotov's departure. Half a dozen officials were gathered on the platform. Molotov looked ill-tempered. Ribbentrop, his hands clasped behind his back, aloof.

'The woman, Tam. Look at the woman.'

Moncrieff looked, frowned, then looked again. The woman was tall, as tall as Ribbentrop. Bareheaded on the platform, she was wearing a fur coat that hung an inch or two below her knees. Unlike the men, she had a smile for the cameras.

Moncrieff was staring at her face. This was no close-up but the resemblance was beyond dispute. The same blonde fringe. The same laugh lines around the eyes.

'Bella Menzies,' he looked up. 'She was with the Russians?'

'That has to be the assumption.'

'Has anyone checked it?'

'Not to my knowledge. It would make sense for the Russians to bring her back to Berlin. Not the most tactful move in the book, perhaps, but she speaks good German and she knows the city inside out. If nothing else, we should accept that she's played her cards well. Our Soviet friends obviously value her many talents. As they should.'

Moncrieff could only nod. Barely two years ago he'd been in this very city, Berlin, a novice agent trying to wrestle Germany away from the madness of its leadership. One of his consorts had been Wilhelm Schultz. Another was Isobel Menzies, whom he'd met at the British Embassy. Bella had helped him on a number of occasions, and watched his back after the death of an American businessman, and to their mutual surprise the relationship had deepened until the moment the Gestapo stepped in. The rest – the interrogations, the torture, the screams from neighbouring cells – was something Tam did his best to forget until the news arrived that Bella, the one woman he might have loved, had defected to the Soviets.

He was still gazing at the photo. Did he need proof that she'd been wedded to a greater cause all the time? That their plans for some kind of post-war life together had been nothing but a fairy tale? If so, here it was. A good-looking woman standing beside a railway carriage. Smiling for the camera. En route back to Moscow.

Liddell was studying him carefully. He gestured at the paper. 'Keep it,' he said. 'It's yours.'

Moncrieff folded the paper and handed it back. Then a knock on the door brought Ursula Barton into the room. She'd been on the phone to the Air Ministry. As expected, last night's raids had led to widespread damage in Birmingham and Southampton, but a much smaller visitation had also appeared over the capital.

'How many aircraft?' Liddell enquired. 'Do they know?'

'Yes, sir. Six.'

'*Six?*' The Director's gaze had swung to Moncrieff. 'Hesketh told us seven.'

'One turned back, sir.' It was Ursula again. 'Some kind of problem over Southend.'

6

Thanks to Hermann Goering, Dieter Merz was able to stay in Berlin for nearly a week. He and Beata took it in turns to sit at Georg's bedside in the Charité hospital. Every hour a male nurse appeared to check his vital signs but nothing seemed to provoke a response of any kind. Then, as the days went by, he began to show flickers of consciousness. Tiny tremors in the right eyelid. Reflex motions in both hands. And finally, towards the end of the week, a muttered demand for water.

It happened to be Merz at the hospital. He stared down at the pale, unshaven face on the pillow.

'Don't you say please any more?'

One eye opened, then the other.

'Merz?' he whispered.

'Me,' Dieter agreed.

'Water?'

There was water in a jug beside the bed. Dieter drew his chair closer and tried to spoon a little into the slackness of Georg's mouth. Most of it ended up on his chest.

'Again.' Georg licked his lower lip.

Dieter did his best. This time there was enough for Georg to swallow.

'More?'

Georg nodded. Another spoonful. Then a fourth. Georg's eyes were closed again and the rise and fall of his chest beneath the single sheet seemed fainter. For a moment or two, Dieter thought he must have gone to sleep but then the eyes flicked open, an expression close to panic, and one hand crabbed up towards his nose.

'What's this?' He began to pluck at the tube that descended to his stomach. Dieter caught his hand before he could pull any harder, surprised at how strong he was.

'Leave it, *compadre*. It's for the stuff they feed you. You need to eat.'

Georg stared up at him. *Compadre?* He didn't seem to understand. Then his eyes flicked left and right, trying to tease some sense from these strange surroundings.

'It's a hospital, Georg. You've been in an accident.' Dieter paused. 'Accident? You remember the car? The trolley bus?'

Georg shook his head and then winced with pain. A nurse approached and stood on the other side of the bed. When Georg tried to struggle upright, his arms flailing, they both had to hold him down. The flurry of movement attracted two more nurses. Then came the doctor who'd been in charge of Georg from the start. He was an older man, approaching late middle age. He'd served in the trenches on the Somme during the previous war as a medical orderly and had plenty of stories about concussion.

'My name is Alster, Herr Messner. Don't fight us, please. We're here to make you better.'

His voice was firm. He had a natural authority. Georg gave up the struggle, his head back on the pillow, his eyes closed.

The doctor studied him for a moment, and then told Dieter to use the telephone in his office and summon Georg's wife.

'Tell her she's married a submarine,' he said. 'Herr Messner just came up for air but it might not last. The sooner she gets here the better. But no speeding, please.'

Beata arrived within the hour. She'd brought Lottie with her. Dieter met them at the entrance to the ward and explained the situation. Georg was asleep, unresponsive, but the right voice in his ear might bring him to the surface again. She nodded. She thought she understood. Her eyes didn't leave the small group of nurses around Georg's bed. On Dieter's arm, she stepped closer. The nurses parted to make space for her. She bent low, her lips to her husband's ear.

'It's Noo-Noo,' she whispered. 'And your Lottchen.'

Dieter stared at her. Noo-Noo?

'It's me,' Beata was saying. 'Your wife. Lottie, too. We've come to see you. Can you hear me? Just nod.'

Nothing. Beata moistened a fingertip, then kissed it and placed it softly on Georg's lips. The intimacy of the gesture made one of the nurses turn her face away. When there was no response, Beata did it again and then made space on the bed for her infant daughter.

'Talk to him, Lottie. Tell Daddy about Noo-Noo.'

'You're Noo-Noo.'

'I know. Just tell him that. Just tell him I'm here.'

Lottie did what she was told but she seemed frightened by the face on the pillow. Not Daddy at all. Someone else. She held her arms out, wanting to get off the bed. It was Dieter who picked her up.

Beata was back beside Georg. One of the nurses had found

a chair. Beata sat down and began to caress the lifeless hand on the whiteness of the sheet.

'Noo-Noo,' she murmured. 'Noo-Noo's here.'

She looked up. She wanted to be sure that earlier he really had regained consciousness. To her this was the same Georg she'd seen day after day, unresponsive, inert, out of reach. One of the nurses fetched the doctor. Beata had never liked him much.

'Frau Messner?'

She said nothing. Just gestured at the lifeless figure on the bed. Your fault, she seemed to be implying. You got me here for nothing. The doctor began to explain about how fragile a patient's contact with consciousness could be. Here one minute, gone the next. Then, as if in agreement, Georg's eyes flicked briefly open. It was Lottie who saw it. She was sitting on her mother's lap. She gave a little gasp, part surprise, part delight, the way children greet a conjuring trick.

'Again, Papa,' she said. 'Do it again.'

Nothing happened. The doctor had stopped in mid-sentence. Everyone's attention was back on the face on the pillow. This time, Georg's eyes stayed open. His gaze moved slowly from face to face, careful, deliberate, almost thoughtful. Then he settled on Merz.

'*Compadre*...' A tiny motion with his right hand that might have been a wave. '*Lloviendo?*'

Lloviendo? Is it still raining? The daily squadron greeting in the chill of a hundred Asturian dawns.

'*Si.*'

'*Que lastima,*' Georg managed a smile. What a shame. His eyes were still on Merz. Dieter nodded down at Beata, who still occupied the chair, but Georg didn't seem interested. He wanted to know when the aircraft would be ready, when they were flying.

Dieter told him he was in hospital. In Germany. In Berlin.

'Guernica? Again?'

'Berlin, *compadre*. Tempelhof. Wannsee.'

'Noo-Noo.' It was Lottie's piping little voice. 'Say hello to Noo-Noo, Papa.'

Georg frowned, examined the watching faces once again. His gaze settled briefly on Beata, then moved on. Finally, he shook his head.

'Noo-Noo?' His voice was faint. Then his eyes closed again.

Gordon Hesketh was arrested the same day, shortly after lunch. Discreet checks in the morning had established his continuing presence at The Limes hotel and it fell to Moncrieff to lead three uniformed policemen to his room on the second floor. They stood aside while Moncrieff rapped on the door.

Hesketh was in bed, naked, beneath a woman who must have been twice his size. The sudden presence of strangers in the room didn't seem to surprise her in the least. She disentangled herself from a sizeable erection with some care, stooped to kiss Hesketh on the mouth, and then stood beside the bed to gather up her clothes. Her face, thought Moncrieff, must once have been beautiful. She wore nothing but a simple gold chain looped around her fleshy neck. Her breasts were enormous and there was a gleam of defiance in her eyes when she asked one of the policemen to pass her brassiere.

Hesketh lit a cigarette from a packet under the pillow and watched her dress. The expression on his face as he followed her every movement spoke of a sense of pride as well as contentment. They'd plainly shared a great deal in this airless little room and now it was over he wanted to savour the memories. When, for the second time, the sergeant in charge told him to get up he shook his head.

'Ladies first,' he murmured. 'Does anyone have a difficulty with that?'

They drove him to a gloomy looking Victorian villa on the edge of Ham Common. A barbed-wire fence surrounded the property. There were armed guards on the double gates and the grounds were dotted with Nissen huts where the detainees were lodged between interrogations. Moncrieff, who was a regular visitor to Latchmere House, had the use of an office on the second floor. While Hesketh was processed through the admissions procedure, Moncrieff settled down to make a phone call.

Guy Liddell was at his desk in St James's Street. Moncrieff confirmed that Agent Souk, as Hesketh had been code-named, was safely in custody. Arrest hadn't disturbed him in the least and his only request en route was that someone might make arrangements to pay his consort for her services to date. She preferred cash to cheques and Hesketh thought a sum of four pounds ten shillings might be more than satisfactory. He offered Moncrieff an address in King's Cross and checked it for accuracy after Moncrieff had written it down. He would, of course, repay the debt as soon as his circumstances permitted it.

'He had a bill at the hotel as well?'

'No. The woman who seems to be in charge says he paid in advance.'

'For how long?'

'Two weeks. He arrived ten days ago.'

'From where?'

'She thinks Lisbon. That's what he told her.'

'He'd stayed before?'

'Twice. The first time was a couple of years ago. She says 1938. On that occasion he told her he was living in Berlin.'

'He's had other visitors? Apart from his lady friend?'

'She thinks not.'

'And now we know where she lives?'

'Yes, sir. And that's because he wants us to talk to her. Getting the woman paid is a blind. Hesketh never does anything by accident. And I mean that as a compliment.'

The interrogations started that same evening. Hesketh had been lodged in a locked two-bedded room in one of the Nissen huts. His companion, carefully selected, was a Pole with fluent German and respectable English. His job was to win Hesketh's trust and open him up for the hidden microphones which would transmit every conversation. Moncrieff, already impressed by Hesketh's coolness under pressure, could only assume that he'd anticipate a trick like this but even attempts to use the eavesdropping to his own advantage might backfire.

In this new world of mirrors, of bluff and counter-bluff, Moncrieff knew how hard it could be to pin down anything as slippery yet absolute as the truth. Was Hesketh as well connected as he claimed? Could he really summon seven German bombers and make the earth shake around targets he'd personally selected in Central London? And if the answer was yes, what kind of man had the sheer nerve to station himself under the falling bombs? To offer himself as a potential target?

Questions like these, heavily disguised beneath a torrent of other more routine enquiries, formed the launch pad for the days and evenings to come.

Moncrieff favoured working in two-man teams. The available interrogators were an ex-Seaforth Highlander called Tar Robertson, and another ex-soldier, Robert 'Tin-Eye' Stephens. Both men had amassed a great deal of experience in the busy months since the outbreak of war. Stephens, with his screw-in monocle, sought to offer himself as a near-caricature of the serving Army officer: short-tempered, choleric and all too easy to underestimate. Robertson, with his Edinburgh manners and easy charm, seemed an altogether softer prospect. Together, in one encounter after another, they'd developed a talent for quickly disentangling fantasy or straight lies from something closer to the truth and Moncrieff had yet to meet a detainee who could avoid their artful traps.

Hesketh, however, had their measure within minutes and to Moncrieff's quiet satisfaction, he listened to the man they'd dubbed Souk parrying every thrust. While Stephens carried a bludgeon, Robertson favoured the rapier, but as the interrogation sessions lengthened Moncrieff became aware of just how deftly Hesketh was laying out the goods on his market stall.

He was, he said, a trader. His mission in life was to make money because, by and large, money opened a number of doors in which he had an interest. If this made him self-indulgent, sybaritic, a mere plaything of the gods of *luxe,* then so be it, but over decades of both opportunity and amusement he'd learned a very simple truth. That you could have anything you wanted as long as you held your nerve.

At this point, in the very first session, Hesketh had very definitely won Tar Robertson's attention. Detainees very rarely had either the mental dexterity or the self-belief to play the interrogation game at this level, and in terms of performance alone Hesketh was frankly exceptional. Every trader, he pointed out, was at the mercy of the iron laws of supply and demand. In times of war, the commodity for sale was information. It had to be very carefully acquired, weighed, assessed. Then came the crucial issue of the customer. *Cui bono?* Who stands to gain? And – most important of all – who might have the deepest pockets?

So far, so good. But where were the quality controllers in this high-stakes game? Who was on hand to vouch for the accuracy of the information? And what might happen if the trader was simultaneously acting for two parties? Or three? Or even more?

These questions had come from Tar Robertson and drew a nod that seemed to indicate approval from Hesketh. Such obvious enquiries. So elegantly phrased.

'If you think I've been having conversations with some of our German friends then you'd be right. How could I not? Where else could I get the kind of information you might buy?'

'I could think of a thousand places,' Tar replied. 'But that's not the point. The point isn't opportunity. It's motive. Why is this information coming your way? Knowing one day that it will arrive on our doorsteps? Why are they telling you this? You've been admirably blunt about your own motive. You want our money. But what do *they* want? Should that question have any importance in your world? Because it certainly does in ours.'

So far, as the days sped by, there'd been no hint about the information itself. Simply that Hesketh had very close friends in very high places and was therefore very well qualified to serve the Allied cause. The latter phrase had caught 'Tin-Eye' Stephens' attention at once.

'And what might that cause be?' he barked. 'Do we detect just a tiny hint of patriotism?'

'Good Lord, no.' Hesketh had laughed. 'I use the word Allied simply as an adjective, a descriptor. I'm with Palmerston here. Personally I have no allies. Only interests.'

'Chiefly your own.'

'Solely my own.'

'At least you're bloody honest.' Stephens again. 'So what, exactly, might we be buying?'

This was the question that dominated session after session, the honeypot to which – under Hesketh's subtle guidance – the faces around the table returned. Like any trader, Hesketh permitted a glimpse or two of the goods on offer – a role in a set of negotiations that might end the war – but refused to add hard details in terms of personalities or deadlines. When pinned briefly in a corner during the final session, he would only admit that the peace initiative (or 'the lollipop' in Tar's droll phrase) had come, in the first place, from Hitler but was, at every turn in the carefully constructed plan, deniable.

'The bloody man wants the British taken care of,' Hesketh had murmured. 'Back in the summer, Goering told him the *Luftwaffe* would do the job. It turns out Goering was wrong and so now there has to be a better way. Our Hermann is the jack-in-the-box. He's irrepressible. You can't keep him down. He has a very big finger in this particular pie and that's why his smell is all over it. Beyond that, gentlemen, I'm not prepared to venture. Not until my lovely bank manager tells me you've paid up. The Banco Espirito Santo. My favourite stopping-off point on a sunny morning in downtown Lisbon before it gets too hot.'

The interrogations complete, Guy Liddell called a conference back at St James's Street to tease out the threads, test their strength and draw a conclusion or two. Stephens thought Hesketh a greasy little shit and said so. He also, if you listened hard enough, had a grudging respect for his honesty. Challenged by Liddell to justify the word 'honest' he said it had nothing to do with his character and everything to do with his greed. The little bastard wanted money, lots of it. And his sole redeeming feature lay in saying so.

'Fair, Tar?'

Robertson was circumspect. What interested him most was Hesketh himself. Over the years he'd had lots of dealings with individuals, mainly men, who'd slipped their moorings at a tender age. Some of them, like Hesketh, had been adopted and forced into a social mould they'd first resented, and then broken. Others, less fortunate, had been abandoned for whatever reason and obliged to cope on their own. Europe was currently full of these characters. They were debris on the tides of war, flotsam and jetsam from a thousand disasters, and a handful had already come to MI5's attention. Either way, these individuals carefully constructed a version of themselves that would keep the real world at bay and in that regard, to be honest, he found Hesketh all the more interesting.

'He writes with real passion about fortifications,' he pointed out. 'I've read a couple of his books. One of his heroes is Vauban. Vauban was a genius. He knew more about fortifications than any man alive. Are we assuming that's some kind of coincidence?

I rather think not. Hesketh has dug himself a moat, thrown up earthworks, built his walls high, readied the boiling oil. That's why no questions of ours really made any impact. He's probably lived through situations like these a million times. There was no way we could take him by surprise.'

Moncrieff, listening carefully, could only agree. There was something incomplete about Hesketh, some absence buried deep in his brain that might account for his immunity from the rude messiness of normal life. By his own account, he seemed to have spent most of his life avoiding personal commitments. He found it hard to interest himself in concepts like loyalty or perhaps even friendship. When it came to sex, he preferred to buy it, and when it came to emotions he was truly a man alone. In Lisbon, he was happy to confirm that he lived in an agreeable flat with views over the city and neighbours who knew not to ask questions. No surprises there.

Liddell wanted to know about the information. Every working day the agency was besieged by strangers, British and otherwise, trying to sell something. One of MI5's many responsibilities was to sieve for the diamonds in all this dross but the Director had a suspicion that Hesketh might truly be someone special. Moncrieff nodded. In essence, as far as they could tell, Hesketh was simply peddling the same story that Moncrieff had already brought back from Stockholm. That British prospects were bleak. That Europe belonged to Hitler. And that two civilised nations should recognise the moment when an honourable peace might be in order.

'You think this is the same offer that Schultz tabled?'

'I don't know, sir. And to be fair to Schultz, he didn't table anything. He simply told us our fortune. Like they all do. First they tie us up, give us a thorough basting, tell us the facts of life. Then, if we let them, they pop us in the oven.'

'So what makes Hesketh different?'

'I don't know. Except that he's educated. He understands the way history works. He knows what will and won't matter in the longer term and he's canny enough to put a price on that knowledge. Whether we're prepared to pay it is another matter, but every time we sit down and talk I get the feeling we'd be foolish to dismiss him.'

Liddell nodded. A buff file lay at his elbow. He extracted what looked like a letter and handed it to Tar Robertson.

'This was intercepted by the Censor some weeks ago. Copies have gone to the Foreign Office, MI6 and the Inter-Services Research Bureau. I'd like you each, please, to read it. Take your time.'

Moncrieff sat back, waiting for the letter to circulate. The Inter-Services Research Bureau was the official designation of what the secret world preferred to call SOE, or the Special Operations Executive. Just now, charged by Churchill to 'set Europe alight', they were tramping all over MI6's turf and upsetting some powerful figures in their Broadway headquarters.

At length, it was Moncrieff's turn to read the letter. It was dated 23 September and addressed to 'My dear Duglo'. After a rather formal expression of sympathies for the death of the addressee's brother-in-law at Dunkirk, it suggested that Duglo might find some merit in getting together for a meeting on neutral territory. The letter was signed 'A'.

Moncrieff looked up.

'Duglo?'

'The Duke of Hamilton. His first name's Douglas.'

'And "A"?'

'We think Albrecht Haushofer. He's an academic. He's widely travelled and he's been a pal of Hamilton's for some time. We also believe he's active in resistance circles in Berlin. His father, Karl, was a professor at Munich University, and taught Rudolf Hess after the war. We have it on good authority that the pair of them have stayed very close. Hess, of course, is Hitler's Deputy.'

Moncrieff took a second look at the letter. Post boxes in Lisbon served as a neutral channel between Britain and occupied Europe and this one appeared to have come through a box registered to a Miss V. Roberts at Post Box 506 in Lisbon.

Moncrieff wanted more details.

'The original letter came from Berlin. It was addressed to the Duke of Hamilton and Brandon at the House of Lords. It was then sealed inside another envelope and sent to a Miss Violet Roberts at the Post Box.'

'She's on file?'

'Yes. She's a widow in her seventies. She and her husband knew the Haushofers before the Great War and they stayed friends ever since.'

'And she lives in Lisbon?'

'Cambridge. We've checked her movements over the past few months and she hasn't left the country. Our assumption has to be that someone else monitors the Post Box on her behalf.' Liddell nodded at the letter. 'Read the marked paragraph, Tam. Aloud, please.'

Moncrieff returned to the letter. The paragraph in question had been lightly scored with a pencil.

'If you remember some of my last communications in July 1939, you and your friends in high places may find some

*significance in the fact that I am able to ask you whether
you could find time to have a talk with me somewhere
on the outskirts of Europe, perhaps in Portugal. I could
reach Lisbon any time within a few days after receiving
news from you. Of course I do not know whether you can
make your authorities understand so much that they give
you leave.'*

Moncrieff looked up. It was Tar Robertson who put his
finger on the key phrase.

'*Friends in high places,*' he mused. 'What do we make of
that?'

Liddell smiled. The Duke of Hamilton, he said, had a wealth of
excellent connections. As Lord Steward of the Royal Household
he was effectively the King's representative in Scotland. As the
Marquess of Douglas and Clydesdale he'd served as an MP in
the House of Commons.

'He's a flyer, too. Am I right?' Tar again.

'Of some distinction. Currently he holds the rank of Wing
Commander. He's in charge at RAF Turnhouse and flies Spitfires
and Hurricanes operationally most days.'

'And pals with the Nazis?'

'That's excessive. Pre-war, he certainly admired what
Goering achieved with the *Luftwaffe*. That's a matter of record.
He was in Berlin for the Olympics and met Hitler on a couple
of occasions. But the man's a patriot. Which is where it might
get interesting.'

'How, pray?' The question, typically blunt, came from 'Tin-
Eye' Stephens.

Liddell reached for the letter and carefully returned it to the
file. Several days ago, he'd asked the Foreign Office whether

they had any objection to the letter finally making its way to the addressee.

'You mean Hamilton?'

'Of course.'

'And then what?'

'We make it our business to monitor what happens.'

'You think he might collude?' Stephens nodded at the file. 'With Herr Albrecht?'

'I imagine that's a possibility.'

'And if he doesn't?'

'Then nothing changes. Albrecht Haushofer remains interested in a conversation and that might offer us an opportunity or two. In which case we'd require someone from our end. Someone plausible. Someone who knows the territory. Someone who could play a role. Someone who could speak for Duglo's England.'

There was an exchange of glances around the table but it was Moncrieff who offered the obvious candidate.

'Hesketh,' he said softly. 'Perfect casting.'

Dieter Merz drove Beata and Lottie back to the waterside house at Wannsee. It was late now, nearly midnight. They'd stayed at Georg's bedside all evening as he flitted in and out of consciousness, articulate one moment, comatose the next. Under these circumstances, even the most basic conversation became a kind of lottery. Sometimes he'd understand, other times he just looked blank, but what was most hurtful was his seeming hostility towards Beata. Whenever she bent to talk to him he frowned and shook his head. When, on two occasions, she tried to take his hand he withdrew it. And finally, when Dieter had said his goodbyes, he shut his eyes and turned his head on the pillow, ignoring both his wife and child.

'Did you have a row that day? When you last saw him?'

They were on the final stretch of road before the turn towards the lake. Lottie was asleep on her mother's lap.

'No. We never quarrelled, ever. I know it sounds strange, but Georg never saw the point.'

'Because he was always right?'

'Of course. You know what he was like. He had views on everything. He was the most logical person I've ever met. That was part of the attraction. He was so sure of himself, so certain. With Georg life was always black and white. Nothing in between. Agree with him, and life was sweet. In his world, he had to be in control.'

Dieter nodded. With the handful of men he trusted Georg would occasionally relax, and after a good day's hunting among the Ivans he could be excellent company. But even after a night in the bodega and a flask or two of the harsh *vino rojo*, he'd still be categorically right about everything. Do yourself a favour, he'd say. Just believe me.

Dieter was slowing. Beata held Lottie a little tighter in anticipation of the turn.

'You think it'll pass?' she said. 'Whatever it is?'

'Of course it will.'

'You sound like Georg. How can you be so sure?'

'I can't. But the last thing you need just now is me telling you he might be this way forever. Have faith...' he shot her a look in the darkness, '... Noo-Noo.'

Beata's father, Friedrich, was waiting up for them at home. Earlier, he'd been the one who'd taken the phone call from the hospital about Georg and now he wanted to know how the conversations at the bedside had gone. Beata had Lottie in her arms. The child had just woken up and was beginning to struggle. Beata held her for a moment, then caught Dieter's eye.

'Please? Do you mind?'

Dieter took the little girl and tried to comfort her. Beata's father asked again about the hospital. Georg had been unconscious for days. Was he cogent? Did he know where he was? Could he remember anything?

Beata just stared at him.

'I've no idea, Papa,' she said at last. 'Except that he hates me.'

Her eyes were moist and when her father put his arms round her she buried her face in his jacket and began to sob. Dieter did his best to explain. Georg, he said, was confused. The aftermath of the accident was playing tricks with him. Soon he'd be a husband again, and a father. In the meantime, a good night's sleep might put things right.

Beata was drying her eyes. She clearly resented letting her guard down like this and she retrieved Lottie before saying goodnight and heading upstairs. Dieter listened to her footsteps overhead. He knew that mother and daughter had shared the same bed since Georg's accident and within less than a minute all movement had ceased.

'You'll have a drink with me?' Beata's father had found a bottle of Schnapps. Friedrich was tall, with thinning hair and a store of amusing stories from his days as a teacher. Dieter could imagine his sense of humour being lost on his son-in-law, but children sensed his gentleness and lately Lottie had taken to spending hours watching him saw logs in the garden overlooking the lake. His wife, Hanni, had been taken by cancer some years earlier and, according to Beata, her father had never quite recovered.

Now he wanted to know more about the hospital, but Dieter could add very little.

'He really turned his back on them? Beata? Lottie?'

'I'm afraid so, yes.'

'Any idea why?'

'No. I thought maybe you could help.'

Friedrich nodded. Before the accident he'd been living nearby, in a rented flat in the local village. These last few months, with Georg away so often, he'd seen a great deal of what he called 'my two girls'.

'And?'

'They coped.'

'With what?'

'Georg. I'm afraid this isn't just the accident. He was changing already.'

'Towards Beata?'

'Towards family life. I'm not sure Beata was aware of it. Too close and you don't see what's under your nose.'

Georg, he said, had become a distant presence in the house, not simply because of the demands of his job but because he seemed to have lost interest.

'He'd go for long walks alone. He'd take that little rowing boat of ours out on the lake for hours on end. He said he needed the peace and the silence and Beata believed him. Flying our lords and masters, being at their beck and call, would break most people. Beata knew that. And it was in her nature to give him space.'

'And you?'

'I agreed. At first.'

'And then?'

Friedrich studied his glass for a long moment, and then emptied it before reaching for the bottle. Dieter shook his head. He'd barely touched his own glass.

'And...?' he asked again.

'I met someone in the village, someone I know very well. He used to be a flyer in the last war and sometimes he'd find himself in the *Weinstube* next to the bakery talking to Georg.'

'Georg was in there by himself?' Dieter didn't try and hide his surprise.

'He was. My friend would walk in and he'd be there in the corner, always the same table, and always writing.'

'Writing what?'

'My friend said it looked like a letter. Every time. But he could never be sure.'

'Anything else?'

'Yes.'

'Like what?'

Friedrich stole a look at the stairs. He clearly found the conversation deeply uncomfortable.

'You've known Georg a long time. Am I right?'

'You are. He's my best friend.'

'How was he with women?'

'Before Beata, you mean?'

'Yes.'

'Shy. Awkward. Guarded. Certain women, serious women, he sometimes liked. Most of them were married. That made them safe. He could talk to them, put them right about this and that. But anything flirtier, anything light and frothy...' Dieter shook his head, '... he'd take to the hills.'

'Until my daughter came along.'

'Yes. And to be frank I couldn't get over how lucky he was.'

'Why?'

'Because she can be so...' Dieter shrugged, '... sexy, as well as serious.'

'Sexy' was a risk. Dieter knew it. But the word put a brief smile on Friedrich's face.

'You're right,' he said softly. 'I've always thought that. Her mother did, too. That's what made Beata so special. And Hanni would have been pleased about Georg, just the way I was.'

'But?'

'But nothing. This is about a single conversation, that's all. My friend could have misheard. He could have jumped to the wrong conclusions. That probably goes for me, too. So pay no attention. This is an old man talking. We get it wrong. All the time.'

'Get what wrong? You've told me nothing.'

Another gulp of Schnapps. Friedrich's eyes were beginning to moisten. He bent towards Dieter, his voice low.

'This is recently, two or three weeks ago. My friend found Georg at the usual table, scribbling away. The moment he walked in, Georg covered the pad with a newspaper. They had a few drinks. They talked the way they always talked. Then Georg mentioned an actress, Olga Helm. You know her?'

'Of course. Everyone knows her. Especially Goebbels.'

'Exactly. They must have met on some flight or other. She was part of the Goebbels circus until recently. Made appearances all over Germany. Strictly for propaganda purposes, of course. Remarkable woman. And a great actress.'

'And you're saying…? Georg and Olga Helm…?'

'I'm saying nothing, except what my friend suspected. He said Georg was a man possessed.'

'By Olga Helm?'

'Yes. That was the phrase he used. A man possessed.'

'Possessed enough to sit in a *Weinstube* and write to her?'

'Yes.'

'Letter after letter?'

'Yes.'

Dieter sat back, nursing his glass, thinking about the proposition. It was, on the face of it, wildly unlikely. To the best of his knowledge, Olga Helm was Russian. Hence the sculpted cheekbones and slightly Slavic eyes. Attractive? Without question. Talented? Undeniably. But risky, too, not simply because Georg was himself married but because one of the senior chieftains had put his smell on her. Goebbels was said to have a stable of mistresses, many of them actresses, but had never been keen on sharing. Once fucked, always fucked.

'I'm not sure I believe this,' Dieter said slowly. 'It's not what Georg would do. It's completely out of character. He'd never expose himself like that.'

'Then so be it. You've put my mind at rest.'

'Have I?'

'Of course not. My friend's no fool. And neither am I.'

'I see,' Dieter nodded. 'And Georg? What does this make him?'

'It makes him very unlucky.'

'To have fallen for a woman like Olga Helm?'

'To have gone through a windscreen the way he did. And survived.'

Tam Moncrieff telephoned the Glebe House from the privacy of his office, returning to St James's Street after an evening at the theatre. Ursula Barton had acquired two tickets for Flanagan and Allen at the Stoll Theatre in Kingsway and *Hi-de-Hi!* had been light relief for both of them after the sheer pressure of work over the recent weeks. Moncrieff was aware that many calls from the office were monitored but he anticipated nothing of any interest to listening ears. Wrong.

The number rang and rang. Moncrieff was about to give up, thinking that Cathy Phelps must have gone to bed, when she picked up the phone. The sound of Moncrieff's voice put a smile in her voice.

'Lovely to hear you,' she said. 'At least you're still alive.'

'You thought I might not be?'

'I'm not sure you'd tell me if you were. Does that make sense? Probably not.'

Moncrieff wondered whether this was some kind of reprimand. It had been days, after all, since he'd received her letter. *If it felt right*, she'd written.

'You've applied for that job? The one you mentioned? Buckingham Palace? Court Jester? By Royal Appointment?'

'I have not.'

'But it still interests you?'

'Only if you approve.'

'Why's that?'

'Because I like to think you might be part of it.'

'But you'd have gone. No more Glebe House.'

'That's not what I meant. And you know it.'

Moncrieff blinked. The phone was in the hall in the big old house. He was trying to imagine her in the chilly gloom. He knew she wore a long nightshirt in bed. He'd seen it hanging on the washing line, a creamy white with lace around the low neckline, and once – all too briefly – he'd looked up from the courtyard late at night and glimpsed her at the bedroom window in the attic quarters where she lived. He visualised her now, her bare feet curling on the cold flagstones.

'Did I wake you up?'

'No. I've been waiting for this call. I just need to know, Tam.'

'Know what?' He smiled. She'd never called him by his Christian name.

'Know whether there's something else between us. You're a lovely man. Am I allowed to say that? Probably not.' She paused. 'Are you still there?'

'Go on.'

'There's nowhere to go. Which is rather the point. I'm glad you employed me. I'm grateful for this job of mine. But I'd be lying if I said it's all about the house. It's a lovely house. I love the silence, the views, the wind in the trees, everything. But that's not the end of it and in some ways it's not even the beginning. This house is you, Big Man, and it's empty if you're not here. Is there any chance of you coming back in the near future? On a regular basis? The answer's no. Do I want to see you more often? Be with you? The answer's yes. But only if it feels right. And that judgement has to be yours.'

This time the silence stretched and stretched. Moncrieff admired the way she'd been so candid. She'd quickened the pace, just like a good RSM, and in so doing she'd forced him to a decision he should probably have taken months ago. What the hell.

'You say the job is there for the asking?'

'Yes.'

'Then take it.'

'I will, Boss,' she laughed. 'And I promise you won't regret it.'

7

Winter came late to Berlin that year. It was early December before a hard frost and freezing rain made the roads and pavements treacherous underfoot, and the first blizzard had yet to sweep in from the east. Beata continued to come to the Charité hospital every day, and whenever he was in Berlin Dieter Merz was happy to drive her.

By now she seemed hardened to her husband's apparent indifference and she still took up her post by the bed and tried to coax him into conversation. Most of the time it was hopeless. Georg simply feigned sleep or turned his head away. Dieter watched her at the bedside, keeping vigil, her hands in her lap, composed, still, watchful, as if she was trying to conjure back the man she'd known and loved. Once a nurse paused beside her and quietly asked whether there might be days when she'd prefer to stay at home and rest, but she shook her head.

'We're husband and wife,' she said. 'We must go through this together.'

In many respects, Georg was getting better. He had full movement in every limb, his speech was unimpaired, he was beginning to put on weight again and he could even manage the walk to the toilets at the end of the ward. Then, late in the evening on 20 December, he had an epileptic fit. Two nurses held him down for nearly a quarter of an hour while his body convulsed. Afterwards, exhausted, he slept.

Next morning, when Beata and Dieter arrived, they found him slumped in bed, his eyes closed, his face sagging, and a thin dribble of saliva moistening the roughness of his chin. From time to time there were tiny spasms of involuntary movement in his right hand and his eyes would open and he'd stare at it with fierce concentration, as if it had appeared from nowhere, a mysterious addition to the wreckage of his body. On these occasions Beata tried to help him, calm him down, tell him to relax, but he always ignored her. He was angry, as well as helpless, and the anger began to overwhelm him.

As Christmas approached, decorations appeared in the ward. One of the porters had acquired a tree from somewhere and a couple of the nurses wrapped tiny presents to hang from the boughs. On Christmas Eve, children from a local school sang carols in a circle in the middle of the ward and afterwards they took the presents down from the tree and circulated from bed to bed with fetching little curtseys. Beata unwrapped Georg's present. It was a tiny replica of a Bf-109. Georg ignored it.

The following day, shortly before noon, the Matron stepped in from the corridor and clapped her hands. The ward, to her delight, had been selected to receive a visit from a pair of very special guests. Dieter was at Georg's bedside. He'd been reading a novel Friedrich had lent him and he looked up to see Joseph Goebbels at the entrance to the ward. Beside him, unmistakable in her trademark black dress, was the Slav cinema goddess, Olga Helm.

The Minister of Propaganda limped into the ward, Olga on his arm. Behind him was a two-man camera team. Goebbels paused at the foot of each bed to offer a nod and a seasonal greeting. Then came the moment when he recognised Georg Messner. His rubber smile widened. He whispered something to Olga. She, too, was gazing at Georg. And she, too, was smiling.

Beata and Dieter got to their feet. Georg was staring at the actress. Dieter was dreading a *Heil Hitler* from Goebbels but instead he turned to his cameraman. He wanted this scene recorded. Back with Georg, Goebbels asked how he was. Georg, who seemed to recognise the minister, struggled to frame an answer. His gaze kept returning to Olga. He couldn't take his eyes off her.

The Matron was hosting the visit. At a word from Goebbels she summoned two nurses to raise Georg into a sitting position. Then Goebbels told Olga to perch on the bed beside the Führer's favourite pilot. When she was comfortable, he took a seat on the other side. The cameraman was ready with his tripod. He rearranged the cards on Georg's bedside cabinet and then returned to his camera. He wanted three smiles, *drei frohe Weihnachten*. Olga and Goebbels obliged. Happy Christmas, they chorused. Both had an arm round Georg. He seemed dazed. His eyes had lost focus and tears were pouring down his face.

Dieter stole a glance at Beata. Her expression gave nothing away, but he suspected that she wasn't fooled by this vintage piece of Nazi pantomime. Her poor mute husband had become the focus for Goebbels' attention and there had to be a reason.

The cameraman had finished. Goebbels was already on his feet. Olga whispered something in Georg's ear and squeezed his hand. When Georg wouldn't let go she kissed him on the cheek and then sought the help of the Matron to disentangle herself. Moments later, without a backward glance, the circus moved on and silence descended once again. Outside, Dieter caught the distant whisper of a Christmas trolley bus.

Two days later, a uniformed SS orderly appeared with a parcel at the house beside the Wannsee. For once, Beata's father had accompanied her to the hospital and so Dieter was in the house alone.

'You're *Major* Merz?'

'I am.'

'Sign here, please.'

'This is for me?' Dieter was staring at the package.

'Yes.'

'From who?'

'The Promi.'

The Promi was Berlin slang for Goebbels' Ministry of Propaganda. Merz scribbled a signature and watched the orderly return to his motorbike. The door closed, he opened the parcel. Inside was the previous day's copy of the *Völkischer Beobachter* and a bundle of what looked like letters. There must have been at least a dozen of them. They were written on ruled Luftwaffe-issue notepads and Dieter knew at once that these were Georg's work. He recognised the handwriting, the way the words crabbed carefully across the page. *Meine Liebling*, the first one began, *Wo kann ein Mann anfangen?* My darling? Where can a man start?

Dieter swallowed hard, already embarrassed by the way his friend had let himself down. The first of the letters was clumsy but explicit. Georg and Olga had obviously been meeting at her apartment, presumably somewhere in the city. Georg described the look of her bedroom, the smell of her perfume, even the way her dachshund would join them in bed. He was obviously obsessed by her – by her smile, by her body, by the way she made love to him – but he lacked the language to do this passion justice. Parts of it read like the work of a fourteen-year-old. Other passages, more prosaic, might have come from a post-mission combat report. She'd attacked him from a direction he'd least expected. And he'd surrendered totally to what followed. More, he kept begging. I need more.

Need? Dieter shook his head. The rest of the letters he wouldn't bother to read. They'd be simply variations of the same theme – a loyal servant of the Reich, a pilot charged with the safety of the Führer, the co-star of the pre-war dogfights on the air show circuit, in thrall to a Slavic film goddess with a following of millions. Under pressure, Dieter could dream up a number of ways Georg Messner could make a fool of himself, but nothing was as cheap and as hopelessly disloyal as this. Talking to Beata's father last night, Dieter had fought hard not to believe the suspicion that Georg was cheating on his wife. Now, faced with the evidence, he had no choice.

But why had the letters come to him? And what, exactly, was he supposed to do with them? Dieter didn't know. Showing them to Beata wasn't an option. His loyalty to Georg was too strong. But maybe, in due course, there might come a time when he could share the billets-doux with his ex-wingman. Beware of temptation, he'd say. And beware, above all, of the bastards who'd baited this little trap and turned up in Georg's hour of need to make him look a fool.

He picked up the copy of the *Völkischer Beobachter* and began to thumb through it. He found the photograph and the accompanying story on page five. Georg Messner, the Führer's brave pilot, was recovering in the hands of expert doctors following a car accident. The Minister of Propaganda and one of the Reich's leading film stars had been happy to pay him a visit and wish him a Happy Christmas, secure in the knowledge that they carried with them the good wishes of the entire Reich.

Dieter's gaze returned to the photograph. This was the real nastiness behind Goebbels' little game, the reason he'd planned the hospital visit in the first place. Georg Messner had crossed a line and now he was sending this drooling cretin a message. One of my women, he was saying. Leave well alone.

The New Year came and went. The atmosphere at the house beside the water was glum. Dieter did his best to find ways of comforting Beata without upsetting her further but in the end he was relieved when Friedrich suggested that the pair of them could cope without *der Kleine*'s aid. Maybe it's best if you get on with your life, he said. We'll give you a call if we need you.

And so Merz found himself spending more and more time with Rudolf Hess. The Deputy Führer's daily schedule of meetings and speeches across the Greater Reich was as demanding as any of his fellow chieftains' and, when the pressure of events obliged him to attend to his paperwork in the air, he was happy to let Merz fly him from city to city. On these occasions Merz was careful to let Hess handle both the take-offs and the landings. Winter weather often complicated both but Hess's performance at the dual controls, as he reported to Goering, never left him with a moment's doubt that the Deputy Führer was an extremely accomplished pilot.

In mid-January, Merz attended a conference with Hans Baur at the *Reichsregierung* at Tempelhof airfield. Baur wanted to know whether, in Merz's opinion, Georg Messner would ever be fit enough to return to the Führer Squadron. Merz shook his head. He hoped against hope that Georg might one day find his way back to a pilot's seat but, given what had happened, Merz was certain that his friend's days of flying premium cargo were over. The latter phrase amused Baur.

'You don't think these people wouldn't relish the company of a fellow madman?' he asked.

Later that afternoon, Merz ran into Goering again at Tempelhof. The *Reichsmarschall* had just got off a flight from Paris. He took Merz aside and asked him about Hess's navigational skills. Merz didn't understand the question. Hess had been flying for two decades. Of course he could find his way around.

'But a really long journey? More than a thousand kilometres? With somewhere in the dark to find at the end of it all?'

At the time Merz had simply repeated that Hess was amply qualified in the air. Pilots with his experience could always find their way home. Only months later did this innocent question acquire greater significance.

At the Glebe House, meanwhile, Cathy Phelps was taking pains to make Christmas especially memorable. With a full week's holiday at his disposal, Tam Moncrieff had taken the train north. He was now in regular contact with Cathy by telephone, and he knew that she'd been accepted for the post at the Palace, but the abrupt change in their relationship still felt slightly unreal. How easy would it be for his former housekeeper to occupy a far more intimate role in his life? Or was he, the

Laird of Glebe House, simply the victim of some middle-aged fantasy?

He needn't have worried. Cathy picked him up at Laurencekirk station. He hadn't seen her for more than a month and she looked radiant. They sat in the old shooting brake for a moment or two, watching the steam from the engine shredding in the wind as the train headed north. Then Moncrieff felt her hand close on his.

'Kiss me?'

He looked at her for a moment, then cupped her face in his big hands, knowing that Archie Gasgoigne had been right. Housekeeping had been a blind alley, a needless trick he'd played on himself, a source of unspoken torment. Time wasted, he thought, at a moment in the nation's fortunes when time was no longer something you could rely on. Such cowardice on his part. Such indecision. She was there. She wanted him. She'd said so.

He kissed her softly, then again. Her eyes were open. She pulled away slightly, told him he needed a shave. She'd do it herself, the moment they got home. The water was hot. The towels were freshly laundered. She'd cover him with shaving soap, working up the lather exactly the way men liked, and afterwards she'd take him to bed.

'You approve?'

'I think I might.'

'Might?' She laughed. 'Relax, Boss. We've nothing to lose.'

They stayed in bed all evening. The bed itself had once belonged to Tam's parents. After his father's death he'd treated himself to a new mattress but after he and Cathy had made love for the second time he lay back, her head on his chest, staring at the darkness beyond the window. Had it ever been like this between his mother and father? In truth he'd never know. Cathy was the most accomplished lover he'd ever met and she'd acquired a repertoire of tiny tricks that first surprised then delighted him. There wasn't a corner of his body off-limits to her busy tongue and later that night, after she'd returned from the kitchen downstairs with a bowl of soup and fresh bread, he'd asked her about previous relationships.

'Are you checking up on me?'

'Christ, no. You've made me a very happy man. I'm just curious, that's all.'

She nodded, kissed him, said nothing. They ate in silence. At length, she asked him whether he minded her being honest.

'Not at all. Go ahead.'

'Good,' she nodded in approval. 'The truth is I've wanted you since we first met. Enjoy the moment, Mr Moncrieff. Because these days there's nothing else.'

Moncrieff had never known a Christmas like it. Even the gods of the weather were on their side. Snow began falling on Christmas Eve and the pair of them had to make their way through knee-high drifts to the sturdy stone-built kirk at the far end of the village for the midnight service. The congregation was thinner than usual and a handful of the older women seemed to sense that something important had happened up at the Glebe House. One of them, who'd been a favourite of Moncrieff's father when the old man was still alive, took Tam aside as they filed into the darkness after the last of the hymns.

'You're a lucky man,' she said, knotting her scarf against the cold. 'Take great care of her.'

Moncrieff needed no prompting. In the normally dead time between Christmas and New Year's Eve, he filled the bright, cold days with expedition after expedition, sometimes an amble through the surrounding forests, sometimes a more ambitious trek down the glen towards the distant gleam of the River Dee. In the garden behind the house Cathy built a snowman with a fine view of the mountains. She gave him unmatched buttons for eyes, a woolly bonnet to keep out the cold and an old pipe where his mouth should be. She beckoned Moncrieff over for a formal introduction and together they crouched in the wind to name each of the neighbouring peaks for the benefit of the lumpy little snowman. Tam, who'd known this landscape since childhood, could only marvel at how a handful of days was changing his life. More, please, he told her.

On New Year's Eve, he and Cathy awoke to a sudden thaw. Meltwater was dripping from the roof and they stood in the window as the snowman began to vanish in front of their eyes. Moncrieff wondered whether this sudden passing might break the spell but, when he asked, she shook her head.

'The moment lives on,' she kissed him. 'If the poor thing melts any quicker we'll be sharing the garden with a ghost.'

On New Year's Day, the heather and peat soggy underfoot, they hiked to the top of the nearest peak. A week of overeating should have taken its toll on both of them, Cathy especially, but Moncrieff was surprised by how fit she was. When they finally reached the stony lip at the mountain's summit, she seemed barely to have drawn breath. Despite the thaw, and fitful sunshine through rags of cloud, it was cold up here and he put his arms around her. Below, a tiny dot in the wildness of the landscape, was the Glebe House, but what really took his eye was her face. Her cheeks were pinked with the climb. She looked beautiful.

'You remember Archie?' Moncrieff was holding her at arm's length. 'My bootneck friend? The one who called me Boss?'

'Yes.'

'Did he pay you a visit that night he stayed?'

'Yes.'

'And?'

'I told him he was too late. A respectable woman only loses her heart to one man at a time.'

'Is that a compliment?'

'It's whatever you make it,' she smiled. 'Boss.'

Back in London, waiting for Cathy to join him once her job started, Moncrieff moved briskly from meeting to meeting. Ever-tighter restrictions were bringing queues of people to MI5's attention, and some of the files – after preliminary investigations – landed on Moncrieff's desk. Normally he'd battle to keep up with this kind of workload, but Christmas seemed to have revived him.

Everyone said how well he looked, how buoyant, how cheerful. There was gossip about someone new in his life. Liddell hazarded a guess about Isabel Menzies. Maybe Tam had found some way of making contact with his old flame. Maybe he'd tracked her down in Moscow. Maybe they were planning to meet, in Stockholm, or Geneva, or even Lisbon. The rumour drew a shake of the head from Moncrieff, and a murmured reminder about sleeping dogs. Only Ursula Barton, who was privy to the telephone intercepts, knew the truth. That Tam Moncrieff had fallen in love.

The price of her silence, not entirely playful, was an invitation to meet the lady. Moncrieff was delighted to oblige. Cathy moved out of the Glebe House in early February, having found someone to take her place until Tam could make more permanent arrangements. She was allotted a draughty attic room on the top floor at the Palace – a bed, a washstand, a battered old wardrobe plus a crisscross of sticky tape on the single window to protect her from bomb blast – and settled into her duties as a housemaid. Making contact with Tam wasn't as easy as she'd imagined. All calls from the Palace had to be routed through the main switchboard and waiting one's turn in the queue could, in the words of her supervisor, be tiresome. Under the circumstances, Moncrieff found it easier to leave messages. 'Miss Phelps needs to be at the Antelope in Marlowe Street at half past seven,' he told the voice on the switchboard. 'I'd be obliged if you could tell her.'

In the event, Cathy was late but Ursula Barton and Moncrieff were no strangers to the Antelope and they had more than enough to talk about. Ursula, Moncrieff knew, had the Director's ear. Liddell trusted her completely, a compliment she returned by being extremely careful about what she let slip.

In-house, Hesketh had by now officially become Agent Souk. Since the sessions at Latchmere House, he appeared to have vanished and Moncrieff wanted to know why.

'I thought the Director told you?'

'No. I'd remember if he had.'

'Then I'm puzzled. I thought I typed you a confidential note.'

'I'd remember that, too.'

'I see.' She glanced around. On a wet Tuesday evening the pub was nearly empty. 'He's back in Lisbon.'

'We've let him go?'

'On the contrary. We've agreed a modest retainer for the time being and given him a list of errands to run. Tar did the negotiations. It wasn't the fortune Souk expected but Tar can be very persuasive.'

Moncrieff nodded. He wanted more.

'Errands?'

'You'll have seen the letter that came to us through the Censor.'

'From Albrecht Haushofer? To Hamilton?'

'Exactly. It turns out that Souk has met young Albrecht on a number of occasions. They go back a long way.'

'We know that?'

'No. We mentioned Haushofer's name *en passant*. We said that he might be a person of interest to us and that's when he told us that they were friends. This is his account, no one else's, but the Director is minded to believe him. Haushofer is an academic. It runs in the family. Souk likes to put himself in the same box. He knows Munich well. They speak each other's language. And I'm not just talking *Englisch und Deutsch*.'

Moncrieff smiled. Ursula was herself German. She'd been married to an English diplomat at the Hague embassy and had been a key asset for MI6. After the debacle at Venlo, she'd jumped ship in disgust and ended up in the arms of the Security Service, much to Guy Liddell's delight. It had taken a while for the penny to drop but Moncrieff now realised that Ursula

Barton was probably privy to more secrets than anyone else in St James's Street. Hence, perhaps, her near-runic ability to predict air raids.

'So Souk has been despatched to knock on a few doors. Probably in Lisbon. Am I right?'

'Yes.'

'And one of them will be young Haushofer's?'

'Yes.'

'But Albrecht lives in Germany. Which might pose a problem, *nein*?'

'Not if he's come to collect the mail.'

'A letter, you mean?' Moncrieff was smiling now. 'In answer to his own?'

'That might seem logical.'

'So Hamilton's written back? And Souk's playing postman?'

Ursula's gaze had drifted to the door. Already she was getting to her feet.

'This must be your young lady,' she murmured. '*Very* pretty.'

The evening was a success. Cathy had found her feet in the Palace within days. It was a much bigger operation than Balmoral, and light years away from her solitary months at the Glebe House, but it was evident that she had the guileless knack of making new friends and Moncrieff wasn't remotely surprised to learn that she was already in the running for a promotion.

'The woman who helps run the appointments secretariat has just found out she's pregnant. That puts her out of the running for a while so they've asked me to stand in.'

Ursula wanted to know what kind of appointments. Was this a question of the Civil List? Gongs and honours for the favoured few?

'Not at all. These people organise the public appearance schedules. It helps to know who's doing what where. That's something I learned at Balmoral. The royals work hard for their money. They're on the move all the time.'

Ursula seemed impressed. So was Tam. Only a couple of days ago he'd imagined Cathy toiling away below stairs, surrounded by baskets of laundry. Now this.

'Will you get to join them on any of these outings?'

'Who knows? Maybe. Maybe not.' She glanced towards the bar. 'Do you think they have Mackeson?'

After the pub, Ursula insisted on taking them both for a meal at an Italian restaurant in Covent Garden. She had the ear of the owner, a Genoese émigré who seemed to be able to call on an endless supply of fresh fish. Abelone was always packed but a phone call secured them a discreet table away from the noise.

They settled at the table and Ursula asked a series of questions about Cathy's young life. None of these enquiries seemed remotely personal, just conversational chit-chat, but as the evening drew to a close Moncrieff realised that he'd just witnessed a masterclass in interrogation. Without ruffling a single feather, Ursula had established that Cathy Phelps came from a big family in Canning Town, that her father was a stevedore in the Prince Albert Docks, that she'd imbibed left-wing views as a child from an uncle who sold copies of the *Daily Worker* on street corners in Plaistow, and that her mum was mad about *Wuthering Heights*. Hence Cathy's name.

The meal over, Tam hailed a taxi to take her back to the Palace. Tomorrow morning she was due to start work at six but she had the weekend free and she couldn't wait for her first night in Tam's flat. They kissed goodbye at the kerbside and Moncrieff stepped back as the taxi sped away. Then he turned to Ursula.

'As an exercise in PV, that was extremely accomplished,' he murmured.

'You think so?'

'I do. *Gut gemacht*. Congratulations. I don't think she felt a thing.'

PV meant positive vetting, a normally brutal test of a stranger's virtue. Ursula was still watching the taxi.

'You've fallen in love with a Communist again,' she said thoughtfully. 'Once is careless. Twice might make some of us wonder.'

8

'*Ah...*' Hess shook his head, '*... die Roten...*'

Dieter Merz was sitting in the Deputy Führer's study at his home in Munich. Hess was drinking boiled water. Downstairs, his wife had poured a glass of wine for Merz. He'd just flown in from Berlin, summoned by his new pupil.

Die Roten meant the Reds. Dieter assumed Hess was talking about Communists.

'You're right, Merz. This was after the war. Some days it feels like a lifetime ago. It's hard to put it into words sometimes. You fight them night after night. You get yourself injured. You see your comrades perish around you. For some reason you're chosen to survive. And then, when you think you've got them on their knees, there's only more fighting. Not because you want to. Not because you've become some kind of animal. But because you *have* to.' The flat of Hess's palm descended on the desk. 'No choice. Not if you care.'

Merz didn't know how far to take this conversation. Days at Georg's bedside and nights trying to get through to Beata had been exhausting. In both cases, neither party really wanted to talk. Georg because the physical act of talking was still beyond him; Beata because she'd turned her back on the world. Then had come the summons to Munich. Hess had a mission for Merz. Might *der Kleine* be good enough to fly south and discuss it?

'*Der Kleine*' Merz took as a compliment. Hess, as a shy man, hid behind a certain formality. Only very recently had he begun to use Merz's nickname. It meant, thought Dieter, that he was beginning to let his guard down. In the cockpit and on the ground he knew he'd won Hess's respect. Beyond respect lay trust, and maybe even friendship. Friends with Hitler's Deputy? Merz would never have believed it. Yet here he was, listening to a man desperate to share long-ago moments in his past.

'You fought the Reds in Spain,' Hess said. 'You know about Communists.'

'I know about shooting them down. I'm not sure I ever met any.'

'Then let me tell you, young man, that makes you lucky. We broke heads, looked them in the eyes, fought hand to hand. No quarter. Not in those days. We shed blood for the cause. *Die Blutfahne* didn't happen by accident.'

Die Blutfahne was the Blood Flag, a relic from the failed Nazi attempt to seize power in Munich back in 1923. Wrapped around a Party trooper who'd died in the abortive putsch, it had become an object of reverence and had featured at Party rallies ever since. Merz, along with most of his friends, regarded this piece of Nazi theatre as mawkish but was careful not to say so.

'Do you miss those days?'

'Never. They were necessary. They brought us to power. Communists only understand the language of violence. Remember that.'

He nodded, looking Merz in the eye, and Dieter caught a glimpse of the ruthless self-belief that lay behind the Nazis' climb to power. Nothing mattered. Except their ever-tighter grip on the German soul.

'You were in prison with the Führer after the putsch? Am I right?'

'Yes. Nine months in Landsberg. I had the adjoining cell. The people who ran the prison made life easy for us. Every day the Führer and I had use of another room where we could work.'

The Führer, Dieter thought. The Leader. Even then.

'And that's where you wrote *Mein Kampf*?'

'Yes.'

'Both of you? Is that true?'

'Not quite. The force, the inspiration, came from Hitler. I was the clerk, the housemaid, keeping things nice and tidy, making sure it read well. We worked every day, chapter after chapter. I was happy to contribute an idea or two. *Lebensraum*, for instance. The need for us to move against the east. That came from my teacher at the university here in Munich. Professor Haushofer. The Führer, I'm glad to say, needed no persuading. He saw at once why Russia was wasted on the Soviets. We need the living space, the wheat, the oil and a thousand other things. One day, young man. And not a moment too soon.'

'We invade?'

'Of course.'

'But the Russians are our allies. We have a pact, an agreement.'

'The Russians are Slavs. We have a duty to kick down their door and take what we need. My admiration for the Führer is boundless. It knows no limits. No one else in this country could have crushed the Communists and worked such miracles since. But even he has moments of weakness. At Dunkirk, I was frankly dumbfounded. Stop the Panzers to spare the English their blushes? Madness. And I told him so.'

Dieter nodded. Hitler had ordered his generals to pause in sight of Dunkirk to let the *Luftwaffe* finish the job. To the bewilderment of the tank commanders, the order had lasted three days.

'You never thought the English would get their men away?'

'Never. And neither did Hitler. But that's not the point. In war, you always fight the battle to the finish. The English were there for the taking. We could have played the policeman and arrested them all. Instead, God help us, they still have the remains of an army. So now there has to be another way.'

'Of what?'

'Of keeping them quiet. Of making them understand their proper role in the world. The British Empire commands the Führer's respect. It's there in *Mein Kampf*. All they have to do is mind their own business, look after their own affairs, and leave everything else well alone. It's a rule that any child can understand. So why is that man Churchill so difficult?'

Merz heard footsteps on the staircase. Frau Ilse appeared at the open door. She had the bottle of wine in one hand and a plate of biscuits in the other. Albrecht, she said, had arrived and was downstairs playing with young Wolf.

Hess asked her to show Albrecht up. Then he gestured at the bottle. Merz was to help himself. Dieter didn't move.

'Is this the Albrecht I met at Augsburg? Albrecht Haushofer?'

'Yes.' Hess was on his feet. 'You don't speak English. Am I right?'

'You are.'

'*Gut.*'

Albrecht appeared at the door. Tieless in a rumpled linen jacket, he looked a great deal more relaxed than the man Merz had met at the Messerschmitt factory. Hess found him a chair. Albrecht tapped his watch and began to explain, in German, that time was short. He had to be at his father's house across the city within the hour. Regrettably, they had fifteen minutes to agree arrangements.

Hess nodded and said something in English that Dieter didn't understand. Then the two men were speaking German again.

'Tomorrow I want you to fly Haushofer to Lisbon,' Hess was looking at Merz. 'You will refuel at Barcelona. At Lisbon you will accompany Haushofer at all times unless he decides otherwise. Accommodation has been arranged and paid for. Please keep a note of all other expenses you incur.'

'We're staying at the embassy?'

'No. And neither will you have any contacts beyond the people Haushofer deems necessary to meet. In this respect and all others during the trip Haushofer has my complete authority. Is that clear, Merz?'

Dieter could only nod. Over the previous weeks, Hess had been softening towards him. Now, for whatever reason, this sudden show of teeth.

'Understood, Herr. Hess.'

There was a brief discussion of the take-off time. Haushofer needed to be in Lisbon by dusk. According to Hess's calculations, they should therefore be in the air no later than mid-morning.

'I'm taking your 110?'

'No. Another machine has been readied.'

All being well, Merz should expect to be back in Germany

within a couple of days, though provision had been made to extend the accommodations, should that prove necessary.

'Any questions, Merz?'

'None, Herr. Hess.'

'Excellent.' A rather stiff bow. 'I wish you fair weather and a safe flight. Take care of my friend here. His is work of some importance.'

Hess turned back to Haushofer and began to speak in English again. Dismissed, Merz made his way downstairs. Half expecting an invitation to stay the night again, he found himself being conducted towards the front door.

'My husband has made arrangements for you to stay at the Drei Mohren.' She sounded apologetic. 'They keep a good table. If you like wild boar, you won't be disappointed. But please don't tell my vegan husband.'

Late that same afternoon, Guy Liddell drove out to Northolt airfield to take the long flight to Halifax, Nova Scotia. Ursula Barton was at the wheel of the Humber Super Snipe, and they conferred for several minutes in one of the RAF briefing rooms before Ursula slipped her notes into her bag and returned to the car. The following morning, she mounted the stairs to Tam Moncrieff's third-floor office, entered without knocking, and carefully shut the door behind her.

'All well?' Moncrieff was in the middle of a particularly tricky report on a Polish agent he'd recently managed to turn. He didn't look up.

Ursula ignored the question. The Director, she said, would be away for at least five days. He'd managed to coax a handful of luminaries from the American intelligence establishment to meet him on the very edge of the continent. She hinted that their deliberations might pave the way for the day when Washington finally entered the war but in the meantime the management of certain 'B' Section operations was in her hands. These included developments surrounding Agent Souk.

'Delighted to hear it.' Moncrieff put his paperwork to one side. 'How can I help?'

Ursula at last sat down, her hands in her lap, her legs crossed. Moncrieff knew that every corner of her life was meticulously organised but even so he marvelled that she never wore stockings that had been laddered. These days, that spoke of powerful connections, almost certainly in the black market.

'Souk will be delivering the letter tomorrow. In Lisbon. This is a copy. You should read it with some care.'

She handed him two sheets of paper. The letter was typed. The signature at the end was difficult to read.

'This comes from Hamilton?'

'Not exactly,' she nodded at the scribbled Duglo at the foot of the letter. 'That was as close as we could get. According to Registry it's near perfect.'

'And it's going to Albrecht Haushofer?'

'Yes. Souk already has a copy.'

'And Haushofer knows he'll be meeting Souk?'

'That's the message we passed. Gordon Millord Hesketh. A name you wouldn't forget.'

Moncrieff bent to the letter. Hamilton thanked Albrecht for his letter of 23 September last year and apologised for the long delay in replying. He'd been extremely busy seeing to the prosecution of the war, and to dealing with a number of other responsibilities. As Albrecht might imagine, life had become extremely complicated and, like so many other of his family, friends and colleagues, he longed for the return of peace. Such a profligate waste of treasure, he'd written. And such a needless spilling of blood.

In the second paragraph, Hamilton directly addressed the proposition that the two of them might meet up on neutral territory, perhaps Lisbon, in order to talk about matters in general and perhaps one or two issues in particular. While he, Duglo, could think of nothing more agreeable than seeing his old friend again, in all conscience he could visualise no immediate prospect of such a meeting coming to pass in the very near future. For one thing, his service obligations precluded such a commitment. And in another, he suspected that it might be wise to take soundings among like-minded patriots before embarking on such a trip.

In the latter instance, the letter went on, it would be immensely helpful if Albrecht could be a little more specific about what he had in mind. Time spent in reconnaissance, he reminded his old friend, is time seldom wasted.

Moncrieff looked up. 'Who wrote this?'

'You don't need to know that.'

'Liddell?'

She smiled, said nothing. Moncrieff went through the letter again. He especially liked the sentence that referred to 'like-minded patriots'.

'Very clever,' he said. 'Very deft. It's a fishing expedition, isn't it? A fly to tempt Haushofer onto the hook.'

'Nicely phrased.'

'Because we need to know who these people are?'

'Because we need to know how serious they might be.'

'About?'

'Mounting some kind of peace initiative. These people can see no end to the war and that disturbs them.'

Moncrieff nodded. For a Security Service charged with safeguarding the country's elected leadership, this made perfect sense.

'So how do we make sure this doesn't get back to Hamilton?' he asked.

'Everything has to go through Lisbon. To date, that's meant Violet Roberts' Post Box address. Souk, as you know, claims he knows Haushofer already. That might turn out to be a godsend. We can only hope it's true.'

'And does Souk also know the letter's a fake?'

'God, no.'

'And he's going to be spending time with Haushofer in Lisbon?'

'Yes.'

'So what happens if Haushofer takes it upon himself to make direct contact with Hamilton?'

'He can't. That can only happen through Souk. For the time being we've closed down the other Post Box.'

'And Souk himself? What if he goes freelance? Makes some kind of approach to Hamilton?'

'He won't.'

'Why not?'

'Because you're going down there. Tomorrow. Once Haushofer's gone back to Germany, we want you to make contact with Souk. We need to know what Haushofer had to say. Once you're satisfied you know exactly what happened you have to make it worthwhile for Souk to bide his time in Lisbon, to maintain contact with Haushofer, but to otherwise keep his mouth firmly shut. I've read the transcripts from Latchmere. Hesketh's a self-important little man. Appeal to his vanity. Make him feel part of the operation. We've intercepted the letter from Duglo and we need to know where it leads. That's the script. That's the legend. Make him feel *wanted*. Money will undoubtedly help. Depending on the way things go, you're authorised to double his retainer and perhaps hint at more largesse as events unfold. Does that make at least a modicum of sense?'

Moncrieff didn't answer. This whole operation depended on Hesketh already knowing Albrecht Haushofer. The interception of his letter to Duglo Hamilton had happened within a week of Hesketh's appearance on MI5's radar. All his life Moncrieff had mistrusted coincidences. And he'd rarely been proved wrong.

'Well?' Ursula wanted an answer.

'Souk remains in the dark about the letter being a fake?'

'Of course he does.'

'And we really believe he's known Haushofer for a while?'

'I've no idea, Tam. But he's been your *Kleines Säugling* from the start.' *Kleines Säugling*. Little baby. She glanced at her watch. 'You're booked on tomorrow's flying boat. You need to be at Poole by half past ten. The tickets and everything else you'll need are in my office.' She got to her feet, adjusted her skirt. 'Do I detect just a flicker of enthusiasm?'

Dieter Merz took off from the long concrete strip adjoining the Messerschmitt works at 10.05 the following morning. In the seat behind him was Albrecht Haushofer, his leather briefcase stowed securely in the rear gunner's space. At Haushofer's request, Merz had plotted a route that skirted Switzerland to the south, offering a grandstand view of the Austrian and Italian Alps. Haushofer, who'd skied many of these slopes before the war with his father, was on first-name terms with many of the peaks, blinding white in the bright sunshine. Weisshorn. Signalkuppe. Matterhorn. The list read like a monument to a world that was now beyond reach.

'You miss St Moritz? Klosters?'

'I do,' Haushofer acknowledged. 'But those days will be back. And very soon, I hope.'

With the blueness of the Mediterranean ahead, and the grey sprawl of Marseilles on the nose, Dieter wondered what clues an answer like that might hold. Both Hess and Haushofer himself had been tight-lipped about the purpose of today's mission. Merz's job was to get Haushofer to Lisbon and back. He assumed that some kind of rendezvous awaited his charge in the Portuguese capital, but he had no idea who Albrecht might be meeting.

Merz had never been to Lisbon but it was common knowledge in most squadron messes that this city on the very edge of Europe had become a playground for spies, black-marketeers, and anyone else with the nerve to cash in on a war that had brought blockade and rationing to every corner of occupied Europe. Were Albrecht Haushofer and the Deputy Führer part of this demi-monde? He rather doubted it.

At Barcelona, with Haushofer translating, Merz bought more fuel and kept an eye on the Catalan mechanic in charge of refuelling. A hour later, after coffee of a quality he hadn't tasted since the outbreak of war, Merz was in the air again, routing south-west over the yellowing body of Spain. From the border it was forty minutes to the Atlantic coast and, as they lost height over the broad estuary of the River Tagus, it was Haushofer who gazed down at the waterside city that was Lisbon.

'Magnificent,' he murmured.

The airfield, in the neighbouring town of Sintra, was busy. The Controller directed Merz to join the line of aircraft parked on the hardstanding and after he'd climbed down from the cockpit Merz stood in the spring sunshine for a moment or two, letting the warmth seep into his bones. Two men in white overalls were loading mail sacks into a nearby Ju-52 with Reich markings. Beyond stood a DC-3 in the colours of a British airline, while ground crew were refuelling a battered Potez in the colours of Air Afrique. In Portugal at least, he thought, commerce trumps war.

In the terminal building Haushofer led the way to a cubicle that served as the information desk. The woman in charge spoke good German and recognised the proffered name at once.

'Herr Hesketh has arranged a car for you. Herr Haushofer? Am I right?'

She summoned another woman who led the way out of the building. Parked nearby was a rusting Mercedes. Haushofer bent to the open window. Behind the wheel was a swarthy half-caste with the whitest teeth Merz had ever seen. The two of them were welcome in Sintra. Please get in the back. The journey will take perhaps an hour.

They drove north, leaving the broad reach of the Tagus behind them. The driver, to Haushofer's visible irritation, was keen to practise his German. He lived in Lisbon. He had a Portuguese wife and three children. Portuguese women were the best mothers in the world. Also the best cooks. Were his honoured guests staying long? Might they like to sample his wife's *sopa de cação*?

'No,' said Haushofer, staring out at the fields ablaze with early spring flowers.

The long dusty road led to a low line of what looked like fortifications, stretching left and right into the misty distance: raised earthwork ramparts, grassed-over strongpoints, footpaths winding in between. Then came the outskirts of a small town.

'Torch Verdsh,' the driver said.

The sound was incomprehensible. An invitation? A question? The name of something important?

'Torres Vedras,' Haushofer muttered. 'I'm guessing this is where we stop.'

He was right. The dense cluster of red roofs was dominated by the ruins of a castle atop a hill. Within the castle walls stood a white church. The driver had slowed. He was consulting a scrap of paper on which someone appeared to have scribbled directions. Finally, in the middle of the town, he pulled into the side of the road where an old man was tethering a donkey. Shown the directions, the old man shook his head. He couldn't read. Try the shop. The driver disappeared into the darkness behind the open door. Merz was gazing at knobbly, misshapen potatoes spilling out of a big wicker basket. A minute or so later, the driver was back, waving the directions in triumph. Nearly there.

In the shadow of the castle, where houses lapped up against the yellow sandstone walls, he finally came to a halt. No. 49.

He pumped the horn several times. At length the front door opened and a small, neat figure stepped into the sunshine. He was wearing a baggy black suit and the open white shirt beneath badly needed a wash, but the greying beard was neatly trimmed and there was a smile of open anticipation on his face. Merz judged him to be middle-aged, maybe older, and the moment he opened his mouth he knew where he came from. Only the English spoke German like this.

'Herr Haushofer?' The face was peering into the rear of the car through the open window.

There was a moment of indecision while the stranger's eyes flicked from face to face. Then Haushofer opened the door and got out.

'Mr Hesketh?'

'Indeed. Please call me Gordon.'

There was an exchange of handshakes and a word of introduction for Merz before Hesketh bent to the driver's window. The driver had no problem with his Portuguese. He grinned at Hesketh and tapped his watch. Seconds later, he'd gone.

'It's been a long drive, gentlemen. My apologies. Come. The exercise will be good for us.'

Without waiting for an answer, Hesketh led the way through a narrow alley that in turn led to a breach in the encircling castle walls at the foot of the hill. From here, the path steepened through rocky scrub. Within seconds, conversation was difficult, then impossible. Merz brought up the rear of the column, his feet sliding on the loose dirt, his balance threatened at every step, his head tipped occasionally backwards, aware of the bulk of the castle above them.

At last they made it to the top. Entry to the castle itself was through a medieval arch that led to a paved courtyard beyond. The courtyard was empty. From its edge the town sprawled below. Beyond the town, in the middle distance, Merz could make out the pattern of the defence works.

Hesketh and Haushofer had been speaking in English. Already, they appeared to be friends. Now, Hesketh switched to German.

'You know about the wars?' He was looking at Merz. 'Napoleon? Messéna? The Duke of Wellington?'

Merz shook his head. He could tell the Englishman a great deal about the Messerschmitt 109, and moments of exaltation in the *Kanalkampf*, but Napoleon had always been a mystery.

'A shame, Herr Merz, because history does nothing but repeat itself. Over there, for instance.' Merz followed the pointing finger north, towards the far horizon. 'That's where Napoleon's army turned up. That's as far as it got. You know why General Messéna was here? Because the Portuguese refused to close their ports to the English. And you know what the English did to return the favour? With the help of the locals, they built all this. They built it over a period of months. They built it for the sake of Lisbon. They kept it a secret from the French and when the conquering army finally arrived it was far too late. The English kicked their arses and Napoleon never recovered. This was his high-water mark. He wanted the whole of Europe but he couldn't get further than here. Thanks to the Duke of Wellington. And the English. And, of course, our Portuguese friends.' He produced a packet of cigarettes. One each. 'We should always listen to history,' he smiled, and struck a match. 'Because history never lies.'

*

Tam Moncrieff's departure for Lisbon was delayed by two days. When Moncrieff asked why, Ursula Barton told him that negotiations in Lisbon were taking rather longer than anyone had anticipated, a development which was, in her view, deeply promising.

'Why?'

'Because they've obviously got a great deal to talk about.'

'Who says?'

'Souk,' she held Moncrieff's gaze. 'Which is all we have to go on until you take a view.'

Accordingly, Moncrieff busied himself with a tangle of other commitments – all of them wearisome – until, forty-eight hours later, the moment came to leave for Poole. Of Cathy Phelps, a little to his disappointment, he'd seen very little. The one occasion they'd managed to share a brief weekend together, she'd spent most of the time sleeping. Royal service at the Palace, she'd mumbled, was bloody hard work. Memories of life at the Glebe House seemed rosier and rosier.

Poole, in late February, was umpteen shades of grey. Grey for the limitless expanse of the harbour. Grey for the open water beyond. Grey for the heavy overcast sky and the threat of imminent rain. Half close your eyes, and even the Empire flying boat, rocking gently at her moorings beside the long pontoon, was grey. A landscape in tune with the times, thought Moncrieff. Spiritless. Monochrome. Infinitely depressing.

Departure fell victim to an abrupt fall in oil pressure in one of the engines. The captain abandoned the take-off run moments before lift-off and returned to the pontoon for checks. More than two hours later, after mechanics had found the ruptured lubrication line, the captain tried again. The roar of the engines stilled conversation in the cabin and, in the thickening dusk, the big flying boat finally lifted clear of the harbour. Transit to Lisbon was nearly six hours. By the time Moncrieff awoke to find the lights of Lisbon beneath the port wing, it was nearly midnight.

Hesketh was waiting in the arrivals hall at the end of the pontoon. A light tan told Moncrieff that the weather in Lisbon had been far from grey. When Hesketh offered to take him to the hotel he'd booked, Moncrieff shook his head. He'd slept on the plane. If Hesketh cared to find them a café, a discreet table and a decent bottle of wine, he'd be very happy to pick up the bill.

'Done, sir.' Hesketh was beaming. 'Exactly what I expected. *Bem vindo a Lisboa.*'

The café was deep in a working-class area a fifteen-minute taxi ride from the flying boat terminal. Stepping into the crowded little space beyond the half-closed door, Moncrieff was reminded of Stockholm: the colour, the fug of cigarette smoke, the swirl of a dozen conversations, a lone guitarist on a stool in the corner, the promise of fresh ingredients and a woman's touch at the stove. The only problem was privacy.

'Upstairs,' Hesketh nodded at a door in the corner at the back. 'Maria's a good friend. Trust me.'

The room was perfect: small, intimate, insulated from the world outside. One of the two tables was bare. On the other was an uncorked bottle of wine and two glasses. Beside the wine was a basket of bread and a bowl brimming with olives.

Moncrieff realised he was starving. He tried the bread. Even at this time of night, it was warm from the oven.

Hesketh watched him eat. Then he poured the wine and pushed one glass gently towards Moncrieff.

'This is a red I ordered specially. It comes from the Alentejo. If you're sensible enough to order Maria's goat stew we'll have another bottle and you'll sleep a happy man.'

Moncrieff tasted the wine and smiled. If the rest of whatever Hesketh had to offer was as good as this then MI5 had acquired an asset of genuine value.

If.

'Haushofer's gone?'

'This morning. I'm glad to say he arrived in some style. Personal plane, his own pilot. The Reich know how to look after their own.'

'And we don't?'

'I didn't say that. It was a pleasure to catch up with Albrecht. And, I must say, something of a surprise.'

Moncrieff wanted to know about the letter Hesketh had been sent from London.

'You gave it to him?'

'Of course I did.'

'And?'

'Albrecht was delighted. I think he'd assumed the friendship was dead, or at least shelved for the duration. He holds Duglo very close to his heart. I suspect he was disappointed that they won't be getting together down here but, as I tried to explain, there might be other ways.'

'Of what?'

'Of achieving the same ends.'

Hesketh let the sentence hang in the air. Then came the clatter of footsteps on the wooden stairs and the door opened. Hesketh was on his feet and for a split second Moncrieff assumed the worst. After the long flight, his defences were down. He'd been here before. Police, probably armed. A hand on his shoulder, a rough descent to the restaurant below, a windowless van parked outside, and the beginnings of a long journey to God knows where. Instead he found himself looking at a woman in late middle age with burn marks on the plumpness of her arms.

'Maria.' Hesketh did the introductions.

Moncrieff got to his feet, hoping the relief didn't show. After an awkward conversation, fathered by Hesketh, he seemed to have agreed to a dish of *chanfana*.

'*Chanfana?*' Maria had disappeared.

'Goat stew, my friend.'

They'd sat down again. Two middle-aged Englishmen, Moncrieff thought, perched above an artists' café in the depths of Lisbon. The door was an inch or so ajar and the conversation below had stilled to make way for the guitarist. He strummed a couple of mournful chords before a woman began to sing. Her voice was bold, almost incantatory, swelling and dying as the guitarist played on.

'*Fado*,' Hesketh said. 'The music of fate. The Portuguese adore melancholy. They call it *saudade*. They set out to discover the New World and ended up missing the old one. Maybe that's the price of empire, though our lot seem untroubled.'

'Our lot?'

'The English. It's something that Albrecht's always remarked upon. We painted half the world pink and it never crossed our mind it might belong to someone else. No guilt. And absolutely no melancholy. Personally speaking, he's honest enough to find that rather admirable. I suspect someone in his bloodline got fucked by an Englishman. Male or female, it probably doesn't matter. Either way, that might explain his passion for Duglo.'

'You think...?'

'I'm making no assumptions. Albrecht is extremely good-looking in a rather un-German way and judging from photographs Duglo more than holds his own. Here and now you want me to report on what happened over the last couple of days and that's very sensible. I just offer the thought *im Vorbeigehen.*'

In passing? Moncrieff reached for his glass. Nothing Hesketh brought to the table was by accident.

'You think they had some kind of relationship?'

'It's possible. Duglo's a man of action. Boxing champion. Record-breaking aviator. Fighter pilot. In fact a true Corinthian.' He smiled. 'And you know what those Greeks got up to.'

'Proof? Evidence?'

'None. As I just said, they're good-looking chaps. They have lots in common. He and Duglo shared times together back in the thirties. Which I suspect is rather the point.'

'So what did he have to say? Haushofer?'

'Probably more than might have been wise.'

'I don't understand.'

'I wined and dined him. Not here. I took him to a hotel in the Baixa. Proper tablecloths, silver service, and some seriously expensive wines. Please don't blame me when you see the bill. This was last night, by the way. Bear in mind the man's always trusted me. Most Germans, especially nowadays, like to think of themselves as locked doors. It goes with the uniforms and all the Blood Flag nonsense. Not our Albrecht. He's subtler than that.'

'You got him drunk?'

'Very.'

'And?'

'More wine?' Hesketh was reaching for the bottle. He was plainly enjoying this. Moncrieff shook his head and covered his glass with his hand.

'Explain,' he said. 'Tell me what happened.'

Hesketh paused a moment, then shrugged and refilled his own glass. Haushofer, he said, had arrived as an envoy. From his father, he'd inherited an understanding of what bound nations together. From his connections in Berlin, he understood the inner workings of the Reich. And his knowledge of history had given him an extra insight or two.

'Last night Albrecht put it rather well. At this point, he was still sober, still cogent. We were talking about the earthquake that flattened this place, back in the eighteenth century. It's 1755. It's All Saints' Day. It's mid-morning. One minute you're at your window looking out at a medieval city. Six minutes later most of those buildings are rubble. But one escaped and the clinching evidence, which Albrecht understands only too well, is that the building is still there.'

'Where?'

'At the top of the hill. Where you'll always find them.'

'You mean a castle?'

'*The* castle. *Castelo de São Jorge.* I'll show you tomorrow, but you don't have to see it to understand.'

'About the earthquake?'

'About Albrecht. He understands fortifications, buildings designed to protect, buildings designed to *last*. That, dare I say it, is what history teaches us, and it's a lesson that applies equally to nation states. Some, like France, fall over. Others, like ours, don't. Lisbon surrendered herself to an earthquake. France lay down in front of the *Wehrmacht* and spread her shapely legs. Hitler had something similar in mind for us but I gather he's now decided that it isn't going to happen.'

'Meaning?'

'Meaning there has to be another way. By and large, Hitler is a man without weaknesses. Except for one. He loves the English, he counts them as *Blutsbruder*, and, worse still, he thinks he understands them. He's wrong, of course, but life is all about opportunity and here, dare I say it, is the perfect example.'

Blutsbruder. Blood brothers.

Moncrieff nodded. After the first couple of sips, he'd barely touched his wine.

'Go on,' he said.

'Hitler, of course, has other things on his mind. History is full of pleasing little ironies and here's one of them. Albrecht's father, as you may know, planted the seed of *Lebensraum* in Hitler's fertile little brain. It came via Hess, Hitler's Deputy, and it stuck there among all the other rubbish. Living room in the east. The prospect of ceaseless plunder, of limitless blood and untold treasure. Hitler needed no prompting. If I was a Russian I'd have taken a good look at *Mein Kampf* before I had anything to do with Ribbentrop, but now it's probably too late. In certain circles in Germany they're laying bets on exactly when the men in grey will roll east. Albrecht's bet the family fortune on late May. Hitler always invades on a Sunday.

It's become a habit. Barring accidents, that means either the eighteenth or the twenty-fifth. A war on two fronts, if you're sane, would be unthinkable. No one's quite sure about Hitler's sanity but everyone assumes he can count. Heading for Moscow with Churchill up his arse conjures all kinds of nightmares. So there has to be a better way.'

'According to Hitler?'

'Emphatically. Horse's mouth.'

'Says who?'

'Our Albrecht.' Hesketh reached for his glass. 'And we hadn't even started on the third bottle.'

Moncrieff slept at a hotel elsewhere in the city. Before turning out the light, he made notes on the evening's discussions with Hesketh and awoke twice in the middle of the night to add one or two afterthoughts. Next morning, he made his way downstairs to the hotel's restaurant to find Hesketh already at a table beside the window. He was enjoying a cigarette and crumbs on his plate suggested he'd already had breakfast.

'Try the *pastéis de nata*.' He gestured towards a pile of golden tartlets on the table beside the door.

Moncrieff preferred to wait for coffee. The view from the window seemed to take in half the city: a tumble of red roofs falling towards the startling blue of the water. Tiny yellow trams rumbled up the hill towards the hotel and from the river came the distant parp-parp of a departing freighter. Watching the sheer busyness of the city, Moncrieff was reminded of Napoleon's luckless attempts to throttle Portuguese trade. These people lived to barter, he thought. Much like Hesketh.

After breakfast, at Hesketh's insistence, they left the hotel to make for a nearby park. The park was huge, acres and acres of carefully tended grassy slopes that offered yet more views of the city. Near a soaring greenhouse towards the top of the park lay a pond full of lazy carp. Children, often in the care of much older women, fed the carp with scraps of bread before running off to a play area shaped like a galleon in full sail. Hesketh found a bench. It was already mid-morning, and Moncrieff could feel a thin warmth in the early spring sunshine.

'I should take you to the Jerónimos Monastery. Vasco da Gama's buried there. And we ought to pay the Belém Tower a visit. That's where the imperial story begins and ends.'

Moncrieff shook his head. He hadn't come here as a tourist with a list of must-see locations. He was more than content to let the city grow on him, street corner by street corner. It was a scruffy place and he liked that. Every time they'd stopped en route to the park he'd noticed faces at the tram stops, housewives shopping for bread and pastries, huddled in endless conversations, queues of refugees seeking visas outside the foreign consulates, an old man with a pigeon on his shoulder gazing thoughtfully into a fountain. The city was full of these little glimpses. What the Portuguese seemed to treasure above all was peace.

Moncrieff asked where Hesketh lived. He'd just lit yet another cigarette. He waved vaguely across the city beyond the castle.

'There,' he said. The gesture meant nothing.

'An apartment? A whole house?'

'The former. Nothing grand but perfectly serviceable. Everyone here lives in layers, floor by floor. Fundamentally it's a balance between privacy and neighbourliness. It's a trick you learn when you stop being so poor that you rely entirely on others. They've spent centuries practising and now they're very good at it.'

'And it's cheap?'

'Extremely. That's one of the charms of the place. In case you're wondering, I have a modest trust fund. I owe my dear pa for that. This far south it buys you everything you need. Not that a little extra wouldn't be more than welcome.'

They spent several minutes wrangling about money. Moncrieff made it plain that he could authorise a supplementary payment but it had to be against results. So far he knew that Haushofer was representing powerful elements within the Reich and seemed to carry authorisation from the very top. It seemed that Berlin was in the process of finalising a peace offer and Moncrieff was now relying on Haushofer's intelligence contacts to nominate the British faces they wanted to see at the table.

'Last night you told me anyone but Churchill or those warrior chums of his,' Moncrieff said. 'As it happens, they wouldn't be interested anyway. Churchill won't let anyone in his circle close to a German. House rules.'

'So I gather,' Hesketh was smiling. 'Which leaves us spoiled for choice. Senior businessmen, perhaps? A handful of backwoods aristocrats? And a sprinkle of the *haute juiverie* to add a little *savoir faire?*'

'You mean bankers?'

'I do.'

'And Duglo?'

'I'm not sure. That's a personal view, of course. Albrecht believes the good Duke is aching for an outbreak of sanity and, God knows, he might be right. Duglo is Albrecht's key to lots of doors.'

'You know he's Lord Steward of the Household, now? The King's representative in Scotland?'

'Of course I do, and so does Albrecht. These people are highly intelligent. They have the finest army in Europe. They eat entire countries for breakfast. But they have very strange ideas about the way we run our constitution. Albrecht and his father are the same. They both think that real power rests with the monarch. All you have to do is to gain Bertie's ear. Remind him what happened to the Romanovs. Assure him that Berlin will put the Communists out of their misery. Do that, they say, and we'll all be watching the ink dry on the peace treaty. I do my best to point out that we English live in a democracy. That power lies in Parliament. And that Churchill, as Prime Minister, wants nothing to do with peace treaties. But all this tiresome detail falls on deaf ears. The Germans assume that Bertie can snap his fingers and Churchill will be gone. Sadly, they're wrong.'

Moncrieff nodded. 'Bertie' was Palace-speak for King George VI. He'd heard Cathy Phelps use the same nickname.

'They have a meeting place in mind? For these negotiations?'

'Albrecht mentioned Sylt.'

'That's where it happened last time. Is this Goering's little party?'

'Albrecht wouldn't say. Sylt's an island, of course. It's part of the Reich now but Berlin would guarantee safe passage. And there's something else that might please your lords and masters.'

'What, exactly?'

'Hitler would be there. As long as we're in good faith.'

Good faith. Moncrieff had no idea whether Hesketh was bluffing. He was both plausible and fluent but there was absolutely no proof that any of these stories were true. A well-spoken fantasist, he thought. Relaxing in the Lisbon sunshine.

'Well?' Hesketh still wanted to know about the money.

'I need more detail from Haushofer.'

'In what respect?'

'I need to know exactly where we go from here. I need an assurance that Haushofer can deliver what he's promising. And I need sight of the terms of the German offer.'

'And after that?'

'We have another conversation.'

'About a bigger fee?'

'Yes.'

'I see.'

There was a long silence. Hesketh tapped ash onto the grass, and then tipped his face to the sun. Moncrieff was looking across at the pond.

'Over there,' he said. 'Beside the water.' Hesketh opened his eyes and followed Tam's pointing finger. 'Did you ever come across the parable of the dog with the bone?'

'I'm afraid not. Is this something I need to know?'

'It might be. Just listen. A dog is standing beside a lake. It's a sunny day, much like this one. The dog has a big meaty bone in its mouth. The water is totally still, mirror-still. The dog looks at his reflection in the lake. He sees another dog. With another bone. And so he snaps at it. And what happens? He drops the bone in his mouth,' Moncrieff smiled. 'Might I assume you get the point?'

'Of course. The dog's greedy. And pays the price.'

'You're right. But it's more than that. The other dog was a mirage. It never existed.'

Moncrieff left Lisbon late that afternoon. Hesketh, as urbane and opaque as ever, accompanied him to the flying boat terminal. They exchanged handshakes in the sunshine outside the departures hall and Hesketh confirmed that his personal PO Box was still the best way of staying in touch.

Moncrieff thanked him for his time. He'd given Hesketh a confidential telephone number at St James's. Should anything happen over the next couple of days, he'd welcome a call and a conversation.

'Are you happy with that?'

'*Sim. Perfeito. Boa viagem.*'

Moncrieff held his gaze for a moment and then turned to leave. The pontoon stirred on the outgoing tide beneath his feet. When he next checked the departures hall, Hesketh had gone.

The flight back to Poole filled up quickly. Seats were preassigned and Moncrieff found himself sitting beside a suited figure in his early thirties with carefully parted hair and a light stammer. Deep in a novel, he looked up when Moncrieff eased his long frame into the adjoining seat.

'Bit of a squeeze, I'm afraid,' Tam smiled. 'Think on the bright side. Only six hours to go.'

The stranger nodded. He agreed that conditions were foul. Pre-war, he said, everyone had time. Time meant three days at sea, possibly more, but pay a little extra and you could expect service in your cabin and a choice of champagnes at dinner.

He returned to his book. His English accent was wedded to a strangely deferential charm.

The flying boat, exactly on schedule, took off at a quarter to five. The captain carved a path across the waters of the Tagus and then hauled the aircraft into a shallow climb. Above a thin layer of cloud, the sun was already beginning to settle in the west.

Thanks to Hesketh, Moncrieff had laid hands on a copy of *The Times* before embarkation. The newspaper was three days old but after briefly scanning the headlines he settled down to the crossword. It was hot in the cabin, the air still thick with cigarette smoke, and within minutes Moncrieff's head began to nod. Seconds later, he was asleep.

By the time he awoke, three and a half hours later, it was dark outside the half-curtained window. His companion, his book still open on his lap, was nursing a glass of what looked like Scotch. Aware of Moncrieff stirring beside him, he reached inside his jacket and produced a silver flask.

'Fancy a snort? It's only Laphroaig, I'm afraid.'

Moncrieff liked the single malt and said so.

'You have to be north of the border with an accent like that.'

'I'm afraid so. Scots through and through.' With some awkwardness in the confined space, Moncrieff offered a hand. 'Tam Moncrieff.'

'Philby. Say when.' He'd found another glass. Moncrieff watched him pour.

'Thank you,' he said. 'More than generous.'

They settled down again. Even at cruising speed, the thunder of the four engines didn't encourage conversation. Moncrieff, back with his crossword, sipped at the malt. Seven across.

Four letters. *Coarse person, unknown character becoming top.*

Spiv? Caid? Tam shook his head, looked at the clues for the surrounding spaces. Nothing seemed to fit. Three pages earlier, he'd noticed a lengthy review for a book on the Highland Clearances. The fate of Scottish crofters had always fascinated him and he took his time reading the piece. Then he returned to the crossword, hoping the malt might have summoned a little inspiration.

'*Apex,*' said a voice at his elbow. 'And I rather think that makes six down *Marxism*. Do you mind terribly? Or should I be reading my book?'

'Not at all. I'm grateful.'

Moncrieff pencilled both words in. His companion, to his slight irritation, was right. He gazed at the crossword a moment longer. Should he persevere? And invite further humiliation? Or should he just fold the paper and call it a night?

'He's a little shit, you know.' Philby again, his mouth close to Moncrieff's ear. 'The man Hesketh. If he told you he went to Lancing College, he's right, but what he won't tell you is what happened after they caught him with his sticky little fingers in the till. And as for the Balliol tie, he's never been near the place. I'm afraid he's a bottom feeder. Lisbon's full of them. They pick up all the rubbish and simply sell it on. If you've got deep pockets by all means go ahead but when it comes to product you'll find the stuff stinks. Just a thought, old boy.' He smiled, tipping his glass. 'Here's to crime.'

Moncrieff said nothing. His mind was racing. He had to assume that Philby, too, lived in the shadows of the intelligence world. Had he seen Hesketh at the departures hall? And drawn his own conclusions? Or did he know a great deal more?

Moncrieff reached for his pencil. Most of the crossword was still empty.

'SIS?' he wrote. The Secret Intelligence Service. MI6. The Broadway-based agency charged with gathering intelligence abroad.

Philby nodded, and beckoned Moncrieff closer.

'I head the Iberian Station,' he said. 'A small parish but intensely interesting. Madrid? Gib? Tangier? Lisbon? A man could do worse.'

'And Hesketh?'

'We used him for a while. He's good at what he does but what he does, alas, has very little connection with the truth. Those history books earn him peanuts. He should recognise his own talents and write fiction. I told him once, back in the early days when we thought he was some kind of prospect, but he just laughed. That was when the courtship was still young. He's getting older now, and it shows.'

Moncrieff nodded, said nothing. Albrecht Haushofer? Some kind of peace offer from the very top of the Reich? How much did this man know? Where, exactly, had he been these last two days? Had the pair of them – Souk and his lanky handler – been under surveillance? Had MI6 agents been watching them at the restaurant? At the hotel? On the bench in the park? And if so, why?

The aircraft droned on. Philby had returned to his book. Feigning sleep, Moncrieff badly wanted the flight to end. Hours later, an abrupt change in the roar of the engines signalled the beginnings of a descent. At the same time, a uniformed sergeant advanced down the aisle, checking left and right. Seat belts on, please. Landing in fifteen minutes.

The flying boat touched down with a series of jolts. Moncrieff, peering past Philby into the darkness, saw dancing crescents of sea spray in the throw of light from the cabin. Minutes later, the aircraft nudged the pontoon as the pilot finally throttled the engines back.

Passengers were already on their feet, plucking at stowed luggage. Moncrieff joined them, elbowing his way into the queue that had formed in the aisle. Only Philby hadn't moved.

Moncrieff gazed down at him.

'Not joining us?'

'Alas, no,' Philby shook his head, 'I'm flying back tonight. Line of duty, old boy. And just for the record, we think you might be straying off the reservation.'

9

Georg Messner had left hospital by the time Merz made it back to Berlin. For the time being, the *Luftwaffe* had lodged him in a convalescent home for badly wounded flyers in the Harz Mountains. The doctors and medical staff at the Charité had, according to Beata, decided there was nothing further they could do for her husband. Surgical intervention would be pointless. Best to leave any further improvement to the onset of spring and a dose or two of the bracing mountain air.

Merz toyed with making the long trip down to Bad Harzburg but Beata's father dissuaded him. The real victim of all this, he pointed out with some asperity, was his daughter. Her near-total rejection by the man she'd loved had first exhausted and then depressed her. All her young life, Beata had been a believer. As a child, she never skipped Mass. As a student, she'd clung to her faith despite endless temptations. And her prize at the end of all this devotional fervour, undoubtedly the best day of her life, was the hot summer afternoon back in 1938 when she'd married Georg Messner. At the bridegroom's request, *der Kleine* had displayed in front of a gardenful of guests in one of the new 109 Emils. They'd drunk champagne until dusk settled over the lake. Truly a day to remember.

'She's looking for a miracle, Dieter, which is why I've sent her to Vierzehnheiligen. She's alone there. Her decision, and a bad one. Depression thrives on solitude. She needs company, someone to talk to, someone to *listen* to. I get the impression your bosses keep you on a long leash. Just a couple of days, *ja?*'

Merz couldn't say no. He'd never heard of Vierzehnheiligen but Friedrich fetched out a map. A shrine had been erected on top of a hill near Bamberg where a shepherd had seen repeated visions of fourteen children. The kids, he said, had announced themselves as The Fourteen Holy Helpers, invoked for protection against disease, and the miracle cure of a local milkmaid prompted the building of the shrine. Beata was staying at the nearby town of Bad Staffelstein.

Next morning, Merz telephoned the Air Ministry. By now he was on good terms with the *Luftwaffe* staff sergeant who ran Goering's private office. Bad Staffelstein was a couple of hours' drive from Augsburg. Did anyone have any objection to Merz returning the Me-110 to the Messerschmitt factory, rather than taking the train down? The staff sergeant thought there wouldn't be a problem but, just to make sure, he'd check. Less than a minute later, Dieter recognised Goering's bellow on the line.

'Merz? Is that you?'

'Yes, *Herr Reichsmarschall.*'

'You took Haushofer to Lisbon?'

'Yes, *Herr Reichsmarschall.*'

'And?'

'And we made it there and back. Just the way you wanted.' Dieter was staring at the phone. He was a pilot, not a diplomat.

'But was it successful? Did he get to meet the Englishman?'

'Yes, *Herr Reichsmarschall*, though you should be talking to Haushofer, not me.'

'Of course. And Rudi? He's still flying? You're still keeping him out of trouble?'

'I am, yes.'

'*Gut*. Of course you can take the bloody plane. Help yourself. Rudi thinks well of you, Merz. Proof the man's losing his wits.' A final bark of laughter, and the *Reichsmarschall* was gone.

The 110 was still out at Tempelhof. The squadron adjutant confirmed that the Air Ministry had authorised its release to Merz and that it had been fully refuelled. As Merz was about to leave the office, the adjutant called him back.

'Has anyone talked to you about night fighters?'

'No.'

'And you're still going down to Augsburg?'

'Yes.'

'See if you can raise an engineer called Pauli Hahn. He phoned this morning. Asking for you.'

Night fighters? Merz walked out across the hardstanding, none the wiser, his maps under his arm. Beside the aircraft, he spread one on the tarmac and contemplated his options. The direct route would take him SSW to Augsburg but only a modest diversion to the west would put him among the Harz Mountains. To the best of his knowledge, the *Luftwaffe* convalescent home was in a valley beneath the Brocken, the tallest hill in the range. Why not pay his ailing wingman a brief visit? Bent over the map, he quickly plotted a course that would take him to the Harz. Thereafter, an 83 degree turn to port would route him south to Augsburg.

His calculations complete, Merz waited for one of the squadron ground crew to settle him in the cockpit. It was a cloudless day, with a light wind from the south, perfect conditions for the kind of flying Dieter had in mind. In less than half an hour, as long as he found the convalescent home, he could be adding a little excitement to Georg Messner's day.

The ground crew engineer was still bent over the open cockpit, checking the tightness on a control valve. Merz showed him the map.

'Here,' the engineer produced a pen and marked a tiny dot south of the Brocken.

'You've been there? You were ill?'

'Not me. A friend of mine.'

'And they cured him?'

'Sadly not.' He slipped the pen back into the pocket of his overalls and gave Merz a pat on the shoulder. 'Take care, eh?'

Merz took off a minute or two before noon. He stayed low, maximum power, roaring across the Brandenburg flatlands. This kind of flying drank fuel, but he had full tanks and plenty of reserve if he got into trouble. At 540 kph, the lush green fields were a blur. Within a quarter of an hour, the gentle swell of the Harz Mountains began to fill the windscreen. Twice, thundering across farmland, he was aware of herds of cattle scattering beneath his wings and once, on the edge of a tiny hamlet, he waggled his wings at a woman in a red skirt. She'd got off her bicycle and he caught the briefest glimpse of her upturned face and a waving arm as he flashed by.

The Brocken was easy to spot. Merz pulled back on the joystick and felt the aircraft lift beneath him. By Alpine standards, at just over a thousand metres the summit was a mere pimple. Dieter gazed down at the thickly wooded hillsides, amused by the birds exploding from the darkness of the forest. Fun, he thought. Georg, in another life, would have appreciated this.

Minutes later, exactly where the engineer at Tempelhof had indicated, he found what must have been the convalescent home. From the air, it was 'H'-shaped. There were ambulances parked outside, painted in *Luftwaffe* grey, and as Dieter dropped a wing for a better view he spotted a gaggle of wheelchairs on a terrace in front of one of the wards. The terrace was angled due south, and Dieter wondered whether Georg was out here, his face in the sunshine, maybe feeling a little better. One of the tiny figures below lifted an arm in salute. Georg? Dieter had no way of knowing.

He was climbing for height now, one hand on the joystick, the other pushing the twin throttles against the gate. Most pilots were reluctant to test their aerobatic skills on the rugged fighter bomber, largely because it lacked the nimbleness of a single-engined fighter. Put your life in the hands of this machine, fly normal missions, and it would certainly look after you. Try anything fancy and it might bite you in the arse.

Dieter Merz had built his entire career on judging the fine line between calculation and risk. He had a great deal of respect for his own talents but even more for gravity. He certainly owed Georg Messner a twirl or two in this big old plane but he knew its limitations.

At the top of the climb, at four thousand metres, he dropped a wing again and rolled into a dive. The convalescent home was a dot among the trees. Merz lowered the nose a couple of degrees to increase speed and began to feel the aircraft shaking around him. Recommended top speed was 560 kph. The needle on the speedometer was flickering above 583 kph.

Dieter's eyes returned to the windscreen. The dot was getting bigger by the second and the judder of the airframe had got worse. He eased back a little on the joystick, checking that he still had control. Then came the moment, perfectly judged, when he pulled out of the dive, fed in lots of left rudder and hauled the aircraft into the tightest turn his own body could sustain. Already he could feel his chest trying to squeeze out through his arse. He was struggling to breathe and for a moment he thought he'd overcooked it. Colour was draining out of the landscape. No greens. No blues. On the edge of blacking out, he lifted a gloved hand in salute as the terrace flashed by beneath him. Word had spread about the madman in the Bf-110. The terrace was full of faces, wheelchairs, bodies shrouded in blankets. Men were waving. One of them blew him a kiss. Then, in less than a second, it was over and Merz was climbing again, fighting for altitude, that final image imprinted on his brain. Georg, he thought. I did it for him.

He landed at Augsburg an hour or so later. By now, Dieter Merz was a familiar face at the Messerschmitt factory. Ground crew fetched a ladder to let him de-plane.

'Good flight?'

'Superb.'

'Any problems?'

'None.' Merz was trying to remember the name of the engineer he'd been given. 'Pauli Hahn?'

'Upstairs,' the crew nodded at the block where the draughtsmen worked. 'Office at the far end of the corridor.'

Merz took the stairs two at a time. His visit to the Harz Mountains had left its mark. He felt revived, exhilarated. He knocked twice on the office door and pushed it open.

'Herr Hahn? Dieter Merz.'

Hahn had been working at a drawing board. He was a slight man with thinning hair and a ready smile. Ignore the Party badge on the lapel of his jacket and Dieter might have been looking at Sol Fiedler, Beata's friend, a Jewish physicist who'd fled to America after the terrors of *Kristallnacht*. The same alert intelligence. The same eagerness for a conversation.

'Please...' Hahn drew up a chair. 'You want coffee?'

Merz said yes. While Hahn was out of the office, he stole a look at the drawing board. The side view of the Bf-110 was instantly recognisable, except for the addition of what looked like four stubby pipes protruding from the top of the fuselage aft of the canopy. New, too, was an ugly array of aerials poking from the aircraft's nose.

Hahn was back with the coffee. The sight of Merz in his flying suit behind the desk sparked a grin.

'Know what it is?'

'A 110, obviously.'

'Of course, but what else?'

Merz asked about the pipes. Was there an auxiliary engine in there? Was this some kind of exhaust system?

'Nice try. I'm afraid the milk's powdered. You prefer it black?'

Merz nodded. He was still looking at the drawing board. Hahn circled the desk, then gestured at the window. Dieter's 110 was still on the tarmac.

'So what do you think of the "E" version?'

'You want the truth? I think it's shit. The basic design is still good but we need more power. You're asking the aircraft to do too much. New engines would solve that.'

'They're on their way.'

'Really?' This was news to Merz.

'Yes. Originally we planned for a whole new aircraft. We called it the Bf-210. It's in production but we won't be building as many as we expected. Instead we'll be giving you the "F" variant, and then the "G". Every day will be Christmas, believe me. These will be lovely aircraft.'

Dieter grinned. All well and good, he said, but what about the design on the drawing board?

Hahn had recently been in Berlin. Goering, to everyone's quiet astonishment, had put together a group of aircraft designers in anticipation of heavier raids over the Reich's major cities. The British would no longer be relying on *Scheisse* aircraft a child could shoot out of the sky. Even now, they'd be working on big multi-engined bombers with a long reach and a huge payload. The *Luftwaffe* had to be prepared for that. And they had to have an answer.

'Easy. We shoot them down.'

'I agree. And so does Goering. But how? These bombers will be flying at night. First you have to find them. Then, unless you're crazy, you have to stay well clear of their own guns. Mid-upper turrets? Turrets in the tail? Turrets in the nose? These will be castles with wings. No pilot got old by underestimating the enemy.'

Merz shot him a look. He was impressed.

'Is this you talking?'

'No. As it happens, it's Goering. But that's not the point. This is pure logic. Pretend you're the British. Get inside their heads. This is what you'd do. It's obvious. And so we have to have an answer. Now. Before these machines appear and we no longer sleep at night. So,' – he gestured at the board – 'it's very dark. You're carrying a radar set. It's the job of the man behind you to work that set and find the target. He does well. You slip into the bomber stream. You've found your target. You're one of the best, Herr Merz. What do you do next?'

'I shoot him down.'

'Of course. But how?'

Dieter was trying to visualise the situation and this man, to his credit, was making it easy.

'The blind spot,' he said softly.

'And where might that be?'

'Underneath. Where none of the crew can see you.'

'How close?'

'Close enough not to miss.'

'Aimed shots?'

'Possibly not.' Dieter's eyes were back on the side view of the 110. The four stubby little pipes, he thought. Pointing directly upwards.

'We're talking formation flying,' he said. 'Same speed, same direction. You hold station for as long as you need to. If your guns are vertical, or near-vertical, the rest is down to physics.'

'A kill every time?'

'Yes. And a very big bang if you hit the target's bomb bay. You've thought of that?'

'We have.'

'And you've got the answer?'

'Not yet.'

'So is that why I'm here?'

'I'm afraid so.' Hahn nodded at the desk. 'Drink your coffee. It's getting cold.'

Dieter emptied his cup. Hahn had yet more meetings to attend but was happy to let Merz have the run of his office while he was away. With Hahn gone, Dieter settled behind the desk, trying to test this elegant theory against the million rogue factors that made real-life combat such a satisfying challenge. By the time Hahn came back, he thought he had at least a couple of answers.

'Imagine this,' he said. 'We tell every pilot to fly immediately below the centre line of the bomber. The safest place to hide is between the wing roots. Agree an ideal vertical separation between you and the target, offset the cannons left and right, and you're guaranteed hits on the engines and the fuel tanks. That way you avoid the bombs.'

'Number two solution?'

'The brains of any plane are the pilots. Kill them both, pilot and co-pilot, and the game's over. So this time you angle the cannons slightly forward, so they chew up the cockpit. Same principle. Number one, you put holes in both wings. Number two, you put holes in both pilots. Both times you're leaving the bombs alone. But both times the aircraft's fucked.'

'Excellent,' Hahn was grinning again. 'And you think all that's possible? In combat?'

'I've no idea,' Dieter checked his watch. 'One day we should try and find out.'

*

In his borrowed Mercedes, Dieter made excellent time on the run north to Bamberg. He skirted the city to the west and then made for Bad Stiffelstein. By now it was late afternoon, and nearly dark. Beata's father had given him the name of the hotel where his daughter was staying but, instead of checking first at reception, Dieter decided to follow the signs for the shrine.

The Basilika Vierzehnheiligen stood on a low hill three kilometres east of the city. In peacetime a spiritual landmark like this would be floodlit at night, a beacon for lost souls, but nowadays darkness was Germany's best friend. An entrance gate looming suddenly out of nowhere took Dieter by surprise. He slowed for the turn into the drive. Dimly, in the gathering gloom, he could make out the mass of the church.

He hadn't expected something so enormous. He parked the car and stood beside it, gazing up at the twin towers. It was a cloudless night, colder than he'd anticipated, and the black outline of the cupolas was etched against a thin crescent of moon. He stood a step backwards, then another, still looking up. A gigantic prayer for the needy and the lost, he thought. A hymn to the afflicted, sculpted in the local stone, then aged by centuries of weather.

To the left Dieter found the entrance to the church, a huge wooden door, the big iron latch cold beneath his fingertip. Curious, he lifted the latch and pushed hard on the door. To his surprise, it swung open. At once he could hear chanting, the low, haunting murmur of male voices, and with it came the sweetness of incense. Dieter closed the door behind him. The interior of the church was cavernous, lit by a handful of candles. Stone arches receded into the darkness. After the chill of the night air outside, the temperature seemed to have plummeted still further.

Already, Dieter felt a sense of trespass. All his life he'd had a lazy rapport with his Maker, a relationship untroubled by regular church attendance. In some dim, unspoken way he'd always taken a degree of divine protection for granted but when it came to the business of survival he preferred to trust his own instincts. He'd known a number of fellow pilots who'd always crossed themselves before take-off and most of them were now dead.

He was advancing down the aisle now, step by careful step. At the far end of the church, half a dozen faces, strangely disembodied, were chanting plainsong in the soft yellow glow of a nest of candles on the altar. Dieter paused, buoyed by the voices, letting the sombre chords, plaiting and replaiting, carry him away. Then, way above the bass tread of the plainsong, he heard another sound, piercing, shrill, high-pitched, and he looked up in time to catch a flurry of bats criss-crossing in the gloom, and as he watched them he thought of Pauli Hahn and his carefully angled cannons and all the technical cleverness that would take flyers like Dieter Merz to within touching distance of the bellies of enemy bombers. Pauli had called the device *Schräge Musik*, the Devil's jazz, and Dieter had known exactly what he meant.

Merz had always trusted his instincts. He liked to think that no one – in the air or on the ground – ever took him by surprise. Until now.

'My father told me you'd come.'

He spun round. It was Beata. He hadn't seen her, hadn't even been aware of her presence, yet here she was, another face in the darkness. She offered a cold cheek for a kiss.

'Thank you,' she murmured. 'Thank you for being here.'

She led him to the pew where she'd been sitting. He recognised her bag on the neighbouring seat. Georg had bought it for her in Ulm, a memento after a particularly successful air display back in the hot summer days before the Polish adventure. Beata put the bag on her lap and gestured for Dieter to sit beside her.

'How long have you been here?' he whispered.

'All day. All day yesterday and all day today.'

'And has it helped?'

'That's a fighter pilot's question. You're always so impatient. In life you have to choose the right tense. Helped? A little. Is it help*ing*. Yes, definitely.'

'And tomorrow?'

'Back here. You must see this building in daylight. Then maybe you'll understand.'

They settled down in silence to listen to the plainsong. Dieter quickly lost track of time. The bats came and went overhead, curious, noisy, mapping this huge space with their tiny squeaks. God's radar, Dieter thought, aware of Beata's hand closing softly on his.

It was mid-evening by the time they finally left the church. The singers had long extinguished their candles and vanished into the darkness, leaving Dieter and Beata alone with the bats. When Merz asked whether anyone ever locked the place up, Beata said she didn't know. Just now, for the first time in her life, she'd put worries like that behind her. If God willed someone to turn a key in the door, then so be it. If they had to spend all night here, she'd be more than content.

As it turned out, the door remained open and it was Dieter who suggested they eat in a small, half-timbered tavern he'd noticed during the drive though Bad Stiffelstein. The place was empty, but a log fire added to the snugness of the dining room and the owner, a big woman with an Austrian accent, was able to offer them freshly caught trout from a local stream as well as schnitzel or goulash. They both settled on the fish and Beata insisted on buying a pricey bottle of French Chablis to toast Dieter's arrival. It wasn't until they'd finished the trout that she mentioned Georg.

'Have you seen him at all?' she asked. 'Have you paid him a visit at that new place?'

Dieter nodded. Then he described his lunchtime fly-by, a surprise get-well card for a bunch of flyers with far too much time on their hands.

'And you think Georg was there? On that terrace?'

'He might have been. I can't say for sure. But if he wasn't, I'm guessing the rest will tell him. He only knows one pilot who'd take that plane so close.'

'So close to what?'

'Them.'

'So it was dangerous? What you did?'

'It left no margin for error. One pass. One opportunity. In my business you have to get it exactly right. And I did.'

Beata nodded. She had a smear of butter at one corner of her mouth. Dieter proffered a napkin.

'It's yours.' She ignored the napkin. 'These days we waste nothing. Am I right?'

Dieter shot her a look. This wasn't a Beata he recognised. 'Lick it off,' she said.

Dieter moistened a fingertip and reached out. The butter was skin temperature, and slightly salty. Delicious. He eyed the menu.

'Dessert?'

Beata shook her head.

'You're staying tonight?' she asked.

'Of course.'

'Have you booked a room at the hotel yet?'

'No.'

'Good. I have a double bed. Do you mind sharing? Under the circumstances, it might be a kindness.'

'I don't understand.'

'I'm trying to spare your blushes. Papa is right. You're a gentle man. I need some of that.'

They drove to the hotel. It was bigger than Dieter had expected, a sombre building in reddish brick that dominated the town square, and the night porter barely lifted his head as they walked through the reception area towards the lift.

'Top floor,' Beata murmured. 'I wanted a view of the shrine but apparently it's too far away.'

The room was generous, if a little cold. There was a scatter of clothes on the floor and the bed was unmade. Another mystery. When Dieter asked why the hotel didn't stretch to a chambermaid, Beata told him she'd asked for complete privacy. No interruptions. No phone calls. No room service.

'Why?'

'Because I needed time to think. Time to be me again.'

'So who were you before?'

'Frau Messner.'

'And that's over?'

'Yes. My father told me about the Russian woman, the film star. When he called her a whore I told him he'd got the wrong person. If he was looking for someone to blame, he should start with his son-in-law. You know something about Georg? Something I'd never realised? Beneath all the bluster, all the certainties, he was a weak man. I can pardon lots of things, truly, but not weakness.'

'And your father?'

'He agreed. I'm not even sure he ever liked Georg.'

Dieter nodded. They were sitting side by side on the bed, chaste, companionable. They might have been brother and sister.

'And now? Here?' Dieter nodded down at the bed. 'What do you want?'

'I want to be held. I want to be talked to. Whatever else happens doesn't matter.'

'But it might. Have you thought about that?'

She studied him a moment. She wasn't a beautiful woman, far from it. She wasn't even pretty. Her face was long. Her hair was lank. She didn't smile a great deal. And her teeth, like her husband's, needed a little attention. But Dieter had always liked her intelligence, and the way she listened so attentively to other people's stories, and that affection – since Georg's accident – had been thickened by something close to admiration. No one deserved the scene that Goebbels had stage-managed at the Charité, and Merz knew very few people who could have weathered the past few weeks with such grace and fortitude.

'You're right,' he said. 'You deserve someone much stronger than Georg.'

She looked at him a moment and then smiled before kissing him lightly on the lips.

'Don't worry,' she said. 'That needn't be you.'

It was early afternoon before Moncrieff finally made it back to St James's Street. The morning express from Poole had broken down in Southampton and hours passed before a relief engine appeared. The train had come to rest half a mile from the city centre. Staring out at the wreckage left by the last major bombing raid – tottering walls supported by baulks of timber, kids scavenging for coal in the mountains of rubble – Moncrieff could think only of the warmth and the colour he'd left back in Lisbon. Anyone with any kind of choice, he told himself, would gladly abandon scenes like these for the promise of sunshine and the blessings of peace. Another small victory, perhaps, for Agent Souk.

'So how was he?'

The question came from Ursula Barton. Within minutes of stepping into the building, Moncrieff had been summoned to her office. They had just half an hour before she was due to conference with 'B' Section's Director on the secure transatlantic line. Liddell knew that Moncrieff was due back from Portugal and was bound to demand a proper briefing.

'Souk's in rude health. Lisbon suits him. He loves it down there.' Moncrieff produced a file and slipped a sheet of paper across the desk. Ursula picked it up.

'What's this?'

'It's a bill for two. Hesketh and Albrecht Haushofer. They dined together the evening before I arrived.'

'Ninety-three US dollars?' She looked up, appalled. 'Doesn't the bloody man know there's a war on? How can I ever justify a sum like this?'

'I'm afraid I've no idea. We asked Souk to pass on the letter and that's exactly what he did. Afterwards he poured a great deal of wine down young Albrecht's throat and listened carefully to what he had to say.'

Moncrieff summarised the main points. Top-level negotiations leading to a peace treaty. Venue to be decided. The English to turn their backs on Europe and attend to their precious empire. Leaving the Germans with a free hand everywhere else.

'Like Russia?'

'That would seem a reasonable presumption.'

'They really mean to invade?'

'I gather they do.'

'Do you know when?'

'Haushofer thinks the eighteenth or the twenty-fifth of May. That's according to Souk.'

'And the Germans think we'd simply stand aside? Has this man Haushofer ever heard of Churchill? Oldish chap? Drinks a fair amount? Fine radio voice? Big popular following? And Prime Minister, to boot? Does he feature anywhere in these people's calculations?'

'Only in the most negative sense. They refuse to believe he speaks for England.'

'Then who does? In their view?'

'The King. He's the top of the pile. Then they have a long

list of trusties who see no point in continuing a war we can't possibly win.'

'Is this you speaking, Tam? Or them?'

Moncrieff blinked. His relationship with this woman was based on total candour but she'd seldom been so aggressive.

'Them. I'm simply the messenger, as you doubtless know.'

Moncrieff held her icy gaze. Sometimes he hated this war. Southampton, he thought. And the sight of kids hunting desperately for lumps of coal.

Ursula was making notes prior to her imminent conversation with Guy Liddell.

'Anything else I should know?' Her head was down. She was still writing.

'Yes. It's a postscript really. Make of it what you will.'

'Postscript?' She sounded irritated. 'What on earth does that mean?'

Moncrieff described his flight back from Lisbon, his companion in the adjoining seat, the crossword clues, the shared Laphroaig, and then the message he'd been waiting to deliver since the moment they'd taken off.

'MI6, you say?' Ursula at last looked up. 'And this new friend of yours has a name?'

'Philby.'

'And he has an interest in Souk?'

'Had, I think. Past tense.'

'So why warn you off?'

'I've no idea.'

'But they hate us. You know that. If Souk's such a waste of time, why bother marking our card? They love it when we foul up. A word in the right ear and we're the talk of clubland. Again.'

Moncrieff nodded. He'd seen the gleam in Ursula's eyes. She knew MI6. She'd worked for them in The Hague. She knew how arrogant they could be, how careless, and he rather suspected she knew a great deal more.

She asked him for the name of the agent again.

'Philby. His first name's Kim. Apparently he's head of their Iberian Station. He struck me as a decent operator. Urbane. Nice sense of timing. Kept his nerve. Good at crosswords, too.'

Ursula had written the name down. Now she underlined it twice and then glanced at her watch.

'You did well.' She nodded at the door. 'Stay near a phone.'

Close of play for most of the staff at St James's Street was six in the evening, though working hours could extend deep into the night when operations ran into trouble. It was ten to seven when Ursula Barton appeared at Moncrieff's door.

'It seems your postscript has touched a nerve or two. This has gone to the very top. The good Brigadier, no less.' Brigadier Oswald Harker had been the acting Director-General of MI5 since last year, though a full-time replacement was rumoured to be imminent.

Moncrieff nodded, said nothing. At length, Ursula settled uneasily in the spare chair.

'My apologies for this afternoon. I'm afraid I was a little testy. To tell you the truth, I've been getting tired of us having to deal with all these peace merchants, all these middlemen, all these Germans wanting to tie us hand and foot. Dahlerus. Your friend Schultz. I thought Haushofer and Souk were simply more of the same. It appears I'm wrong.'

'Who says?'

She shook her head. Moncrieff pressed her harder. Souk, after all, was his baby. As she'd already pointed out.

'We think Souk has value,' she said briskly. 'Certainly enough to warrant a series of precautionary actions on our part. We are, after all, charged with keeping enemies of the state at arm's length.'

On the basis of what he'd learned in Lisbon, she asked Moncrieff to prepare a list of targets for the MI5 watch list. Some would warrant full-time surveillance. All would have their post and phone calls monitored.

'These are names of interest to Haushofer?'

'Of course. What Souk appears to have identified, whether he knows it or not, is a fault line at the very top of what the Director-General likes to call the Establishment. If anyone has a willingness to sit down and talk peace to the Germans we need to be aware of them. I know it sounds blunt but that's the way it is. We can only have one leader. And he'll have no truck with anyone from Berlin unless they're offering the *status quo ante*. And that, we assume, is unlikely.'

Moncrieff offered a nod of agreement. The *status quo ante* would reinvent the pre-war countries of Western and Middle Europe, all of them sovereign and independent, unmolested by Hitler's armies.

'You want names, then?' he said.

'Absolutely. Anyone whom Haushofer mentioned. And anyone, in your judgement, who might also qualify.'

'I'm not sure I understand.'

'I'm talking about fellow-travellers. Take the Duke of Hamilton. As you know, we took liberties with the letter to Haushofer and any real interest on the good Duke's part in peace negotiations may be a gross slander. On the other hand he had some kind things to say about the Third Reich a couple of years ago and so did a number of others in his circle. Take that into account, Tam. We're not short of bodies among The Watchers. If any of this troubles that conscience of yours, call it spring cleaning. We need to be ready for what I understand is going to be a difficult year. Forewarned is forearmed, especially when we're dealing with the enemy within.'

The enemy within.

She got to her feet, the conversation evidently over. Then, beside the door, she turned back.

'One thing I forgot,' she said. 'We took a call this morning. I should have mentioned it.'

'About Souk?'

'About your place up in the wilds. You've had a break-in. The facts aren't clear and that in itself may be troubling. Esther McFaddon? You have her number? I know she'd appreciate a call.'

Esther McFaddon was Tam's temporary stand-in for Cathy Phelps. She was an older woman from the village, a family friend of long standing who'd agreed to keep an eye on the Glebe House in Tam's absence. With Ursula gone, Moncrieff found her number and reached for the phone. It took an age for Esther to answer. When she finally lifted the receiver, she recognised Tam's voice at once.

'Thank goodness,' she said. 'I've been so worried.'

She said she'd been checking on the house every couple of days. This morning, she'd arrived to find a small pane of glass smashed in the back door that led to the scullery. It had been snowing overnight and there were tyre marks on the drive. The back door had been opened and there was melted snow on the flagstones inside.

'Did you have a look round?'

'I did.'

'And?'

'Everything looked normal. That struck me as odd.'

'Did you contact the police? In Laurencekirk?'

'Aye. They came out. Two of them. But we can't know what's gone missing until you take a look yourself.'

She'd had the glass replaced, she said, but being in the house like that wasn't really to her taste any more. The thought of the presence of strangers upset her. They might have been there for hours.

Moncrieff was checking his watch. The Edinburgh sleeper left King's Cross fifteen minutes before midnight. He could be up at the Glebe House by mid-morning and back in London by the day after that.

'I'll take the train tonight,' he told her. 'Expect a knock on your door.'

10

The summons to the phone found Dieter Merz and Beata at breakfast at the Hotel Franconia.

'It's a call for you, Frau Messner. Your father, I think.'

Beata nodded. She was looking at Dieter.

'Will you talk to him? Please?'

Dieter was about to protest but she put her fingers to her lips and offered a rare smile so he got to his feet and followed the waiter out of the dining room. The phone awaited him at the reception desk.

'Beata? *Liebling?*'

'It's Dieter.'

'Really?' The waiter was right. Beata's father. 'You made it down there? You're staying at the hotel?'

'I am.'

'And is all well?'

'Very well.'

'You've talked to her?'

'I have.'

'And what do you think?'

'I think you have a lovely daughter. I think she's strong and

I think the break has done her good. She's taking the train back after lunch.'

'Tell her I'll meet her at the station.'

'Of course. I'm sure she'll phone you later with a time.'

There was a longish silence on the line. For a moment, Dieter thought Friedrich might have hung up but then he was back again.

'About Georg,' he said. 'I had a call this morning.'

'From the doctors?'

'From Georg himself. It was a message. For you.'

Dieter was staring at the phone. Georg? Well enough to make a call?

'How was he?'

'That's the point. He sounded normal. He said he felt much better. And he said to say thank you.'

'For what?'

'For yesterday. You dropped in? You saw him?'

'Only briefly. Very briefly.'

Dieter described the fly-by, the moment he swooped low over the terrace and glimpsed the whiteness of the faces below. He could hear Friedrich laughing at the other end of the line.

'Well, it worked,' he said. 'I was talking to the old Georg.'

Dieter took the news back to the breakfast table. Beata pushed the remains of her boiled egg to one side.

'I'm glad,' she said. 'For his sake.'

'And yours?'

She held his gaze for a moment and then reached across the table. Her hand was warm in his.

'I want to take you back to the church,' she said. 'In daylight.'

She checked out of the hotel and Dieter drove her to the Basilika Vierzehnheiligen. The church, with its twin towers, dominated the surrounding countryside. Standing in the thin sunshine beside the car, Beata slipped her hand under Dieter's arm.

'Come,' she said, 'I need to show you something.'

They crossed the gravel towards the big oak door. Two Nazi banners hung on poles outside, rippling in the cold wind from the east. The door was slightly ajar and Dieter half expected the chanting of male voices again but the huge building appeared to be empty except for an old lady on her knees in the aisle.

Dieter looked around. This kind of heavy ornamentation depressed him at first sight. Huge pillars soaring towards the richness of the decorated ceiling. Patterned marble floors. A vast set of organ pipes. Ornate frescos on the walls. Plump angels cavorting above an eiderdown of fluffy clouds. A building like this, thought Dieter, might have been designed by a confectioner. Half close your eyes and the basilica was almost edible.

'I think I preferred it in the dark,' Dieter murmured.

'That's because you're a good Lutheran boy,' she was smiling. 'May God forgive you.'

She tugged him towards one of the side aisles. Portraits of local worthies hung in the gloom. Finally, she brought him to a halt in front of a sculpture in white marble. The gowned figure gazed sightlessly over rows and rows of wooden pews. The expression on the smoothness of the face was deeply mournful and something strange seemed to have happened to his hands.

'Saint Pantaleon,' Beata was crossing herself. 'He was a famous healer. You see his hands?'

'Yes.'

'They're nailed to his head. That was me yesterday. Me the day before. Me in Wannsee. Me in that horrible hospital. Saint Pantaleon cures headaches. Also depression.'

'And it works?'

'It does.' Beata dropped to her knees and began to murmur a prayer. From the back of the basilica came a hollow clunk as the old lady left the building and hauled the door closed behind her.

Finally, Beata got to her feet. She stood beside Dieter and reached for his hand again.

'You were asking forgiveness?'

'I was giving him thanks.'

'For stopping the headaches?'

'For last night.'

Moncrieff took a taxi to the Glebe House from Laurencekirk station. He'd slept badly on the train, half awake for most of the night trying to fathom just who might have broken into the Glebe House. The remoteness of the place had always been something he'd taken for granted. The village was tiny, a mere speck on the edge of the wilderness that was the Cairngorms, and the house itself, a brisk half-hour walk from the kirk and the tiny village shop, was yet another step into the yawning emptiness of the mountains. No one came here by accident.

The taxi dropped him at Esther McFaddon's house. She had her coat readied beside the door. An overnight thaw had melted most of the snow and when they finally made it to the Glebe House, Tam could find no traces of tyre tracks in the drive.

'Did the police look for fingerprints?'

'Yes. Most of them were mine and the rest were probably yours. They need to talk to you. They want to check.'

She had the key to the front door. Tam stepped into the chill of the entrance hall. Already, in some unfathomable way, it felt sullied, interfered with, a home that was no longer entirely his own. Someone had been here, a stranger, maybe strangers. They'd probably come in the dead of night, aware that they had time and privacy on their side. He tried to imagine the beam of a torch in the darkness, shadows moving from room to room, the creak of an unoiled hinge on a door, the scrape of a drawer being carefully opened.

Esther went to the kitchen. It must have been a long journey, she said. She'd make him tea and rustle up something to eat. Tam thanked her, grateful to be left alone. No hurry, he said. This may take a while.

It didn't. The last time he'd been here was at Christmas with Cathy Phelps. She'd served out her time afterwards and, as he'd expected, left the place spotless. In room after room, everything was exactly where he remembered it should be. Only in the snug, where Tam had always attended to his paperwork, did he find signs of disturbance.

His father's escritoire had been his pride and joy, a treasured piece of Louis XVI furniture that had passed down the generations before him. Tam had moved it carefully into the snug where it now occupied a space between the corner of the room and the window. The hinged top lifted to reveal a series of compartments beneath and Tam had taken some care to index letters, bills, diaries and sundry other items he might need in the future.

Now, studying the contents of the desk, he knew someone had been through it. The smallest of the battered cloth-covered notebooks he'd filled with jottings should have been here, not there. And the big address book on which he'd always relied had been replaced upside down. Someone had paid the Glebe House a visit because of this desk, and these contents. But why?

Checks upstairs revealed nothing beyond Cathy's immaculate stewardship before her final departure. Everything neat and tidy. Everything in its place. Back in the kitchen, Tam settled at the long oak table. Esther had conjured a bowl of porridge with water and spoonfuls of honey. Tea, as well, without milk.

'Well, laddie?' Esther wanted to know what he'd found.

'Nothing, really. Bit of a mystery.'

'Nothing at all?' She sounded disappointed.

Moncrief shrugged. Just now he was keen to minimise the importance of what had happened. The last thing he needed was for Esther to decide that the Glebe House could look after itself.

'You'll still keep an eye on the place?' Tam gestured around. 'It was probably a stranger looking for shelter. Snow? That evil wind off the mountains? There's no damage I can see. Certainly nothing missing. I'll talk to the police, of course, but I think we can chalk it down to a rough night and an absence of good manners. Always ask first. Even if the answer's going to be no.'

'But there was no one here, Tam, and that's not right. You can't just break in, help yourself.'

'I know. But I think we'll just have to forget it.'

'Are you sure?'

'I am. But thank you for doing what you did. Dad would have been grateful, too, I know he would.'

She nodded, unconvinced. Then, struck by another thought, she gestured towards the hall.

'You didn't see it? Upstairs in that bedroom your father used at the end? Before he went down to London?'

'See what, Esther?'

'His wee red beret. The one with the silk tassel on the back. The one he always kept on the back of the door.' She was frowning now. 'It took me a while to realise but it's nae there any more.'

Back in London next morning, Tam got in touch with Buckingham Palace. By now he was on first-name terms with two of the voices on the switchboard.

'Miss Andrews? The usual message, if you'd be so kind, for the usual recipient.'

'A pleasure, Mr Moncrieff. I'll make sure Miss Phelps telephones at lunchtime.'

Moncrieff was at his desk when Cathy returned the call. Her morning, she said at once, had been bloody awful. Travel arrangements falling apart. No one knowing their arse from their elbow.

'Tonight?' he enquired. 'As we planned?'

Moncrieff could hear the hesitation in her voice. So far they'd seen far less of each other than he'd anticipated. When plans fell through for her to stay the night – Cathy having to cover for someone on compassionate leave, or a last-minute alteration in one of the senior royals' schedule – he'd at first blamed the ongoing muddle that was the war. More recently, though, he'd begun to wonder whether she wasn't beginning to regret the move south. At the Glebe House, Cathy had been her own mistress. At the Palace, she was merely one face among hundreds.

On the phone a couple of days earlier he'd invited her to a show called *Hay Fever*. Thanks to Ursula, Moncrieff knew he could lay hands on a couple of tickets. On the phone he and Cathy had agreed seven o'clock in the upstairs bar at the Lyceum Theatre and now she confirmed she'd do her best to be there.

'Best? What does that mean?'

'It means I might be a bit late. Hold the curtain, Big Man. This place is madness.'

Moncrieff was at the theatre ten minutes early. He bought a Mackeson for Cathy and a light ale for himself and found an empty table at the far end of the bar. Cathy joined him moments later. She'd had her hair cut since he'd last seen her and it made her look boyish.

She kissed him, and then sat down.

'You've been in the sun,' she said at once.

'You're right.'

'Where?'

'Lisbon.'

'Lucky you.'

'Right again.'

'So why Lisbon?'

Moncrieff shook his head. He was always careful about sharing operational details with anyone in his private life.

'No clues?' Cathy was feigning outrage.

'I'm afraid not. Tell me about your lords and masters. As mad as ever?'

'Actually, they're rather sweet, some of them. The Queen still makes a fuss of me, thank God, and that bloody portrait's finally finished. The artist delivered it yesterday morning. I'm not sure the Queen's very impressed but Bertie loves it. He even thanked me for filling in. That was his term, not mine. He's a darling, that man, and he's crazy about her. I told my dad he should take a leaf out of the King's book. Treat Mum the way he treats the Queen. I was wasting my time, though. Dad never listens. Never has and never will.'

'You've been seeing them recently? Your mum and dad?'

'Of course.' She shot him a look and then changed the subject. 'Exciting, was it?' she enquired. 'Lisbon?'

'Sunny. And lots to eat.'

'That's twice lucky,' she said. 'Bertie thinks we all ought to be setting an example. If I have another slice of Woolton pie I'll be like that girl on the posters. All teeth and good intentions. One of the people I work with came up with the perfect answer. He says he's given the pie up for Lent and they believe him. He even got an extra egg last week. Lucky bastard.'

The barman was ringing the bell. Five minutes to curtain up. There was a surge of movement as people began to head for the door.

Cathy reached for her Mackeson and emptied the glass before wiping her mouth on the back of her hand, a gesture Tam had never seen before. He downed the last of his beer and helped her to her feet. London has begun to coarsen her, he thought. Ironic, when she's working for the King.

They made for the nearest exit leading to the stalls and Moncrieff led the way to their seats. The performance was played with immense brio. Cathy sat beside Moncrieff, rocking with laughter, and in the half-darkness, whenever Tam stole a glance, she looked younger than ever. In theory, he'd always assumed that this new job of hers would take its toll but despite her impatience on the phone she appeared to be thriving on the non-stop pressure. Her responsibility, she said, was to help keep the senior royals out of trouble. At Balmoral, she'd seen lots of evidence of just how quickly things could go wrong and so now she was only too happy to play the sheepdog and head off the more unruly members of the flock. Pressed for a name in the interval, Cathy checked carefully around her.

'The Duke of Kent,' she murmured. 'Even the Queen can't cope with him.'

The second half was, if anything, better than the first and as the curtain fell the four members of the Bliss family tiptoed offstage, turning their backs on the untold disorder behind them. As the pair of them queued in the aisle to leave, Cathy beckoned Moncrieff closer.

'It's like that every day at BP,' she said. 'Noël Coward must be psychic.'

The play over and the theatre-goers flooding onto the darkened streets, Moncrieff was looking for a taxi. When a cab finally appeared, he stepped into the street, brought it to a halt and opened the rear door. Cathy gave him a brief peck on the cheek and climbed in.

'Move over,' Moncrieff bent his long frame to get in beside her.

'What are you doing?'

'Coming with you. I thought we might go back to my place for a nightcap or two.'

His face was inches from Cathy's. With one leg still in the road, he felt slightly ridiculous.

'But I've got to go back to BP.'

'Why?'

'They give me hell if I'm late. I thought you knew that.'

'Really?'

'Yes.'

Moncrieff held her gaze for a moment or two, then stepped back in the road and shrugged.

'Ah...' he straightened his coat. 'My mistake.'

Next morning, tired looking and a little hungover, the Director returned from Nova Scotia. Ursula Barton conferred with him for a little over an hour and then despatched Liddell home. Moncrieff was in his office putting the finishing touches to the MI5 watch list when she appeared at his door. She was carrying a thickish file. When she asked for a look at the list of names he'd compiled, Moncrieff pushed it towards her.

She scanned it quickly, tiny nods of her head.

'Perfect,' she said. 'No real surprises.'

She sat down, the file on her lap. Expecting at the very least some kind of discussion about the weight of surveillance these people could expect, Tam found himself on the receiving end of an entirely different operation.

'September the 14th last year?' Ursula began. 'The Blitz barely a week old? You remember what happened at the Savoy?'

Moncrieff leaned back. The late summer of last year already seemed an age ago. Aerial dogfights over the Weald of Kent, he thought. The front-line RAF airfields suddenly spared as Goering switched his attentions to London. But the Savoy Hotel? He shook his head.

'It was occupied,' Ursula said. 'Briefly, I admit, but the mob got its way.'

She selected a number of photos from the file and spread them on the desk. The first showed a thinnish column of marchers on the Thames Embankment. One of the banners read *Stepney Young Communist League.* Another, pithier, *Ration the Rich!*

'These people were en route to the Savoy?'

'Yes. Eight nights of the *Luftwaffe* had worn them out. Air raid provision in the East End isn't all it might be. One of them knew a chambermaid at the hotel. What she had to say about the shelter under the Savoy won their full attention and so they decided to move in. Strictly speaking it wasn't illegal. All shelters are obliged to accept visitors during a raid. But you can imagine what the guests had to say.'

More photos, this time of the shelter itself. It was a biggish space with a dance floor on one side and some kind of dormitory on the other. According to Ursula, there were separate sleeping arrangements for single men, single women and couples. The hotel supplied mattresses with matching sheets and pillows in pink and red, plus a discreet recess for the Duke and Duchess of Kent on the descent from their suite above.

'They also have a Snore Warden,' Ursula observed drily, 'for when times get really trying.'

Moncrieff was back with the column of marchers. In a third photograph, they'd been snapped milling around outside the hotel itself.

'So who are these people?'

'Workers from the rag trade. Dockers. Bootmakers. Salt of the bloody earth. You get their point, of course. One war for the rich, another for the poor. The face we're really interested in is this one.'

A perfect fingernail settled on a young looking figure beside the open doors of the hotel. Moncrieff recognised him from the earlier shot on the Embankment. Grubby trousers, open-necked white shirt, unruly black hair and a clenched right fist, raised above the milling crowd.

'His name's Doherty,' Ursula said. 'Patrick Doherty. Irish by birth. Big Catholic family. Grew up in Liverpool. Now then, something a little more recent— '

'But what happened at the Savoy? Did they get in? Spend the night there? Make friends with the Snore Warden?'

'They got in for fifteen minutes. Most of them reckoned that was a major victory. In the end the police escorted them out but it was very peaceable. Here. Take a look at this…'

She handed him yet another photo. This time Moncrieff was looking at a hall bursting with demonstrators. Many of them were on their feet, cheering a handful of speakers on the low stage. He recognised the venue.

'That's the Royal Hotel in Bloomsbury,' he said. 'It's just round the corner from where I live.'

'You've been inside?'

'I have. Once. And that's the big public rally they had last month. The People's Convention? Am I right?'

'You are. Were you there, by any chance?'

'No.'

'But you'd recognise this chap?'

Another photograph, a close-up this time. Same trousers. Same clenched fist. But it wasn't Doherty who won Moncrieff's attention. It was the figure beside him. Smaller. Younger. And far prettier.

'That's Cathy Phelps.'

'Indeed.'

'So tell me more about Doherty.'

'Bright boy. A Bolshie, of course. Hard left. But unlike most of them he made an investment or two in the class war.'

'I don't understand.'

'He wanted, in his own phrase, to get to know the enemy. And so he made it his business to enlist in their ranks.'

Moncrieff nodded. He was still staring at the two faces in the photo. The truth, much though he tried to resist the word, was slowly beginning to dawn.

'He was a footman,' he said softly. 'At Balmoral.'

'He was indeed.'

'Sacked?'

'In the end, yes. I gather they rumbled him the morning they found sand in the fuel tank of one of the Rolls-Royces. He denied it, of course, but it made no difference. He was gone by lunchtime.'

She reached for the file and extracted yet another photograph.

'One last glimpse of the enemy,' she said. 'Are you ready?'

Moncrieff nodded, said nothing. The invasion of the Savoy appeared to be over. This shot had been taken in some pub or other. The scene had all the makings of a victory rally. Doherty was standing on a table. Cathy was beside him. Their hands were linked and they were acknowledging roars of applause from the faces below.

'She's obviously a girl with a taste for the limelight,' Ursula murmured. 'We think that's remarkably brave of her, given the position she now holds. Brave or perhaps foolish.'

Moncrieff was still staring at Doherty.

'He's wearing a beret,' he said. 'Do you happen to know what colour it was?'

'I do. I was there.'

'And?'

'It was red.' She smiled. 'With a rather fetching silk tassel on the back.'

Moncrieff nodded. At last he understood. Cathy Phelps hadn't turned her back on the Glebe House to spend more time with him. She'd come south to be with Doherty, and his socialist friends, and perhaps her own family. In the shape of the Irishman she'd found a cause.

Moncrieff shook his head, wondering whether he should have read the weather earlier. Her recent reluctance to spend the night with him. Last night's scene in the taxi outside the theatre. The fact that she was always so busy, so beyond reach. And lately those other little indications that she'd been keeping rough company. Did he feel betrayed? No. Angry? A little.

Ursula was watching him carefully. At length she gathered up the photos and returned them to the file.

'Shall I inform the Palace or will you?'

'Neither,' he nodded at one of the names on the watch list. 'We keep her in post. For when we might need her.'

'An agent in place?'

'Indeed.'

'Run by your good self?'

'Exactly.'

'Very neat,' Ursula was smiling. 'If I may say so.'

Three days later Dieter Merz was summoned to the Führer Squadron out at Tempelhof. It was early afternoon and the squadron adjutant told him that an aircraft was inbound from Paris with Goering and Hess on board. An Me-110 was out on the hardstanding and ground crew were busy with the refuelling hose. Merz, it seemed, was on call to fly the machine.

'Why? Where?'

'No idea, I'm afraid. I get the impression the sortie is local, up and down and some nonsense or other in the middle. Talk to Hans. He knows.'

The aircraft appeared from the south-west minutes later. Expecting one of the fleet of Ju-52s, Merz found himself watching a four-engined Focke-Wulf Condor pull off a perfect landing. Named *Grenzmark*, the huge plane had been fitted out to Ribbentrop's personal specifications, yet another monument to the Foreign Minister's vanity.

Merz met Hans Baur, Hitler's personal pilot, at the foot of the aircraft's steps. He wanted to know what Baur had in mind.

'I want you in the 110,' he nodded at the fighter bomber on the hardstanding. 'Remember the conversation you had with Hahn in Augsburg the other day? About flying the blind spot under enemy bombers? Goering wants a demonstration. I get the impression the Fat One's not a believer. Hess is interested, too. He wants to go up with you and take a look for himself. Back seat, though. You'll be doing the fancy stuff.'

Merz nodded. Hess was already emerging from the Condor and returned Merz's salute when he reached the bottom of the aircraft's steps.

'Do you mind?' he said at once, nodding towards the 110.

'Not at all, Herr. Hess. Glad to be of service.'

Merz returned to Baur. They had a brief conversation about comms frequencies and altitude. Baur would be flying gentle circuits north of the airfield, well away from approach and departure paths, while Merz did his best to slip in beneath him and remain invisible. The *Reichsmarschall*, he said, would be on board the Condor to try and spot him.

'He's in an evil mood,' Baur warned. 'Beware.'

Both aircraft were airborne within minutes. The Me-110 had a much better climb rate than the Condor but Merz throttled back immediately after take-off, letting the larger aircraft slowly gain height over the gleaming stripe of the Wannsee. The Condor, thought Dieter, offered a glimpse of what the new generation of transports and heavy bombers would look like. With its streamlined body and sleek nose, it put the trusty old carthorse, as Hans Baur termed the Ju-52, in the shade.

At two thousand metres, the Condor levelled out. Behind Merz, in the second seat, Hess had readied a borrowed Leica camera. Merz was to hunt for the perfect blind spot beneath the Condor's silver belly and it was Hess's responsibility to photograph the results.

On the radio, Baur announced that he was starting the turn that would take him into the circuit. Merz, trailing by a hundred metres, could see a big pale face in one of the windows towards the rear of the Condor. Goering, he thought. Taking a look for himself.

Merz pushed the joystick gently forward and fed in a dab of throttle. The 110 nosed down and picked up speed. A little too quickly, the vast spread of the Condor grew bigger above the canopy and Merz eased the throttle back. Earlier, with Baur, he'd agreed a minimum ten-metre vertical separation between the two aircraft but already the sheer size of the Condor had masked the scatter of clouds and fitful sunshine. Looking up, Merz could count the rivets on the wing roots where they joined the fuselage. He'd never been this close to an aircraft this big.

He checked with Hess in the rear seat. The Deputy Führer, to his evident delight, was taking photo after photo with the Leica. Like Merz, he was struck by the sheer novelty of this manoeuvre.

'A little closer?' he suggested.

Merz was happy to do his bidding, knowing that a formation this tight, this intimate, would shield the fighter bomber from the watchers above. Up and up he went, closing the gap centimetre by centimetre until the giant aircraft seemed within touching distance.

'*Genug*,' Hess whispered on the intercom. 'Enough.'

They were back on the ground forty minutes later after Merz had experimented with a series of other configurations. None had the sheer drama of that first embrace and after the two aircraft had landed, Merz and Hess were summoned for a conference aboard the Condor.

Merz had never been on Ribbentrop's personal aircraft before. Upholstered leather seats on the left of the cabin were separated by polished wooden tables and a soft glow came from lamps recessed above the curtained windows. Merz stood in the narrow aisle for a moment. He knew that this was the

plane which had carried Ribbentrop to Moscow in the weeks
before the outbreak of war. He half closed his eyes, trying to
imagine the Foreign Minister flying back to Berlin with the
precious treaty in his pocket. Was there champagne on offer?
Had the Soviets contributed a giant jar of caviar and a supply
of blinis to be warmed in the on-board oven? Was Ribbentrop
already savouring the welcome he'd get from an ecstatic Führer
and a grateful nation?

Merz couldn't answer any of these questions, neither was
he about to ask Goering. The *Reichsmarschall* had always
dismissed the Foreign Minister as a social upstart and an
arrogant fool, and their mutual loathing had been one of the
deeper wounds that disfigured the upper reaches of the Reich.
Now, Goering was sprawled over two seats and one look at his
face told Merz that Baur had been right. The *Reichsmarschall*
was spoiling for a fight.

He gestured for Merz to take a seat across the table beside
Hess. Hess was fiddling with the Leica. At length he looked
up at Goering.

'Did you see us?' he demanded. 'Be honest.'

Goering grunted a negative but pointed out that it didn't
matter. The *Luftwaffe* were taking the battle to the enemy.
Soon, the British would have no aircraft factories left. Without
assembly lines, there'd be no giant bomber formations to shoot
down. Pretty flying on Merz's part, he said, but it proved
absolutely nothing.

At this point, Baur made an appearance, stepping into the
cabin from the cockpit. Uninvited, he took a seat across the aisle.

'The English bombers will come, *Herr Reichsmarschall*,' he
said quietly. 'You have my word that it will happen.'

'How on earth do you know?' Goering turned on him.

'Because they'll do what we do. They'll move the factories around. Build somewhere else. Make it tough for us to find them. Give the English a year or two and they'll be all over us.'

'Nonsense. You're lucky the Führer's not here. Talk like that, he'd have you shot.'

'Or you, *Herr Reichsmarschall*,' Baur had a twinkle in his eye. 'You only win wars by assuming the worst.'

'You really think they'll come?'

'I do, yes.'

'Then we'll shoot them down,' Goering lifted a dismissive hand. 'Better planes, better pilots, men like Merz here. Eh, Rudi?' He cocked a bulging eye at Hess. 'What do *you* think?'

Hess was looking at the canister of film he'd extracted from the camera. He appeared not to have heard the question. Goering, growing more heated by the second, leaned across the table. It was just conceivable, he hissed, that the English would produce enough bombers to survive the wall of fire that would greet them on the edges of the Reich. It was even possible that one or two might make it to Berlin. But if that were ever to happen in earnest, then the likes of Dieter Merz would send them packing.

'Am I right, *der Kleine*?'

'Of course, *Herr Reichsmarschall*.'

'And you, Rudi? You agree?'

Hess looked pained. Merz knew he loathed confrontations like this. At length he checked his watch and then glanced up.

'There'll be no need,' he murmured. 'We'll soon have no quarrel with the English.'

BOOK TWO

11

Saturday 10 May 1941.

Dieter Merz awoke to the insistent trill of the Messner family telephone. Careful not to disturb Beata, he slipped out of bed and tiptoed downstairs.

'*Compadre?* You're still there?'

'I am.'

'Thank God for that. Is she OK? The little one?'

'She's well.'

'And her mother?'

'She's well also.'

It was Georg. Since his discharge from the convalescent home, the name Beata had never passed his lips. Only 'Lottie's mother' or 'my once-upon-a-time wife'.

'Listen, *compadre*,' Georg sounded excited. 'Good news. The best.'

Dieter bent to the phone. *Der Eiserne*, Georg said, had given him the OK to join a bomber force going into action this very night. He'd be flying as a spare pilot in a Heinkel 111. After five months in the hands of a surgeon, and unforgiving nurses, and a turd of a psychologist determined to prove that he was insane, Georg Messner would finally be airborne again. Not once had Goering ever let him down but for this act of faith he was truly grateful.

Act of faith? Dieter had last seen his ex-wingman just four days ago. They'd shared a beer or two in a café overlooking the Spree. Now that Georg was back on his feet, physically intact, everything in perfect working order, it was plainer than ever that the accident back in November had stolen the essence of the man he'd once been. Dieter didn't have a moment's doubt that Georg could still fly an aircraft, but that wasn't the point. The old Georg, the man he'd gone to war with in Spain, measured, loyal, committed, had gone.

'And tonight's target?' Dieter enquired.

'I can't tell you.'

'London?'

'Of course.'

'Then take care, *compadre*. It's a long way down if you get it wrong.'

A strange cackle of laughter brought the conversation to an end. Naked in the slant of early morning sunshine, Dieter glanced round. Beata could move like a ghost but on this occasion a creaking stair had let her down.

'Georg again?' She pulled her dressing gown a little tighter around her.

'Yes.'

'You think we can do without the phone? You think we might get rid of it?'

'That may not be necessary. He's flying tonight. One shell. That's all it takes.'

*

The stranger who met Tam Moncrieff on the steps of the Air Ministry was full of apologies. Not simply for the absence of the expected weather forecaster, at present nursing a broken leg after a fall from his bike in last night's blackout, but for the non-availability of the Ministry's lifts, both the victim of a breakdown in the winding gear. The Met Office, alas, was on the top floor. Within touching distance of the cloud base.

The latter remark, Moncrieff assumed, was a joke. London had awoken to a perfect late spring morning: bright sunshine, a cloudless sky and a warm easterly breeze. The replacement forecaster, a bluff man in his late fifties, was carrying far too much weight for the endless flights of stairs. By the time they made it to the Met Office, he was scarlet with the effort.

The office was smaller than Moncrieff had expected. The forecaster dismissed the woman behind the desk and then cleared a space in the middle of the floor to unroll a map. Barometric pressure rings had been overlaid on the familiar outlines of north-west Europe. On his hands and knees, the forecaster weighed down the corners of the map with books and then rocked back on his haunches.

A huge bubble of high pressure, he said, had settled over the British Isles, extending deep into the Eastern Atlantic. It wouldn't last forever but for the next forty-eight hours the country would be cursed with cloudless skies and near-perfect visibility.

'Cursed?'

'Of course,' a fat finger settled on the Belgian coast. 'There's a full moon tonight, believe it or not. If we're expecting any kind of visit, all the Germans have to do is follow the Thames.

Moonlight that bright, it's as good as a flarepath.' He paused, looking up. 'That *is* why you came, I assume?'

Moncrieff said nothing. His gaze had tracked north, towards Scotland. The Duke of Hamilton's country seat lay south of Glasgow. Moncrieff had paid Dungavel House a quiet visit only last week. The estate included a private airstrip, equipped with landing lights.

'The high pressure extends into Europe,' Moncrieff said. 'Am I right?'

'Yes. Aren't you from Bomber Command? Or have I got the wrong end of the stick?'

Moncrieff didn't answer. He took his time looking at the map and then indicated the curl of Friesian islands off the German/Danish border.

'Assume you were routing west from thereabouts. What conditions might you expect?'

'Over the North Sea, you mean? Today?'

'Tonight.'

'A light following wind, nothing more than ten knots or so, and maybe a little sea mist off the coast around here...' he tapped the edge of Northumberland above Newcastle.

'And over the border country? Still heading west?'

'Bright moonlight.'

'Visibility?'

'Excellent.' The forecaster paused. 'You want me to look up the sunset time?'

'No need,' Moncrieff stepped back from the map. 'But thanks for the offer.'

Ursula Barton was waiting for Moncrieff in the Director's office. Guy Liddell was on the phone.

'Sunset's at nine minutes past ten, BST,' Moncrieff folded his long frame into the spare chair.

'And you're still sure someone's coming?'

'I am.'

'Because Souk says so?'

'Yes.'

'Any idea who?'

'Souk thinks Albrecht Haushofer. He's got the contacts. He speaks excellent English. He suspects they'll fly him into Hamilton's place.'

'A plenipotentiary?'

'Indeed. And when the talks are done and the war's over he'll get safe passage home.'

'*Over*? Are you serious?'

'I am.'

'Because of what might happen tonight?'

'Yes.'

Ursula shot him a look. These past few months, Moncrieff had been banging the drum about the dangers posed by the peace party, but no one appeared to be listening. Least of all, it seemed, the Director.

Liddell had just come off the phone. Lately he'd been under intense pressure from a number of quarters and it showed on his face. Every week brought more arrests, more suspects to be interned, more names on the ever-lengthier interrogation lists, more holes in the fragile dyke that MI5 had thrown up against untold enemies within. And now, if Tam Moncrieff was to be believed, the country was facing another threat of an entirely different order.

Ursula confirmed the imminence of a big raid on London.

At least a hundred aircraft expected. The first wave to arrive around eleven this evening. Stumps to be drawn by three in the morning. Much *Sturm und Drang* in between.

'Evidence?'

'The usual source, sir. Orders went out to *Gruppe* this morning. We deciphered the bomb loads, too. A mix of HE and incendiaries. Not much sleep for anyone tonight.'

The Director turned to Moncrieff.

'And you, Tam. What news from the north?'

'You'll have seen the surveillance reports, sir. And the telephone intercepts. We're looking at the makings of a reception committee. So far, unless I'm mistaken, peace negotiations have always been discreet. Lisbon. Geneva. Stockholm. Sylt. Neutral territory. This is different. This is far closer to home.'

'And you still think Dungavel House? Hamilton's place?'

'Yes, sir.'

'And you say the great and the good are gathering up there?'

'In the vicinity, some of them, certainly. Others are keeping their distance. Which may prove very wise.'

'Care to give me a name or two?'

''C', for one.'

'You said that last week.'

'I did.'

'And you still believe it?'

Moncrieff nodded. 'C' was the Director of MI6, Sir Stewart Menzies, and every particle of intelligence Moncrieff had analysed over the past few months supported his belief that 'C' had quietly thrown his weight behind the peace lobby. He was highly placed in Court circles. He got on famously with the King. His perch in clubland, above all his membership of

White's, put him alongside most of the key figures arguing for a negotiated treaty with the Germans. Take a cold look at the jigsaw of impending events and Menzies might well end up with a seat in a reformed Cabinet.

'For what it's worth, sir, I suspect our friends in Broadway have been in touch with the people around Hess for some time. We've barged into their party with that letter of yours from Duglo and that upset them somewhat. At the very least they think we're guilty of trespass.'

'Their turf?'

'Indeed. And they're not shy about keeping us at arm's length.'

Moncrieff mentioned the break-in at the Glebe House.

'You think Broadway were responsible?'

'It's possible, yes.'

'Sending us a message?'

'Telling us to mind our own business.'

Liddell fell silent for a moment, then nodded.

'So you think 'C' is up there now? In Scotland? Expecting some kind of development?'

'I know he's in London, sir. Watching and waiting. For my money, the overthrow of the PM might serve him very well.'

Liddell smiled. If he was shocked by the suggestion that Winston Churchill might be under threat it didn't show.

'I thought we were discussing covert negotiations,' he murmured. 'Not a *coup d'état*.'

Ilse Hess awoke with a pounding headache and a slight fever. She lay still for a moment, aware of the splash of water from the nearby bathroom. Rudi, she thought. Up early again.

These last few weeks, he'd been acting out of character. Normally, he was predictable, immaculately organised, a glad prisoner of a thousand routines. Every Sunday, he'd make a point of sharing his diary for the coming week, explaining where he was going and why, fitting in time with his family whenever he could. For this, Ilse had always been grateful, only too aware of how rare her husband was among the other big shots in Berlin. For Rudi, time spent in stealing a march on a rival, or spreading ugly rumours about this person or that, was time wasted. He had no further ambitions for higher office. He was a stranger to any kind of conspiracy. He owed his sole allegiance to his Führer, to the Reich, and to his beloved family.

This much Ilse knew, and the knowledge was a source of constant reassurance. And yet recently, especially the last few weeks, something seemed to have happened to the husband she thought she knew. He'd become fretful, often visibly nervous. The smallest things – a missed phone call, a perceived slight from the local herbalist – would trigger a long diatribe and then an abrupt withdrawal into total silence. The diatribes she could cope with – her Rudi had never known how to end a sentence – but the sudden mood changes were something new. More often than not she was able to put them down to the ever-faster pace of events. But the times when there appeared to be no rational explanation had begun to alarm her.

Then, barely days ago, Rudi had got himself measured for a brand new *Luftwaffe* uniform. After years of dressing in a plain brown shirt with the barest of insignia, she was confused. Why the change of plumage? What was so important that merited the collar tabs of a *Luftwaffe* Captain? Both questions had gone unanswered yet last night she'd noticed the uniform carefully readied on a hanger in the spare room.

Now, Rudi stepped in from the bathroom, still towelling himself dry. He paused beside the bed, as solicitous as ever, asking whether she needed any more medication. She shook her head. She wanted to know what he had planned for the day. Hess said he'd like a walk in the woods with their son and the dog and her new pups. Alfred Rosenberg, one of the regime's big brains, was due for lunch. Then, in late afternoon, he'd be leaving for Augsburg.

'You're flying?'

'Yes.'

'In that lovely new uniform?'

'Yes.'

'When will you be back?'

'Tomorrow, I hope. If not, then certainly Monday.'

He held her gaze and for once she resisted the temptation to ask where he might be going. Minutes later, with Rudi dressed for the woods and attending to their son, Ilse returned to her book. It was an account of a flight over Mount Everest, a present from English friends. The author, the Marquess of Clydesdale, now the Duke of Hamilton, had been the pilot on the flight and Ilse knew that her husband had always treasured the gift.

Hearing a peal of laughter from her son's bedroom, she flicked idly back to the personal dedication inscribed at the front of the book. '*With all good wishes and the hope that out of personal friendships a real and lasting understanding may grow between our two countries*', it read. The dedication was unsigned but the clue, Ilse thought, was in the script itself. A male hand, definitely. Carefully measured. Confident. Full of the best intentions.

Georg Messner flew himself from Berlin to one of the bomber airfields in the Pas-de-Calais. Approval from Goering would have been enough to win him a ride in any *Luftwaffe* squadron for tonight's big raid but Messner knew the *Oberstleutnant* from their days in the Condor Legion and it was a pleasure to see him again.

'Messner! What an honour!'

Otto Klopp was a big man, famously foul-mouthed, physically imposing. Conversationally and in every other respect, he always set a fierce pace. Tonight, he said, would be an early birthday present for his new wife. A couple of thousand tons of Third Reich high explosive might just be enough to teach the fucking English the error of their ways. They'd wake up to find some familiar London landmarks gone and with luck they'd at last see sense. By midsummer, he and Hildegarde might find themselves quartered in one of those fancy houses overlooking the upper reaches of the Thames. They'd play polo, and drink thin beer, and have hundreds of kids. They might even consent to learn English and acquire a taste for overboiled vegetables.

'Tonight, Messner, you and I will make history.' He got to his feet and reached for his cap. 'Happy to have you along.'

Rudolf Hess took off from the Messerschmitt airstrip at Augsburg at 5.46 p.m. in perfect weather. He was flying alone.

On his personal orders, the cannons and machine guns were packed in grease to disable them, and he carried no bombs or ammunition. The specially fitted auxiliary tanks contained an extra 1,800 litres of fuel, extending the aircraft's range to more than 1,500 miles. He'd also demanded radio equipment he could tune as a navigational aid.

According to the account he offered later, Hess flew north-west across Germany and Holland, reaching the coast at Den Helder. A ninety-degree turn to starboard then took him north-east towards Germany before a second turn to port routed him up the North Sea until he intersected the radio beam from Kalundborg in Denmark. By now it was gone half past eight and the sun was beginning to sink in the west.

Riding the radio beam due west would deliver the Deputy Führer to the English coast just south of the Scottish border but he was wary of entering enemy airspace in daylight and so he flew back and forth for an hour until darkness stole towards him from the east. Locked onto the radio beam from Kalundborg, he began a shallow dive towards the distant smudge of the British Isles. At twelve minutes past ten, residents in the coastal town of Bamburgh heard the roar of an aircraft approaching from the North Sea. Travelling low-level at more than 350 mph, it thundered overhead, disappearing within seconds towards the Cheviot Hills.

Hess, at the controls, had spent weeks rehearsing the next thirty minutes, poring over maps of the border country, memorising the key features, aware that already his presence would have been registered on RAF early warning radar screens. His life was now in the hands of the Me-110. A lone target in the near-darkness, it could outrun most enemy fighters. He had enough fuel – just – to make his destination. Duglo's country seat, Dungavel House, lay directly under the Kalundborg beam. The Duke's private airstrip was equipped with lights. And there, praise God, his journey would end.

In his early days as a pilot Hess had loved flying at low altitude. This barnstorming dalliance with gravity had won him many admirers and now – in the last of the twilight – he took the aircraft as low as he dared. Thirty metres. Twenty metres. The soft contours of the border country were a blur below him.

Somewhere ahead, blacked out, lay the sprawl of Glasgow. Hess lifted the nose and began to climb. This final stage of the journey were the moments he'd dreaded. After five hours in the cockpit he was physically and mentally drained but now he had to rely on the Danish radio beam, and the map of local features he'd so carefully committed to memory.

Throttling back to save fuel, he peered down at the landscape below, trying to orientate himself, but he sensed already that he must have overshot Dungavel House. Ahead, he caught the gleam of moonlight on what must have been the Firth of Clyde. In thirty brief minutes he'd crossed Scotland and would soon be heading for Northern Ireland. Except that his fuel was now critically low.

Already, with the needle on the gauge at zero, he was braced for the moment when the first engine would miss a beat. Then would come another cough, and then another, and then the nose would go down and he'd have no option but to bale out. The thought filled him with horror. He stared out at the curl of the coast and dropped a wing to take him back inland. He'd never made a parachute jump in his life.

*

At about the same time, 10.52, the first wave of Heinkel-111s droned into the Thames estuary, following the silver thread of the river towards the heart of the city. Georg Messner was flying as co-pilot in *Oberstleutnant* Klopp's aircraft, and Klopp had given him control as soon as they'd climbed to their cruising altitude over the English Channel. As the *Gruppe* weather forecaster had promised, conditions were perfect for a night of sustained violence. Already, looking down at the long finger of Southend Pier, Messner knew that target identification would be no problem. In the brightness of a full moon, even with perfect blackout, there was nowhere for London to hide.

Messner relaxed at the controls. On Klopp's recommendation, he was wearing earplugs but even so the noise from the two engines, one either side of the cockpit, was deafening. Klopp would be taking over in the next few minutes for the run-in to the target, and the bomb-aimer, who was in a makeshift perch behind him, would take his place flat on his belly in the nose.

At the *Gruppe* briefing, just a couple of hours earlier, Klopp's wooden pointer had settled briefly on the square mile of Westminster he and his pilots were tasked to help destroy. Direct hits on the Houses of Parliament would go down very nicely in Berlin but the whole area offered rich pickings for bomber crews with talent as well as iron nerves. Downing Street, where Churchill held court. Whitehall, heart of the administrative machine. Famous hotels like the Savoy and the Ritz. Lately the British had started to learn a thing or two about marrying their searchlights to effective anti-aircraft fire, but blow these targets apart with high explosive, add a top dressing of incendiaries and even Churchill might have second thoughts about a war without end.

The cockpit of the Heinkel was cramped. The all-glass cockpit forward of the controls offered a front-row seat for the evening's entertainment and, once Klopp had taken over again, Messner shifted his weight in the narrow seat, trying to ease the pain in his back. Only days before, a *Luftwaffe* doctor had conducted a thorough examination before declaring him fit to fly. When he'd asked Messner whether he still had any residual pain after the accident, Messner had shaken his head and said no. It was a lie, of course. His lower back was on fire after just an hour sitting down but he'd had months in hospital contemplating the years to come and he knew he'd die if he couldn't get back in the air.

Flying with the Führer Squadron had been pleasant enough. There were rewards as well as glamour in shipping Hitler and his top chieftains around the Reich, but this was the real thing. This was why you went to war. This was where all that training led. You hung in the night sky, three kilometres above the enemy, and you rained terror onto the heads of those who deserved it. Beautiful, Messner told himself. Truly a work of art.

Ahead lay a picket of searchlights, sweeping left and right, restless, hungry, impatient. In Spain, the Republicans had barely had guns, let alone searchlights, and for Messner this was already a new experience. As the river looped left and right beneath them, always narrowing, Messner watched the light show as they closed on the jigsaw of docks on both banks. Then, abruptly, the Heinkel was coned, at least two searchlights, maybe even three, and the cockpit was full of a blinding whiteness. Beside him, Klopp cursed the fucking English. Then the bomber reared up and shook itself as the first shells exploded and the anti-aircraft gunners began to find their range.

Klopp was silent now, tight-lipped, and Messner detected fear as well as intense concentration in the way he crouched over the controls. This wasn't like being a fighter pilot. There were no options, no ways of answering back. There was nothing to chase, nothing to shoot at, nothing to get your teeth into. You were in the delivery business. Your sole responsibility was to fly straight and level, hold a steady course and listen very hard to the bomb-aimer in the nose who'd tell you when your moment of glory had finally arrived. What kind of flying was that? Assuming you made it at all?

The aircraft was still webbed in the searchlights. Klopp was flying blind, relying on sheer courage, sheer obstinacy, refusing to yield. The bomber, he was showing the pilots around him, will always get through. Always. A pleasant trip up the Thames had become a suicidal test of will.

From somewhere in the depths of the Heinkel came a smell of cordite as another shell exploded, and then a third. By now, Messner was praying for Klopp to do something, anything, drop a wing, corkscrew down, give the searchlights and the hungry ack-ack the slip, dive into the big, black cave that was the darkness below. Then came yet another shell, an explosion even brighter than the searchlights with a molten golden core that scorched itself onto Messner's retina as red-hot shrapnel shattered the Perspex panels on Klopp's side of the cockpit.

The blast of icy air took Messner's breath away. He tried to swallow, couldn't. Instinctively, he'd thrown his hands up, trying to shield his face. Something warm was trickling down his chest. He was grateful for the warmth. Then he looked left, towards Klopp, and he knew they were in deep, deep shit. The man beside him had no head. It just wasn't there any more.

The aircraft, nose up, was heading for a stall. Messner reached for the control column and pushed it forward. At the same time he kicked the right rudder bar as hard as he could. The aircraft responded slowly, dropping a wing and spinning out of the bomber stream. Engulfed by darkness, Messner wondered for a moment whether he was dead, then he forced himself to concentrate, to ignore the roar of the wind through the ruined canopy, to concentrate on the altimeter and the compass, and to use what little strength was left to him to make a plan. Kill the spin, he told himself. East, he told himself. Away from the searchlights. Away from the guns. And as low as possible. Where the cold wouldn't kill them.

Leaving the Firth of Clyde, heading east again, Rudolf Hess was lost. All his preparations, all his hours at the map table, had come to nothing. Beyond the starboard wing he could just make out the darker edges of what must have been Glasgow. South of there, with luck, was Dungavel House but he knew his chances of finding it had gone. He was down to his last litres of fuel. The rest of his flight was now measured in minutes.

He stole a look at the altimeter: 1,400 metres. He knew he needed more height. He lifted the nose, praying for the last few drops of gasoline to keep the props turning, and then gripped the control column between his knees as he sought to get out of his seat harness. At 2,100 metres he levelled out. He thought he'd heard a misfire in the port engine, but he couldn't be sure. Either way, he knew he had to bale out while he still had the option.

He pushed hard at the canopy. Against the press of the airflow, it was a bitch to open. Then he pushed again, all his strength, and the catches suddenly sprung back and his head was out in the night air. He was fighting to get out now, to release himself from the seat and to somehow escape from the narrow cockpit, but it was impossible. Think, he told himself. There have to be easier ways. Pilots do it all the time. And survive.

The cough of one engine again. This time, he was certain. He still had one hand on the joystick, he was still in control, but the propellers were beginning to windmill, no real bite, and the nose was going down. He closed his eyes a moment, forced himself to concentrate, then he remembered. Invert. Turn upside down. And let gravity do the rest.

It worked. He rolled the aircraft very slowly, feeling for the moment when the sheer weight of his body would release him, and then came a sudden blast of air in his face as – upside down – he slipped free of the cockpit. For a split second he was flailing in the darkness, then he felt a hot jolt of pain as his ankle hit the tailplane and dimly, looking up, he watched the Me-110 disappearing into the darkness.

Falling now, his hand found the loop that operated the ripcord and he pulled as hard as he could. Moments later, the parachute blossomed above him, slowing his descent. His injured ankle hung uselessly from his right leg, but the pain told him he was still alive. He looked down. He could see nothing. Not at first. Then, field by field, a farm appeared, a copse of trees, hedgerows, ploughed furrows thinly veiled in mist. All too quickly, the oncoming field got bigger and bigger and he was still trying to remember how to roll his body on impact when the force of the landing knocked him out.

When he came to again, he was aware of something on fire a couple of hundred metres away. Then he saw the figure of a man running clumsily across the ploughed field. He wasn't a soldier. Apart from a pitchfork, he didn't seem to be armed. And when he finally arrived it was to offer nothing but help.

Hess allowed him to remove the parachute harness and then struggled to his feet. The moment he put any weight on his ankle it gave way.

'You're hurt?'

'*Ja.*'

'Was there anyone else in that plane of yours?' The man nodded across the field towards the burning wreckage.

'*Nein.*'

'You're not British?'

'No,' Hess mustered what dignity he could and extended a hand. 'My name is Alfred Horn. Please tell the Duke of Hamilton I have arrived.'

12

The news from Scotland reached the Duty Officer at St James's Street half an hour after the departure of the last German bomber. He alerted Brigadier Harker, who in turn telephoned the Director of 'B' Section.

'It seems we have an intruder in the camp, Guy. He gets an RAF designation all of his own. Raid 42. Your baby, I think.'

Liddell summoned a meeting at St James's Street. Central London was in chaos after last night's raid, but officers were urged to attend as soon as they could. Moncrieff, after half the night in a shelter beneath a pub in Gower Street, made the briefest detour to view what was left of the House of Commons. He joined a thin crowd behind the barriers in Old Palace Yard and gazed at the smoking ruins of the Commons chamber.

Like many in the capital, he'd regarded the Blitz as a minor inconvenience. If you had the misfortune to live anywhere near the docks, the long winter nights had been hellish. East Enders, in particular, would emerge from their shelters to find whole streets wrecked but anyone living upriver was relatively undisturbed. Until now.

Moncrieff, about to make his way to St James's Street, caught the attention of a policeman beside the barrier. The officer had been on duty all night, helping the fire crews contain the conflagration. His uniform was coated in a thin film of ash and something heavy had dented his helmet. He nodded at the smoke still coiling upwards from the piles of rubble, and pinched the exhaustion from his eyes.

'The bastards'll be back tonight, sir. To finish the job.'

Liddell decided to hold the emergency meeting in the basement cellar. Blast from nearby bombs had again shattered most of the windows upstairs and wind off the river carried the sweet stench of a ruptured sewer main. The basement was used for storing sensitive files which would otherwise have found their way to the Registry at Wormwood Scrubs. Cobwebbed and damp, it was lit by three bare bulbs, one of which kept flickering. Moncrieff, who was the last to arrive, counted the faces in the gloom: Tar Robertson, 'Tin-Eye' Stephens, Ursula and Guy Liddell.

Liddell told Moncrieff to close and bolt the door. An Me-110, he said, had crashed in open country south of Glasgow. As far as anyone could ascertain, only the pilot had been on board. He'd managed to bale out and after being arrested by the local Home Guard he was now in custody in a Scout hall in the village of Giffnock. So far he was giving his name as Alfred Horn but an officer from the Royal Observer Corps was convinced this was an alias.

Liddell glanced down at a sheaf of hastily scribbled notes. The officer's name, he said, was Major Graham Donald. Before the war, he'd spent some time in Munich. He was familiar with a number of faces from the leading ranks of the Nazi Party and this was one of them.

Liddell glanced up. It was Tar Robinson who voiced the obvious question.

'So who is he?'

'Rudolf Hess.' A thin smile. 'We think.'

'Christ, he's the Deputy Führer. Hitler's little helper. What on earth's he doing in Scotland?'

'Good question. I suspect we owe Tam an apology. Herr Horn, it seems, has come to talk to the Duke of Hamilton.'

'About what?'

'He won't say. Not yet.'

A search of Herr Horn, he said, had yielded two visiting cards, one for Karl Haushofer and one for his son Albrecht, as well as homeopathic medicines and a hypodermic syringe. A black and white photograph of a woman holding a baby might well turn out to be Frau Hess and the officer who'd conducted the search had also found a lengthy letter.

'Does Hamilton know about any of this?' Robertson again.

'I gather he's been alerted.'

'So where was he? Last night?'

'On duty at RAF Turnhouse. He's Commanding Officer there.'

'Neat.' Stephens this time. 'The perfect alibi.'

Liddell acknowledged the point with the slightest inclination of his head. Horn, he said, had been taken in the middle of the night to Maryhill Barracks in Glasgow for treatment to an injured ankle. As far as he could gather, Hamilton was due to visit him this morning. Around about now.

Moncrieff stirred. He was watching the Director carefully.

'How do we know all this?'

'That, I'm afraid, I can't tell you. Not yet. But there's a person of interest we need to talk to. His name's Kacper Wojcek. He's employed as a clerk by the Polish Consulate in Glasgow and he speaks good German. He also works for Polish Intelligence. According to Major Donald, he met Horn in the small hours of this morning and spent some time with him. Wojcek is known to us. He works for our friends in Broadway.'

Broadway housed the headquarters of MI6. Moncrieff permitted himself the ghost of a smile.

'So the Deputy Führer appears from nowhere. Might we assume Wojcek was expecting him? Or did he just happen to be in the vicinity?'

'A scurrilous suggestion, Tam, but I suggest you explore it further. Downing Street have been kind enough to put an aircraft at our disposal. RAF Northolt. As soon as you like. Ursula has a Glasgow address for Wojcek. I doubt he'll be pleased to see you.'

Dieter Merz was still in bed when the Gestapo arrived at Beata's door. Visitors to the house by the Wannsee lake had dwindled since Merz had moved in, and intrusions on a Sunday were virtually unknown. After the thunderous knocking came vocal protests from Beata. Merz was halfway down the stairs when the two men appeared in the narrow hallway. They were both uniformed – standard SS grey-green – and one of them had unholstered a service Luger.

'*Major* Merz?'

Merz nodded. Asked what they wanted.

'Get dressed, please. We'll wait here with the lady.'

'And then?'

'And then you'll come with us.'

Merz held his gaze for a moment and then shrugged. He'd done nothing wrong. He had nothing to be worried about. Not that these people had the slightest interest in either proposition.

They drove him back into the city. Within a kilometre of their destination he knew exactly where they were going. The lifeblood of the Reich ran through the big ministries on the Wilhelmstrasse and some of it was spilled in the sombre building on Prinz-Albrecht-Strasse, a smaller street to the left, which housed Gestapo headquarters. Like most Germans, Merz had heard chilling accounts of what you might expect on a visit to the basement interrogation suites but so far he'd never been near the place. *Scheisse*, he thought.

An older man in plainclothes was waiting inside the big reception doors. He looked like a schoolmaster wearied by a term that never seemed to end. He greeted Merz by name and apologised for disturbing him on a Sunday. There were one or two issues they needed to discuss, and before they got down to business he'd like to place on record his admiration for *Major* Merz's flying skills. He'd been at Nuremberg for the last of the party rallies in '38 and he'd never forget that final low pass over the Zeppelinfeld.

'Outstanding,' he said. 'Please follow me.'

Merz did his best to go along with this pantomime, grateful that they weren't heading for the stairs to the basement. His new fan, who'd neglected to introduce himself, led the way along an interminable corridor. Marble floors. Framed black and white photos of a stern-looking Führer. Even a flower vase or two. An abattoir, Merz thought, disguised as an office of state.

The room at the end was bare, except for a metal desk and two filing cabinets. Scuffed linoleum on the floor and a view of what Merz assumed was the rear courtyard from the single window.

'I'm a detective, in case you're wondering. Please take a seat.'

Merz didn't move. He was watching the man as he produced a handkerchief and began to flick dust off the desk. A borrowed office, he concluded. On loan to someone probably important, embarrassed by his circumstances.

'What am I supposed to have done?' Merz asked. 'Do you mind telling me?'

The detective looked up. He seemed slightly pained by the question.

'Please sit,' he nodded at the chair in front of the desk. He was tall and thin and he was studying Merz the way you might assess an item at an auction.

'You'll be aware he's gone,' he said at last.

'Who?'

'*Der Stellvertreter.*' The Deputy Führer.

'You mean Hess?'

'Yes.'

'Gone where?'

'We think Britain. That makes him either a madman or a traitor or perhaps both. What's your opinion?'

Merz took his time to frame an answer. All those training flights, he thought. All those questions about range and fuel load. All that navigational expertise, so carefully gathered, so perfectly mastered.

'Did he get there?' he asked.

'You haven't answered my question.'

'I know. As it happens, I liked the man.'

'You think he's dead?'

'I've no idea. I hope not.'

'So you think he could have made it? All that way? Flying alone?'

'Yes. He's a natural flyer. He's brave. He understands aircraft.' Merz paused. 'But why would he want to go?'

'That's my question. And I suspect you know the answer. Here, in this room, we can bring this business to a happy end. Otherwise...' he shrugged, '... it's your choice.'

The detective seemed to resent the need for the threat, no matter how subtle. Merz recognised weakness when he saw it.

'How many other people have you arrested?'

'Personally? None. You've met Pintsch? *Der Stellvertreter*'s adjutant?'

Merz frowned. Munich, he thought. The night Hess emerged from the *Bierkeller* and Pintsch drove them both home.

'Yes,' he said.

'I understand he was detained this morning. At the Berghof. Also Herr Haushofer. And Herr Messerschmitt.'

'Willi?' Merz was incredulous. 'You think he's a traitor?'

'We think he helped Hess on his way. As did you.'

'We helped Hess learn to fly a particular aircraft. And we did that because he was the Deputy Führer and he asked us. Goering asked, too. And guess what? I said yes.' Merz paused, angry now. 'So have you arrested the *Reichsmarschall* as well? Is he down the corridor?'

The detective ducked his head and Merz had the brief satisfaction of knowing the man felt uncomfortable. Press your advantage, he told himself. Close the distance between you. Go for the kill.

'Why would Hess fly to Britain?' he asked.

'I have no idea.'

'Of course you have. This is speculation on my part. These are bullets for your gun. Hess is an educated man. He understands a great deal more about this war than most of his sort. And my guess is that he's gone to try and talk some sense into the English. I'm a fighter pilot. I see the war through a single gunsight. The British did well over the Channel back last year. The Spitfire is a superb aeroplane. But they're fighting the wrong enemy, and so are we. Ask any aviator, any soldier, which direction we should be going next. Ask Hess, if he ever gets back. And you know the answer? Well? Do you?'

The detective wouldn't reply. At length he circled the desk and folded his long frame into the other chair. Then he steepled his fingers and looked at Merz.

'Is this you talking or *der Stellvertreter*?'

Merz held his gaze and then started to laugh.

'If that's a serious question,' he said, 'then we're all in the shit.'

Moncrieff hadn't been to Glasgow since before the war. The address he'd acquired from Ursula took him down to an area of tenements near the Clydeside shipyards. Mid-afternoon, even on a Sunday, he could feel the heavy industrial pulse of the city. The insistent clang of metal on metal. The throb of dozens of generators. The frieze of giant cranes silhouetted against the hills beyond the river's northern shore. Ship launch after ship launch, war had brightened Glasgow. The streets were packed, the pubs were full and the men who'd avoided the call-up were duly grateful.

Kacper Wojcek lived in the end house of a terrace that straggled up from the shore line. Moncrieff's insistent knocking finally brought him to the door. He was a tiny man, red pyjama bottoms, no top. He looked exhausted, as well he might. Spend half the night talking to the Deputy Führer and you deserved a proper lie-in.

'May I?' Moncrieff stepped past him without waiting for an answer. The place smelled ripe.

A woman had emerged from the steam of a kitchen at the back of a narrow hall. Moncrieff at first assumed she was foreign, like Wojcek, but he was wrong.

'So who are you?' she said, wiping her hands on the remains of her apron. 'And why are you so bloody tall?'

She was a big woman, handsome. Her bare arms were blotched with scald marks, her shoulders were slightly hunched and her eyes had the wariness Moncrieff always associated with a good boxer.

He was peering into the scullery. Half a dozen nappies cut from old towels had been pegged to a line across the back of the room.

Moncrieff felt a movement behind him, then a hand on his arm. Wojcek again.

'You never gave me your name,' he said. 'Or have I forgotten it already?' Thick foreign accent, softened with a smile.

Moncrieff introduced himself. He said he'd just come up from London on government business. Was there somewhere they might talk?

Wojcek led him into a tiny living room at the front of the property. It was overfurnished but spotless. A wooden crucifix hung from the picture rail above the mantlepiece and there was a framed photo of a young girl among the clutter on the sideboard. Her face was sombre beneath an explosion of white taffeta and her gloved hands were pressed together in prayer.

'Roseanne,' Wojcek nodded towards the hall. 'Her first communion.'

'She's your wife?'

'My landlady. I rent a room.'

'You've been here long?'

'Long enough,' he pulled a face. 'How can I help you?'

Moncrieff wanted to know about Wojcek's job. He understood he worked at the city's Polish Consulate. Was that true?

'Are you a policeman?'

'In a way, yes.'

'And you're telling me I've done something wrong?'

'I'm telling you we need to talk.'

'Why?'

The door burst open. Roseanne was carrying a baby, a tiny thing pressed against her huge bosom. She gave it to Wojcek, raised an eyebrow in Moncrieff's direction, and left. From somewhere else in the house came the cry of another child.

'Yours?' Moncrieff was looking at the baby in Wojcek's lap, a little girl, huge blue eyes, chubby arms and legs, beautifully dressed in pink.

'Mine,' Wojcek agreed. 'Agata.'

'And upstairs?'

'Tomasz.'

'Not just a lodger, then?'

'No.' He dipped his head low, and nuzzled the tiny face, cheek to cheek, avoiding Moncrieff's gaze. 'You want to know about last night?'

'I do.'

'And you know who this man is? The man I talked to?'

'Tell me.'

At last his head came up. He badly needed a shave.

'You say you're from London?'

'Yes.'

'Who do you work for?'

'That's of no consequence.'

'You're not going to tell me?'

'No.'

'Then maybe you should be talking to someone else. There were many people there last night. Soldiers. Airmen. The man landed in the middle of nowhere. A ploughman arrested him, called for help. Can you imagine that? A man like Hess? Held prisoner in a *Scout hut*? You know something? I felt sorry for him. Me, a Pole, feeling sorry for a German, after Danzig, after Warsaw, after everything. He conducted himself well. He was in pain but he didn't let it show. He was polite, too. That was another surprise.'

'But what were you doing there?'

'I speak German. Someone called the Consul. The Consul was drunk. Useless. Worse than useless. So I went instead.'

'To translate?'

'Of course. Sometimes you get to look the enemy in the face. It doesn't happen often.'

'So what did he have to say? Herr Hess?'

'He didn't say his name was Hess. He said it was Horn, Alfred Horn, but I recognised him at once.'

'Had you met him before?'

'No, but I'd seen his picture.'

'How? Why?'

'I don't know. I can't remember. Maybe a newspaper.'

'So what else did he say?'

'He wanted to know whether we could take him to the Duke of Hamilton.'

'Did he explain why?'

'He said he was on a mission for humanity. You speak German?'

'*Ja.*'

'*Eine Mission für die Menschheit.*'

A mission for humanity. Moncrieff produced a notepad and scribbled down the phrase. Then he looked up again.

'And were you there when he was searched?'

'No. That must have been earlier.'

'Was there a list of any kind? An inventory that you might have seen?'

'No.'

'Did anyone mention a letter?'

'No.'

'Not Hess himself? When he asked about the Duke of Hamilton?'

'No.'

'Did you get the impression he was expecting some kind of reception committee when he arrived? Had he planned to land the plane?'

'I've no idea. He didn't talk about that.'

'And you? Were you expecting him? Was that why you were there? On hand? With your perfect German?'

'Me? Why should I be there?' He held Moncrieff's gaze, unblinking.

'So who were these people who came to collect you?'

'I've no idea.'

'They wore uniforms?'

'Yes.'

'What sort of uniforms?'

'They were Army. Army uniforms. Army people.'

'And they came here? Woke you up? Woke Roseanne? Maybe the babies, too?'

For the first time Wojcek hesitated. 'No,' he said at last.

'They didn't come here?'

'No.'

'So where were you?'

Wojcek wouldn't answer. He was back with the baby. Finally he muttered that life was complicated, awkward, often a bitch. A man could make mistakes, many mistakes. His wife believed in God. He'd never had that pleasure.

'You're telling me you were with another woman?'

'Of course.'

'What's her name? Where do I find her?'

Wojcek shook his head. He was rocking the baby now, gazing down at her. It was none of Moncrieff's business, he muttered. It was nobody's business. It was a weakness, something he needed to do from time to time. He didn't want to talk about it any more. And he didn't want anyone else to know.

Moncrieff let the silence stretch and stretch. One last question. Then maybe an entirely different conversation.

'So how did these people know where to find you?' Moncrieff asked softly. 'When you'd hidden yourself away like that?'

At last his head came up. It was a woeful performance and he knew it. He looked distraught.

'Who do you really work for?' he asked.

'The government. I think I told you.'

'But that should make us friends?' His eyes drifted back to the baby. 'Shouldn't it?'

Moncrieff had noticed a pub down the road towards the shipyards. When he pushed the door open, it was packed. The single bar was thick with tobacco smoke and heads turned as he asked the landlord for a phone.

When Ursula Barton finally answered Moncrieff did his best to shield the conversation with his body. She already had Wojcek's address. He wanted her to book him a room for the night at the Caledonian Hotel. Then he asked her to talk to the Glasgow police. They were to raise two search warrants, one for Wojcek's place, the other for the Polish Consulate, both under the provisions of the Defence of the Realm Act. When Ursula pointed out that the Consulate might be tricky because it had diplomatic protection Moncrieff said it didn't matter. In these circumstances it paid to make a noise, kick a few doors in, see what happened. Shooting pheasants in the hills you always started in the denser parts of the heather.

'Ask any beater,' he laughed. 'Never fails.'

Moncrieff paid the landlord for the call and left the pub. A shop across the road still had a pile of Sunday newspapers for sale. Moncrieff bought a copy of the Glasgow *Herald*. From the corner of the street he had line of sight on Wojcek's front door. He'd already established that the terrace houses were back-to-back, no rear access, and within minutes the front door opened. It was Roseanne. She didn't have the kids. She was carrying a bag. She set off up the hill, away from the river. She was walking fast, her head down. She seemed preoccupied and Moncrieff was tempted to follow her but knew he should wait for the police. He wanted to be there when they tore the place apart. He wanted, above all, to be watching Kacper Wojcek.

The police arrived within the hour. Moncrieff was deep in an article about the black market in venison. He crossed the road and walked up the hill. The van was dark blue and had seen better days. Two uniformed constables were on the pavement staring up at Wojcek's house while the sergeant in charge sat in the driving seat studying a form.

Moncrieff opened the door of the van and showed the sergeant his Security Service Pass.

'Pain in the fucking backside,' the sergeant gestured at the DORA regulations. He was an older man, at least fifty, and his thick fingers were stained yellow from years of cigarettes. He'd scarcely glanced at Moncrieff's pass. 'So what are we after here?'

Moncrieff asked him to search the house. Cupboards. Hidey holes. The kids' room. The attic. The lot.

'Looking for what?'

'Documentation. You find anything, I'll take care of the details.'

'Aye. That'd be a blessing. And then?'

'You leave.'

'With the householder?'

'No.'

'You're serious, laddie? All this way for no arrests?'

At last Moncrieff had the sergeant's full attention. He repeated the brief. Lift every floorboard. Leave no corner unmolested. And then leave.

'Remarkable,' the sergeant shook his head and tossed the DORA form onto the passenger seat. 'At least you're a fucking Scot.'

Wojcek was holding the baby Moncrieff hadn't seen when he opened the door. This one was a boy, older, noisier. The sight of two policemen pushing past him didn't appear to come as any surprise. Neither did the search warrant the sergeant thrust beneath his nose. From upstairs came the noise of splintering wood.

Moncrieff was in the hall now. Already he could smell burning.

'Something on the stove?' He nodded towards the kitchen.

Wojcek shrugged, said he didn't know. The little boy in his arms must have been nearly two. The drumbeat of boots on the thin boards overhead had made him cry. Wojcek tried to comfort him, turning his back on Moncrieff.

'Your mummy's back soon,' he whispered.

Moncrieff wanted to know where she'd gone.

'Shopping,' Wojcek said vaguely. 'She's gone shopping.'

'On a Sunday? You'll have to do better than that.'

Wojcek shrugged. They were in the kitchen now. The little girl he'd seen earlier was asleep on a blanket in a cardboard box and the bottle of vodka on the table was nearly empty. *Monopolowa*. Polish. Moncrieff took a look round. There was nothing on the gas rings on the cooker, nothing to explain the lingering smell. Footsteps clattered down the stairs. Moncrieff turned to find the sergeant holding a book.

'Upstairs. Room at the front.' He thrust it towards Wojcek. 'Bedtime reading, laddie?'

It was a copy of *Mein Kampf*, the spine nearly broken.

'Hess wrote some of this,' Wojcek had taken the book. He offered it to Moncrieff. 'Did you know that?'

Moncrieff ignored the question. He thumbed carefully through, looking for annotations, phrases circled, finding nothing.

The sergeant had disappeared upstairs again. Then came the crash of something heavy and an oath from one of the policemen. He clattered down the stairs and out into the street. When he came back he was holding a crowbar.

'The wardrobe's fighting back,' he said. 'Very Polish.'

Moncrieff smiled. He'd forgotten how witty people in this city could be, and how unforgiving. He pushed at the door into the sitting room and stepped in. The smell of burning was suddenly stronger. He gazed down at the tiny hearth beneath the mantlepiece. The delicate curls of ashes hadn't been there earlier. He knelt beside them and reached for the stub of a poker. Paper, he thought. Pages and pages of paper.

He gave the remains a gentle prod and watched them settle in the grate. Just one curl had survived, scorched brown by the heat. He lifted it carefully out. It was no more than a fragment, the corner of a single sheet. He held it up to the light from the window. Heavy-gauge paper, he thought. Official looking.

The scrape of the door opening wider brought him to his feet. It was Wojcek. God knows what he'd done with his son.

'What happened there?' Moncrieff nodded at the ashes in the grate.

'Rosanne gets cold. She wanted a fire.'

'Very funny. What were you burning? What was it?'

'Old stuff. Stuff she didn't want any more.'

More lies, Moncrieff thought, but the man didn't care. His work in the shadows had brought strangers to his door and now he was looking at four lives in ruins. Later, if he had to, Moncrieff might try and get the rest of his story but in the meantime he'd let events take their own course. In circumstances like these it paid to be patient.

'My friends upstairs have the worst manners in the world,' he said. 'If there's anything you think might interest me, now is the time to say. Otherwise there's no knowing what they might do.'

'There's nothing to find,' he said. 'You're wasting your time.'

'And this?' Moncrieff still had the curl of singed paper.

'That's nothing. That's less than nothing. If that's all you've got then you might have saved yourself the journey. You know what someone told me recently? About your sort of people? They said you were all *Bauern*. And you know something else? They were right.'

Bauern. Peasants. Exactly what MI6 would say.

Moncrieff smiled. He could smell the alcohol on Wojcek's breath.

'Do you have an envelope, by any chance? A bag, perhaps?'

'I have nothing.'

Moncrieff turned and left the room. The police van in the street was locked. He returned to the house and made his way upstairs. The search party had begun on the floorboards, the sergeant on his hands and knees among the contents of the emptied drawers. He looked up at Moncrieff.

'There's nothing here,' he said. 'If there was we'd have found it.'

Moncrieff told him to keep looking. In the meantime, he needed an old envelope, a bag of some kind, somewhere he could store an item he needed to remove. One of the policemen tossed him the keys to the van.

'Bag in the back,' he grunted. 'Full of all kinds of shit.'

By late afternoon, the search was finally over. When the sergeant offered to make a start on tidying up, Moncrieff told him not to bother. They'd done a thorough job and he was duly grateful. The lady of the house might be back soon and she was the one who knew where everything belonged.

'And your wee man downstairs?'

'Leave him be.'

'You mean that?'

'I do.'

Moncrieff followed the three men downstairs. Wojcek was in the kitchen nursing the smaller of his two children. The older one stared up at Moncrieff, baleful, angry, uncomprehending.

Moncrieff had torn a sheet of paper from a pad in the van. He handed it to Wojcek.

'My name's Moncrieff,' he said. 'If you've anything else to tell me, that's where I'll be tonight.'

Wojcek glanced at the address.

'The Caledonian? Isn't that the one in Sauchiehall Street?'

'It is.'

Wojcek nodded, and then swallowed a yawn. The last of the vodka in the bottle had gone.

'*Eine Mission für die Menschheit*,' he muttered. 'A mission to save mankind. Very funny, *ja*?'

*

Dieter Merz spent the rest of the day in the detective's office at Gestapo headquarters. The detective himself had long gone, carefully locking the door behind him, leaving Merz with nothing except the interminable silence of a Berlin sabbath.

The knowledge that even the Gestapo didn't work on Sundays amused Merz. It seemed at first a relic of a more civilised Germany but as the afternoon wore on the absence of any activity – footsteps, conversation, doors slamming, the trill of a distant telephone – began to gnaw at him. Twice he got to his feet and prowled round the bare desk, pausing beside the window. From this height he'd survive a jump, and when he unlocked the catch on the central bar the lower frame moved easily under his fingertips, but he knew only too well that any serious escape attempt would itself have consequences. Nobody was safe any more in Hitler's Reich. Whoever you were, wherever you hid, they'd find you.

And then what? The basement suites downstairs? The rumoured Hungarian sadists imported from Budapest? The pale men in the white gowns whose speciality was pain? Who had a thousand ways of taking you to the very edge of the ugliest death and then leaving you dangling there? Was that what he really wanted? To put those animals, this regime, to the test?

The answer, Merz knew, was no. And so, as the shadows lengthened in the courtyard below, he knew he had no choice but to sit and wait. Someone would make a decision. Someone would come. And after that, God willing, things might be a little clearer.

He needed to think about what might have happened over the past twenty-four hours. He closed his eyes, trying to imagine Rudolf Hess, his distinguished pupil, alone at the controls of the Me-110. In truth he'd never quite believed the Deputy Führer's explanation for making the jump to a bigger aircraft. Merz knew he was a busy man. He knew he prided himself on meeting a schedule of public appearances that would have broken a lesser mortal. And in that context it made perfect sense to fly from city to city. Hess was an accomplished pilot. The cockpit was his second home. But why not stick to a single-seater? A Bf-109? Enjoy himself? Avoid the tedium of the three-month conversion?

The answer, Merz knew, was the range of the aircraft. He himself, when he was still a barnstorming display pilot before the war, had flown himself from venue to venue. The longer flights, especially after the Anschluss had brought Austria into the Reich, might need the odd refuelling stop, but that would be no hardship for a pilot like Hess. Unless, of course, he'd had another destination in mind.

The detective, before he'd gone, had hinted at some kind of peace mission. *Der Stellvertreter*, he suggested, must have cooked up some crazy, half-baked plan to bring the English to the negotiating table. To do that, of course, you had to be mad, clinically insane, because no one in his right mind would ever entertain a conversation with a warmonger like Winston Churchill, not for a single second, and at that moment in the conversation Merz had recognised that the price of his own freedom was to agree.

Hess was mad. That's why he'd planned the whole thing. That's why he'd turned his back on his Führer, on the Reich itself, and flown away. Poor, mad Rudi. The believer in herbal cures and magical spells. The stern-faced vegan. The one old fighter who'd never touch a drop of alcohol. Rudi the family man. Rudi the Führer's favourite. Rudi the king of the crosswind landings. Rudi the fervent believer who'd lost his heart to the cause of peace. Was that madness? God, no.

And so, in the ever-longer silences towards the end of the interview, Merz had declined the detective's far-from-subtle invitation to parcel up the Deputy Führer and lock him away in the cupboard marked 'Mad'. Why? Because Rudolf Hess was anything but insane. A man with more than his fair share of obsessions? Definitely. A man half-crippled by his own sincerity? Again, yes. But mad? Dribbling, certifiable, 110 per cent crazy? Never.

The detective had mentioned Scotland as a possible destination and Merz, genuinely intrigued, had asked why, but no details were forthcoming. In their absence, now, Merz tried to visualise the realities of a flight that long. The bomber boys, and elite pilots in the Führer's *Reichsregierung*, were used to eating that kind of range but getting to Scotland from Augsburg in an Me-110, even with extra drop tanks, would call for rare precision when it came to navigation.

Hess, it seemed, had taken off around six o'clock in the evening. The last part of his journey, therefore, would probably have taken place in darkness, with half the RAF up his arse. The Me-110, with its sheer power, would be a friend in circumstances like these but you still needed real guts for a challenge like that.

Merz tried to concentrate, to think the proposition through properly. One possibility, of course, was the fact that the British might have known he was coming. Safe passage. Maybe even an escort. With a big fat flarepath at journey's end. Was that the real story? Was that the reason that big names like Willi Messerschmitt had woken up this morning to find the Gestapo at their door? Had poor Rudi found himself in a nest of vipers? The plaything of some bunch of old-school conspirators? Neanderthal Prussians with their dreams of a nicer, more virtuous Reich? Had Rudi clambered into his brand new 110 and closed the lid, determined to fly to Scotland, to bang the right heads together, and thus save the Führer from his wilder excesses?

Merz didn't know, couldn't possibly even hazard a guess, and after a while – awoken this morning far too early – he fell asleep, jerking awake hours later to hear the sound of footsteps approaching in the corridor outside. The detective, he thought, come to check up on me.

He was wrong. He forced himself upright in the chair and rubbed his eyes. Beyond the window, it was dark. The figure in the open doorway, pocketing the key to the office, was wearing the collar tabs of a *Luftwaffe* officer. He was young, exquisitely barbered and probably spent every weekend practising his Hitler salute.

Merz responded with a tired lift of his right arm but didn't get up.

'Who are you?' he asked.

'*Oberstleutnant* Heider.' The voice was clipped. 'A pleasure to meet you, *Major* Merz.'

The fact that he had the manners to use Merz's rank, Dieter took as a good sign. He struggled to his feet and yawned. For a brief second, he fancied that he might have the advantage.

'I'm free to go now?'

'You are, *Major* Merz. But first I have some news you might like to hear.'

Merz tried to hide his surprise. The best part of a whole day awaiting the pleasures of interrogation. And now this. Crazy, he thought. Completely insane.

'Your colleague, *Major* Merz. Your *Kamerad*.'

'You mean Messner?'

'Indeed. We gather you know he was flying last night. In a Heinkel. Against the English.'

'And?'

'I'm glad to tell you he brought the plane back in one piece. The cockpit blew out before the bombing run. Had Messner not been on board, the whole crew would have perished.'

'They're all safe?'

'Sadly not. *Oberstleutnant* Klopp is no longer with us. The *Reichsmarschall* has recommended Messner for the *Ritterkreuz*.' He paused, standing respectfully aside to let Merz leave the office. 'The *Reichsmarschall* presents his apologies for the loss of your Sunday. My car is outside. It will be a pleasure to drive you back to Wannsee.'

Moncrieff ordered his dinner from room service. Liver and onions with duchesse potatoes, carrots and cauliflower florets. When the meal was finally delivered, nearly an hour later, it was swimming in a thin gravy that proved to be lukewarm and in place of the cauliflower was a stringy greyish vegetable he didn't recognise. He was tempted to lift the phone and send the whole lot back, but hunger got the better of him. Besides, he suspected the evening's real entertainment was yet to come.

He was tidying up the remains of the liver when he heard a soft knocking at the door. He put his tray carefully to one side and checked his watch. Nearly half past ten. Early, he thought.

He paused beside the door. He hadn't carried a weapon for nearly a year but Ursula Barton had insisted and now he knew why. The neat little Beretta had been waiting for him at Northolt, and the carefully labelled box had included fifty rounds of ammunition. Ursula again. Clearly expecting some kind of war.

'Who is it?'

No reply. Then came a second knock, louder, more insistent. Moncrieff asked again for a name. This time he got an answer.

'Wojcek. It's Wojcek.'

Moncrieff opened the door. Wojcek was so drunk, he could barely stand. Moncrieff reached for him as he began to buckle at the knees and as he did so he became aware of another figure, bigger, taller, dressed entirely in black, and then a third. The pair of them stepped around Wojcek as he fell and the one in black stooped to drag Wojcek into the room. In his spare hand, Moncrieff had time to glimpse a knife before a blow to his midriff forced the air from his lungs. He stepped back from the open door, gasping with the pain, and managed to duck a second punch. Then the sight of the black automatic in Moncrieff's hand brought everything to a halt.

'Fuck.' The man in black looked first at Moncrieff, then at Wojcek. 'You should have said, my friend. We'd have come prepared.'

Wojcek was face down on the carpet. He appeared to have gone to sleep. Moncrieff gestured at the door.

'Shut it,' he said.

Neither men moved. Then the one in black began to laugh.

'You think we're staying?' he nodded at Wojcek. 'Tell him it's the usual address. And tell him we just doubled the fee.' He looked up at Moncrieff. 'You can remember that, mister? A nod will do.'

Moncrieff watched them leave. Thick Glasgow accent. Gorbals swagger. Once they'd gone, he locked the door and then hauled the little Pole to his feet. Wojcek gazed blearily up at him and then began to be sick. Moncrieff slipped the gun into the waistband of his trousers, stepped round the pool of vomit and pushed Wojcek into the bathroom, forcing him to his knees over the lavatory.

'More,' he said. 'Get rid of it.'

Wojcek began to throw up again. Soon he was dry-retching, groaning with the effort to empty his stomach. Moncrieff checked the door and then lifted the telephone and dialled reception. He wanted to know whether two men had left the hotel recently and described one of them. The woman on the line said she'd no knowledge of anyone dressed entirely in black, either coming in or going out.

Moncrieff thanked her and hung up. A service entrance, he thought. People who knew what they were doing. Thank Christ they hadn't been armed.

Wojcek had appeared from the bathroom. He was weaving across the carpet, trying to make it as far as the door. Moncrieff got there first. He told the Pole to fetch two towels from the bathroom. Wojcek stared at him, uncomprehending. Then his gaze drifted to the vomit on the carpet.

'*Two* towels?'

'Yes.'

He did what he was told. Moncrieff draped the bigger of the two towels over the pool of vomit and then led Wojcek to bed and pushed him gently backwards. Wojcek collapsed with a sigh, his eyes closing again.

On the windowsill stood a tall glass vase with a bunch of late daffodils. Moncrieff tossed the flowers onto the carpet and refilled the vase with fresh water from the bathroom. Then he returned to the bed and rearranged the thin body until Wojcek's head was hanging over the side of the counterpane. Two hotel dressing gowns were on hangers in the wardrobe. Moncrieff removed the cords from both and tied Wojcek's wrists together. Then he did the same with his ankles. Bound hand and foot, the Pole was now helpless.

He gazed up at Moncrieff. He looked troubled now. Through the fog of vodka he sensed something very bad was about to happen.

Moncrieff made a space for himself on the bed and sat down beside him. He had a number of questions he needed to ask and he'd be grateful for some answers. If all went well, Wojcek would be on his way.

'Or?'

Moncrieff didn't answer. He wanted to know who the two men were, and who'd ordered them to the hotel.

Wojcek closed his eyes and shook his head.

'You must have talked to somebody. After we searched your house. Who was that somebody?'

No response.

'What were they here to do? Hurt me? Something worse?'

'I don't know.'

'I don't believe you.'

'It's true. I've never seen them before. I was told to meet them at the back of the hotel. They said you'd answer the door to me.'

Moncrieff was watching the Pole very carefully. He thought he saw tears, but he couldn't be sure.

'Let's talk about last night,' he said. 'No one came to look for you. No one came to fetch you. You were out there already. You were waiting. Because you knew Hess was coming. So here's the question, my friend. Where exactly were you waiting? Dungavel House? The Duke's place?'

Wojcek turned his face to the wall. He wanted no part of this conversation. Moncrieff stooped lower, his mouth to Wojcek's ear.

'Dungavel House? You don't have to say anything. Just nod.'

An imperceptible movement of his head. A nod? Moncrieff couldn't be certain.

'You're working for MI6, for the Secret Intelligence Service. Yes?'

'I work for the Consulate. I'm a Pole.'

'But MI6, as well. Yes?'

Wojcek tried to turn over, to bury his face in the pillow, but Moncrieff stopped him. He was rougher now, pinning Wojcek's bony shoulders against the counterpane.

'One last chance,' he said. 'Who else was with you? Last night? When you were waiting for Hess?'

'Nobody. Nobody was there.'

'You're lying. You've lied from the start. And you're a bad liar, Kacper. Which is something you might regret.'

Moncrieff reached for the smaller of the two towels and draped it carefully over the Pole's face. The vase of water was beside the bed. Moncrieff picked it up and poured a little over the towel, then a little more before inching Wojcek's head over the edge of the bed so the water trickled into his nose and down his throat. Wojcek coughed and then began to retch again.

Moncrieff poured more water onto the towel. Wojcek's whole body was convulsing now and in the struggle to keep him pinned to the bed the rest of the water spilled over the towel, filling the passages at the back of his throat, reaching deep into his lungs.

Moncrieff had been here before, as helpless and as frightened as Wojcek, and he remembered the chill of the water triggering the body's most primitive responses. No one ever wanted to drown. Not like this. Not so slowly. So helplessly. In Berlin, he'd been in the hands of experts, but the principles were the same. The water robbed you of everything. Except raw terror.

The water was gone. The vase was empty. Wojcek had been sick again. Moncrieff could hear the vomit bubbling in his throat. Soon he'd have to stop. Attend to the man. Empty him.

'Last night, Kacper. Just tell me.'

Wojcek's face emerged from beneath the towel. He nodded. Anything. Anything to make this nightmare stop.

'Talk to me, Kacper. Who was there last night?'

Wojcek tried to talk, couldn't.

'I'm going to the bathroom again, Kacper. I'm going to fill that vase. You understand me? You understand what I'm telling you?'

The Pole nodded, croaked, coughed, but couldn't shape a single word. Moncrieff got to his feet and reached for the vase. Wojcek shook his head. His eyes spoke for him. No. Please. I beg you. In the name of God.

'Names, Kacper. Names.'

Wojcek stared at him. Finally, one pale hand circled his head and his eyes drifted upwards.

'What does that mean, Kacper? Tell me.'

The Pole made the gesture a second time. Then came another knocking at the door, raised voices shouting Moncrieff's name, and finally the scrape of a key in the lock.

Moncrieff swore softly, abandoning Wojcek on the bed. He crossed the room, the gun in his hand, stepping aside as the door burst open. Moncrieff recognised the man in the suit from reception. With him were two uniformed policemen. One of them had drawn a truncheon. The other was making for the bed.

He bent briefly over Wojcek and gave him a shake. Wojcek groaned and then whispered something in Polish. A splatter of bile had stained the whiteness of the pillow.

'The gun, sir?'

The policeman by the door extended his other hand. Moncrieff shrugged and gave him the Beretta. The policeman removed the clip of ammunition and put the gun to one side before Moncrieff found himself surrendering to a search. The search was thorough, every pocket, trousers and jacket, and while the policemen went through the tidy pile of objects on a neighbouring chair Moncrieff kept his eyes fixed on Wojcek. He was still alive, still moving. That, at least, was a blessing.

'Put your hands behind your back, please sir. Wrists together. And turn round.'

Moncrieff gazed at him for a moment. Handcuffs, he thought.

'You're arresting me?'

'We are, Mr Moncrieff. If that's your real name.'

13

Moncrieff jerked awake in the chill of a police cell. Fully clothed, beneath a single blanket, he'd passed an uncomfortable night trying to doze on the concrete slab that served as a sleeping platform. A thin grey light had penetrated the thick glass of the barred window and from time to time he caught the screech of an early morning tram. Twice he crossed the cell and banged on the door, demanding to talk to someone, but his pleas were ignored.

At around nine o'clock he was escorted to an interview room where a uniformed inspector asked him to account for the events of last night. The duty officer, he said, had taken a call about an incident at the Caledonian Hotel. An armed man had barricaded himself in Room 633. The staff had seemed oblivious, but the tip had proved to be all too accurate. The Pole, Kacper Wojcek, was mercifully recovering in the General Infirmary. Might Mr Moncrieff care to explain why he'd so nearly killed him?

Moncrieff declined the invitation. Last night, with the aid of his MI5 pass, he'd tried to establish that he worked for the Security Service and he would appreciate the opportunity to talk to a Miss Ursula Barton. This request had been refused but now the Inspector made a note of the number and left the interview room to make the call himself. When he returned he offered no apology for the arrest, neither did he volunteer any details about any conversation with London. Instead, Moncrieff was escorted back to his cell and told to wait.

Ursula arrived in person nine hours later. It was early evening. An enormous woman with a thick Glasgow accent had brought him a curling spam sandwich and a cup of lukewarm tea around lunchtime but he was still starving. Ursula was standing at the open cell door in the company of a grim-faced turnkey. She was carrying a small suitcase. She gazed at the cell and then wrinkled her nose.

'Nice,' she was looking at the stains on his shirt. 'You might be glad of this.'

Ever practical, she'd brought him a change of clothes. The turnkey guarded the door while Ursula looked the other way. Moncrieff could have done with a wash but didn't want to tempt fate by asking for water.

A minute or two later they were leaving the police station. There were no forms to sign, no conversations to be had. The sergeant at the front desk barely lifted his head as they stepped out into the gathering dusk. The right word in the right ear, Moncrieff thought, and any door in this country would open.

Ursula took him to a restaurant near the railway station. The least she owed him, she said, was a decent meal somewhere moderately discreet. A word to the maître d' on the door took them to a private room at the back of the restaurant. He left her with the key and Ursula locked the door behind him.

Moncrieff was looking at the single table. It was laid for two and included flowers in a vase. A bottle of red wine had already been opened. Ursula poured.

'How is he?' Moncrieff was still looking at the flowers.

'Your little Pole? He'll live. Christ knows what you did to him.'

'It was an old German trick. I picked it up in Berlin. Another couple of minutes and we'd be drinking champagne.'

'Saint-Emilion not good enough for you?'

'Saint-Emilion's perfect. *Prosit...*'

The wine softened what was left of Moncrieff's anger. After his experiences in Prague and Berlin, he'd never again wanted to spend time in a prison cell but life, unaccountably, had banged him up again.

'He's still in hospital? Wojcek?'

'Of course he's not. Our friends removed him this morning. Took him somewhere safe. Even that woman of his hasn't a clue where he might be.'

'You've met her?'

'I paid her a visit when I arrived. I think she liked the flowers but I'm not sure. That's a joke, by the way, in case you were wondering.'

Moncrieff forced a smile. Ursula, as she would, had obviously coaxed a full account of the incident from the police.

'You said *they*. Care to elaborate?'

'MI6. Obviously. Whether or not they're running this whole operation is still moot but we're beginning to think they've been rather clever.'

'So where's Hess?'

'They took him to a military hospital attached to a castle

next to Loch Lomond yesterday afternoon. He's still got trouble with his ankle.'

'This place is secure?'

'Of course. At the moment the Army have control but guess who'll be standing guard from tomorrow?'

'MI6.'

Ursula nodded. 'C', she said, was playing the security card for all that it was worth. Hess was a foreign asset of immeasurable worth. Hence the three armed agents to be assigned outside his door.

'He's lodged in the hospital?'

'In the castle. Upstairs in the servants' quarters. Thick walls. No heating. He was officially identified yesterday, around ten in the morning. This was at Maryhill Barracks down the road here.'

'By whom?'

'Guess.'

Moncrieff stared at her. Wojcek had recognised the Deputy Führer from newspaper photographs. Another soldier, the night he landed, had seemed to know who he was. But official confirmation had to come from another source.

'Someone in the swim,' Ursula rarely smiled. 'Someone who met him before the war.'

'You mean Hamilton? The trusty Duke?'

'The very same. He motored over and shook the man's hand on Sunday morning. Then they spent some time together.'

'Alone?'

'Yes. Hamilton had brought an RAF interrogation officer across from Turnhouse but he dismissed him.'

'Hamilton speaks German?'

'Very badly. But Hess has good English.'

'Really?' Moncrieff was thinking about Wojcek. Why summon a translator when your surprise guest doesn't need one?

Ursula hadn't finished. So far no one knew what the two men had been talking about. Churchill, she said, was spending the weekend at Ditchley Hall, the country seat of Ronnie Tree and his wife. Another house guest was Sir Archibald Sinclair, the Air Minister, and she rather suspected that Sinclair had been alerted by RAF officers on the spot within hours of Hess's arrival. Either way, Hamilton had been summoned to Ditchley Hall yesterday afternoon to offer the PM a full briefing.

'He flew himself down,' she said. 'And arrived in time for dinner. Afterwards they all watched a film. The Marx Brothers. Knockabout comedy. Very apt under the circumstances.'

'So what's Hamilton saying?'

'To be honest, we haven't got the full story, just scraps from the feast, but I get the sense that Herr Hess never meant to arrive by parachute. He expected to land and that, of course, raises a number of questions. Like where. And for how long.'

'He expected to fly himself back?'

'That would be our assumption.'

'So who would have supplied the fuel?'

'An excellent question. We gather he's been asking for a guarantee of safe passage from the King. This in itself is an interesting request. No one's quite sure that it carries any constitutional weight.'

'Least of all, Churchill.'

'Exactly. The PM knows precisely where real power lies and you won't find it at Buckingham Palace. He motored into

London this morning. Hamilton was in the car with him. And afterwards it was the Duke's job to brief the King.'

'And Hamilton's own story? He was really on duty when Hess turned up?'

'He was. We've checked. He was at RAF Turnhouse. Near Edinburgh. That means nothing of course. He could have come off duty, driven himself back to Dungavel, extended a decent welcome. He's not living at Dungavel House just now, incidentally. He and his wife have a property nearby.'

'Where he and Hess might have talked?'

'Indeed. And whoever else had been invited.'

'Any clues?'

'Just one. Thanks to you.'

'Wojcek?'

'Yes.'

Moncrieff nodded. He had nothing but admiration for Ursula Barton in situations like these. She had an icy ability to marshal the facts, decide probabilities, come to a conclusion or two. Very German, he thought.

'So where's Hamilton now?'

'The PM despatched him back up here with a diplomat, Ivone Kirkpatrick. Kirkpatrick served in Berlin before the war and speaks good German. He also knows Hess, which is more than useful. The pair of them, Hamilton and Kirkpatrick, are due to land about now. They're expected at Buchanan Castle before midnight. That's where they'll find Hess.'

Moncrieff emptied his glass and enquired about food.

'They'll serve when we're ready, Tam. Business first. Then, perhaps, another bottle.' She refilled his glass and invited him to sit down.

Moncrieff looked up at her. One or two elements in this extraordinary story were slipping into focus.

'Hess was searched when he was first arrested,' Moncrieff said.

'Of course. That would have been routine.'

'Have you seen the list? The inventory?'

'Not personally, no. But I understand it included some cranky medicine, some photos and a couple of visiting cards. The latter from the Haushofers.'

'That's right,' Moncrieff nodded. 'And a letter.'

'What letter? Addressed to whom?'

'Exactly. I've not the first idea. No one's talking about it. And that, I suspect, is because it's disappeared.'

He described his return visit to Wojcek's house. While the police tore the place apart upstairs he'd found the remains of a fire in the grate of the living room below. Earlier, when he'd first met Wojcek in the same room, the grate had been empty.

'What sort of remains?'

'Paper. Definitely.'

'So what are you telling me?'

'I'm telling you that Wojcek was there when the search was under way. He was there afterwards. He would have known about the significance of that letter. And I'm suggesting he removed it from the evidence bag.'

'And then burned it?'

'Yes.'

'Why would he do that?'

'I don't know. Except that it might have been deeply revealing.'

'Naming names?'

'That's a possibility.'

'There's another?'

'Of course. It could have been proposals, detailed proposals, proposals backed from the very top.'

'For what?'

'For a peace treaty.'

Ursula was frowning now. She fingered her glass, then checked her watch.

'You don't, by any chance, have any evidence for this?'

'Yes. As it happens, I do.'

He took a moment to check the inside pocket of his jacket where he'd stored the tiny surviving fragment from Wojcek's grate, the tiny curl of paper that had survived the fire. It had gone.

Dieter Merz was packing a suitcase when German radio officially announced Hess's departure. Earlier that day Merz had been summoned to the Air Ministry where the head of Goering's private office had officially confirmed that Merz was no longer under suspicion with regard to the Deputy Führer's treasonous theft of an aircraft. The reasons for his flight, indeed its very destination, was still a mystery but Merz had been cleared of all responsibility.

The *Reichsmarschall* regretted his absence on important state business but wanted Merz to know that he still had his full confidence. That very morning he'd given the new night fighter initiative his official blessing, and wanted Merz to be in charge of all experimental – and later operational – flying. He was to report to the Messerschmitt factory at Augsburg for further detailed orders.

Now, in the kitchen of Beata's house, Merz turned up the radio and gazed out at the grey waters of the lake. The announcement about Hess came in the trademark parade-ground bellow of Goebbels' Ministry of Information. Party member Rudolf Hess, after suffering from an illness of some years' standing, had been strictly forbidden to embark on any flying activity. He had, nevertheless, come into the possession of an aeroplane for training purposes. At about 6 p.m., just two days ago, he'd set off on a flight from Augsburg from which he had yet to return. A letter he left behind had given rise to a fear that Party member Hess had been suffering from a mental disorder and hallucinations. The Führer at once ordered the arrest of anyone who had prior knowledge of Hess's flying activities. It was feared, finally, that Party member Hess had either jumped out of his plane or had met with an accident.

The news report gave way to martial music, slightly funereal, and Merz reached for the off switch. The report had the fingerprints of Goebbels all over it: the blatant lies, the demotion from Deputy Führer to 'Party member', the repeated claims that – all these years – one of the Reich's most loyal servants had, in fact, been crazy.

Merz shook his head. To his certain knowledge, dozens of people, possibly hundreds, must have known about Rudi and his brand new Me-110. His was a familiar face at the Messerschmitt works and he flew everywhere in the Reich. Since late last year he'd been learning to master the aircraft and yet now, at the stroke of a pen, Goebbels had presented the nation with a very different story.

Merz was staring out at the lake where a pair of swans were drifting slowly in the wind. The man was a lunatic. He'd stolen an aircraft. At best he was a common thief. At worst, a traitor. How many of them out there would believe this fiction? How many in the Reich would even care?

Merz felt the presence of Beata behind him. She'd been up in the bedroom and she too had heard the Goebbels broadcast.

'Is it true?' she asked.

Merz turned round and embraced her.

'No,' he muttered. 'It's a lie.'

14

A heatwave had settled on Lisbon. Most mornings, as Hesketh knew, the city always took its time to shake its feathers and prepare itself for the day to come, but this particular Tuesday the streets were emptier than ever. A handful of people at a tram stop. An old woman in black pushing a bicycle up the long hill below the apartment building, her face filmed with perspiration. A lone refugee with a cheap suitcase, squatting in the shade beneath a tree, trying to sell a handful of onions. Hot, he thought. And barely ten in the morning.

He stepped back into the apartment, clad only in a pair of khaki shorts, grateful for the first stirrings of breeze from the river. He'd listened to the news at dawn, Deutscher Rundfunk on the short-wave radio, out there on the terrace. A leading figure had fled the Reich. Not Albrecht Haushofer at all, but Rudolf Hess. He'd somehow acquired an aircraft and flown away. There was no hint of a destination, neither was there any indication whether he was still alive, simply that he'd gone. He was mad, of course, and doubtless a traitor, but they were bound to say that.

The Deputy Führer? Hesketh shook his head, sensing that this had to be the peace initiative. It was unbelievable. If he'd only known, if he'd only worked it out, he might have made so much more money. Hundreds of thousands of escudos. Maybe more. Maybe millions. He looked around the new apartment. Five rooms. A balcony. A wonderful view of the boats and the river. As it was, he'd earned a decent sum from his hasty liaison with Albrecht Haushofer, but the sad truth was that a flight by Hess, if he'd only guessed, if he'd only have passed the word on, could have made him a very rich man.

He stepped through to the big airy room where he slept. The woman in his bed was Senegalese. She had a habit of never rising until mid-morning and her eyes were still closed, one plump arm thrown out across Hesketh's pillow. He'd dubbed her Cou-Cou and was glad to have her in this new nest of his.

Hesketh sank into a new wicker armchair he'd acquired only last week. He loved watching her sleeping. She had a languor and a fullness he'd always looked for in women. She was generous in bed and amusing over a drink or two and she'd taught him how to make a foolproof crème brûlée.

In Dakar, if he was to believe her, she'd been the mistress to one of the top Vichy admirals and had been obliged to flee the country after a complex financial scandal. She'd arrived at Hesketh's door on her way north, to join de Gaulle's circus in London, but showed no eagerness to move on. His address, she'd told him, had come from contacts at the British Embassy, which meant she'd been a present from Kim Philby, Head of Station for the SIS, but the fact that she'd obviously been installed to keep an eye on him didn't bother Hesketh in the least.

In her luggage, of which there was a great deal, he'd found a small fortune in uncut blood diamonds – carelessly wrapped in a sheet of newsprint – and he'd taken the liberty of helping himself to a couple of the smaller gems. Either she wouldn't miss them, he told himself, or she'd sensibly regard them as a down payment on the rent. Either way, they were having a fine time.

Hesketh stirred. She'd brought coffee beans, too. The tiny kitchen was at the back of the apartment and he carefully shut the door so that the rasp of the grinder wouldn't wake her up. He treasured that delicious moment when he could perch himself on the side of the bed and let the waft of the fresh coffee open her eyes. Sex, she always said, was best in the mornings, *en plein matin*, when the body was rested and eager, and she kept a selection of lotions in the cabinet beside the bed. One of them, her favourite, carried the scent of coconut and under Cou-Cou's firm direction it was Hesketh's responsibility to oil her huge breasts before she straddled him. Coconut. Cou-Cou. A perfect pairing.

The beans were done. Hesketh was still waiting for the water to boil when he heard a woman calling his name out in the narrow alley at the back.

'*Senhor* Hesketh? You're up there?'

Hesketh inched the kitchen window a little wider. She was standing in the shade of the building opposite. She was blonde, tall. She was carrying a small suitcase. Hesketh studied her for a moment. Her voice sounded English.

He made his way downstairs and unbolted the big wooden door that led to the alley. The heat down here was intense. The woman was still in the shadows.

'You're Hesketh?'

'I am.'

'Thank Christ for that.'

She sounded tired, irritable, and she was very definitely English. She was also, for a woman, very tall. Hesketh studied her a moment, amused.

'Everyone's got a name,' he said. 'What's yours?'

'Isabel. Isabel Menzies.'

'And there's some way I can help you?'

'Yes,' she gestured round. 'Is it always so bloody hot here?'

He took her upstairs, carrying the suitcase. It was lighter than he'd expected. In the big living room he left her to enjoy the breeze off the river while he prepared the coffee. From the bedroom, there was no sign of life.

By the time the coffee was ready she'd settled on the low banquette that offered the best views of the river. She'd lit a cigarette and relaxed against the rug that Cou-Cou had draped across the back of the banquette. Her eyes were closed and some of the irritation appeared to have gone. Wonderful bones. Full mouth. A hint of laughter in the lines around her eyes.

Her pack of cigarettes, together with a lighter, lay on the occasional table beside the banquette. Hesketh deposited the coffees. The cigarettes were Russian. *Kapteal.*

'May I?' Hesketh had extracted a cigarette, sniffed it, reached for the lighter.

'Help yourself. Keep the whole pack. It's the least I can do.'

'For what?'

'For letting me in like that. A perfect stranger? Is Lisbon always this hospitable?'

'Always. It's the charm of the place. How did you know where to find me?'

'I have friends in Berlin. Albrecht Haushofer? He sends his regards and thanks you for the new address.'

'You've come from Germany?'

'Moscow. I flew to Berlin yesterday. And now here I am. Flying's a wonderful thing but you can overindulge. If it wasn't so hot I could sleep for a year. You know that feeling? When there's no room left for argument? Even for negotiation? When the only option is surrender?'

Clever, Hesketh thought. A woman with a talent for metaphor.

'Are we talking about the weather?'

'Of course.' For the first time, she smiled. 'What else?'

'And you have somewhere to stay? To surrender?'

'Yes.' She rummaged in her bag and produced a slip of paper. 'The Hotel Convento do Salvador?'

'It's a five-minute walk from here. I can take you there.'

'That's very kind.'

'But that's not why you've come here.'

'No.'

'So how can I help you?'

She took her time, reached for the coffee, took a tiny sip, rolled her eyes with pleasure.

'Christ,' she said. 'Where did you get this?'

'Senegal. It's a long story full of interesting asides. If you're here a while I'm sure we could discuss it further. The Convento's a fine hotel. I haven't had the pleasure since God knows when. This city is dedicated to illusion, by the way. When something seems obvious, it isn't. Even the street signs are put there to fool you. But then I imagine that Moscow is probably the same. Stalin hasn't stayed in power by playing the Boy Scout. Rule number one, confuse the enemy. Rule number two, eliminate him. My name is Gordon, by the way. More coffee?'

She was smiling now. She seemed to feel at home.

'Very good,' she said.

'The coffee?'

'You. It's true what they say about the English. They always know how to make a girl laugh. The Russians can be glum. Witty but glum. And you're right about Stalin. The Motherland is no place for Boy Scouts.'

'You've been in Moscow a while?'

'Three years.'

'The Party badge? The black market contacts? The dacha for weekends?'

'All three. The dacha's too small, by the way. A bigger one's on order.'

'These people appreciate you?'

The question stung her. Hesketh detected a small spark of anger.

'It's *my* people, not *these* people,' she said. 'And, yes, they do.'

Hesketh fetched more coffee. He very badly wanted Cou-Cou not to wake up. Not yet. Not until this business was finished. But back in the living room, to Hesketh's disappointment, Isabel Menzies was on her feet. She was truly exhausted. The coffee had been delicious. But now it was time to find the hotel.

'You still haven't told me why you came.' Hesketh refilled her cup.

'You're right. It's a long shot, really, but Albrecht said you might be able to help.'

'I'm sure Albrecht is right. In what respect? Precisely?'

'I've got a name for you. Tam Moncrieff? You've met him? You know him?'

'Very well.'

'And you're in touch?'

'Yes.'

'You have a number for him? A telephone number?'

'Yes.'

Hesketh held her gaze. She hadn't touched the coffee. Finally, she turned away and looked out at the view.

'Shall we say tomorrow afternoon?' she murmured. 'At the hotel? Who knows, the view might be as lovely as this one.'

Hesketh nodded and found himself a pen. The view, he assured her, would be perfect. He asked her for the scrap of paper on which she had the details of the hotel. He'd memorised the number that would take her to Moncrieff and he wrote it down.

'You might be talking to him today?'

'I might.'

'Good,' she smiled again. 'Then tell him Bella will be in touch.'

Hesketh walked her down to the street. As the door opened, she braced herself for the blast of heat and thanked him for the coffee.

'*Bis morgen nachmittag,*' he kissed her lightly on the cheek. See you tomorrow afternoon.

Back upstairs, Hesketh returned to the kitchen and reheated the remains of the coffee before making his way to the bedroom. Something was troubling him and he didn't know what it was. Then, as the coffee came to the boil, he remembered. Not once during his conversations with Albrecht Haushofer had he ever mentioned Tam Moncrieff.

*

Ursula Barton and Tam Moncrieff took the night sleeper back to London on the Monday night. Guy Liddell convened a meeting of 'B' Section principals on Tuesday morning. Repairs had been effected to the Director's office since the Saturday night raid and he took the chair to review the latest developments. He'd been talking to contacts in Downing Street and had, in his own phrase, been testing the waters on what might lie ahead for Herr. Hess.

The Prime Minister, it seemed, had been all for taking Hess at his word. It seemed he had a sneaking regard for the Deputy Führer's courage and wanted to confirm in public that he'd arrived 'on a mission to save humanity'. This had sparked fierce opposition in the corridors of Whitehall, chiefly from the Foreign Office. Both Anthony Eden, now Foreign Secretary, and Alex Cadogan, his Under Secretary of State, preferred to keep information to the very minimum. Hence last night's terse announcement from the Ministry of Information that Hess had arrived and was now under arrest.

'Their thinking, sir?' This from Tar Robertson.

'They want to wrongfoot Goebbels. They want to keep the Germans guessing.'

'And longer term?'

'They'll do what the Germans have done. They'll say he's mad.'

There was an exchange of glances around the table. Nobody in this room had actually met Hess so the allegation was totally unproven.

Moncrieff cleared his throat. He wanted to know whether, in his dealings with Downing Street, the Director had caught wind of a letter Hess might have brought with him.

'What kind of letter?'

Moncrieff explained briefly about the item that had mysteriously disappeared from Hess's belongings, and about the ashes he'd found in Wojcek's grate.

'This is the house the Glasgow police searched?' The Director was smiling.

'Indeed, sir.'

'A very shrewd move, Tam. Our friends in Broadway regard it as a declaration of war.'

'But the letter, sir?'

'No one's mentioned it. Not in my hearing. What might it contain?'

Moncrieff glanced across at Ursula. Clearly she'd yet to brief Liddell.

'It might have been peace proposals, sir,' Moncrieff explained. 'Developed in some detail and properly authorised.'

'By whom?'

'Hitler.'

'You're serious?'

'I am, sir. But sadly we're unlikely to ever know.'

'That would be unfortunate. In the extreme.'

'I agree.' Moncrieff paused. 'Do you think they're even aware of this letter? In Downing Street?'

'I've no idea, Tam. Conceivably not. The PM would give it very short shrift indeed. In fact, he'd erupt if he thought that was the basis for the visit. No one talks to the Germans about peace. Not while he's Prime Minister.'

'No, sir. Unless the plan was to get rid of him.'

Liddell nodded but said nothing. This was old ground, Moncrieff's conviction that MI6 were up to their collective necks in the Hess conspiracy, but so far Moncrieff had been proved right.

There was a moment of absolute silence. Then Ursula came up with a suggestion.

'Maybe Tam should talk to his old friend Schultz again,' she said. 'If this document exists, I'm sure he can get hold of a copy.'

Liddell nodded. In principle, he said, he had no objection. How would Tam manage the mechanics of such an exchange?

'Easy, sir. I'd talk to Sir Harold Wernher. He's the Chairman of Electrolux and reports to Birger Dahlerus in Sweden. He lives out at Luton Hoo. He has a reliable contact with Schultz through Dahlerus in Stockholm. That's where we met last time, back in November.' He hesitated a moment, uncertain about Liddell's memory. 'You might remember, sir. You marched me to the Foreign Office on my return.'

A frown briefly clouded Liddell's face. Then he nodded.

'You're happy to talk to Wernher by phone?'

'I'd prefer face-to-face, sir. And I'm sure he would, too.'

'Then make it happen, Tam,' a thin smile. 'And sharpish, eh?'

Luton Hoo lay beyond St Albans, thirty-three miles north of London. On the phone, Moncrieff had established that Sir Harold was in residence and would be happy to spare half an hour of his time. Ursula laid hands on a Super Snipe from the Home Office car pool and insisted on a driver who was happy to put his foot down. Early afternoon, the big saloon was nosing up Wernher's drive.

The estate, Moncrieff already knew, was a cherished slice of English country life. The house itself had been designed by

Robert Adam, the grounds by Capability Brown. The sheer scale of the place was breathtaking yet it had retained a style and a colonnaded grace that told Moncrieff everything he needed to know about the England the peace lobby were determined to protect.

It was a beautiful day. Moncrieff checked to make sure he had the letter for Schultz and then eased his long frame from the passenger seat and stood in the sunshine, gazing at the ornamental gardens. A pair of ducks were canoodling on the circular pond and beyond a row of trees Moncrieff could hear the growl of tank engines. According to Ursula, the Wernher family had allowed the Army to establish the headquarters of Eastern Command here, though Sir Harold retained the use of a suite of rooms.

A busy woman in a black skirt and white blouse met Moncrieff beneath the entrance to the house. A beautiful staircase, carpeted in the deepest red, swept them both up to the first floor. The woman paused on the landing beside a portrait of a bearded figure in full dress uniform.

'Nicholas II,' she said. 'The last Czar of Russia. Lady Anastasia's uncle.'

Lady Anastasia? Moncrieff assumed this must be Wernher's wife but didn't like to ask. The woman marched on. Sir Harold, she said, normally worked in one of the big rooms overlooking the pond but this was currently in the hands of the decorators. Sir Harold had therefore been banished to a little shoebox of a cupboard that wasn't the least bit to his taste. The move had left him out of sorts, but Moncrieff wasn't to take it personally.

Expecting to find the next half-hour slow-going, Moncrieff was surprised to find himself in a beautifully proportioned space that must once have been a bedroom. There were flowers everywhere, and the deep-pile carpet was striped with sunshine through the tall windows.

Sir Harold Wernher was a tall man, balding, with a long face and impeccable manners. He wore a suit and a tie, despite the warmth of the weather, and his brogues, when he rose from behind the desk, were highly polished. His handshake was firm. He thought he'd met Moncrieff before.

'I think not, sir. I'd remember.'

'Royal Marines? Am I right?'

For a moment, Moncrieff was nonplussed. Then Wernher roared with laughter.

'Just testing, young man. I get many visitors, more than you might think. I always pretend I've met them before. The weak-willed say yes because they don't want to offend me. You avoided that temptation. If you're wondering how I know about the Marines, I have to confess it came from that nice young lady of yours. Miss Barton? Hint of a German accent? I took the precaution of making a call. Unforgiveable, I know, but these days you can't be too careful. Now then. How can I help you?'

Moncrieff was still thinking about the last Czar. The Establishment was laced with royal bloodlines, and here was the living proof. No wonder Sir Harold had an interest in a timely peace settlement.

'Back in November I made a trip to Stockholm,' Moncrieff began. 'And I met with an *Abwehr* man, Wilhelm Schultz. He happens to be a friend of mine but that's another story.'

'You want to meet him again?'

'I do. But first I have something I need him to read.' Moncrieff extracted the envelope from his jacket pocket and laid it carefully on the desk. Shultz's name was on the front.

Wernher looked at the envelope but didn't pick it up.

'May I enquire why you're going to these lengths?'

'I'm afraid not.'

'Even if I ask nicely?'

'Especially if you ask nicely. We spies get trained in the arts of subversion. Charm butters no parsnips.'

Wernher beamed his approval. He was tempted, he said, to write the phrase down. *Charm butters no parsnips.* How wrong could a man be.

He steepled his fingers and sank a little deeper in his chair. Moncrieff had the feeling he was being inspected.

'Tell me something, young man. Do you mind awfully? Off the record? Strictly *entre nous*?'

'That depends, sir.'

'On what, pray?'

'On what you want to know.'

'Very sensible. Very prudent. My question is this.' He gestured vaguely towards the window. 'Out there, where the land rises and the going gets tough, there are boffins putting the new tanks through their paces. They're at it day and night. We hate it, the pheasants hate it, even the poor bloody foxes are probably stone deaf as a result. But in the end I'm assured it's going to be worth it. Why? Because that's what Winston wants. This war, young man, has become an act of faith. We've become a nation of believers. And that's because, for once in our history, we're obliged to look evil in the face. Many of my friends, people I deeply respect, are bankers. They're also Jews who have had the foresight to make a home on this side of the water. Naturally, they want to protect their wealth. And happily they're still able to do that. So my question is this. Birger Dahlerus, bless him, is an apostle for peace. But what kind of peace can you negotiate with the Nazis?'

Moncrieff held his gaze. Before he lifted the phone, Sir Harold wanted to check his bearings. Very sensible, and under the circumstances, rather heartening.

'None,' Moncrieff said. 'Even if there was a peace to be had.'

'A peace to be had. My point exactly. Deeply gratifying, if I may say so, and something that appears to be entirely lost on another family I could name. The Romanovs left a terrible legacy. No one disputes that for a moment. But the future of royal blood lies with Churchill, not Hitler, and our monarchy would be a great deal wiser if they understood that small truth.' He put Moncrieff's letter to one side. Then he got to his feet and extended a hand once again. 'My pleasure, young man. Leave Herr Schultz to me but remember one thing. If you sup with the devil...' he offered a cold smile, 'use a very long spoon.'

Moncrieff was back in London by late afternoon. In Scotland, according to the Director, Hess was still talking to Ivone Kirkpatrick and the Duke of Hamilton though no one else was privy to these interviews. In due course, he said, Hess would be brought south once arrangements had been made to keep him somewhere secure. MI6 were looking for premises in Surrey but in the meantime a suite of rooms was being readied in the Tower of London. Hess, Churchill had ordered, was henceforth to be treated as a prisoner of the state.

The Tower of London? Moncrieff slipped behind his desk. Quaint, he thought grimly. Rudolf Hess spending his days in the company of Beefeaters, a colony of ravens and centuries of history he seemed determined to protect. He sat back for a moment, staring at the window. Wernher, only hours ago, had hinted at royal fingers in the Deputy Führer's pie. What, exactly, had he meant? And how far did this complicity extend?

His phone began to ring, the dedicated line only a handful of agents were authorised to use. Moncrieff picked it up. It was Hesketh. Agent Souk.

'*Grüsse aus dem sonnigen Lissabon.*' Greetings from sunny Lisbon. 'Is our friend in good order? Everything working the way it should?'

'Our friend is fine. Apart from his ankle, he's in rude health. A flesh wound, we think. Nothing serious.'

'Have you made his acquaintance yet? Talked to him? Berlin thinks he's slipped his moorings, gone mad. Next they'll discover he's got syphilis. You know something about this little episode? I rather fancy Goebbels is losing his touch. Round one to Rudi. What's your feeling?'

'It's early days,' Moncrieff grunted. 'You've heard from Albrecht?'

'Alas, no. I imagine Albrecht will be behind bars by now, pleading for his life. Berlin can be unforgiving. Had things gone to plan, the war with the English should be over. You can accuse Hess of lots of things. Albrecht always said he talked too much. But the man's timing, you have to admit, is impeccable. Belgrade levelled? Greece occupied? Crete waiting to be invaded? Us Brits on the run in North Africa?

This is more than bad luck, my friend, and the whole world knows it.'

'Apart from Churchill.'

'Indeed. A man in love with history. One day he'll be writing it so he has no interest in defeat. I bring glad tidings, by the way, from a very good friend of yours.'

'Who?'

'Do you want clues? Or just a name? She's currently in a hotel just down the street from where I am now. The manager happens to be a good friend of mine. He keeps Krug from the German Embassy in his personal kitchen and this afternoon, I'm glad to say, he presented us with no less than two bottles.'

'Us?'

'Me and your lady friend. These days it takes a lot to keep an old man amused but she has limitless talents. And that was before we started on the Krug. Hurry on down, Tam. I get the impression she's missing you.'

The line went dead. Moncrieff frowned. Then the phone began to ring again. Hesketh, he thought. With more drivel from sunny Lisbon.

'You're still there?'

'I am...' a woman's voice, '... and it's lovely. Why were we so keen on Seville when we could have been fantasising about this place instead?'

Moncrieff was staring at the receiver. He hadn't heard this throaty laugh for nearly three years, but he knew exactly who it was. The same intonation. The same hints of self-mockery. Not Souk's drivel at all but Isabel Menzies. For once in his life, Moncrieff was speechless. When they were in Berlin, Seville had been code for a future together. It had never happened but here she was again, Bella Menzies, still with the word Seville on her lips.

'You're in Lisbon?'

'Yes.'

'Why?'

'It's a long story. We need to meet. Tell me you'll come.'

'When?'

'As soon as you can.'

'That could be difficult. More than difficult.'

'So I gather.'

'You know about our visitor?'

'Of course. Churchill's best-kept secret. Isn't that the line?' She laughed again, and Moncrieff had a sudden image of the pair of them, Bella and Souk, together in some hotel room, toasting the Deputy Führer in looted French champagne. The thought made him feel deeply uncomfortable but he'd no idea why.

Bella hadn't finished.

'A big fat plum falls into your lap...' she said, '... and no one has a clue what to do with the wretched man. Am I getting warm here?'

'You might be.'

'Then come down. Take the flying boat. It can't be worse than Air Hitler. The Alps were invented to frighten people like me. At least my bit of Russia's flat. No mountains.'

'You flew in from Moscow?'

'Via Berlin. Our German allies can be very accommodating but flying's still flying and I hate it.'

'And Moscow?'

'Moscow is a state of mind. Just now the snow's gone but nothing seems to get any warmer.'

'Why might that be?' Moncrieff enquired.

'I've got a shrewd idea but in our game you need to be certain. Maybe Hess knows. He's a special kind of German. He doesn't like us much but he seems to have some regard for the truth. This pact of ours was always a marriage of convenience but at least we're not killing each other. Not yet.'

A marriage of convenience. Was this why she'd taken her courage in both hands and flown to Lisbon? Was this why she'd phoned? Everyone knew that Hitler would one day turn on the Russians. That was a given. That was what he'd been telling the rest of the world for years. But a date would be useful. Especially if there was some prospect of the English suing for peace.

Bella wanted to know whether Moncrieff had talked to Hess personally.

'No.'

'Will you?'

'I've no idea. It's possible, I suppose.'

'You could talk to him in German. Make friends with the man. I gather he expected to be home by Monday. Which must be something of a disappointment.'

'Is that what they're saying in Berlin?'

'It is. He flies. He lands. He talks. He tells the King to get rid of Churchill. And then it's Monday morning and he's off again. Porridge and kippers in Scotland. Wife and baby waiting in Munich. Sweet.'

Moncrieff smiled. He could hear the old Bella, the Bella who'd cut a swath through the diplomatic parties along the

Wilhelmstrasse, the Bella who'd made a name for herself in the higher reaches of the Nazi dung heap. She'd quietly attended to MI5 business from her desk in the British Embassy and no one had realised, least of all Moncrieff, that in the smallest hours she'd been reporting to her masters in Moscow. A woman with a true centre to her life, he thought. No matter how misguided.

'Do you ever miss it?' he asked. 'England?'

'Not at all. Most Russians I know live on porridge oats, and they do smoky things to fish from the Baltic. Shut your eyes and it could be a cold day in Arbroath. Does that help at all? Only I'd hate you to be sorry for me.'

'I'm not sorry. I was never sorry. Just confused.'

'That you hadn't spotted it? My little passion? Hadn't drawn the obvious conclusion?'

'Yes.'

'And the other thing?'

'What other thing?'

'Us?'

'We were good. Or I always thought so. We laughed a lot. That mattered.'

'So why did you go? Why did you leave?'

'They threw me out. You might have remembered.'

'That's not what I meant. Why did you leave *me*? Why no letters? Why no attempt to stay in touch? We weren't at war, not then. The phones still worked. Air mail was still getting through. Just a word would have been nice. Just the knowledge that it had really happened and I didn't make the whole fucking thing up. Leading a double life isn't quite as simple as it might sound. Even women have needs.'

Moncrieff nodded. Everything she said was true. Under different circumstances they'd have made that trip to Seville. And probably stayed.

'You sound hurt,' he said at last.

'I was.'

'And now?'

'Now's different. Don't ask me for the details because that's another conversation. Something important in your life, you take care of it. I thought I'd done that. I honestly did.'

'You mean Communism? The cause?'

'I mean you. There were certain things I'd never said to anyone. But you were there. You were listening. And yet you still went. I couldn't work that out. I tried for days, weeks. I got ill. That's pathetic. That's a confession. But here's the truth. After something like that you get tougher. God has a role for heartbreak. It's not very pretty and I'm not sure it turns you into a nicer person, but it's a bit of a lifeline and I was grateful for that. So I'm different now, if that's your question, and, no, there's nothing I miss about bloody England.'

'You want to see me again?'

'I'd love to see you again. I'd love to take you to bed and fuck you witless and I probably will. But the woman you wake up with won't be the woman you left in the middle of the night. You remember that? After I picked you up from our Gestapo friends? You had to get to the airport for the morning flight. Otherwise they'd lock you up again. I had that planned. I had it all worked out. There was a bed upstairs in that flat of mine, our bed, the bed where we'd say a proper goodbye, and maybe make a plan or two to meet later, neutral territory, any bloody place as long as we were both there, and yet you wouldn't even step foot inside the building. I offered to drive you out to Tempelhof but even that didn't work. You said you wanted to walk. You said you needed to be alone. A girl understands language like that. It meant all bets were off. It meant I'd failed completely. Alone is the perfect description. And I've been alone ever since. Did it hurt then? Yes. Does it hurt now? No. I'm lying in bed with a phone to my ear. I don't know whether you want to make the effort to imagine any of this, but I haven't got very much on and it's very hot outside and there's still a bottle of Krug in the fridge and your eager little friend knows where to lay hands on a great deal more. So take the flying boat, Mr Moncrieff, and let's talk a little more...' she laughed, '... while there's still time.'

15

The following day, Wednesday 14 May, German radio made another announcement about the ex-Deputy Führer. By now, it was known that Hess was in Scotland, a prisoner of the British. He had grounds, in the words of Goebbels' Ministry of Propaganda, for believing that the Duke of Hamilton and a group of his friends were opposed to the warmonger Winston Churchill and were determined to get rid of him. Hence his flight across the North Sea. His intention? Perhaps a little less crazed than it might have seemed: to bring the British to their senses.

This bombshell exploded in Whitehall in mid-morning and prompted a tart response from the Ministry of Information. Churchill wanted to make a lengthy statement to the Commons but once again he was dissuaded. Instead, word was quietly passed that the German broadcast was pure mischief, a barefaced lie trying to spare German blushes. They'd lost one of the top figures in the Reich, and they were trying to make the best of it. At MI5 headquarters in St James's Street, the Director of 'B' Section had drawn the appropriate conclusions.

'Downing Street are going to bluff it out,' Liddell said. 'They're going to put Hess on the shelf, keep him safe, and not say a word. That way they keep everyone guessing. The

Germans. The Russians. Even MI6. It's ruthless, of course, but you wouldn't expect anything else. Churchill is the key to everything. He was never good at spotting plots, but I suspect it's dawned on him just how dangerous the situation might have become. It was Churchill's good luck that Hess ran out of fuel. Otherwise anything might have happened. The PM has to emerge from this thing intact. That, gentlemen, will dictate the passage of events from this day forth.'

Heads nodded around Liddell's office. The Director asked Moncrieff whether he had any news from Wilhelm Schultz. Moncrieff shook his head.

'These things take time, sir,' he said. 'You'll be the first to know.'

The meeting over, Ursula beckoned him into her office and asked him to close the door. She'd been quietly keeping her eye on the People's Convention, the Communist group that had so briefly helped themselves to the comforts of the Savoy's air raid shelter. There was to be a meeting in an East End pub this very evening and she wondered whether Tam might pop along.

'Harry Pollitt will be there. And Willie Gallagher and maybe that MP, Denis Pritt. All the usual suspects.'

'And Pat Doherty?'

'Him, too. And maybe even our little princess.'

Our little princess was new. Moncrieff wondered whether the appellation was Ursula's or had come from someone else. Miss Cathy Phelps. *Our little princess.* Deeply fitting.

'You think it's worth a visit?'

'I think it's time we cocked a listening ear. She works at the Palace. Places like that are full of gossip. The royals always assume that the staff are deaf and blind, that they lack the intelligence or the interest to take much notice of what's really going on. They also believe in a degree of loyalty that might be misplaced. Are we getting my drift here? Or should I spell it out?'

'You want me to talk to her about the Hess thing.' Moncrieff's voice was flat. In truth, he had no appetite for another meeting.

'The Hess thing. Exactly. These last couple of days I've had two conversations which suggest some kind of royal welcome might have been prepared for our German friend.'

'In Scotland, you mean?'

'Yes.'

'At Dungavel House?'

'There or thereabouts.'

'Care to give me a name?'

'I'm afraid I can't. And that's rather the point. Our little princess struck me as very acute. Judging by the company she keeps, she's also no friend of the royals. A conversation would be more than welcome. It might even yield a name.' She offered Moncrieff the ghost of a smile. 'It was your idea to leave her in place. Do I hear a yes?'

The pub was called the Roaring Donkey and lay in a maze of streets between the Whitechapel Road and the river. No German bombers had appeared over the capital since Saturday night, but the smell of ashes and ruptured drains still hung in the air. It was impossible to round a corner, Moncrieff quickly concluded, without confronting more rubble heaps, more shards of glass swept into tidy piles, more front walls ripped off to reveal – with a terrible intimacy – the domestic lives within.

Just yards from the pub, people were still pausing to inspect an upstairs bedroom, complete with pink wallpaper, sagging floorboards and a rather handsome brass-knobbed bedstead exposed to the chill night air. Someone had hand-lettered a rectangle of cardboard and hung it on the end of the bed. *Bombed-out twice,* it read. *Third time lucky?*

The pub – imperfectly blacked out – was cavernous, packed with drinkers, both men and women. Sturdy wooden crates, probably filched from the nearby docks, had been pushed together at one end to form a makeshift stage, and a rather tattered red flag had been fixed to the wall behind. With some difficulty Moncrieff found himself a chair at the back of the crowd, all too aware of his height. Should Cathy turn up, he wanted – for the time being – to remain unseen.

She arrived barely minutes later, Doherty with her. Moncrieff watched them as they elbowed their way through the crowd, drawing handshakes and pats on the back. They were well known here, welcomed, admired, but the sight of his father's red beret, on Cathy this time, angered Moncrieff deeply. Since Ursula had shown him the surveillance photos he'd made a sort of peace with the way she'd betrayed him, blaming himself for ever believing she'd be genuinely interested in a man his age, but the beret was something different. It was tangible. It had meant a great deal to his poor mad father, even in his twilight years. And yet, in cold blood, she'd stolen it. In the land of Karl Marx he was aware that all property might be theft but this was larceny on an altogether more intimate scale. She'd known exactly what she was doing. And now he'd make her pay for it.

The meeting was in some danger of making a start. A man in a worn black suit clambered onto the stage and called the room to order. The collar of his open shirt was frayed and a blow of some sort had half-closed one eye but his voice carried to the far corners of the huge bar and he had an air of command that stilled the hubbub.

He'd arranged the evening, he said, to push the People's Convention a little closer to where it deserved to be. He, along with a number of other speakers, was here to make the case for the Peoples' War and the People's Peace. Too many men and too many women had already died in battle, or under the bombs, to preserve the rights and privileges of the rich. Society, he roared, was totally out of kilter but thanks to Mr Hitler, in one of history's great ironies, an opportunity was on hand to correct that balance. The day of reckoning, of righting old wrongs, was fast approaching. And no one in the ranks of the so-called mighty could stop it.

The pub erupted in applause. The floor was suddenly wet with spilled beer. Moncrieff was still looking at Cathy. Tiny amid the press of bodies, she was clinging onto Doherty, her eyes ablaze.

Another speaker mounted the stage and added more fuel to the fire. Earlier, making his way to the pub, Moncrieff had wondered quite how this bunch of Communists had adapted themselves to the Non-Aggression Pact that Ribbentrop had so artfully schemed in Moscow. How come you could live with the knowledge that Fascism had just become your very best friend?

This puzzle had preoccupied far bigger brains than his, but watching the evening unfold, Moncrieff realised that none of it really mattered. Ribbentrop's pact was simply the small print of history, a deceit the Nazis had fathered to keep the Soviets off their backs while they attended to enemies rather closer to home, and very soon would come the moment when Hitler turned his armies around and marched them east.

The evening's final speaker was Doherty. He bounded onto the stage and left the pub in no doubt where the people's revolution was heading next.

'War is a confidence trick,' he yelled. 'Germany, Britain, France, they all spill our blood for their gain. Capitalism is a conspiracy against the people. Just take a look down the street. Just ask yourself who does the dying. This will be the war to end all wars. Why? Because at last we've seen through all the lies, all the propaganda. And you know what? Up there, up river, they're shitting in their pants. Because they know their time has come. Remember Robespierre. Remember Danton. *On les aura!*'

Another roar of applause. *We'll have them!* Minutes later, the meeting over, the crowd pushed towards the bar for more beer. Doherty had been mobbed by the people around him, mainly women. They wanted to touch him, to put their arms round him, to give him a kiss, to tell him what a hero he was, to marvel at his passion, and the way he could exactly voice what they all thought, all believed. Moncrieff's gaze found Cathy, the little princess, and he knew she'd seen this wild adulation too, probably dozens of times. She was much closer now, carried towards the door by the swirl of the crowd. And as he watched she turned and caught his eye.

'You,' she mouthed. 'What are you doing here?'

Moncrieff fought his way towards her and grabbed her by the hand. Moments later, they were out on the street. She fought free. She wanted to know what on earth he was doing.

'We need to talk,' he said.

Another pub, close by, Cathy's choice. Moncrieff didn't even know what it was called. The bombing had removed the sign that had once hung over the main door and most of the windows had been boarded up. They slipped inside. Candlelight revealed half a dozen drinkers, bent sorrowfully over near-empty glasses. Cathy led the way to the bar. Moncrieff sensed she wanted to be friends.

'You can have light ale or light ale,' she said. 'They haven't got many glasses, either.'

Moncrieff bought two bottles and they retired to a table at the back.

'You've been here before?'

'Yes. It used to be a proper pub. Once.'

'You were here with Doherty?'

'Yes. That man was probably born in a pub. The drink doesn't touch him.' She reached for her bottle and twisted the stopper. 'You know his Christian name as well?'

'Patrick. I'm guessing Pat for short.'

'Guessing?' She smiled at him in the half-darkness. 'You people never guess. Pat's right. You people *know*.'

'You think I'm one of them? The class enemy? Tam Moncrieff? Laird of all he surveys?'

She ducked her head, took a long pull at the bottle, wiped her mouth with the back of her hand. She might have been a man, he thought. Except she was still very pretty.

'I loved that place of yours,' she said. 'I truly did. It spoke to me. You know that feeling? You can be alone but you're not alone? There were spirits there. On windy nights I'd talk to them. It never frightened me, not for a moment. Odd. The place was always freezing but I'd never felt so warm, so *loved*.'

'Is that why you stole the beret?'

She studied him a moment over the bottle, then took the beret off and laid it carefully on the table.

'It's yours,' she shook her curls out, ran her fingers through her hair. 'Take it.'

'Tell me about Doherty.'

'There's nothing to tell. We met at Balmoral. After a while they got rid of him. All the time I was with you, I never heard a word, not a peep. Then he turned up one night and we were together again.'

'Was that when you decided to come to London?'

'Yes.'

'Because of Doherty?'

'Yes. I made contact with Jack Riordan. He got me the job at Buckingham Palace.'

'So why didn't you tell me? Why pretend?'

She frowned, took her time to answer.

'I didn't want to hurt you,' she said at last.

'I don't believe you.'

'It's true. We were good together. You're a lovely man. It seemed such a shame to wreck all that so I thought I'd just turn the gas down, let things cool off, and fingers crossed we'd end up friends.'

'You could have simply told me. That might have been kinder.'

'I wasn't brave enough for that. I'm sorry.' She ducked her head. She seemed to be crying. Moncrieff wanted to reach out for her but knew it was pointless. Every relationship got one chance to work. And this one hadn't.

'You're still at the Palace? BP?'

305

'Of course.' Her head came up. Her eyes were shiny.

'And you're still organising all those trips?'

'Helping, yes.'

'A German arrived at the weekend. Up in Scotland. You might have heard.'

'Hess,' she said tonelessly. 'Rudolf Hess.'

'You know about him?'

'Yes.'

'How?'

'It's been in the papers, on the radio. People like me take an interest, believe it or not. He was Hitler's deputy. Isn't that right?'

'Yes. So what's the word at BP? About our new friend?'

'I'm not sure I understand. What do you mean?'

'I'm talking about the royals, the people who employ you. Do they talk about him? Have you heard any...' he shrugged, '... gossip? I understand the footmen are there at every meal. They'd listen. They'd know.'

She stared at him. She wasn't tearful any more.

'I've heard nothing,' she said at last. 'But that's not the point, is it. That's not what this is about. You want me to make some enquiries?'

'That would be very helpful. The details are important. We need to know if anyone was planning to meet him.'

'Hess, you mean? In Scotland? When he arrived?'

'Yes.'

'You think that's possible? You think that might have happened?'

'Yes. But the royals are obviously the ones in the swim. And just now I can think of no better way of finding out.'

'And if I say no?'

'Your job will come to an abrupt end. I can also have you arrested.'

'On what grounds?'

'That doesn't matter. You don't need grounds any more. Suspicion is enough, believe me.'

'And you'd do that?'

'I would, yes.'

Cathy nodded. Then she studied her hands, twisting a ring on her little finger that Moncrieff hadn't seen before.

'You want to turn me into a spy,' she said at last.

'You're right.' Moncrieff got to his feet. He hadn't touched his beer. 'Just think of it as an episode in the class war.' He reached down for his father's beret. 'And if that doesn't work, pretend you owe me a favour or two.'

It was nearly midnight when Wilhelm Schultz received the summons to the Air Ministry. He'd left his desk barely an hour before and was enjoying a plate of *Wildschwein* at a discreet restaurant off the Wilhelmstrasse that served as an all-hours canteen for intelligence officers from *Abwehr* headquarters. The waiter with the telephone knew him well.

'For you, Herr Schultz. It's *der Eiserne*'s adjutant.'

The Iron Man? What could Goering want?

Schultz wiped his mouth and bent to the phone. The *Reichsmarschall* apologised for the lateness of the hour but would appreciate a little of Schultz's time. A car was waiting outside the restaurant.

Schultz eyed his unfinished supper and helped himself to a little more gravy.

'Give me ten minutes,' he growled.

The lights were burning late at the Air Ministry. Goering's adjutant escorted Schultz past the guards inside the big main door and up the main staircase to the first floor. Uniformed officers were everywhere, hurrying from office to office, laden with files. The *Reichsmarschall*'s new suite occupied one corner of the building. Schultz hadn't been here before and the moment he stepped in he knew that Goering had stolen a march on his fellow chieftains. The room was enormous. Even Ribbentrop couldn't match this.

'Schultz'.

Goering waved his visitor into the chair that had been set in front of the desk. A soft light from the single lamp pooled on an untidy pile of papers. A box of cigars lay beside them. Goering told Schultz to help himself.

Schultz nodded his thanks and gestured towards the door. What was so important it kept so many men from their beds?

'Crete.' Goering, for once, looked weary. 'The Führer has designs on the bloody island. The *Kriegsmarine* aren't up to it. The wrong ships in the wrong place. So I have to find twenty thousand paratroopers and God knows how many aircraft to fly them there. If this was a training exercise I'd have a month or so to make the arrangements. He wants the island by next Tuesday.'

'So when did you get the word?'

'This morning. The man's all appetite. In principle I have no objection to gluttony but preparing a meal like that isn't simple. Sometimes I wonder whether the people round that man shouldn't answer back. Just a little more notice might have been kind.'

'You think there are limits? You think we're pushing too fast? Too hard?'

Goering gazed at him a moment. Then he roared with laughter.

'*Think*, Schultz? Since when did anyone have an opinion round here? Listen, my friend. You're right. We bite off far too much. We risk indigestion. We fart a lot and stink Europe out. But that's the beauty of the game. It works. The Reich gets fatter by the day. And so far that's all that matters. We take our chances, Schultz. But no one in his right mind should ever rely on luck. This request of yours...' he extracted a message from the pile of papers '... you're telling me it came from our friend Birger?'

'Dahlerus, yes.'

'And thus the English?'

'Yes.'

'This is about Hess. Am I right?'

'Yes.'

'So what, precisely, do they want?'

Schultz at last reached for a cigar. He said that the request had come from an English intelligence officer, Tam Moncrieff.

'I know Moncrieff. You were kind enough to bring him to meet me at Nuremberg. We punished a bottle or two of that shit Spanish brandy. Tall man. Needs to laugh more.'

Schultz nodded. According to Moncrieff, Hess had arrived with a letter. No one knew what was in the letter because it had disappeared. Moncrieff had grounds for thinking that it had been destroyed.

'By whom?'

'He didn't say.' Schultz paused, fingering the unlit cigar. '*Was* there a letter, *Herr Reichsmarschall*?'

'Of course there was a letter. That's why he went. Rudi Hess. The Reich's favourite postman.'

'And what was in it? What did it say?'

There was a long silence. Schultz worked for Army Intelligence. He was highly placed. He had the ear of Admiral Canaris. He knew that powerful figures here in Berlin wanted to bring the *Abwehr* to its knees. But he also knew that Goering wasn't one of them.

'Hess was carrying a peace treaty,' he said at length. 'On Chancellery notepaper.'

'It came from the Führer?' Schultz was astonished.

'Not personally, no. Even he's not that reckless. It carried another signature. But it had our Leader's backing and Hess knows that.'

Schultz sat back a moment. Goering passed him a lighter. Schultz lit the cigar, inhaled, tipped his head back, expelled a perfect smoke ring.

'This was a treaty?' he asked. 'Or proposals?'

'Proposals. Detailed proposals. A treaty in all but name.'

'And might the British buy it?'

'Some of them, undoubtedly.'

'But not Churchill?'

'Churchill won't buy anything. He won't even read a letter with a Berlin postmark. If you want to see the Führer eating the carpet just mention Churchill's name. Hitler loathes the bloody man. He wants him gone.'

'Hence the letter?'

'Of course. And hence Hess. No one expected him to arrive

on the end of a parachute, least of all Rudi, but this is war, my friend, and sillier things happen.' Goering hadn't taken his eyes off Schultz. 'I assume Moncrieff wants a copy of the letter?'

'That would be your decision, *Herr Reichsmarschall.*'

'And you'd play the postman? Be Rudi?'

'Of course. I can contact Moncrieff through Dahlerus. I'd hand the thing over personally. If that's what you all want.'

Goering nodded, then he struggled to his feet. The meeting was evidently over. He said he'd need to make a call or two and if things went well then Schultz should expect to be summoned again.

'To pick up a copy of the letter?'

'*Ja.* The envelope will be sealed, Schultz. If you open it, my friend, I'll have you shot.'

Schultz nodded. When Goering was joking he had a twinkle in his eye. No twinkle. He studied Schultz for a moment or two, and then his gaze settled on the pile of paper.

'Crete?' he murmured. 'By Tuesday? When we have so much else to get done?' He shook his head. 'Madness.'

16

At the end of the week, Rudolf Hess was removed from Buchanan Castle and taken by train to London. There, he was lodged in officers' quarters in the Tower of London, pending a transfer to secure accommodation in preparation elsewhere. Between them, the Duke of Hamilton and Ivone Kirkpatrick had conducted three lengthy interviews with the Deputy Führer and a detailed account was delivered by hand to Downing Street to await the Prime Minister's perusal.

That night Liddell summoned a meeting in the MI5 safe house in Mayfair. Moncrieff had been here before. It was tucked away in the maze of streets around Grosvenor Square, a top-floor perch in a brick-built block of apartments. He attended with Ursula Barton. The gates to the lift were secured with a chain and padlock and so they climbed the six flights of steps from the street. Ursula had a key to the flat. She knocked twice, and then a third time before opening the door. Liddell was waiting in the living room. He had a decanter of sherry in one hand and a glass in the other.

'Perfect timing,' he murmured. 'Sorry about the lift. The wretched thing's broken again. It happens to be a German design, but I don't think they meant it.'

They all sat down. Liddell, it seemed, had just arrived from Downing Street. He'd spent an uncomfortable twenty minutes with the Prime Minister but had emerged, he thought, with some good news.

Ursula wanted to know whether this was about Hess.

'It is. I've been pushing for access to our distinguished visitor but so far to absolutely no effect. Menzies has got him locked away. As well he might.'

'So what's changed, sir?' Ursula again.

'The PM's read the account of the interviews and he's not entirely convinced.'

'Of what?'

'That he's getting the whole truth. He suspects Hess may be withholding something.'

'Hess?' Moncrieff this time. 'Or MI6?'

'That's a nice distinction, Tam, if I may say so. And it goes to the heart of the matter. The PM wants a second opinion. Ideally from someone who speaks German.'

'Kirkpatrick speaks German. He was in Berlin for years.'

'Indeed. And the PM's casting no aspersions. He regards Kirkpatrick as sound. That's why he sent him up there.'

'So what can anyone else bring to the feast?'

'We've no idea, and neither does the PM. Call it an insurance policy. Call it whatever you will. The truth, I suspect, is that the PM and probably the people at the Foreign Office are smelling a rat.'

Moncrieff nodded and then exchanged glances with Ursula.

'Did the PM mention any letter, at all? Something Hess might have brought with him?'

'No.'

'Did you mention it, sir?'

'No.' He reached for the decanter and then paused to glance across at Moncrieff. 'You're expected at the Tower at ten o'clock tomorrow morning, by which time I gather Herr Hess will have had his breakfast. You should be aware that MI6 have a presence at the Tower. They may not be pleased to see you.'

The expedition to the casino at Estoril was Hesketh's idea. After a long winter in Moscow, he suggested, Isabel Menzies deserved a therapeutic peek at the fleshpots of capitalism. With luck, it might revive her appetite for a little recreational wickedness. At the very worst, she might lose an escudo or two.

'This is a regular treat? Are you a betting man?'

'Emphatically not. Life's a gamble as it is. Why lengthen the odds any further?'

They were sitting at a restaurant table overlooking the gaggle of players around the roulette wheel. A sleek woman with an American accent had just won a sizeable pile of chips on 19. An older man beside her was trying to persuade her to cash in. Hesketh pointed the couple out.

'She flew in a couple of days ago,' he said. 'She talks about Hollywood a lot. The locals assume she's some kind of film star but that's because they're too lazy to look any harder.'

'And him?'

'He's her pimp. She sleeps with a variety of clients and he rakes in the proceeds.'

'We're talking lots of money?'

'We're talking information. In this neck of the woods the two things are indivisible. The right information can earn you a fortune if you know where to place it.'

'You'd know that?'

'I would.'

'So does that make you rich?'

'Only in the smallness of my wants.'

Hesketh smiled at her. He loved occasions like these, a new face in town, a fresh opportunity to cast his net, and give it a shake, and see what wriggled out. She Isobel had already impressed him. She was obviously bright, and she seemed undaunted by any challenge, but her days of falling under the Soviet spell were clearly over. She carried a hint of weariness, of faint but perceptible disillusion, and most promising of all was the fact that she didn't bother to hide it. Hesketh had met people like her before. And they always surprised you, especially in bed.

'Can good looks be a handicap in Moscow?' he was still watching the woman at the roulette table. 'Be honest.'

'Good looks can be a handicap anywhere. As it happens, Moscow is full of beautiful women. Russian men don't know how lucky they are.'

'But you, my dear. Tell me about you.'

'There's nothing to tell. I fell in love with a crazy man who thought he'd found God. I was nineteen years old. He was twenty. God lived in Moscow. God knew exactly what was wrong with the rest of the world and was taking steps to put it right. My crazy young man went to Spain to give God a hand. And that's where he died.'

'Fighting the Fascists?'

315

'Of course. In the end they put him against a wall and shot him. He died in the light of car headlamps on a bomb site in Madrid. Later I met someone who'd been there. He visited the place where they took all the bodies the next day. He might even have died happy. I've no idea.'

'And you?'

'I was heartbroken. As a girl should be.'

'And went into mourning? Widow's weeds? An anguished verse or two?'

'I joined the Party. It might be the same thing.'

'And did it work?'

'Oddly enough, it did. For a while. Being a spy can be quite exciting. You pass on all kinds of information. You've no idea what's happening at the other end, whether they even believe you or not, but you tell yourself you're making a difference. That's in the short term. That's when you're fresh to the job. Later you realise that Communism is just another cul-de-sac and you end up trying to manage your own schizophrenia. That can be exhausting.' She smiled. 'But then you'd know that.'

'You think I'm a spy?'

'I think you're a rogue. And you make me laugh. In certain moods, that can be a happy combination.'

Hesketh nodded, and lit another cigarette. He thought she might have just offered him a compliment, but he wasn't sure.

'What about Moncrieff?' he said.

'Tam?' She helped herself to one of Hesketh's cigarettes. 'He was another cul-de-sac. My life's been full of them. Funny, that.'

'But what did you make of him?'

'He's good. He's shrewd. He's brave. He listens. I also lusted after him. He was my Scottish mountain in the wilderness, my very own Cairngorm. I wanted to clamber all over him. I wanted to conquer him. But he was never an easy man.'

'On other people?'

'On himself. He's a throwback, really. The twentieth century is wasted on people like Tam. Even the Victorians would probably be a bit racy for his taste. He'd be a hard person to live with. I never doubted that for a moment. But in a strange way, that was the appeal.'

'And now? Since you've talked to him?'

'Nothing's changed. We are what we are.' She permitted herself the ghost of a smile. 'But a girl likes a challenge, as you might sense.'

Moncrieff arrived twenty minutes early at the Tower of London. Liddell had told him to report to a Crown official called Laidlaw at a side entrance beside the Thames Embankment and Moncrieff was happy to kill time in the warm May sunshine. For nearly a week, the city had been *Luftwaffe*-free at night and Londoners, like the cherry trees in the moat, were beginning to blossom. Lingering beside the water, Moncrieff watched a middle-aged couple on a bench, with an ancient spaniel curled at their feet. Two faces tipped towards the sun. Both smiling.

Laidlaw was a Scot, from Aberdeen. He checked Moncrieff's MI5 pass, matched the fading photo to his face, and took him into the castle. One staircase led to another and the air was chill inside the thick stone walls. The Governor's House had its own entrance, guarded by two plainclothes figures with military haircuts. MI6, Moncrieff thought. Just as Liddell had anticipated.

'Mr Moncrieff?'

'That's me.'

'And you're here for Herr Hess?'

'I am.'

The taller of the two agents asked him to turn his pockets out while the other one patted him down. Moncrieff's joke about Hess outshining the Crown Jewels failed to raise a smile. Finally, they both escorted him through a suite of rooms and up yet another flight of steps. The Deputy Führer, it seemed, was still in bed.

'A word in your ear, Mr Moncrieff.' They'd paused outside the bedroom door. 'Don't believe everything the bloody man tells you.'

Hess, at first sight, was fast asleep. His long body was a hump beneath the grey blanket, his face was pale against the pillow, and he badly needed a shave. Moncrieff closed the door behind him and tiptoed into the room. It was thoughtfully furnished, personal touches in the choice of watercolours on the walls, and when he checked the view from the window he found himself looking down into the keep.

'*Wer sind Sie?*'

Who are you? Hess was awake now, rubbing his eyes. Perfect, Moncrieff thought. We speak German from the start.

He drew up a chair and sat beside the bed.

'You're German? You sound like a Rhinelander.'

'I'm English. Or Scottish, to be more precise.'

'Scottish? You know Hamilton? Young Duglo?'

'I'm afraid not.'

'But we carry on in German? *Ja?* You do me that favour?'

'Of course.'

Hess eyed him. He wanted to know why he was here like this, unannounced, and who he spoke for. He said he was starting to tire of telling his story over and over again, as if people didn't believe him, as if they were trying to catch him out. He'd come to meet the King. The King, at least, might have the courtesy, *die Zucht*, to believe him.

Die Zucht. Breeding. Moncrieff wondered how much a concept like this mattered in a regime run by gangsters. Was this what marked Hess out from the other criminals who strutted around Berlin? A belief that anyone half civilised should conduct himself with some consideration for others? Was this why he'd turned his back on Berlin and sought loftier company in Scotland?

Hess wanted news from the front. Had Greece fallen yet? Was Italy still busy in the Adriatic? And what was happening with Rommel in North Africa?

Moncrieff said he had no news about North Africa. Nor was he certain about Greece. The island of Crete, he said, had been heavily bombed only yesterday, but London, mercifully, was prospering in the absence of German raids.

'You had a big one on Saturday,' Hess said, 'the biggest of the war.'

'I know. I was here.'

'But you think that was an accident? A coincidence? You think there was no connection between my flight and what happened down here? In Germany, with the young ones, we have the stick and we have the carrot. Saturday night was the stick.'

'And you, Herr Hess?'

'I bring the carrot. It's a big carrot. Big and juicy and freshly pulled. You're a gardener, Herr Moncrieff? You understand vegetables? How much better they can taste straight from the soil? At home, my wife tends the garden. She uses horse dung. We have a man who brings it to the house. I fought alongside him in the old days. He's my age. He understands everything. And we pay him not in money but in carrots. And you know why? Because he *loves* carrots.'

Moncrieff was watching Hess carefully. There was something in his eyes that seemed to lasso a passing thought and not let go. One sentence led inexorably to another. Carrots. And yet more carrots. Maybe the MI6 men were more right than they knew, and maybe Goebbels, too. Maybe this man *was* slightly unhinged.

'I understand about sticks and carrots, Herr Hess,' Moncrieff said. 'So what exactly did you bring?'

'From Germany?'

'Yes.'

'I brought hopes of peace. That's why I'm here. Peace and understanding. In Germany we've always known there should be no blood spilled between us, between our two peoples. We're too similar, too close. And that's the Führer's view, as well. He admires you and most especially he admires your empire. That's why the fight you put up last summer came as no surprise. I was sometimes the one who took the Führer the figures about our losses, the *Luftwaffe* losses, the number of planes we'd lost over the Channel that day, and you know what he'd say to me? Rudi, he'd say, these people fight like lions because they're tough, because they conquered half the world, and that's where they still belong, out there looking after their empire, leaving us alone. It's a little like the carrots, Herr. Moncrieff. The British are the gardeners of Europe except their allotments lie overseas. Turn your back on us, Herr. Moncrieff, and I promise you we won't feel insulted. Not for a moment. What belongs to us belongs to us. By birthright? By conquest? It doesn't matter. And what belongs to you British rightfully belongs to you. Exactly the same logic. What you have, you hold. In our two worlds, possession is everything and after that all argument is a waste of breath. Yes? You agree?'

Moncrieff said nothing. France, he thought. Holland. Spain. Portugal. Empires that lasted generations and were now dust in the wind. Maybe that same fate lay in wait for Nazi Germany. Maybe.

'We shouldn't be fighting,' Moncrieff said at last. 'You're right.'

'Good. Very good. You agree after all. That makes you a wise man, Herr. Moncrieff. You know Churchill? You've met him?'

'Once. Very briefly.'

'Then you'll know that we waste our time with such a man. Churchill is the rock between war and peace. We have to move that rock. We have to blow it up. We have to get rid of it.'

'Only we can do that. You'd need an election. I think it's called democracy.'

'What?' Hess's eyes had narrowed. He had little wit. He scented a trap. 'What did you say?'

'We vote our leaders in. And when the time comes, we vote them out again. To think otherwise is not to understand the English.'

'But the English hate Churchill.'

'You think so?'

'I do. They hate him and they fear him and in both instances they're right because Churchill will bring you nothing but blood and sacrifice and piles of the needlessly dead.'

'That's exactly what he promised us.'

'He did. I know. And that shows something else. That he's a madman. All he thinks about is war. What he doesn't understand is peace. He knows that's what we Germans want. People in your country, serious people, wise people, *good* people, tell him all the time but a man like Churchill never listens. That's why I came. To talk to the good people. And to make peace.'

'You brought proposals with you? Peace proposals?'

'I did,' he tapped his broad forehead. 'Up here. Ask Duglo. Ask Kirkpatrick. In Scotland, when they came to me, those two gentlemen, that's all I talked about. Peace. Peace. Peace. How we get there. Together. How we *make* peace. How we hatch it like a big fat egg. And how we all prosper afterwards, once the fighting is done. No one wants to fight, Herr Moncrieff. Not if you're German, not if you're British. Only the warmonger wants to fight.'

'The warmonger?'

'Churchill.' He spat the word out, then lay back against the pillow, his eyes closed, seemingly exhausted.

Moncrieff took his time. He was very close now. He knew it.

'So did these ideas of yours, these peace proposals, exist on paper?'

'Of course they did.'

'In detail?'

'Of course,' his eyes opened. 'You think we're savages? You think we can't read? Can't write? Martin Luther was a good German, Herr Moncrieff. He put his thoughts on vellum and nailed them to a door in Wittenberg. That changed the course of history. And so will we.'

'We?'

'Me, and my people in Germany, and people here, good people, who know that Churchill is wrong. Not just wrong but dangerous. We all agree on that. We all know that there is no peace in the world with that man in charge.'

'And your peace proposals? On paper?'

'You have them. They were in my belongings. I've explained all this a thousand times. Two thousand times. Read them, Herr. Moncrieff. You need to read. It's black and white. Thirteen pages. Ernst Bohle did the translation. He works for the *Auslands-Organisation*. It might not be perfect but everything is there, every proposal, everything we need to discuss. I was promised safe passage. The King must know this. Please remind him. I deserve to be treated properly. And when my work here is over I want to go home.'

Moncrieff stiffened in the chair. He could hear voices outside. An interruption, he thought. Trouble. He leaned forward, sensing that time was suddenly precious.

'These proposals,' he said. 'What are they?'

'You want me to go through them? Explain them? How generous they are? How respectful of the English? All thirteen pages?'

'Just the key points, Herr Hess. That's all.'

'I see...' Hess was frowning now and Moncrieff knew at once that this was a man whose mind functioned only in longish paragraphs. Reducing something to its essence appeared to be beyond him. Odd, he thought, given the fact that he was an accomplished pilot, that he could squeeze the details from a chart, compute compass readings and engine settings and fuel loads, lay a course across the North Sea, and deliver himself intact on the other side of Scotland, albeit by parachute.

Moncrieff was just inches away now, seeking some kind of answer, some kind of clue to what bombshells might lie among Ernst Bohle's thirteen pages, when the door opened to admit one of the two MI6 agents. With him was a much older man in a loosely belted gabardine raincoat. He was carrying a bulky leather case.

'This is Doctor Ellis,' the agent spared Hess a glance and then looked at Moncrieff. 'The overnight nurse has worries about our friend's blood pressure. She also thinks he's in danger of hyperventilating. I'm afraid we have to bring this interview to an end.' A thin smile. 'On medical grounds.'

Moncrieff nodded. He didn't care. He'd got what he came for and he was very happy to leave with that knowledge. He extended a hand. Hess was looking confused.

'You want to know about the peace treaty?' he said in English. 'And you're leaving?'

Wilhelm Schultz received the summons to the Air Ministry late on Friday afternoon. A package was waiting for him in the *Reichsmarschall*'s office. When he got to his feet and reached for his leather jacket an aide offered to run the errand for him, but Schultz shook his head. He needed the exercise. Life behind an *Abwehr* desk was designed to make people fat. He'd be back later.

When he got to the Ministry he was told to wait for Goering's adjutant. He stood in the big picture window, his arms folded, watching a succession of pretty women out in the bright Berlin sunshine. When the adjutant arrived, he was carrying a carefully taped field-grey folder.

'With the *Reichsmarschall*'s compliments, Herr Schultz,' he said. 'When you've made contact with the English and decided on a rendezvous, I'd be obliged if you could give me a call.'

'Why?'

'The *Reichsmarschall* has some ideas about delivery.'

'Me, you mean? Or the letter?'

'Both, Herr Schultz. And I gather speed is of the essence.'

Schultz returned to *Abwehr* headquarters. His aide was going through a sizeable pile of files in his office. Schultz dismissed him and shut the door. The *Abwehr* agent at the German Embassy in Lisbon was an East Prussian called Wolfgang Spiegelhalte. He and Schultz had drunk themselves unconscious in a number of bars across Europe, always at the owner's expense. When he finally answered the phone, he recognised Schultz's voice at once.

'Wilhelm! *Wie geht's?*'

Schultz kept the conversation brief. He knew that Spiegelhalte had a channel to an Englishman called Hesketh who was always trying to sell bits and pieces of information, loose change by and large but occasionally interesting. He also knew that Hesketh made the same approaches to every other player in the Lisbon game.

'Ask him about an English agent. MI5. Tam Moncrieff.' Schultz spelled the name and asked Spiegelhalte to read it back. 'You've got that? You know how to get hold of Hesketh?'

'My pleasure.'

'Tonight, Wolfgang. In fact, better do it now.'

'Of course, my friend. You're down soon? Is that what I'm hearing?'

'More than likely.' Schultz checked his watch. 'I'll wait for your call.'

17

Kacper Wojcek was tiring of life in the MI6 safe house. He'd been there since the transfer from the Infirmary in Glasgow. It was no more than a farm worker's cottage, really, thrown up in the nineteenth century, a pile of bricks and leaky slates with a view of sodden fields to the west, an outhouse that appeared to serve as a rubbish dump, and a manic sheepdog which barked half the night and kept him awake. When he enquired where, exactly, they were they told him not to worry. Glasgow was only an hour away. Soon he'd be home again with fifty pounds in his pocket to thank him for everything he'd done.

The stay, already far too long in Wojcek's opinion, had been sold to him as a period of necessary convalescence after his ordeal at the hands of the tall Scot from London. He'd been through it a million times in his head, reliving the nightmare, and twice – in reply to their questions – he'd described what had happened. It was the fear of drowning that still haunted him. For someone who had a dread of water, who couldn't even *swim*, the knowledge that his lungs were slowly filling was impossible to explain.

Then, on what he suspected was the Saturday, they told him his time was up. That evening someone would be coming to drive him home. In the meantime, they thought they owed him a drink or two. Bottles of vodka appeared and a couple of faces he didn't recognise stepped into the tiny kitchen. There was food, too, sandwiches with generous fillings of cheese and early tomatoes and even a slice or two of ham. One of the strangers, who knew he was Polish, had managed to lay hands on a jar of pickled herrings and the men round the table watched him wolfing them down. Glaswegians, he thought. These folk know how to look after you.

By mid-evening his driver still hadn't turned up but by this time, drunk, Kacper had ceased to care. He could go home any time, tonight, tomorrow, the next day, whenever. But for now there was no sweeter prospect than another glass of vodka, another toast to fallen comrades, another song. They asked him to sing them something Polish and he was glad to oblige. As a student in Warsaw, the few times they had money he and his friends would drink in a cheap bar near the station, and the words to the songs had never left him. There were four of them at the table, two Scots, someone from further south, and Kacper himself. He made everyone at the table link arms and sway together, to left and right, as he stumbled into the song, tripping up on the lyrics, making everyone laugh.

> *Ja nie dbam o czerwony nos,*

he sang,

> *I o to że wciąż tyję*
> *Ja biorę kufel w ręce swe*
> *I piję i piję i piję.*

I don't care about my red nose,
I don't care I'm getting fat
I take another pint in my hand
And I drink, and I drink, and I drink.

His new friends wanted more. The songs went on until his memory had gone and his mouth wouldn't work any more and he couldn't stand up when his bladder was bursting and he knew he had to have a piss. And so he wet his trousers, there in the kitchen on the rough floorboards, dimly aware that the laughter had stopped. Then came another face in the room, a stranger, someone he hadn't met before, and unseen hands were carrying him bodily out of the cottage.

He felt rain on his face, and a gale of wind, and then he was lying full length in the back of a car. Mumbled conversation. A cough from the engine. The wheels churning as the car reversed into the narrow lane that ran past the cottage.

His eyes were still shut. The car lurched to a halt. Then it began to move again and the moment it rounded the next bend he started to be sick. Someone in the front was cursing now but he paid no attention. Agata, he thought. Tomasz. Roseanne. How pleased they'd be to see him. The stories he'd have to tell.

He began to be sick again, pawing blindly at his mouth, tasting the vodka in his own vomit. Then, mercifully, there were no more bends, no more sudden stops, and he drifted away, the faintest smile on his face.

When he came to again, it was dark outside and the car had stopped. The moment the rear door opened he could hear seagulls and the howl of the wind. Pulled bodily from the car, he struggled to stay upright. More hands, tugging him forward.

The ground was rough beneath his feet. From somewhere ahead came the growl of the ocean.

He had no idea what was happening, no idea where he was, and so he started singing again, one of the drinking songs, the one about the flirty waitress with the wandering hands, and then suddenly they'd come to a halt. He tried to focus on the faces around him. They seemed to be melting away. Then he looked ahead, into the darkness, struggling to remember the next line, and the line after that, surprised by the small pressure in his lower back, the gentle shove, the ground giving way beneath his feet, and the feeling – quite suddenly – of being weightless.

The ocean was louder now, a thunder in his ears, coming up to meet him, to claim him. And then there was nothing.

Cathy Phelps left the Palace at half past ten by the side entrance into Buckingham Gate. One of the yeomen was on duty, the one she'd made friends with, and he asked when she'd be back. She smiled, and said it might be early in the morning, or maybe even later than that, depending what kind of mood her boyfriend was in, and he grinned back at her and winked to say he understood.

'Lucky man,' he said, opening the gate to let her through. 'You know where to come if he ever lets you down.'

She stepped into the half-darkness of the blackout. She knew the way by heart, not simply because of Tam's place, but because Doherty lived only ten minutes or so further on, in a chaotic basement flat near the Angel. Down the Mall, she thought. Then left to Piccadilly. Then on through Soho and up to Oxford Street and into the peace and quiet of the

Bloomsbury squares. Half an hour if she got a move on. Forty minutes if she took her time.

She took her time. The warmth of the day had lingered in the capital and she loved the freedoms you found here at night. Very little traffic. The odd passer-by in the Mall. A nod from a stranger. A muttered good evening. When she reached Soho it was suddenly busier, and twice she was propositioned by men who took one look at her and drew the wrong conclusion. On both occasions she told them she was flattered and when the second man became more insistent, offering her money on the spot if she accompanied him down the nearest alley, she looked him in the eye and told him she hated strangers with bad teeth.

'You're drunk, as well,' she nodded at the pub across the road. 'Why don't you spend your money in there?'

She walked on, not looking back, and when she knew he could no longer see her she stopped in a shop doorway and checked her bag. The letter for Tam was still there, still safe. She'd written his name on it in case he wasn't at home. In his stern Scots way he'd demanded a settling of accounts, and she'd been happy to comply. As it happened, the fruit of her labours – a casual question here and there, a peek at schedules that should have been locked away, a couple of checks to make sure she hadn't got this thing completely wrong – had first amazed, and then shocked her. At first she hadn't quite believed it but then the moment came when any possibility of doubt vanished. The Duke of Kent, she thought. Sheep in any family wouldn't come blacker.

Should she share the news with Doherty? She didn't know, couldn't decide. On one level she loved getting involved in the political side of his life – the hours of preparation for the speeches that sounded so spontaneous, the faces in the meeting halls and busy pubs, the all-day marches despite weather that wouldn't disgrace the Highlands. All this was new to her, an excitement she'd never experienced before, but what really mattered about Doherty was the way he took care of her, made room for her, so natural, so unforced. Tam had never been less than a gentleman, but there was something much rougher about Doherty that she found irresistible.

She rounded the corner and stepped into Woburn Square. Tam's little flat was at the end of the terrace. From here she couldn't see the front of the house and so she crossed the road to look up at the first-floor window. If the curtains were drawn he'd be at home.

She faltered. Then stopped. The curtains were drawn. Did she really want to knock on the door? Be invited in? Risk whatever scene might follow? Wouldn't it be wiser simply to post the letter through the door and leave him to find it next day? What did five hours matter? Every detail was there, carefully spelled out in her neatest hand. All he had to do was read it, draw his own conclusions and take whatever actions he thought necessary. Would there be repercussions in the Palace? Some kind of enquiry? A hunt for whoever had raised the alarm? She didn't know, and in truth she didn't care. Doherty was right. The royals were leeches. They sucked the blood of the people. The moment was fast approaching when they'd get their comeuppance. And by that time, she'd be gone.

She felt in her bag for the letter and stepped off the kerb to cross the street. As she did so, she became aware of the car

parked beside her. Two doors were opening. Two men got out.
One of them stood in front of her, stopping her dead. She began
to protest, told them to leave her alone, but then she was lifted
bodily off the tarmac. The interior of the car smelled of cigars.
Both doors slammed shut.

One of the men was laughing.

'Easy,' he said. 'So easy.'

18

Summoned to meet the Director as a matter of urgency, Moncrieff lingered on the pavement outside the Kensington church. Lately, according to Ursula, Guy Liddell had begun to attend services regularly. His marriage, she thought, was in trouble and he seemed to find solace in making space among the press of events for an hour or so when he could reflect in peace.

He was one of the last to leave St Benedict's, and to Moncrieff's surprise he had Ursula Barton in tow. She spotted Moncrieff at once and she crossed the road to join him.

'Is this a regular thing?' Moncrieff nodded towards the church.

'It's the last Sunday before Ascension. Back home my mother always celebrated it. We always went with her.' She smiled. 'Old habits die hard.'

The Director joined them on the pavement. He'd been out of London for a couple of days. A light tan suggested a country house with a south-facing terrace. He wanted to know about Hess.

'You saw him? Yesterday?'

'I did, sir.'

'And?'

Moncrieff did his best to pick the flesh off the bones. Hess was something of an obsessive, definitely. Not crazy, not mad, but a man who'd committed himself to a certain course of action and was determined not to be deflected.

'He believes in peace. I don't doubt that for a moment.'

'Peace with whom?'

'Us. He likes us. If we were a club, he'd join tomorrow.'

'That won't be necessary. I gather he's here for the duration.'

MI6, Liddell said, had been tasked by Churchill to find the Deputy Führer a permanent home within reach of London. They'd settled on a Victorian pile near Aldershot and were turning the place into a fortress.

'You're serious?'

'I am, Tam. Earth embankments. A moat. Two lines of barbed wire. Watchtowers. And a couple of companies of Coldstream Guards in case he gets homesick for Scotland. Anyone visiting Mytchett Place needs three passes and an alias. This is theatre. The PM's idea of a joke.'

'On whom?'

'MI6, I fancy. They've been rumbled. Churchill's taken a good look at all the clues and drawn his own conclusions. Hold your friends close but hold your enemies closer. Sir Stewart Menzies is no friend. He's brought Hess to the table and now he must pick up the bill. In some respects, Tam, it's the sweetest of ironies. A week ago you were right. We were probably looking at a *coup d'état*. Now, thanks to a navigation error on Hess's part, it's 'C' who's lost his bearings. Not that he'll ever admit it.'

'So what's he saying?'

'He's telling everyone that Hess was the *Sicherheitsdienst*'s comeuppance for Venlo. Tit for tat. A clever act of vengeance. As an explanation it holds a little water but not enough. The PM knows that, of course, and so does 'C'. Which takes us into the realm of pantomime.'

Ursula checked her watch and then led them into the nearby park. They settled on an empty bench.

'Did Hess mention the Russians at all?' Liddell unbuttoned his jacket and lifted his face to the sun.

'No.'

'No hint of an invasion date?'

'I'm afraid not.'

'Did you ask him?'

'No. I would have done but our MI6 friends had other ideas.' Moncrieff described the abrupt arrival of the physician. The interview had been cut short, he said. For the sake of their precious guest.

'Golly,' Liddell opened one eye. '*That* blatant?'

'I'm afraid so.'

The Director nodded. He looked suddenly cheerful.

'They're panicking,' he said. 'That's a very good sign.'

Ursula wanted to know about the existence of a letter, of a possible peace treaty.

'He definitely bought a letter. Thirteen pages. Translated by Ernst Bohle.'

'He works for the *Auslands-Organisation*,' she said. 'Under Hess.'

'That's right.'

'So what's happened to the letter? Does Hess know?'

'No. I suspect he thinks it's still in circulation. He hasn't given up. Not at all. Any minute now he thinks the King's going to come to his rescue, bang a few heads together and do the sensible thing.'

'Like?' Liddell this time.

'Get rid of Churchill. Open negotiations. Declare the last year and a half a terrible mistake. And then turn our attention to the east.'

'Our?'

'Their.'

'But definitely no date?'

'I'm afraid not.'

Liddell nodded. The smile was back on his face.

'What a lovely idea,' he said.

Even Ursula was slightly shocked.

'I hope you're joking,' she said quietly.

'Of course I am.' His hand settled lightly on her knee. 'Do we have any idea about a signature on these proposals? Under whose name were they issued? Might Hitler be a possibility?'

'I doubt it, sir. But Hess told me they were typed on headed Chancellery notepaper.'

'Really?' The Director was beaming now. 'And you think there's some chance of us laying hands on a copy?'

Hesketh made contact that same afternoon by telephone from Lisbon. He said he had news from Berlin that Moncrieff's masters might consider worth buying.

'News about what?'

'Our German Pimpernel. He's been with you an entire week now. Is his English any better? Have you got him eating bacon and eggs yet? Is Churchill sleeping easy at night?' One question followed another until Moncrieff brought them to a halt.

'News about what?' he said again.

'Some kind of package. I've been talking to your friend Schultz. He sends his compliments. As does your lady friend. A small but eager queue appears to be forming for your attention. It might be good manners to make yourself available and I'm only too happy to put the appropriate arrangements in place. It's nearly summer, Tam, and I've never seen the city looking more alluring. London can be a demanding mistress. So can this wretched war. Sunshine and a bottle or two of that outstanding Alvariño? Does that sound too much of a cross to bear?'

'This package. Do you know what's inside?'

'I can guess.'

'When is Schultz due?'

'He's flying here tomorrow. I'm booking him into a hotel of my choice. That's where I suggest the pair of you meet. Another thousand US dollars should cover it nicely.'

'The hotel?'

'My fee. I sense a certain eagerness on Mr Schultz's part. Perhaps on yours, too. Hurry on down, Tam. Peace demands no less.'

The line went dead. On the basis of the Director's description, Moncrieff was trying to imagine Mytchett Place, the next port of call for Rudolf Hess. Defensive earthworks. Fields of fire. A once genteel country property converted into a stockade. Hesketh would love it, he thought. Another lazy afternoon circling the battlements. Another book in the making.

He still had the phone. Ursula, even on a Sunday, would be

in her office until close of play. When she answered he told her
briefly about the call from Hesketh.

'Go down there,' she said at once. 'I'll sort out the tickets.'

'He wants more money.'

'How much?'

'A thousand dollars. US.'

'We'll pay it.'

'Shouldn't you check with the Director?'

'He's with me now. And he's nodding.'

Dieter Merz hadn't seen Schultz since Nuremberg in '38. They
met on the oil-stained crescent of tarmac outside the Führer
Squadron mess at Tempelhof.

'Merz,' Schultz grunted. 'Still drinking like a newt?'

'Still drinking.'

'And the last three years? They've treated you well?'

'No complaints. They gave me a front-line squadron and
then found me a war to fight. I was grateful on both counts.'

'You flew against the Poles?'

'I did. They gave me one of those.' Merz nodded towards
the waiting Me-110. 'The aircraft's a brute. There isn't a trench
deep enough to hide, not if you're a Pole and you're digging in
a hurry. We'd fly over a day later and they were still spading
out the remains. It was the same against the Belgies. Against
the Dutch. Against the French. You play God at thirty metres
and don't look too hard at the results. Refugees were the worst.
Families never learn how to dig.'

'And the British?'

'The British were different. I was back in the 109. Some

days they kicked our arses. After the Poles and the French that's not the kind of welcome you expect. Goering switched to bombing the cities but that just made things worse. Wasting your last drop of fuel flying *escort*? That's not what we were trained for.'

Schultz grunted. Two years of war, Merz thought, were beginning to show. Not just the scuff marks on his battered leather jacket, but the darkness under his eyes. Schultz was either ill or exhausted, Merz didn't know which, but until now he'd never realised how much the *Abwehr* man loathed flying.

They began to stroll towards the aircraft. Ground crew had finished with the fuel bowser.

'You hear from her at all?' Schultz asked. 'Your Japanese lady?'

'Never. The Japanese are all the same. They come, they go. She used to say the same thing about *sakura* but I never paid much attention.'

'*Sakura?*'

'Cherry blossom. The Japanese live for moments of beauty. That's what I always believed but what they really love is the way the blossom fades and dies. They're in love with death, those people. I should have taken more notice. All the clues were there.'

They paused beside the Me-110. Three years ago, Merz had been living in Berlin with the daughter of a Japanese industrialist, little suspecting that she was a spy. At the time he'd almost worshipped her, an act of submission – or perhaps an error of judgement – he'd come to regret.

'But that fool Ribbentrop was filling his boots as well, isn't that right?' Schultz offered him a rare smile.

'She always denied it.' Merz shrugged. 'So I imagine the answer is yes.'

Merz helped Schultz into the rear seat. Schultz was looking round, one hand checking the inside pocket of his jacket. He looked acutely uncomfortable. Everything was too tight, too restricting, too intimate. Real life was full of options. Flying as a passenger wasn't.

'What happens if we end up in the shit?'

'We won't.'

'How do you know?'

'I'm a fighter pilot. Trust me, Herr. Schultz. Fighter pilots know everything.'

Merz lowered himself into the front seat and settled down to run the pre-start-up checks. He was still thinking about Keiko and the times they'd spent together. For months the regime had been kind to them and then he'd found the little camera and the rolls of film, irrefutable evidence that her heart still beat to Tokyo time. This, he reflected, was the real hurt, not some passing affair, not the odd fumble with the Reich's Foreign Minister, but the knowledge that he'd never really known who she was. *Sakura*, he thought. Those intense yet weightless moments that come and go.

The wheel chocks had already been removed. Merz signalled the ground crew to stand clear and then hit the starter button. Two coughs, two ragged puffs of dirty smoke and they began to roll.

'Look after me,' Schultz grunted on the intercom. 'Nothing fancy, you hear what I'm telling you?'

The flight south was uneventful. Twice Merz adjusted his mirror to check on Schultz in the seat behind him and both times he appeared to be asleep. Refuelling in Barcelona, Merz shook him awake and led the way to a small bar the engineering boys used, attached to the main airport building. Schultz, it turned out, had taken a double dose of sleeping tablets ahead of the flight. Hence his drowsiness.

'Why Lisbon?' Merz asked.

'I'm the post boy,' Schultz patted the tiny bulge on the front of his leather jacket.

'You're delivering something?'

'I am.'

'To Moncrieff? The English spy?'

'Spy?' Schultz nearly choked on his beer.

'You're telling me different? At Nuremberg he put a crazy idea in my head about shooting down the Führer. He knew I sometimes flew in the *Reichsregierung* with Georg Messner. He knew I had access to the flying schedules and a 109.'

'And he knew you were crazy, too?'

'Yes.'

'Because of the Jap lady?'

'Yes. As it happens, I fucked up but that man played me like a fish. He's a Scot. Am I right?'

'You are. And he's learned a lot since Nuremberg. In my business you get to meet the English from time to time. Most of them are fucking devious, which they have to be, but they're snobs, too. They think they own half the planet, which might have been true once, but they're in the shit now and they hate admitting it. Moncrieff's different. He looks the facts in the face and acts like a grown-up. He also leaves the pretty boys alone. That makes him rare.'

Merz nodded. He was drinking bad coffee.

342

'You know Albrecht Haushofer?' he asked.

'Rudi's adopted son?' Schultz nodded. *'Ja.'*

'And another Englishman? Husketh? Hisketh? Hesketh? Beard? Moustache? Shrimp of a man?'

'Never heard of him.'

'As far as I know he lives in Lisbon. I flew Haushofer down to meet him.'

'And?'

'We spent half a day together and I took a good look at him. He likes to think he speaks perfect German. He doesn't. The man's a piece of shit. Haushofer, poor fool, thought the world of him.'

Agent Souk was waiting for Moncrieff at the flying boat pontoon at the Tagus terminal in Lisbon. He tossed the remains of his cigarette into the river and extended a hand.

'Welcome back, *mon brave.* The Brits have turned travelling light into an art form.' He offered to carry Moncrieff's single bag.

Moncrieff shook his head.

'Schultz?' he enquired.

'Delayed in Barcelona. Some technical problem with the aircraft. I gather it's a question of flying spares down from Augsburg. In these situations, happily, Lisbon gives you only one option. The lady's waiting for you at your hotel. Rest those old bones of yours. Schultz won't be here for a day or two.'

They took a taxi from the terminal into the old town. When the driver slowed behind a tram labouring up the steepness of the hill, Moncrieff found himself staring at a sizeable queue outside a pharmacy. Rumpled suits. Overdressed women perspiring in the heat. Kids looking lost.

'Refugees,' Hesketh murmured. 'They haven't got visas yet but they're determined to lay hands on seasickness tablets before supplies dry up. You're looking at an act of faith, *mon brave*. Even if they get a visa the boats are booked up for months ahead.'

Moncrieff nodded, said nothing. Lisbon, he thought, was where you finally ran out of options. Perched on the very edge of Europe, living God knows how, you could only dream of a passage out.

The taxi was moving again. Hesketh wanted to know about his fee.

'A thousand? Dollars, of course? US? I trust that meets with everyone's satisfaction?'

'We'll see,' Moncrieff grunted. 'Once Schultz turns up.'

When they got to the hotel, Hesketh led the way inside. The man behind the reception desk rose to his feet. Hesketh introduced him as the manager.

'Madame is waiting in the restaurant, *Senhor*,' the manager was looking at Moncrieff. 'We've given you the table with the view.'

Moncrieff nodded. Then he asked Hesketh whether he'd booked a room for him.

'I haven't but under the circumstances I suspect that won't be necessary. *Bon appétit*, my friend. And enjoy the food as well.'

Hesketh left the hotel without a backward glance, sauntering down the street in the bright sunshine, and Moncrieff watched him until he crossed the road and disappeared into the maze of alleys that stretched down towards the water. Then he turned back to the manager, recognising the churning in his stomach.

Bella Menzies, he thought. Waiting for him just yards away. Was it wise to risk another meeting? After the spectacular collapse of their last relationship?

He eyed the street again, knowing it wasn't too late to walk away, then glanced at the manager.

'The restaurant?' he enquired.

'Through there, *Senhor.*' The manager gestured towards a nearby door. 'We've kept the kitchen open for you, but the chef's mother has fallen ill. Might you and the lady be ordering soon?'

The restaurant was empty except for two diners. One of them was a man sitting alone at a table in the far corner, bent over a newspaper and a half-empty glass. Centre parting. Heavy glasses. Well-cut suit. It was hard to judge at first glance, but Moncrieff put him in his late thirties, perhaps a little older. The other figure had to be Bella. She was smoking a cigarette and studying the view.

Moncrieff picked his way between the tables and stood over her for what seemed an eternity. She must have felt his presence, sensed his approach, but she didn't move.

'Bella?'

At last she looked round. The same tilt to her chin. The same frank appraisal in her eyes. Nothing appeared to have changed. Except she looked much, much older.

'Shocked?' She'd always been able to read his mind.

'Surprised.'

'Don't be. Another week of this...' she gestured at the view, '... I might be back in shape again.'

Shape.

When he'd first met her in Berlin it had been high summer. Bella – tall, athletic, bronzed, fit – had been rowing twice a week on one of the Berlin lakes with a crew of expatriate girls from the foreign embassies. On one occasion, at Bella's invitation, Moncrieff had joined them. He'd rowed competitively at university and the moment he stepped carefully into the slender racing eight he knew he still had it. A two-kilometre sprint had tested him to the limit but he hadn't let the pain show and Bella, afterwards, had been delighted.

'You've just done my reputation no end of good,' she'd said. 'Those girls couldn't believe how fit you are. They've told me you're welcome any time, Mr Moncrieff. My thoughts entirely.'

Now, nearly three years later, Moncrieff slipped into the vacant seat across the table. Already, in what felt no time at all, he knew they were at peace with each other. He wanted to know how she was. He wanted to know what she was doing here. And above all he wanted to know about Moscow. She'd told him a certain amount on the phone but he suspected there had to be more.

Bella shook her head. She had very little to add. Every particle of her being, she said, every cell in her body, had once believed in Communism and on a good day – a *really* good day – that was still true. The only drawback was the real thing. A winter that seemed never to end. Every second face on the street bloated with moonshine vodka. Endless queues for all the essentials you couldn't do without. Early March slush, the colour of death. And then the briefest glimpse of the *nomenklatura* behind the curtained windows as another limousine swept past.

'January in Scotland used to depress me,' she lit another cigarette. 'Imagine five months of that.'

'No rowing?'

'Absolutely none. You'd need a sense of humour to fill in all the paperwork and a saw to get through the bloody ice. You know the saddest truth of all? Communism works brilliantly on paper. That's where Marx and Engels and Lenin and the rest of them got it so right. But there isn't enough vodka in the world to make Communism work in real life. You can't live on good intentions. Not properly.'

'So what happens next?'

'I'm not with you.'

'You go home? Back to Moscow?'

She looked at him. There was warmth in her laughter.

'Home's quaint. I like that. I have a government flat in a block quite close to the Kremlin. When the wind's in the east I can hear the bells at night. It's meant to be a privilege, a thank you, and in a way it is. I have a kitchen bigger than the normal cupboard. I have fully lagged pipes, water that works, a functioning lavatory, free heating when there's enough fuel for the boiler, and I have neighbours who ration their drinking to a bottle of vodka a day. That, believe me, makes yours truly a very lucky girl. When the summer arrives, like now, I can take the tram out of town to the end of the line. An hour's walk through the pine woods and there's a lake I can swim in, and a very nice man called Yuri who sunbathes *au naturel* and is happy to share his blanket. Yuri, of course, is married but there are times when a girl has pressing needs of her own and Yuri is very happy to take me to his flat when his wife and kids are away and do his bit for international solidarity. I happen to like Yuri. He's gentler than most Russians. He also cooks like a dream. Far better, frankly, than he fucks. But *home*? I'm not at all sure.'

'What about the dacha? The one you mentioned on the phone?'

'That was make-believe. A fib. A fantasy. That's what Communism does to you. Lying becomes a way of life. You start off by lying to other people and you end up kidding yourself. There is no dacha, Tam, and I doubt there ever will be.'

'But you have to go back? Is that what you're telling me?'

'Yes, for two reasons. The first is that they'd come and find me and that could have very ugly consequences. My people don't mind who they hurt and they seem to reserve the really special treatment for their own kind. Trotsky, so I'm told, got off lightly. An ice pick in your head would only be the hors d'oeuvre.'

'And the other reason?'

'There's nowhere else to go. Can you imagine little me turning up at St James's Street? Trying to make my peace with the brethren? After everything I've done? After making you all look such fools? Such amateurs? And then there's my beloved stepdad, all that investment he made in me. Time. Money. Trust. Can you picture the moment I knock on his door and step back into that nice tidy life of his? It won't happen. Because it can't happen. I learned good manners very early on and I know when a girl should say no. So I won't be going back. Probably ever.'

Moncrieff nodded, eyeing his empty glass.

'You said "amateur",' he murmured.

'Did I?'

'Yes, you said you made us look so amateur. What exactly did you mean?'

'You're taking this stuff personally? Is that what I'm hearing?' Bella was picking at a cuticle on one of her nails.

'Just a little. I work for the brethren and I'm glad to, if you want the truth. *Amateur?* Are you serious?'

'That was '38,' she said defensively, 'before you all sharpened up.'

'You mean before I joined?'

'Yes. Back then it was a game. You know how I got into Intelligence. I could speak a couple of languages. I was a game girl. I had the right connections, the right pedigree, even the right fucking accent. I knew how to behave on social occasions and I was very, very good with certain kinds of men, chiefly Germans. That's not difficult, by the way. All you have to do is watch them at work, at play, at the restaurant table, even with their wives and kids. You smile. You drop a conversational curtsey. You play the helpless female. You seed just enough mischief to make the poor darlings believe they might be in with a chance. And then you go home and write down everything they've told you.'

'And send it to London?'

'Moscow. That was the thrill. Sometimes it felt better than sex.'

'Betrayal? Treason? You're serious?'

'Yes, even when you turned up. Don't get me wrong. I loved you. You were very different and I adored that. You were also, and you'll hate this, sweetly innocent. Our world hadn't corrupted you, not then. You were this tall ex-Marine who spoke mysteriously wonderful German and in your own interests you needed a bit of a steer, someone to guide you around Berlin, someone to point out the nastier bars you should try and avoid. And that someone was me.'

'And now? You think it's got to me? Your world? You think I'm tainted?'

'I don't know. Except I understand you're very well thought of in Moscow and that doesn't happen by accident. You must like the job. Because the job certainly likes you. So... can I buy you a drink? Do the rules allow that?'

A waiter brought a bottle of Marqués de Riscal Rioja. Bella insisted on pouring.

'Your little friend's choice,' she tipped her glass, 'and a good one. He's a con man, by the way, but you'd know that already. Quite a decent con man, quite accomplished, amusing too but still a con man. You're going to tell me this city's full of them but there's no need because he's told me already. In a way I suppose that makes him unusual. Not just a con man but proud of it.'

'He told me you shared a couple of bottles of Krug.'

'Champagne? He's lying. I'd have said yes, by the way, but it never happened.'

'Did you invite him up to your room?'

'Absolutely not. Was he after an invitation? Emphatically, yes. He's honest in that respect, too. And he didn't sulk when I said no. Do you pay him lots of money? Be honest.'

'Yes. Far too much.'

'And is he worth it?'

'I'm not sure. Give me a couple of days and I'll let you know.'

'Ahhh...' she smiled. 'You think I'm some kind of prospect? Is that why you've come? You think I'm going to tell you more about Moscow than the state of the plumbing in that flat of mine?'

Moncrieff ducked his head and took a sip of the wine. For the first time it occurred to him that she might know nothing about Schultz's impending arrival.

'It's good to see you,' he said, touching his glass to hers.

'That means nothing. That means less than nothing. What it also means is that there's something else in the wind, something else that might have brought you down here. Am I allowed a clue? Just one?'

The waiter was back. The kitchen, he said, had enquired whether they might be eating. Moncrieff reached for the menu. Bella caught his hand.

'Later,' she said. 'We'll eat later.'

Moncrieff began to protest but she pulled him to his feet. The other diner in the restaurant looked briefly up, offered a faint smile, and then folded his newspaper as they made their way past his table.

They took the Rioja up to her room. Bella had been right about the view. The gleaming waters of the Tagus filled the window. Look left, and the river was full of shipping. Look right, and you could glimpse the open ocean.

Moncrieff turned away from the window. Bella was stepping out of her dress.

'This is what the Soviets like to call *perestroika*,' she said. 'It means no promises, no regrets, no ties, nothing. Do you think you could cope with that, Mr Moncrieff? A chance to check everything works the way it should? The way it used to?'

Moncrieff was looking at her. There was something emotionless, something almost dispassionate about the way she'd framed this invitation. She was still striking – full breasts, flat belly and the longest legs he'd ever seen on any woman – but the warmth in her smile had gone and she seemed to find comfort in the very absence of anything remotely intimate.

'Do I frighten you?' he asked.

'Yes, a little. But I suspect that's me.'

'You frighten yourself?'

'Yes.'

'Why?'

'Because once I let you too close.'

'And?'

'You hurt me. I told you on the phone. In my life that only happens once.'

'And yet here we are. Again. At your invitation.'

'Indeed. And if you need it there's another bottle, and another, and another, until your little friend is running out for more.' She paused. She was naked now. 'You're not taking your clothes off.'

'You're right.'

'You want me to help you?'

'I want you to tell me why you're doing this. And where it leads next.'

'Is that important?'

'Yes.'

'Why?'

'Because what happened in Berlin hurt me, too, believe it or not.'

'Really?'

'Yes.'

'I never knew. I never even suspected it. You seemed so...' she frowned, '... remote.'

'Someone had just tried to kill me. Very slowly.'

'I know. But that wasn't my fault.' She took a step closer. 'What if I told you it won't happen again?'

'We won't go to bed, you mean?'

'No. That you won't get hurt.'

'How does that work?'

'I don't know. Truly, I haven't a clue. But if the little bird tells me anything it's that we owe it a try.'

'Owe who?'

'Each other.'

'A try?'

'This.' She stepped closer still. She put her glass carefully to one side and then cupped his long face in her hands. She began to kiss him, sliding the warmth of her tongue between his teeth.

'This will work,' she whispered. 'I promise.'

It did. Long afterwards, back in England, Moncrieff remembered the moment when she woke him up, hours later, dusk at the window and the siren of a departing freighter echoing across the city. They made love again, less urgently this time, and then she lay beside him, her face on his chest, just the way she used to. The reserve, the caution, had gone, melted away, and in its place was the woman he'd missed so badly when he'd returned to the Glebe House after deportation from Berlin. She was soft, playful, gently mischievous. She reached across and lifted the phone and ordered the promised second bottle and when the waiter arrived at the door with the wine and a plate of tapas she wrapped herself in a bath towel and tipped him with a $5 note she found in Moncrieff's trousers.

'He'll remember that forever,' Moncrieff was laughing.

'Five dollars?'

'You.'

She opened the bottle and re-joined him in bed. Another toast, this time to Lisbon. Then she propped herself on one elbow, exactly the way she used to in Berlin, and smiled down at him.

'I've been meaning to ask you,' she said. 'But a girl forgets.'

'What?'

'The invasion date. When will the Germans march east?'

They talked long into the night. When he pleaded ignorance over Hitler's intentions she told him it didn't matter. She said the coming invasion was common knowledge in certain circles in Moscow though Stalin himself had discounted the rumours. For reasons no one could fathom he appeared to retain the absurd belief that Hitler was a man of his word.

'The generals are on their knees for reinforcements,' she said, 'but Our Leader ignores them. That makes them very unhappy but protesting would make them unhappier still. The last crop of generals got purged a couple of years ago. Purging is code for an early grave.'

'So you expect an invasion?'

'Of course. Uncle Joe's in for a big shock. The rest of us expect the Germans at the gates of Moscow in time for Christmas. Whether we let them in or not is a different issue, though I've noticed that most Russians tend to be fatalists. Maybe it's the serf mentality, I don't know.' She shrugged. '*Que sera...*'

'And you?'

'Me?'

'You believe in the tides of history? Sink or swim?'

'I believed I could make a difference. Tiny. Maybe even minuscule. But important, nonetheless.'

'You said believed.'

'I did.'

'Past tense.'

'Yes.'

'And now?'

'Now?' She looked down at him, and then smiled. 'The Germans are going into Crete on Monday. Expect twenty thousand parachute troops and a lot of reinforcements by the end of the week. You get that for free, by the way. This isn't NKVD gossip. This comes from another source.'

Moncrieff smiled.

'Molotov?'

'Clever man. Not him. You. How did you guess?'

'I saw a photo in the *Völkischer Beobachter*. You and a bunch of diplomats at the Berlin Hauptbahnhof. One of them was Molotov.'

'You're right. It was. I took care of the translations. My Russian is good now. It also gets me out of the country. Another bonus.'

'And your Portuguese?'

'Hopeless. Very strange vowel sounds. Some of the locals sound like cats on heat.'

Moncrieff laughed. She was right about the vowel sounds. Cats on heat, he thought. Clever.

'So what are you doing here?' he asked. 'Who sent you? Molotov?'

'An aide of his.'

'Why?'

'We need to know a little more about Herr Hess. You've talked to him now?'

'I have, yes.'

'And is he as mad as they all say?'

'He isn't mad at all. Eccentric, yes. Crazy? No.'

'That's what Molotov thinks. He agrees with you and that will please him. He's met Hess on a number of occasions and the word he always uses is *chest'nyy*.'

'Meaning?'

'Honest. Sincere. And maybe *nepravil'nyy*, too. That means misguided. Hess sees what he wants to see. The rest, he once told Molotov, is a matter of regret. Maybe you should defect. Talk nicely to Mr Molotov. Get us both a huge dacha in the country. It won't be Seville but this time of year it might be bearable. We could have lots of kids. Little Ivans. Little Anyas. And we'd go to the ballet at least once a week because we're guest defectors and they'll make a fuss of us. The Crimea's OK, as well, as long as Hitler doesn't get that far. Winter sunshine in Yalta? Lisbon beside the Black Sea? Life could be worse.'

'Are you serious?'

'Of course I'm not. You'd hate it, darling. May I call you that? *Dorogoy?* Darling?' She kissed him softly. She wanted a hug. Her mouth was very close to his ear. 'Are you listening, Mr Moncrieff?'

'Yes.'

'There's a man here called Philby. He's MI6.'

'I've met him. He warned me off.'

'And?'

'I paid no attention.'

'Really?'

'Yes.'

'That might not have been wise.'

'Care to tell me why?'

'Because that man is different. He was never an amateur. Ever.' She kissed him again. 'If you remember me for anything, remember me for that.'

19

Merz and Wilhelm Schultz lifted off from Barcelona shortly after nine o'clock in the morning. Engineers had laid hands on spares for the plane locally and at Schultz's insistence they'd worked through the night on a malfunction in one of the engines. Barcelona had been a Republican stronghold during the civil war and negotiations for the extra work had been tricky, but Schultz had called in a favour from a colonel in the Nationalist Army and the engineers, with ill grace, had finished the job in time for breakfast.

Schultz was a little hung-over after an evening in a bar off the Ramblas. Over the dry bony spine of the mountains west of Madrid, he began to drink the water that Merz had stored in a bottle in the rear cockpit. Half an hour later, the bottle empty, he badly needed to piss.

'That funnel thing and tube I showed you,' Merz said. 'Stick the other end of the tube in the bottle. Just remember to put the top back on and take it with you when we land.'

Lisbon appeared just under an hour later, a hazy lattice of streets climbing up from the intense blue of the river. The airfield at Sintra, Merz knew, lay to the north-west of the city. He joined the circuit and radioed for permission to land. He'd filed his flight plan earlier in Barcelona but headwinds had lengthened the journey and he had to wait for an aircraft from Tangier to land first.

Minutes later, they were on the ground. Merz brought the Me-110 to a halt beside a Brazilian Lockheed. The arrival of the fighter bomber with the swastikas on its twin-boom tail had drawn the attention of the Portuguese ground crew. Merz ignored them.

'See the little guy over there? By the arrivals door? Standing where he shouldn't?'

Schultz was storing the water bottle in his bag. He followed Merz's pointing finger.

'Hesketh?' he queried. 'The Englishman?'

'*Ja*. The last time we came here, Haushofer and me, we met him out of town, up near some castle or other. After that he was all over us. Wouldn't leave us alone. Creepy.'

Merz made the introductions. Wilhelm Schultz, he said. From Berlin.

'Herr Schultz,' Hesketh offered a tiny bow. 'I have a car waiting. And a hotel booked. A pity about the headwinds but Lisbon is always worth the wait.'

Merz explained about the overnight repair job. In Schultz's opinion, he said, the Catalans were idle bastards who'd deserved to get their arses kicked in the civil war but they'd done a fine job on the engine. Not once had it missed a beat.

At the sight of the grey-green German passports, the immigration officer in the terminal building waved them through. Out in the sunshine Hesketh led the way to a black Mercedes. The figure at the wheel was Portuguese.

Merz and Schultz sat in the back. Schultz had his bag on his lap.

'Moncrieff?' he enquired.

'We'll be meeting him this evening. At your hotel.'

'Who says?'

'He does. In fact we both do. For most of the day he has other engagements.'

'You're in touch with him?'

'Of course.'

'Then tell him three o'clock.' He checked his watch. 'Make that two o'clock. I don't care where. Just make it happen.'

Hesketh looked briefly shocked.

'Of course, Herr. Schultz,' he said.

Merz looked away to hide a smile. They were in a queue of traffic leaving the airport behind a horse and cart laden with baggage. Something had caught Schultz's attention but Merz didn't know what. He kept twisting round in his seat, looking at the car behind.

At the main road, the horse and cart pulled over to let the rest of the traffic pass. The city lay ahead, half hidden by haze. It was hot by now, gone midday, and Merz wound down the window to get some air.

Schultz wanted to know how far it was to the hotel.

'Fifteen minutes,' Hesketh said. 'No time at all. They do a fine fish stew. The locals call it *cataplana de marisco*. You like seafood, Herr. Schultz?'

'Tell the driver to turn left.'

'Where?'

'Just there. Where the woman's crossing the road.'

Hesketh spoke to the driver. Merz braced himself for the

turn, aware of the woman running for her life, her shopping all over the potholed tarmac. The road here was narrow, flanked by tall houses.

'Faster,' Schultz ordered. 'Go faster.'

The driver put his foot down. A blind bend lay ahead. Anything coming the other way, Merz thought, and they'd be in serious *Scheisse*. Mercifully, once round the bend, the road was clear. Another turn into another street, thirty metres ahead.

'On the right,' Schultz said. 'Take it.'

The driver did his bidding. Watching his face in the mirror, Merz sensed he was enjoying this. The street here was the width of a single vehicle. At this time of day, most of the city had sought the shelter of their houses and the place seemed deserted. Then Merz caught sight of a woman at an open window about twenty metres away. She was up on the first floor, leaning out, watching them. She must have heard the squeal of tyres, he thought. And she badly wanted to know what might happen next.

'Stop,' Schultz said.

The big car juddered to a halt. Schultz had kicked the door open and was running back down the street. Behind them was another car, maybe ten metres away. It was Italian, a Fiat. It had come to a halt. Merz was out of the car. He had time to register the face of the man behind the wheel before Schultz wrenched his door open and dragged him out, wrestling him onto the pavement. The driver was wearing a light cotton shirt and a pair of loose-fitting trousers. He tried to cover his head as Schultz began to kick him, heavy blows to his ribs and his belly. Then Schultz was down on the pavement beside him, a gun in one hand. By now he'd established the man spoke no German, no English, only Portuguese.

'What are you doing?' Merz asked.

Schultz looked up.

'Get the Englishman,' he said. 'And bring that fucking bottle.'

Merz stared at him a moment longer, then did his bidding. Hesketh was already out of the car, trying to explain to the woman in the upstairs window that everything was fine. They were making a movie. It was all fantasy.

Merz took him by the arm but then remembered the bottle. When he unstrapped Schultz's leather bag it was lying on top of a carefully folded shirt.

'What's that?' Hesketh was staring at it.

'Don't ask.'

They ran to the car behind. Schultz had the man by the throat now and was squeezing hard. His pale face had darkened.

'Ask him why he was following us,' Schultz looked up.

Hesketh translated. The driver was beginning to choke. Schultz released his hold.

'Again,' he said. 'Ask him again.'

Hesketh tried a second time and the driver muttered something that Merz didn't catch.

'He said he had orders,' Hesketh told Schultz.

'Whose orders?'

'He won't say.'

'Give me the bottle.'

Merz passed it down. The driver stared at it. He thinks it's petrol, Merz told himself. He thinks this madman is going to set him alight.

Schultz gave the gun to Merz and unstoppered the bottle. Then he forced the man's mouth open and began to pour. The driver coughed, coughed again, trying to turn his head away.

'Whose orders?' Schultz repeated. 'Who sent him to the airfield?'

Hesketh again, trying to be the man's friend, trying to imply that all he had to do was answer the question and then the madness would be over. It didn't work. All the man wanted to do was get rid of the taste in his mouth. He spat towards the gutter, muttered what sounded like an oath.

Then came footsteps down the street, someone running, and suddenly the woman was among them. She was carrying a cudgel of some kind. She started on Schultz, wild flailing blows that he warded off with ease. Other doors were opening down the street, more faces at more windows. Schultz knew it was time to go. He got to his feet and gave the woman a shove. Then he emptied the rest of the bottle over the driver's face before tossing it away.

'The gun,' he gestured at Merz.

Merz gave him the gun. Schultz walked to the Fiat and put three bullets into the front tyre on the driver's side and a fourth through the windscreen. Doors closed again along the street. Faces at windows disappeared. The woman began to scream.

'Enough,' Schultz grunted.

Moncrieff was in Bella's room when he heard the knock at the door. It was Hesketh. For once there was no foreplay. Schultz had arrived earlier than expected. There'd been an incident on the way in from the airfield. Hesketh's careful plans for a get-together in the evening had been abandoned. Schultz wanted a meeting now.

'Where?'

'At his hotel. The Gran Castelo. It's ten minutes away.'

'He's staying the night?'

'I doubt it. I sense they want to get back to Berlin.'

'They?'

'Schultz. And a pilot called Merz.'

'Dieter Merz?'

'Yes.' Hesketh looked surprised. 'You know him?'

Moncrieff didn't answer. Bella was in the bath. He put his head round the door and told her he'd be back later.

She began to ask him where he was going and why but already he was backing out of the bathroom.

'*Zeit um zu gehen,*' he said to Hesketh. Time to leave.

At the Gran Castelo Hotel, Schultz and Dieter Merz had made their way to the room that Hesketh had reserved. Merz was sprawled on the bed, his eyes closed. Schultz was standing beside the window. Through the half-open shutters, from here on the third floor, he had a good view of the street. A heavy automatic, Moncrieff noticed, lay on the windowsill.

'*Der Kleine...*'

Merz roused himself to accept Moncrieff's handshake. Moncrieff perched his long frame on the edge of the bed.

'A good war?' he enquired. 'So far?'

'The best. But only the English fight back.'

'And Messner? He's well?'

'He's better.' Merz yawned and pinched the corners of his eyes. 'He had an accident in Berlin and another over London. One was his fault, the other wasn't. He got four months in hospital for the first and a big fat medal for the second.' He shrugged. 'Such is war. What else should a man expect? You know Wilhelm?'

'Of course.'

'Party time?'

'I doubt it.'

Schultz stepped back from the window and told Hesketh to leave the room. With some reluctance, Hesketh did his bidding. Schultz waited several seconds and then opened the door and checked the corridor. Hesketh had gone.

'Wilhelm thinks he's in a movie,' Merz said. 'That little shit of an Englishman was right for once.'

'So what happened?' Moncrieff was looking at Schultz.

Schultz shook his head. Someone put a tail on them, he said. Mistake number one? The driver followed his orders to the letter. Mistake number two? Schultz produced an envelope from the inside pocket of his leather jacket. He weighed it in his big hands for a moment or two, the way an angler might present a fish he'd just caught, and then gave it to Moncrieff.

'With the Fat Man's compliments,' he grunted. 'Take great care, my friend.'

'Here, you mean?'

'Yes,' he nodded at the letter. 'The Fat One's threatened to have me shot if I take a look at what's inside, but he needn't have bothered.'

'You know already?'

'Of course.'

'And?'

'Read it. And get the fuck out of this city.'

'I can't. Not until tomorrow.'

'Then find somewhere nice and warm. Somewhere safe. Get yourself a woman. Anything. But don't drink too much. There's an *Abwehr* friend of mine at the German Embassy. You'll find it near the park, the Campo dos Mártires. His name's Wolfgang Spiegelhalte. You can remember that? If you get in the shit he'll help you. And take this...' he rummaged in his bag and produced three clips of ammunition, '... and this.' He picked up the automatic and gave it to Moncrieff.

Moncrieff weighed it in his hand. All he could think of was Bella, alone, at the hotel. He swallowed hard. She'd be the easiest of targets. Shit, shit, shit.

He glanced up. Schultz was watching him carefully.

'It's that bad?' Moncrieff nodded down at the gun.

'Worse, my friend. Just watch your back.'

At Bella's hotel the door was locked and when Moncrieff knocked and then called her name there was no answer. Moncrieff returned to reception. The woman behind the desk said that *Senhorita* Menzies had left only minutes ago.

'Alone?'

'I think so.'

'*Think* so?'

'I didn't see anyone else, *Senhor*.'

Moncrieff could see the key to her room in one of the pigeon holes that flanked the desk. When he asked for it, the woman frowned and consulted the register.

'According to our records, *Senhor*, the room is in the name of *Senhorita* Menzies.'

'And me.'

'And you are?'

The hotel's manager emerged from an office behind the desk. He was very happy to resolve this issue. He gave the key to Moncrieff and apologised for the confusion.

Upstairs, Moncrieff let himself in. The room was exactly the way he'd left it: the bed unmade, Bella's suitcase still open on the carpet, the scent she wore still lingering in the airless warmth. Moncrieff opened the window, peered out. Across the street, a shoeshine boy was haggling with a suited man over money. The man in the suit finally gave him a couple of extra coins. The youth looked at them, then tossed them away and spat on the man's shoes. Lisbon, Moncrieff thought, where there's always a better deal to be struck.

He stepped back into the room and searched quickly in case Bella had left a message. In the bathroom, scrawled on the mirror over the hand basin, was a single word: *Sevilla?* Her work, he assumed, and the question both of them still had to answer. Was last night simply the chance for two former lovers to enjoy each other one final time? Or was it a down payment on something else? He stared at the mirror. At the smear of soap on the glass. And at the face that looked back at him. Old, he told himself. I feel old, and a little weary, and it's beginning to show.

Back in the bedroom, he settled down to await Bella's return and fetched out the envelope Schultz had given him earlier. It was thicker than he'd expected and the moment he opened it he understood why. There were two copies of the letter, the original in German and a translation in English. He flicked quickly to the last page of the English version, looking for a signature, some clue about the real weight this document might carry, but all he found was a scrawl in black ink with the name Rudolf Hess typed beneath.

A disappointment? At first sight, yes, but the longer Moncrieff thought about it, the more the seeming authorship made sense. He'd yet to read all thirteen pages but if they proved as controversial as he expected, then Hess's signature at the end would be extremely prudent. This way, if the delivery plan failed for any reason, then it should be child's play for Hitler or any of his senior lieutenants to deny all knowledge of either the flight or whatever might follow. Mad, they'd say. A man with the best of intentions but sadly insane.

Moncrieff returned to page one, reading the original version this time. His years at university had taught him a great deal about the grammar of German bureaucracy, and as he waded deeper into the document he recognised the fingerprints of the Foreign Office committee which must have put these proposals together. Every paragraph perfectly balanced. Every concrete offer freighted with caveats.

Reaching for a pen, Moncrieff began to make notes, trying to extract the essence of what Berlin was proposing. Broadly, in keeping with every peace offer that had followed the Fall of France, Britain was invited to turn her attention away from mainland Europe and content herself with her overseas possessions and protection of the trade routes that knitted the Empire together. Germany, given her dominance on the Continent, would naturally expect the return of her own colonies, surrendered after the last war, but this act of restitution – in the words of Hess – would answer nothing more than the demands of natural justice.

The demands of natural justice.

Moncrieff was sitting in the armchair beneath the window, glad of the breeze from the river on the back of his neck, and he pondered the phrase for a moment or two. *The demands of natural justice.* Would the Czechs recognise a proposition like this? Would the Poles? The Dutch? The Danes? The French? Entire countries dismembered in less time than it had taken Napoleon to advance less than a handful of miles into Russia? He shook his head. Diplomatic sleight of hand, he thought. The mere act of possession turns out to be the key that unlocks a thousand doors. Neglect your defences, ignore the stamp of a million jackboots across the Rhine, and this is where you end up. Having to concede, in evident good faith, *the demands of natural justice.*

Moncrieff read on, scribbling notes as he got to the foot of each page, increasingly surprised what Berlin, for its own part, was prepared to offer the British in return for the cessation of hostilities and a twenty-five-year peace treaty. The withdrawal of all German troops from non-Vichy France, from Belgium, from Luxembourg, from Holland, from Denmark and even from Norway. An undertaking that every trace of German bureaucratic control – that corset of ID checks, local regulations, demands for the surrender of labour, food and other material goods – would likewise be withdrawn. The fruits of the German victory, in other words – so quickly won, so carefully stored – would be returned to their rightful owners.

Astonishing, thought Moncrieff. There were, of course, conditions attached to this seeming act of generosity on the part of the conqueror. Berlin expected her reliance on the supply of Swedish iron ore, shipped to German ports via Norway, to be respected. Important, as well, was the huge larder that was

France. The Reich comprised eighty-seven million Germans. They had to be fed and watered. This happened at the moment by right of conquest but after signature of the Anglo-German peace treaty, Berlin would revert to being just another customer in the brimming markets of Western Europe.

Moncrieff stared at the phrase. Was the Deputy Führer serious? Did proposals this generous really have the backing of the only person who mattered in Berlin? And if Hitler was serious about what Hess was pledging, would he really stand by his promise? Moncrieff thought the answer was no. If his experience at the last Nuremberg rally had taught him anything, it was the sheer duplicity of the man. He remembered the uniformed figure on the tribune at the Zeppelinfeld, his right arm thrust out, bellowing threats to the Czechs in Prague. Rules, he seemed to be saying, were strictly for lesser mortals. Sign a peace treaty one day, and the next you'd find some pressing reason why national survival or the demands of natural justice demanded a wholesale revision.

There was something else, too, Moncrieff realised as he checked through the treaty proposals a second time. The document undoubtedly contained good news for France and the other western democracies but where was Poland? Where was Czechoslovakia? Hess had simply ignored the interests of tens of millions of other Europeans, Middle Europeans, now hapless subjects of the Reich. By choosing to exclude them, he'd consigned them to the dustbin of history. They'd ceased to exist. They'd become nowhere people, subject only to the whims of Berlin.

Did that matter? Moncrieff got to his feet again and stood at the window. In essence, as he recognised only too well, this document returned Western Europe to September 1938. After a taste of German steel, after six terrifying weeks of choked roads and incessant bombardment, would the French really want to surrender the rest of their country for the sake of the Czechs, or the Poles? Knowing what they now knew about the sheer weight of the German military machine? Moncrieff thought not.

And what of the British audience Hess had flown to engage? For the peace lobby and perhaps millions of others, Dunkirk and everything that had followed afterwards had served as a foretaste of what they, too, could expect. The realities of war were already present in every ration book, in every queue for bread, and a thin smear of butter, and powdered eggs, and a pinch of tea. This was the everyday face of fortitude, of sacrifice, of never giving in. This was bad enough but what if it got worse? What if the Russians went under? What if the Americans kept their powder dry? What if Churchill's unbending defiance yielded nothing but the guarantee of more misery?

Moncrieff picked up the letter again, realising at last just how cleverly this document had been drafted. It seemed, at the stroke of a pen, to offer everything that any sane Englishman could ever want. Continued access to the Empire. An end to humiliation in Europe. Properly stocked shops. No more bombers. A good night's sleep. Put proposals like these to the national vote and the outcome would be a stampede to the polling booths. Two and a half years of war had been more than enough and if the presence of Churchill in Downing Street was the only real obstacle to an honourable peace, then so be it. He'd have to go.

Moncrieff carefully folded the German copy of the letter and returned it to the envelope. No wonder, he thought, that

Hess's own copy had so quickly disappeared after his arrest. Make these proposals public and Churchill's days would be numbered. Moncrieff slipped the envelope into his pocket and studied the room for a moment, looking for somewhere to hide the translation. If Hess's copy could disappear in the relative safety of Scotland then so could this one, here in the kasbah that was Lisbon.

In one corner of the room was an ill-fitting metal vent at floor level that seemed to be part of the hotel's heating system. Moncrieff used one of the knives that had come with room service to lever it away. Inside there was just enough room to hide the English translation. He was still replacing the metal vent when he heard shouts from the street outside.

From the window, hidden by the fall of the curtain, Moncrieff looked down. The shoeshine boy had gone. Two men were standing beside a black car. The car was blocking the street. A third man, suited, seemed to be in charge. He was looking up at the hotel.

Moncrieff stepped back into the room. He'd no idea who these people might be, but he'd always discounted coincidence and knew that he had bare seconds to leave. Checking that he still had Schultz's automatic, he made for the door.

Mercifully, the figures in the street had neglected to check the rear of the hotel. Moncrieff rode the lift to the basement and picked his way through a maze of corridors until a blaze of sunshine beckoned him into a narrow alley. Cats scattered as he hurried towards the clatter of traffic from a nearby road. Here, just another pedestrian on the crowded pavement, he felt safer. He checked his pocket for the envelope. Still there.

Hesketh's new address was ten minutes away. Bella had paid him a visit and last night she'd explained exactly where he was living. Familiar by now with the latticework of streets in this part of the city, Moncrieff took care to scout the approaches to the apartment block, alert for signs of surveillance. As far as he could tell, there was no one around. He crossed the road. When he got to the apartment block, the door to the street was an inch or so ajar. He gave it a gentle push. It swung open.

He slipped inside, pulling the door closed behind him. Here it was cooler. He paused a moment, alert for the slightest movement. The place smelled stale. A staircase led upwards. Windows giving onto the street were shuttered against the heat. Moncrieff drew Schultz's gun and moved carefully upwards, step by step. According to Bella, Hesketh lived at the very top of the building. On the first-floor landing, Moncrieff paused. In the shadows, every door was closed. Very faintly, from somewhere above, he thought he could hear the murmur of conversation. Another landing, more stairs. Two people, he thought, a man and a woman. They were speaking in a mixture of French and English and from time to time the woman laughed. The man, unmistakably, was Hesketh.

Moncrieff paused again, then took the next flight of stairs. Finally, he found himself outside Hesketh's apartment. The door was open and on the balcony beyond the sitting room two figures were sitting at a glass-topped table, gazing out at the view. The wine bottle on the table was nearly empty and, as Moncrieff watched, Hesketh reached lazily back to crush the remains of his cigarette in the ash tray. If she really wanted sex again, he sighed, then so be it.

The woman, who was black, caught his hand and raised it to her lips. I want it here, she said. In the sunshine. In the heat of the late afternoon. And afterwards, for a while, we'll go inside and sleep. And then maybe I'll take you to the casino again and you can make us very rich.

It was Hesketh's turn to laugh. He helped himself to the last of the wine in the bottle and lit another cigarette. He had a little business to transact, he told her, but it was nothing that couldn't wait.

Moncrieff had seen enough. Neither Hesketh nor the woman were aware of him crossing the living room. When he emerged into the sunshine, she gave a little gasp of surprise and then covered her mouth. She was a big woman, exactly Hesketh's taste, and she couldn't take her eyes off the gun.

'Tam, my dear fellow,' Hesketh ignored the heavy automatic. 'This is Celeste. Celeste? Say *bonjour* to my friend Tam. We go back a while, Tam and I. Brothers-in-arms.'

Hesketh got to his feet. The occasion called for another chair and at least one more bottle of wine. Moncrieff told him to sit down.

'Not a social visit? How disappointing.'

Moncrieff wanted to know about Bella. Where was she?

'I've no idea. I rather thought she was with you.'

'She's not.'

'You think she might have fled? Found herself a berth on one of those ships down there?' Hesketh waved a languid hand towards the river. 'Gone back to Moscow?'

Moncrieff ignored the suggestion. He wanted to know who had been following Schultz and Dieter Merz in from the airfield.

Hesketh smiled. Herr Schultz, he murmured, was a prisoner of his imagination. He'd been living in Berlin for far too long. The man was haunted by ghosts. He needed a week or two in the sunshine. He needed to relax, unwind, enjoy himself. The car behind had been entirely innocent. Ditto the driver. Hesketh had been there. He *knew*.

'Schultz is a friend of mine.'

'I rather gathered that. You know about the secret police here? Salazar's PVDE? They make sure we all play by the rules. The rules, I admit, can be more than elastic but the one thing they hate is untidiness. Schultz's little adventure had no merit whatsoever. It was coarse in the extreme and it deeply upset the locals. The PVDE like to model themselves on the Gestapo. Herr Schultz might be wise to take that into account.'

'He's gone. He'll be in the air by now.'

'Very wise. The Berlin temperament doesn't travel well and I suspect Schultz is the perfect example.' He paused, reaching for his glass. 'May I assume, at the very least, that he delivered your package?'

Moncrieff didn't answer. Downstairs, in the bowels of the building, he heard a bell ring. A moment later, Hesketh was on his feet, stepping past Moncrieff and heading for the door to the stairs. Moncrieff returned the gun to the waistband of his trousers. He nodded at the woman and asked about the casino.

'You go there a lot? You and *Senhor* Hesketh?'

'*Oui. Bien sur.*'

'And you win?'

'Often we win. Sometimes not.'

'At?'

'Roulette. Always. Never card games. Always roulette. Your friend says he prefers to trust himself to luck. Not skill.'

'My friend?'

'*Senhor* Hesketh.' She put the emphasis on the last syllable. 'I've been at the roulette table many, many times with many, many men but never anyone with the *Senhor*'s luck. Is he brave? Very. Does he love money? Yes. Does he trust his own luck? *Mais oui.* So does that make him wise?' She smiled. '*Non.* Just brave. And a little...' she touched her head, '... crazy.'

Hesketh was back. Moncrieff had learned to recognise the slightly pained expression on his face. This was Lisbon. Something had gone wrong. Again.

'A contact from the German Embassy, I'm afraid.' He gestured back towards the stairs. 'He has news about La Menzies.'

'He's still here? Your contact?'

'Alas, no.'

'So what did he say?'

'It appears that she's in their custody. They're perfectly happy to give her back but there's a price to be paid. They're deeply unhappy about the document Schultz gave you. They're saying he has no jurisdiction in the matter. To be blunt, and Germans are extremely good at this, they want the bloody thing returned.'

'When?'

'Now.'

'How?'

'You give it to me. And I, in turn, pass it to them.'

'And Isobel?'

'She'll be released within the hour. Which gives us plenty of time to do justice to another bottle.'

'You're telling me she'll be coming here?'

'Yes. All I have to do is make a telephone call from the bar on the corner of the street.'

'And Schultz's document?'

'That will stay on the table until she appears. A deal with just a touch of elegance, *n'est-ce pas*? You have the bloody thing? You have it with you?'

Moncrieff didn't answer. Instead he asked why the Germans should so suddenly be having second thoughts about a peace treaty.

Hesketh shrugged. 'That, I'm afraid, remains a mystery. Germans, to be frank, can sometimes be impenetrable as well as bad mannered. Some tribal difference in Berlin? One ministry at another's throat? Your guess is as good as mine. Your good lady, alas, is the meat in the Wilhelmstrasse sandwich. And so, my friend, are you. I suggest I pop along to make the telephone call and leave Celeste here to keep you amused. Under circumstances like these I always find it pays to have a modest celebration. After the first bottle, Schultz's document will have lost its importance, and after the second, we'll have forgotten it ever existed. *Sind wir uns einig?*' We agree?

Without waiting for an answer, Hesketh muttered something in French to Celeste and left. Moncrieff heard the light patter of his footsteps on the stairs receding into silence. Then came the faintest noise of the door to the street opening and closing.

Celeste thought *Senhor* Hesketh might be gone some time. If *Senhor* Tam would like sex she was happy to oblige. Otherwise she would find some more wine.

Moncrieff studied her a moment, and then checked his watch. Nearly five o'clock. He got to his feet and thanked her for the offer of the wine.

'You're going?' She looked surprised.

'I am. Give Souk my regards. And tell him to take care at the roulette table because one day his luck may run out.'

'Souk?'

'He'll understand.'

Moncrieff headed for the door. Out in the sunshine, a minute or so later, the street was empty. Only when he got to the boulevard that ran down to the docks did he find directions to the Campo dos Mártires. A number seven tram, the flower seller told him. A ten-minute journey. Maybe less.

The German Embassy was a grey five-storey building looking onto the park. Over the entrance, a swastika banner hung lifeless in the still air. Inside, a smart-looking woman in a black suit was preparing to leave for the day. When Moncrieff asked to see Wolfgang Spiegelhalte, she frowned.

'You have an appointment?'

'I'm afraid not.'

'*Hauptmann* Spiegelhalte is an extremely busy man. I'm afraid—'

'Tell him Wilhelm Schultz sends his regards.'

'*Oberst* Schultz?' She clearly recognised the name. Her hand reached for the telephone on the desk. The frown had gone. 'My apologies, *Senhor.*'

Spiegelhalte appeared within minutes. He was a small, slight figure in a rumpled suit. He wore a pair of dark-rimmed glasses and obviously took some care to avoid the sun. With his air of faint neglect he might have been a university lecturer without a woman or a wife to look after him. Long, white, ringless fingers. And eyes that missed nothing.

He took Moncrieff by the arm and escorted him up two

flights of stairs. He wanted to know about Schultz. Had he left Lisbon already? And if not, why not?

His office was on the second floor. The big green expanse of the park filled the window, and a black and white photograph of Hitler dominated one wall. Moncrieff took a seat in front of the desk. He'd explained what little he knew about the incident en route from the airfield. Spiegelhalte was watching him carefully.

'Your German is excellent. Do all English spies take so much trouble to learn our language?'

Moncrieff smiled. He mentioned Isobel Menzies.

'I know Miss Menzies. She, too, speaks good German and now Russian, too. I imagine she must be something of a loss from your point of view.'

'Indeed.'

'Professionally?'

'Of course.'

'And in other ways, perhaps?'

Moncrieff ignored the question. Miss Menzies, he said, appeared to have gone missing. Might she be here? At the embassy?

'I have no idea. You want me to find out?'

Moncrieff nodded. Spiegelhalte lifted the phone. A brief conversation established that Bella hadn't paid the embassy a visit. Not today. Not yesterday. Not ever.

'This is to do with Hess, *ja*? And the copy of the letter Wilhelm brought down from Berlin?'

'Yes.'

'You want to tell me more?'

'By all means. I'm told you've had second thoughts about the letter. That you want it back.'

'Us? Here in the embassy?'

'Yes.'

'Why would we want to do that?'

'I've no idea. I just want to find out whether it's true or not. Given the position you hold, I imagine you'd know.'

'You imagine right, Herr Moncrieff. Of course I'd know. Schultz is several ranks my senior. In Berlin he has a very big desk. Unless I want a sudden change of career I'd be very wise to do his bidding. He arrives here in Lisbon with the Hess document. He gives it to you. Why on earth would I ever want it back?'

Moncrieff got to his feet and extended a hand across the desk. He was grateful for Herr Spiegelhalte's time, especially so late in the day. Under the circumstances, he'd been more than helpful. Then he paused.

'You know people in the PVDE? Security police?'

'Of course. We helped train them.'

'I understand they're investigating the incident I mentioned.'

'They are. You're right. I apologised on behalf of Schultz. Occasionally he can be a little forceful.'

'And they're happy with that?'

'They were kind enough to tell me they understood but they, too, have bosses and bosses demand results.'

'You mean an arrest?'

'Of course. In the end there has to be a body. Alive or dead, in this city it doesn't matter. Just as long as someone has accepted full responsibility and paid the appropriate price.'

'But not Schultz?'

'Obviously not.'

Moncrieff nodded. So simple, he thought. And so sweetly *right.*

'Here's a name,' he said. 'Gordon Millord Hesketh. You'll find him in the top apartment in a block on the Largo de Santa Luzia. Number 17. The door to the street is blue and there are tiles on either side.'

Spiegelhalte made a note of the name and address. Then his head came up.

'I know this man,' he said. 'He's one of yours.'

'Was,' Moncrieff smiled. 'Until his luck ran out.'

From the embassy it was a forty-minute walk back to Bella's hotel. When Moncrieff appeared at reception, the manager emerged from his office and asked for a word. Security police had been here earlier and demanded access to *Senhorita* Menzies' room. They'd left after less than twenty minutes. Might *Senhor* Moncrieff throw any light on this surprise visit?

Moncrieff shook his head and promised to ask the *senhorita* when she returned.

'You're expecting her back?'

'I am, yes.'

'I'm relieved, *Senhor.* We always have the welfare of our guests at heart but these days that can sometimes be a complicated proposition. I wish you luck. And the *senhorita*, of course.'

Moncrieff collected the key from reception and took the stairs to the room. It had been torn apart: the bedding all over the floor, the mattress knifed open, drawers emptied, clothes from the wardrobe in a heap outside the bathroom door. Moncrieff checked the bathroom itself. The message fingered in soap on the mirror had been wiped clean. No more *Sevilla*, he thought. Had the PVDE agents taken offence at a message like this?

Had it in some way insulted their sense of order? He returned to the bedroom and stared down at a hole at floor level in the corner. The metal vent had been prised away and now lay on the carpet. Moncrieff knelt quickly, feeling inside, but already he knew that any further search was pointless. The English translation of the Hess document had gone.

It was dark before Moncrieff heard the knock on the door. He'd been lying on the bed for hours, the gun beside him, hidden by the sheet. Either Bella will be back, he told himself, or someone will come looking. His hand found the gun beneath the sheet. Barefoot, he went to the door. Another knock. A pause. And then he opened it, raising the gun.

He'd seen the face in the corridor before, he knew he had. The same centre parting. The same well-cut suit. The same heavy glasses. Recently, he thought. Maybe just a day ago. The restaurant downstairs. When he'd met Bella for the first time.

'Come in,' Moncrieff stepped aside and gestured the stranger into the room. 'You've been following me?'

The stranger nodded. Moncrieff was to call him Rupio. It wasn't his real name but it might make what had to follow more civilised.

'Civilised?' Moncrieff gestured at the wreckage of the room. 'After this?'

'Regrettable, *Senhor*. But doubtless necessary.'

'You're Portuguese?'

'I am.'

'You work for the security people?'

'Only when they meet my terms.'

'You mean money?'

'Of course. In this city nothing talks louder.'

'And now? They're paying you well?'

Rupio shook his head. He wasn't going to say who he was working for. His English was good, if heavily accented. He had presence, too. The sight of the gun hadn't disturbed him in the least.

'We have business, *Senhor*,' he said. 'I am to take you to the lady. The terms of the exchange are very simple. We have her in our custody. In return for Herr Schultz's document, she will be released to your care. You therefore have a choice. You keep either the lady or the document.'

'And if I say no?'

'To what?'

'To giving you the document?'

'Then the lady will suffer. First we will hurt her. And then we will kill her. No one will ever know about either. Except you. In this room. Now. As I say, *Senhor*, it's your choice.'

'And you?' Moncrieff said again. 'Who are you working for? Who's bought your services? The Germans? Unlikely. The Russians? No. The PVDE? I doubt it.'

A smile briefly warmed Rupio's face. Then he nodded down at the gun.

'Unless you want to kill me,' he said, 'I suggest you put that away. We need to stay friends and transact this business as quickly as possible. I have a car downstairs, *Senhor*. At this time of night, your lady is less than an hour away.'

Moncrieff accompanied the stranger downstairs. As they walked through the reception area, the woman at the desk didn't lift her head. Out in the street, parked at the kerbside, was a Citroën. Rupio invited Moncrieff to take the front seat beside the driver before slipping into the seat behind. The driver, who was black, eyed the face in the mirror, spared Moncrieff the merest sideways glance and then stirred the engine into life.

'The plates on this car are false,' Rubio murmured, 'in case you stole a look.'

The car began to move and, as it did so, Moncrieff became aware of another figure in the back. Then came hands reaching over the seat, and the sudden embrace of a blindfold, something soft, maybe even silk, and fingers working busily behind his head, drawing the knot tighter and tighter until he could see nothing but darkness.

'Draw a breath, *Senhor*...' Rupio again, '... and tell me who you can smell.'

Moncrieff knew he had no choice. He still had the gun but the gun was useless if he wanted to get to the end of this journey. He sniffed lightly. Then again. Bella, he thought. Her smell. Her perfume.

The car was moving faster now, slowing only occasionally for other traffic. Once they'd left the city, Moncrieff could hear nothing but the thrumming of the wheels on the tarmac. Twice he half turned in the seat and put a question to Rupio. Why all the drama? And what might he expect if *Senhorita* Menzies was released to his custody? Were they supposed to walk back to Lisbon?

'Bella,' Rupio said softly. 'You call her Bella. I heard you in the restaurant. And so we too will call her Bella. All will be well, *Senhor*. We're civilised people. You have my word.'

After a while, the car began to slow. Then Moncrieff heard the soft clunk as the indicator signalled left and there came the merest whisper from the tyres as the driver made the turn. The road surface here was abruptly much rougher, the car bouncing from pothole to pothole, and Moncrieff could hear the crunch of gravel as the Citroën finally came to a stop.

A door opened, then another. Moncrieff felt a hand on his arm and he slipped out of the car and shook the stiffness from his limbs. From somewhere close came the stir of the ocean and he could hear gulls. A hand removed Schultz's gun from the waistband of his trousers before the gentlest pressure in the small of his back propelled him forward.

Rupio was very close. He promised there was a path ahead, easier going, and then they'd be at their destination. Moncrieff walked slowly forward, one step at a time, feeling his way, trying to imagine what might lie at the end of this surreal journey. Was he really about to meet Bella again? And in this land of deals, was he prepared to meet the price of keeping her alive?

The path came as a relief. He could hear cicadas now and the drip-drip of water from a leaky tap. Then an unseen hand brought him to a halt.

'Reach forward, *Senhor*.'

'Why?'

'Just do it.'

Moncrieff shrugged and reached forward, his long fingers out straight, a blind man seeking reassurance. Then he found something soft, with a hard boniness beneath. Hair. Cheeks. The tilt of a chin. Lips. And the creases of another blindfold. Bella? He couldn't tell.

'Say something,' he whispered. 'Tell me what you wrote on the mirror.'

'I wrote Sevilla.'

'And?'

'Nothing else. It's a city in Spain. Sevilla.'

'Are you OK?'

'Yes.'

'They've threatened you?'

'Yes.'

'Told you what they'd do?'

'Yes.'

'And you believe them?'

'Yes.'

Moncrieff nodded, taking his time. When he asked for the blindfold to be removed the request was refused.

'You've spoken to her, *Senhor*. You've heard her voice. What more proof do you need? This is Bella. You know it's Bella. So now you have to make your decision. We could simply take the document. Help ourselves. Keep the woman. Kill the woman. Maybe even kill you, too. But that wasn't what we promised. We promised you a decision. In good faith. And here it is. Give us the document now, and the woman rides back with you to the city. Keep the document, and there will be consequences. Not for you, *Senhor*, but for the woman, for Bella.'

Moncrieff muttered assent, said he understood. For a long moment his fingertips explored her face again, the tautness of the flesh around her cheeks, the shape of her lips, tiny mole to the left of one eyebrow. When he finally found the pulse point beneath her ear he could sense the steady beat of her heart. She was showing absolutely no fear. Did this mean the threat to her life was a fiction? Had Moncrieff, in this city of lies, fallen into yet another trap?

He paused a moment, realising that the answer was irrelevant. Nothing mattered more than this woman's life.

Not the peace treaty so carefully confected in Berlin. Not the army of conspirators back home, prepared to trade their elected Prime Minister for a new role under the Nazi jackboot. Not even the smaller irrelevance of his own survival.

He pulled the envelope from the inside pocket of his jacket and held it out in the darkness. There was a long moment when nothing happened. Then he felt the weight in his hand lift and disappear and he was being led again, back along the path, back across the roughness of the track, back to the car. A door opened, then another.

'Make yourself comfortable, *Senhor*. You, too, *Senhorita*.'

They rode back into the city. Neither Moncrieff nor Bella said a word. His hand tried to find hers but she withdrew it. Finally, the car rolled to a halt. Rupio told them to take off the blindfolds. After Moncrieff had removed his own he helped Bella loosen the knot at the back of her head. Moncrieff looked out. They were parked in front of the hotel.

'You may leave, *Senhor*. Take great care.'

Moncrieff ignored the proffered handshake over the back of the seat. Opening the door, he stepped into the warmth of the late evening. Bella was already standing on the pavement. She looked pale in the lights from the hotel, as she watched the car drive away.

Moncrieff nodded at the hotel steps. So much to talk about. So much to tease out.

'Shall we?' he said.

She gazed at him for a long moment.

'Thank you,' she said at last.

'You're coming in?'

'No.' She shook her head.

'Why not?'

'One day you may understand.' She forced a smile. 'Is a girl allowed to say that?'

20

Moncrieff arrived back in Britain late the following evening. On his way to Sintra airfield, he'd asked the taxi driver to make a detour via Hesketh's flat. The police presence outside extended to three uniformed officers and a marked car. Moncrieff told the driver not to stop. By now he assumed that Hesketh would have spent an entire night in PVDE custody. Not a pleasant prospect, Moncrieff thought, but richly deserved. Souk had lied for no cause but his own. And now, unless he could weave some of the old magic, he'd doubtless be paying for it.

Ursula Barton, alerted by Moncrieff's phone call from the hotel in Lisbon, was on hand at Hendon airfield to welcome him home. Moncrieff had spent most of the flight north committing every detail he could remember of the Hess document to paper. The offer of an honourable settlement. Freedom in every corner of the Empire. The withdrawal of German troops from most of Western Europe.

'They'd turn back the clock to September 1939?' They were driving into London. Ursula was astonished.

'May 1940. But it still wouldn't pay to be Polish or Czech.'

'Even so…' She shook her head. 'Christ. Don't let the bloody thing out of your sight.'

'It's too late. I haven't got it. It's gone.'

Moncrieff explained about the events of the last two days. Schultz arriving with Dieter Merz. The rumpus in the street. The wrath of Salazar's secret police. And finally Bella.

'You think Souk had a hand in that?'

'I'm sure he did. I don't know how but why's a whole lot simpler. Someone paid him a great deal of money. Blaming the Germans was a blind. The one thing he hadn't taken into account was Schultz's man at the embassy. Get found out in one lie and the rest falls apart. He was drunk yesterday afternoon. That might have been a mistake.'

'So as far as Hess is concerned we have no evidence. Nothing on paper. Is that what you're telling me?'

'Alas, yes.'

'*Status quo ante?* After everything you've been through, that would be a shame.'

Moncrieff shrugged. He said he had perfect recall of the document. Every paragraph. Practically every line.

'But it's not the same, is it? With the document, with words on Chancellery paper, we can beat the enemy to death.'

Beat the enemy to death. Moncrieff permitted himself a smile.

'Which enemy?' he enquired.

'Is that a serious question?'

'Yes.'

Ursula shot him a look and then took the next turn off the arterial road. In a side street, beneath the spreading branches of a chestnut tree, she pulled to a halt. Moncrieff gazed out. Brentford, he thought.

'It's MI6, Tam. SIS. 'C'. It couldn't be more obvious. They stole Hess's copy and now they've stolen yours, probably both of

them. Why? Because they can't afford the likes of Churchill to
take a look. And why might that be? Because Churchill, who can
sometimes be sharper than he seems, will finally know for certain
that this whole pantomime was scripted in Broadway. They made
the first contacts with Hess. They made it their business to lure
him over. To their considerable irritation, we muddied the waters
by taking a peek at that first letter to Hamilton and despatching
a reply of our own. This wasn't in their script and neither was
Hess arriving by parachute. The strength of our interest since
has been a real threat, which is why life has been so hard for
you.' She paused, her face inches from his, intense, concerned,
determined to push this debacle to its logical conclusion. 'They'd
backed both horses, Tam. With a peace proposal like that, they'd
be only too happy to see Churchill gone. The document was eyes-
only for the peace lobby. Had they read it, had they believed it,
everything would have followed. They'd have spread the word.
They'd have found a way to table it in Parliament. They'd have
forced a vote. Their misfortune was that Hess ran out of fuel.
And that the bloody letter ended up in the hands of the Home
Guard. You're with me, Tam. You follow the logic?'

'I do.'

'Good. Because the rest, as the Great Man likes to say, will
be history.'

'Great Man?'

'Churchill.'

At St James's Street, Liddell brought a late meeting to an early
close in order to take Ursula and Moncrieff to his club for
supper. Moncrieff enjoyed the walk across the park, the soft

twilight, the trees heavy with blossom, the squirrels darting from branch to branch. German bombers hadn't paid the capital a visit for more than a week and Londoners were beginning to relax. You could see it, Tam thought, in every passing face. Even the ducks on the pond were looking forward to a good night's sleep.

At the Reform Club, Liddell settled in an armchair and ordered sherry while awaiting the arrival of the menus. Hess, he said, was still in the Tower of London but was shortly expecting a move to Surrey. He was beginning to worry about his health and the food he was expected to eat and plans were evidently afoot for a proper psychiatric assessment.

'On whose part?'

'MI6. They appear to have taken formal ownership of our new friend. In private they refer to him as a pain in the backside. Churchill thinks that's funny. Be careful what you wish for in life, he told me yesterday. MI6 invited him over in the first place so MI6 can damn well keep him amused.'

Ursula beckoned the Director a little closer and asked Moncrieff to outline the proposals in the Hess document. Liddell listened carefully, expressing no surprise. Finally, he plucked at the creases in his trousers and sat back while a waiter arrived with glasses and a decanter of sherry. The waiter gone, he resumed the discussion.

'The PM asked for a full report on the interviews Hamilton and Kirkpatrick conducted with Hess up in Scotland,' he said. 'Once he'd read them, he demanded a redraft. Why? Because Hess had outlined precisely the proposals you've just described. The reports from Scotland now contain no mention of what the bloody man had to say on Berlin's behalf. All that has been expunged from the record and what's left, to be frank, isn't worth keeping.'

'Does Hamilton know that? Does Kirkpatrick?'

'They may. They may not. In any event it doesn't matter. Hamilton is owed fourteen days' leave. The PM has assigned him a Hurricane and despatched him around the kingdom to make house calls on his treacherous friends. The thrust of these conversations is very plain. They've all been rumbled. Downing Street is on top of the plot and they all have a choice to make. The country isn't short of internment camps. Nor is it difficult to find judges prepared to sentence traitors to death. Rather brilliant on the PM's part, if I may say so.'

A choice to make.

Moncrieff sat back in the buttoned leather armchair, nursing his glass of sherry. Hess had made his choice. He'd been unquestionably brave, possibly misguided, definitely reckless. Souk had made his choice, or perhaps choices, playing both ends against the middle. And he, Tam Moncrieff, ex-Marine, current Laird of the Glebe House, had also been confronted with a decision.

Oddly enough, he believed Rupio. He could have returned to the city that night with the Hess proposals in his pocket, leaving Bella to face whatever might follow. But would that have made the slightest difference? Here and now? A stone's throw from Downing Street? Would his physical possession of thirteen typed sheets of paper alter the fact that a *coup d'état* had been nipped in the bud? Moncrieff rather suspected not.

The Director, with the waiter at his elbow, had decided on a saddle of hare with *pommes duchesse* and lightly creamed carrots. Handed the wine list, his finger ran down the champagnes on offer before settling on a bottle of Mouton Cadet. Another choice, Moncrieff thought. Infinitely more civilised.

'I sense a modest celebration might be in order,' the Director glanced up at the waiter. 'Two bottles please...' he turned to beam at Moncrieff, '... and a toast to our vanquished friends in Broadway.'

Moncrieff was back in his Bloomsbury flat by midnight. An envelope with his name on it lay on the doormat beneath the letterbox. He took it upstairs and read it at the kitchen table.

The letter was typed on light blue paper and if Moncrieff believed the signature at the foot of the page it must have come from Cathy Phelps. She said she'd had second thoughts about working in the Palace and had handed in her notice. She'd also got tired of London, of the bombing, of the acres of rubble, of the queues during the day and the blackout at night. She was sorry about the dance she'd led Tam but she wanted him to know that he'd always have a place in her affections. Just now she was undecided about any kind of future but she had a distant cousin who lived in the wilds of Pembrokeshire and needed a little company. There, she wrote, she might at least get a decent night's sleep. As an afterthought, she'd added a PS. 'Ignore what I said about the Duke of Kent,' she'd typed. 'I was wrong.'

Moncrieff stared at the letter for a long time. To his knowledge, Cathy always wrote in longhand. The fact that the letter had been typed rang all manner of alarm bells but he wondered whether he had the energy to enquire further. Maybe someone else had written this. Maybe they'd sat beside her, the way a detective might coax out a statement, keen to explain Cathy's sudden absence at the Palace in case Moncrieff ever tried to get in touch. Maybe they were keen to correct the record as far as the Duke of Kent was concerned. Maybe. But did he really care? Moncrieff knew the answer was yes but just now he was exhausted.

The following day, back at his desk in St James's Street, Moncrieff did some typing of his own. By mid-afternoon he'd prepared a full account of his visit to Lisbon, with an addendum that set out, in full, everything he could remember about the Hess peace proposals.

When he knocked on the Director's door, Liddell invited him in. He put the report carefully to one side. He wanted Moncrieff to know that the Security Service, and indeed Downing Street itself, were deeply grateful for all his efforts. His curiosity about the peace lobby had hardened into something a great deal more menacing and, now that the dust had settled, Liddell said that he had every reason to be proud of himself.

These days there were many threats to democracy, murmured the Director, but the deadliest were often the most unexpected. It was prudent to prepare for more aerial bombardments, and a full-scale invasion was still a possibility, but the last thing you might anticipate was an assault from within.

'A triumph, Tam,' Liddell smiled. 'Maybe a week or two off?'

Georg Messner was back in Berlin for the second week of June. He put a call through to Beata and asked her whether she minded if he spent a couple of hours with young Lottie. She said he was very welcome, and they agreed a time. Surprised and gladdened, he drove out to the house beside the Wannsee, only to find his daughter at the door in the arms of Dieter Merz.

'Beata?' Messner enquired. 'My wife?'

'She's out all day.'

'You live here now?'

'I do, *compadre*. But you know that. You've known that for months.'

'I have. I just...' Messner shrugged, '... hoped things might have changed.'

They hadn't. Merz had bought a small rowing boat from a family further along the lake who'd decided to move away from Berlin before the RAF learned how to bomb in earnest. The weather was perfect: a cloudless sky and a light wind from the east. All afternoon, he rowed Messner and Lottie up and down the lake, trying to ignore the mess of scar tissue that had once been his wingman's face. Messner sat in the stern with his daughter in his lap, trailing his fingers in the water, telling Merz about the night he'd survived to bring Klopp's Heinkel back from near-catastrophe over London.

'Klopp?'

'The *Oberstleutnant*. I was there at his invitation.'

'He didn't make it?'

'A chunk of shrapnel took his head off at the throat. One moment it was there. The next it was rolling around on the floor beneath his feet.' Messner nuzzled his daughter and then gave her a kiss. 'Blood, too. Lots of it. The heart must keep pumping for a bit. You'd never think, would you?' He gazed out across the lake. 'I miss this place, I really do. How's my wife?'

'She's lovely.'

'Missing me?'

'Not at all.'

'Did she send her love? Anything like that?'

'No.' Merz rested a moment at the oars. He'd taken his shirt off and he loved the warmth of the sun on his back. 'Your film star friend was a very bad idea, *compadre*. Didn't that ever occur to you?'

'Of course it didn't, not that first time. She was crazy about body oils and we managed some incredible things. I wanted to stick it to Goebbels, too. And I did. After that I couldn't get her out of my mind.'

Merz nodded. For him, the memory that lingered was the day Goebbels and his Slav starlet turned up at the Charité hospital, not to celebrate Christmas but to teach Georg Messner a lesson. Propped either side of him on the bed, Messner's humiliation had been complete, though at the time Merz suspected he hadn't a clue what was going on.

'So she was worth it? Is that what you're telling me?'

'I'm telling you nothing. Except I'm glad it's you in this boat and not some other fucker.'

Merz knew that Messner was in Berlin to receive his *Ritterkreuz* from the Führer himself. He also knew that he was permitted one guest – friend or family – to witness the happy event, and it came as no surprise when Messner enquired whether he was free tomorrow morning.

'It might as well be you,' he said. 'No one else I know would dream of saying yes.'

Next day, Merz arrived at the Chancellery with five minutes to spare. In deference to the occasion he was wearing full dress uniform, as was Messner. Goering and a small selection of other notables were in attendance, and Merz watched as Messner's name was called and he marched smartly across the endless expanse of Hitler's office and offered a perfect salute, his arm raised, his chin up, the ghost of a smile on his ruined face. Hitler pinned the dull grey metal cross to his uniform jacket, looked him in the eyes, and held his hand for several moments. The pair enjoyed a whispered conversation before a name was called and Hitler turned to be saluted by yet another hero of the Reich.

Afterwards, leaving the Chancellery, Merz wanted to know what Hitler had been saying. Messner stopped on the pavement, aware of curiosity in the eyes of passing women. The weather was still flawless. These days, thought Merz, the sunshine lasts forever.

'Well?' he asked. 'What did our Leader say?'

Messner's fingers were playing with the *Ritterkreuz*.

'He told me Goering has something special lined up.'

'For all of us?'

'For me, *compadre*.' He leaned closer. 'It has to be Russia, hasn't it?'

Moncrieff delayed his windfall holiday, hoping to take advantage of the weather in the hills in high summer. The Germans invaded Russia on 22 June and, in the hectic days and nights that followed, the lights burned late behind the blackout curtains in St James's Street. In the rare hours that Moncrieff had to himself, he thought about neither Cathy nor Bella. Thanks to Hitler, as ungovernable as ever, there were fresh piles of paperwork on his desk every morning. This, Moncrieff counted as a blessing.

Then, in early August, with Stalin shipping entire factories east from Moscow and the Germans closing on Kiev, Moncrieff knew the time had come to cash in the Director's promissory note and take a little time off. The night sleeper delivered him to Edinburgh and by noon the next day Moncrieff was sprawled on a bench outside the Glebe House, munching an early apple from his father's precious orchard.

The days that followed, unseasonably hot, took him to the mountains with a gun. He shot hare and a variety of game birds and spent the evenings after a home-cooked supper enjoying a glass or two of malt whisky while the sun settled slowly over the mountains to the west. Years had passed since he'd been here in high summer and he'd forgotten how the light never quite drained from the night sky.

Then, at the start of his second week, he heard the crunch of gravel under tyres in the drive. He was upstairs in the room that had once belonged to Cathy Phelps, re-laying the floorboards. He got to his feet and went across to the window. He didn't recognise the car. A brisk three-point turn angled the bonnet down the drive again before the passenger door opened and a woman got out. She was carrying a suitcase. A couple of steps took her to the front door. The front door, Moncrieff knew, was open. She knocked twice, then glanced over her shoulder at the driver of the car and gave him a wave. The car began to move. A departing hoot, and it was gone.

Intrigued, Moncrieff made his way downstairs. From his bedroom he hadn't a clue who this woman might be. She was standing on the flagstones in the hall, looking round. It was Bella.

They stared at each other, then Bella began to laugh.

'You're supposed to say hello,' she said. 'You're supposed to fling your arms around me and sob your heart out. Or maybe that's my role. This place is glorious. Why on earth did you ever leave?'

Good question. Moncrieff led her through to the kitchen, sat her down at the table, demanded to know what was going on, how come she'd found her way up here, what might happen next. She gazed at him and then began to giggle. If anyone ever told her again that all was fair in love and war, she'd at last be inclined to believe them.

The Germans, she said, would soon be hammering at the gates of Moscow. Even Stalin had concluded that they had to make friends with the British and the Americans, otherwise all would be lost. And so, with the blessing of her former colleagues in St James's Street, she'd been welcomed back home as a kind of liaison officer, someone who spoke both languages, someone who could help iron out the wrinkles in this hasty shotgun marriage.

'We forgive and we forget,' she said. 'At least that's the theory.'

'So why didn't anyone tell me?'

'Because you weren't there, foolish boy. And who can blame you?' She was looking round again, shaking her head.

Moncrieff was still letting the news sink in. Bella Menzies. Back on home soil. Intact. Then he looked up.

'So who was that?' He nodded towards the window. 'In the car?'

'My lift from London.'

'Does he have a name?'

'Of course he does. Everyone has a name. Philby. Kim Philby. And he's on holiday, too. From Lisbon.' She paused. 'I gather you bumped into him recently. On a flying boat.'

'I did,' Moncrieff nodded. 'So when is he coming back to collect you?'

Bella studied him for a moment, then extended a hand across the table.

'He's not,' she said. 'I thought I might stay a while.'

'You're serious?'

'Always.'

'For how long?'

'Weeks? Months? Who knows?' She shrugged. 'Until my chums in Moscow call me home again.'

ABOUT THE AUTHOR

Graham Hurley is the author of the acclaimed Faraday and Winter crime novels and an award-winning TV documentary maker. Two of the critically lauded series have been shortlisted for the Theakston's Old Peculier Award for Best Crime Novel. His French TV series, based on the Faraday and Winter novels, has won huge audiences. The first Wars Within novel, *Finisterre*, was shortlisted for the Wilbur Smith Adventure Writing Prize. Graham now writes full-time and lives with his wife, Lin, in Exmouth.

www.grahamhurley.co.uk